HE LOVES ME, SHE LOVES ME NOT

EMERSYN PARK

D1607390

He Loves Me, She Loves Me Not, 1st Edition

Cover design and image by Best of You Designs

ISBN: 9798529630990

Library of Congress Control Number has been applied for.

Instagram: EmersynJulesPark

Facebook: EmersynPark

*"Every lie is two lies.
The lie we tell others
and the lie we tell ourselves to justify it."
(Robert Brault)*

K *arma is a bitch, but so is she.*
Yet, I calmly and patiently remained seated beside her embracing the silence and wanting to remember every aspect of this quiet moment. I wanted to get it just right. It might be the last time I sat next to her. Trying to think of the perfect words, I gently held her right hand with both of my hands and rubbed the large vein that extended from her thumb to her wrist.

Her hospital bed was slightly elevated. No IV cords hung from her veins. The white hospital sheets were tucked tightly around her small frame as she took up a minimal amount of space in the twin-sized bed. Two pillows supported her head.

She smelled like an old person; maybe it was the oil on the aging skin or perhaps aging pores secreting decades of toxic chemicals that had entered her body. Maybe odors were actually sins escaping through her pores. The worse the stench given off perhaps symbolized the worse the sins? *Interesting thought.* Among the old lady smell, a hint of lavender lingered from the laundry soap that was used to wash her hospital gown. In my childhood memories, she had smelled like cheap, grocery store perfume. The kind that lingered after she already strutted out of the room. Roses, lilacs and rosemary.

Inhale slowly, exhale slowly. I took a few deep breaths to relax. Years of meditation taught me techniques to calm myself. By relaxing my body and my mind, I would be able to muster up the right words that I needed to formulate.

My eyes settled back on her. Honestly, she looked tired and ready to die. I wondered what she was thinking. *Why is Lily here? Why is she not talking? What does she want now?*

I wondered if my carefully chosen words would help. Push her over the edge. Break her heart. Maybe it would be the nail in the coffin.

As I stood up from my chair next to her bed, I gently leaned over. I buried my nose in her unwashed, wavy hair as I moved closer so I could whisper in her ear. I felt her body immediately stiffen. She didn't appreciate me in her personal space. She wanted to push me away, but her frail body wouldn't cooperate. My coffee-stained breath whispered in her ear, telling her my secret.

Her body tensed up. Her eyelids squeezed shut. Her dry, pale lips pinched as she pressed down on them. A single tear rolled down her cheek.

Blink twice if you understand.

Blink. Blink.

Chapter One

Daddy told me once that they chose the town I grew up in basically because he liked the name of it - Normal, Iowa. "Names are important, Baby Girl. It's like judging a book by its cover. A welcoming, enticing name makes folks like me curious about what kind of life they can create in Normal, Iowa."

In 1854, the town of Normal was established by a group of retired railroad workers, who were exhausted from their nomadic life. They yearned to try something new and settle down. The men worked together to learn how to grow corn and start farms of their own. Native Americans had previously discovered that Iowa had deep rich soil and a perfect growing season for corn. Plus, corn was a sensible choice to cultivate for the simple fact that it fed livestock as well as could be grown for food.

In 1978, Normal's Main Street consisted of a grocery store, an ice cream shop, locally owned restaurant, a post office, a library, a police station, city hall, three churches and four bars. The elementary, junior high and high school were all located at the edge of town near the park and swimming pool. Only one stoplight hung over the streets of our quiet little town. And more often than not, the caution yellow signal flashed at the few cars populating the main drag.

Our town earned a reputation for its small-town values, hard work ethic and remarkable quality of life. Normal's citizens prided themselves on being friendly to travelers and loyal to their neighbors. Crime was almost null due to strict parenting, and most illegal or questionable issues were handled at home rather than in the county courthouse or the town jail.

The large "Welcome to Normal" signs that stood at both the south and north end of Main Street explained, "This is God's country, so don't drive like you are going through Hell."

Legend had it that the town council created that slogan following a traffic incident with a teenager from a neighboring town. Eli Frank raced down Normal's Main Street in his beat-up Chevy pickup. When he was pulled over for speeding, the officer inquired why he was going sixty-five in a twenty miles per hour zone. Eli explained, "I'm going to Hell anyway, so I might as well drive like it." The traffic officer laughed heartily but still ticketed Eli for his excessive speed.

Outward appearances, though, can be deceiving. From the outside, the three of us fit right in. We resembled the classic, normal 1970s American family. Our house was modest, nothing fancy. Curvy Momma was a beautiful blonde who took great pride in her appearance. Hard-working Daddy was a tall, well-built, intimidating man who doted on his wife and only daughter. Daddy was a truck driver, and Momma was a housewife. Momma and Daddy didn't show public displays of affection, but there was no physical abuse either. I was a slightly above average student who stayed out of trouble and minded my parents.

We paid our taxes, voted on Election Day and recited grace before every meal. From all outward appearances, we resembled perfect Normal citizens. We were friendly to our neighbors and owned one car and one colored television set. Normal...average...common... We were like everyone else except that Momma was a pole dancer and the town whore.

Chapter Two

1976

At six feet, four inches tall, Daddy stood like a giant towering over six-year-old me. My neck always arched in an upward angle. He ducked slightly when he passed through any doorway. His dark brown hair was cut military style, short and simple. He always had a clean-shaven face and had a big toothy grin that met his big brown eyes when he smiled. He took care of himself. He told me once that he did push-ups and sit-ups beside his semi-truck when he parked for the night to rest so he could keep himself 'desirable.' Whatever *that* meant!

I never witnessed Daddy smoke a cigarette or cigar, but he had a deep, scratchy voice like many smokers. In conversation, it would crack a bit here and there. If he was mad, that deep voice boomed and echoed throughout the thin walls of our little house. His infuriated voice thundered scarier than any sound created in a horror movie. His anger was hardly ever directed at me, but I heard his deep, angry voice resonate some nights hours after I had already crawled into bed. It was often directed at Momma and at 'the company she kept.'

Daddy smelled like Old Spice and motor oil. He didn't wear actual cologne.

"Cologne is for feminine men. I'm too manly for that!" And he would flex his bulging biceps. After his daily shave, he would splash on a little Old Spice Aftershave. Old Spice reminded me of Daddy, and Daddy was home.

I loved to watch him shave. He would hoist me up onto the bathroom countertop and fabricate some elaborate tale while his straight edge razor glided down his chiseled jaw. I would giggle and shake my head at how silly he was.

"No, Daddy! Her name is Rapunzel, not Momma."

His smile would break out across his face, and he would shush me. "My father created stories for me too when I was a young boy. So, Baby Girl, you pipe down and listen up." He cleared his throat and used his deep, attention-commanding, storytelling voice. "Her beautiful, long blonde hair was the finest in all the kingdom. It was made of gold. Men from far and near would recite stories to each other about the beautiful princess locked in a tall tower. When I heard their tales, I knew that I had to be the one to rescue this damsel. I would be her knight in shining armor. I would rescue her, and we would live happily ever after."

The next weekend when he returned home, we would repeat the same shaving routine, but Momma would be a different princess in a different story. "Momma was a blonde-haired beauty dressed in dirty, old rags. Her stinky undergarments even had huge holes in them."

"Daddy!" I giggled.

"Unfortunately, she lived in a cold, damp, old castle with her evil step-mother who forced her to clean the entire filthy castle all by herself. She also had to wait hand and foot on her two ugly, ugly step-sisters. And boy, they were hideous! Warts on their noses, snarls in their hair, pimples all over their cheeks, teeth that looked like corn kernels because they were so yellow! Even their two pet dogs howled every time the sisters walked into the same room." He produced his version of a dog howling noise that sounded more like a cow on its deathbed.

I remembered giggling so hard that my sides hurt. He loved having a captivated audience who hung on his every word, and I cherished these moments.

6

Momma claimed that I was born a Daddy's girl. She liked to repeat the same story of my birth. "You popped out all slimy and red. Screamin' and hollerin'. As soon as the doctor allowed Daddy into the hospital room, he wrapped you in his big strong arms, and you peered right up at him and cooed. It was love at first sight for both of you."

When she repeated this same story as I grew older, I picked up on a hint of annoyance or jealousy. Same version, but a different tone of voice.

Daddy worked away from home during the week. He drove an eighteen-wheeler all over the country. Most weeks he would leave early Monday morning before I woke up and return late Friday night. He would bring state magnets home for me from every new state he visited. Each funny shape magnet included a story. I never knew if they're stories that Daddy created or actual state facts. Nevertheless, Daddy was a fabulous storyteller, and in the eyes of his biggest, most loyal fan, that fact never really mattered.

"Well, Baby Girl, this funny-shaped state is called Idaho. This great state is known for its potatoes. It grows many, many potatoes for all the fans of french fries."

Hook, line and sinker. He reeled me in.

"I like french fries!"

I enjoyed his lessons about the states and the undivided attention which he granted me when he returned home. I absorbed it all; I was his little sponge.

"Yes, french fries for my Baby Girl. And another fun fact about this state's name I... D... A... H... O... is that the gentleman who suggested the awkward shaped land be named Idaho informed Congress that the word Idaho meant 'Gem of the Mountains.' Congress was impressed with such a grand, unique name and liked it so much that they agreed to name their new state Idaho. However, years later Congress found out that the man lied. He totally made up the word Idaho."

"No way, Daddy. That can't be true. Adults don't lie to Congress."

I wasn't sure who Congress was, but it sounded terrible.

"Baby Girl, unfortunately, adults do lie... even to Congress." His face became serious for a second as if he was personally affected by the story that he revealed to me. "But I will never lie to you, Baby Girl. I dunno what I'd do without you. Get it? Idaho…. I dunno?"

We shared a hearty giggle at his bad dad joke. He was amazing to me: funny, smart, thoughtful. He was my hero, and I adored this giant of a man.

I remember another state magnet that he brought home for me about three years before he died. I was a teenager and really didn't think magnet collecting was cool anymore.

"Baby Girl, I traveled through Tennessee this past week. Did you know Cybill Shepherd is from Tennessee? Isn't she that actress you admire from *Moonlighting*? I drove through this town named Collierville where they posted a speed limit sign claiming nineteen miles per hour was the speed limit! Nineteen miles per hour? Who does that? Nineteen?" He went on and on about how weird it was to use the number nineteen.

"Why not use an even number like twenty? Nineteen is a strange number to choose for a speed limit!"

However, what struck me the most was that he remembered the actress' name from my favorite show. He amazed me all the time. He actually listened to me when I recounted what happened on my favorite Tuesday night program.

When I was young, Saturday mornings were my favorite time of the week. It was my special time to be with Daddy. I would crawl out of bed quietly, so I did not wake anyone up. I would tiptoe down to the kitchen and get everything ready so Daddy and I could make pancakes (I mispronounced them as "panpakes" for the longest time) together. I gathered pancake mix, syrup, butter and the pan. I carefully set the table for two. At Daddy's place setting, I would place his favorite coffee mug that I gifted him with my own saved money last year for Father's Day. It read, "#1 Daddy."

After our Saturday morning pancake and cartoon bonding, I would clean up the dishes while he headed to the garage to tinker on his machines. During the weekends, you could always find him in his garage fixing something. Everything we owned was second or third hand so something was always breaking down or needed a repair. He was handy and didn't mind getting greasy. He loved working with his hands. He was proud he could save money and make something useful with his own two hands.

Cans and cans of motor oil and gasoline were stacked against the walls in his garage. He could never fully wash away the motor oil smell from his greasy hands after he worked on one of our broken-down engines. That was why the smell of motor oil reminds me of Daddy, too.

He could even work his magic with wood. Momma complained that she had to place everything on the floor when she crawled into her bed: her water glass, her magazines and Kleenex. She complained she had nowhere to lock up her valuables, although I am not sure what valuables she actually owned. Their bedside lamps and matching alarm clocks sat on the bedroom floor next to their twin beds. So, for her birthday gift, he cut, sanded, stained and assembled her a one-of-a-kind nightstand. The top drawer even locked with a key so she could lock away her precious valuables. She was elated and claimed he had always been a wonderful creator.

I yelled, "Kiss him! Kiss him, Momma! He did good!"

They both looked questionably at me after my excited demand.

"Do it!" She gave him a quick, sweet peck on the cheek and a slug on the arm. I jumped into his arms and hugged him tightly and begged him to create me one, too.

Momma always slept in on Saturdays, informing Daddy, "I dealt with her all week. It's your turn for one day. It is my only day to sleep in and relax a bit."

He never complained; honestly, he enjoyed spending time with me. But Daddy always defended her and her needs. He never said an unkind word about her even when she was in one of her moods. He would do anything she asked. Daddy would explain to me, "She is the sun, and we are planets that orbit around her. Someone is always the sun in a family, Baby Girl. And your Momma is our sun."

Another lesson by Daddy squeezed in there. It was subtle, but I caught its true meaning.

Chapter Three

1976

Momma was like a Georgia peach. The state of Georgia was known for their peaches of superior flavor, texture and nutrients. When I was six years old, Daddy brought me home a Georgia state magnet and reported to me about how proud the whole state of Georgia was of its peaches.

"Baby Girl, Georgia is famous for three P's: pecans, peanuts and peaches. Not only did I buy you this cool Georgia state magnet for your collection, but I brought home some Georgia peaches." He handed me my first Georgia peach. The outside of the peach was fuzzy, soft and delicate. The magnificent coloring was what initially grabbed my attention. It was a beautiful unique blend of crimson and amber shades. I could smell the fruit's sweetness even before I ingested my first bite. I couldn't wait to sink my teeth into it. Daddy laughed at how much I enjoyed that first Georgia peach. The sweet fruit juice dripped down my chin. I wiped it with my shirt sleeve and went in for my next bite.

"Come up for air, Baby Girl!" Every nibble had me wanting more until I took a huge bite into its hard, brittle core. Inside this sweet, delicious, gorgeous fruit was a hard, jagged seed. One bite of the nut, and a crack of the tooth. And that was what happened to me.

Momma was a natural beauty like a delicious, ripe peach. Long locks of wavy blonde hair fell down her slender back. Her blonde hair contained many hues of yellow, all-natural highlights. She kept it long; it usually fell down past her shoulder blades. When she was home, she often tied it up in a loose bun, but if she vacated the house to go anywhere, she wore it down. Her long, golden hair caught everyone's attention. Her big doe-like, brown eyes were framed by long, dark lashes. Her teeth were white and straight except for one tooth that stuck out a bit like a vampire fang.

People always turned and gawked at her wherever we went as if a blonde woman was an abnormal sighting. It was more the combination of her blonde hair and big, seductive smile and hourglass figure that earned the prolonged stares. It was not only men that noticed Momma - even ladies eyeballed her. However, unlike the men who would whistle or compliment her on how they would like to take her home, the ladies' glances were judgmental, followed by a "tsk" and a head shake of disapproval. Without describing what she was wearing, a stranger might think that these women were jealous and petty of Momma's natural born gifts. But when you added that she accessorized her good looks with a certain style of clothing, a stranger would understand more. Momma's wardrobe consisted of short cut-off jeans and tight tank tops or T-shirts. High heel sandals always showed off her long, slender legs. In the winter, in order to make up for not being able to show skin in bitterly cold Iowa, she wore skintight jeans that still showed off her lean legs.

Being compared to a Georgia peach's beauty should be a high compliment until it's hard, jagged core was taken into account. What made Momma so hard and brittle in her core was a mystery to me. When I was a six-year-old child, I had grown accustomed to Momma's many mood swings. As a young child, her sweet, tender side drew me right in. When she wanted to be near me, I soaked up any attention that she was willing to give. If she wanted to bake cookies together, I was one hundred percent ready for the task. If she wanted to snuggle on the couch and watch *Little House on the Prairie*, I wrapped my arms around her and held on tight. If she wanted to read me a bedtime story,

I eagerly jumped into my bed and made room for her to lay right beside me.

However, as I grew older, the whiplash of her mood swings would sting a bit deeper and stay embedded in my memory a little while longer. When she asked me to bake chocolate chip cookies with her one day after school, I clearly remembered the last time we bonded over baking. She yelled and cursed at me for not putting the oven timer on; one batch of cookies were overbaked. After spending sixty minutes in a timeout, she only offered me the burnt cookies to eat.

"You will learn. When I tell you to do something, you do it."

A week after the last time we cuddled and ate popcorn during *Little House on the Prairie*, I invited Momma to watch the show with me again. I made the popcorn the way she liked it: extra butter. I retrieved her favorite green afghan from the closet. I was ready to enjoy a night in front of the TV with her.

"I am in no mood for that lame ass show tonight, Lily. Paw Ingalls can suck it! I am goin' out. You can watch it alone until Daddy gets home." She was dressed in her high heels, tight jeans and a red tank top. Daddy was never happy on the Friday nights that he rolled into town and Momma wasn't home. He was especially upset that I was home alone.

A few nights, after we snuggled in my bed reading *Charlotte's Web*, I brushed my teeth anticipating the next chapter that we would read. I couldn't wait to discover if Wilbur went to live with Charlotte's uncle. I tiptoed to her room and told her I was ready for my bedtime story. Without an explanation, she slammed the door in my face. Tears sprang into my eyes, and I reluctantly put my six-year-old self to bed.

Momma's Georgia peach inner core was softened with booze and later, I learned - men. My youth and eagerness to please always made it easy to forgive and forget with Momma. Often following a mood swing, I would wake up to donuts and strawberries. She then walked me to school rather than letting me walk the mile alone. As we held hands and skipped along the sidewalk, she would chatter all the way about some funny thing that she read in her magazine or what plans she wanted to make with

Daddy on the weekend. This was her way of apologizing and seeking my forgiveness. I tightly gripped her hand, hoping to hold onto this side of her. I looked up at her with the admiration that she wanted. But my six-year-old self knew that this sweet, kind side of Momma would not last. There was a stale, whiskey smell on her breath that I had come to recognize.

Momma also possessed charisma, but it came with a side of back-stabbing cruelty. Another reason she was like a Georgia peach: she drew you in with her charm and good looks, but the nut was in the center, hard and jagged.

Daddy enlightened me once with a description I never forgot: "Daisy can charm a venomous snake if she sets her mind to it."

I didn't know what that meant, but it sounded impressive. People were drawn to her. Initially, her good looks caught people's attention, but she also made people feel at ease. She could talk to anyone.

To the young, pimply teenager who bagged our groceries, she said, "Thank you so much! I sure appreciate how careful you were with our produce." She would giggle and then throw her head back as she flipped her blonde wave of hair.

At the local bank she would compliment the frizzy-haired bank teller, "You have gorgeous hair. Do you style it yourself?"

The young, unkempt child who held the door open for us at the gas station: "What a gentleman you are. Your mom must be so proud." She ruffled his hair a bit.

These strangers usually beamed back at her proudly, appreciating her kind words.

However, what these strangers did not know was what she said behind their backs, out of ear shot. She would denounce her compliment with a slam for only my ears to hear.

"He literally threw our pears in the grocery bag! Was he trained by monkeys? Has he ever heard of soap? Maybe he should buy some at that fancy grocery store he works at! " Or "Did you see how she looked me up and down when she handed me *my* money like I wasn't worth that much? Well, who is she to judge me? She works at that lousy bank! At least, I have manageable hair!" Or "Damn snot-nosed kid touchin' the door! I wonder where his hands have been? Probably down his pants!"

In hindsight, I realized these days were most common when Daddy had been away too long or one of Momma's special friends hadn't visited that week.

Even as her own daughter, I was often a victim of her cruelty.

"Lily, wow… great job of showin' everyone that you really don't care nothin' about your appearance." My ponytail would be lopsided, or I didn't get all the tangles out of my hair. "You got a B on your spellin' test? Seriously, Lily, you should know how to spell idiot."

Chapter Four

1978

Relationships for me have always been hard to maintain due to the simple fact that I didn't have much practice with friendships. As a child, I yearned for a sibling or a best friend with whom I could share my secrets and depend on as a regular playmate. I had Daddy on Saturdays and shared him with Momma on Sundays, but that didn't fill the void. I yearned for a friend my own age.

Of course, there was the occasional classmate or neighborhood kid that would befriend me for a short period of time. I recall one sweet girl in my third-grade class who moved from Kentucky halfway through the school year. Her name was Genevieve, and she had long, dark curly hair, big green eyes and a wide smile that filled the bottom half of her face. Not only was she completely gorgeous with her flawless tan skin, but she was as sweet as pie - a phrase I learned from her. Since she was new to Normal and I had no friends, we were an easy pairing. We would sit together at lunch and sometimes even swap lunch items.

Words sounded so much cooler coming from her mouth. Our teacher told us it was called a southern drawl. I loved to hear her talk.

"Heavens to Betsy! My momma is always a-packin' me three cotton-pickin' carrots. I am darn-near tired of carrots, y'all." She frowned and pushed them to the side as she was taking out the contents from her Snow White lunch pail.

Even her lunch pail proved that she was too cool to be hanging out with me. My homemade lunch, which usually consisted of a peanut butter sandwich, came each day packed in a brown paper sack that was reused from the day before.

"You can have my pudding cup." *You can have my right arm if you will be my friend*, is what I was actually thinking. I shone my best crooked smile and pushed the pudding towards her. *If she grabs it, we will be friends forever!*

"Well, thanks, Lily, honey! Ain't you precious." Genevieve snatched my pudding and slid her carrots to me. She winked at me.

She had the most contagious giggle, so I was always trying to make her laugh. I tried a few of my daddy's bad dad jokes on her. They would earn her giggle.

This was one of her favorites: "Why can't you hear a pterodactyl go to the bathroom? Because the pee is silent."

Our teacher commented after a few weeks, "You two are like two peas in a pod."

Having a friend to sit with at lunch, someone who saved me a swing at recess, and a pal to partner with for spelling quizzes was worth giving up any dessert. With Genevieve as my bestie, I wouldn't be picked last anymore.

After two months of this ideal third grade friendship, Genevieve informed me that we could no longer be friends. It was recess time, and she met me outside the door. She was not saving swings. She would not look me in the eye. She looked down at her new white Adidas tennis shoes with two navy blue stripes on the side as she informed me.

"Last night, my momma was madder than a wet hen. She said somethin' about your momma havin' loose morals. I don't know what that is, but it ain't no good because she was a-hootin' and a-hollerin' at me and Paw. I ain't allowed to be sortin' with anyone connected to Ms. Daisy. Sorry, Lily."

She slowly turned and walked away. I will never forget how my heart ached that Friday when she broke the news to me during the first morning recess. When she skipped off to the monkey bars, my heart cracked. She knew I would never chase her to the monkey bars; the mean girls played on those. It didn't take long before I heard them welcome her to their part of the playground.

With my tail tucked between my legs and my head down, I kicked rocks and pouted off to the swings. There were two swings left unoccupied like usual; they were the ones we used during every recess. I walked over to the one that was designated as my swing. Tears rolled down my cheeks. I never had a best friend before. Not someone I counted on, looked forward to seeing, and enjoyed their company.

I didn't have a best friend anymore because of something called 'morals', and Momma had lost them somewhere. I was determined to find them for her and claim Genevieve back as my best friend.

When I arrived home from school that afternoon, I was still angry. I purposely slammed the screen door when I walked into the house. Momma casually remained sitting at the kitchen table reading one of her favorite gossip magazines.

"How was your day, Lily?" she inquired even though she didn't even look up.

I couldn't tell if she didn't hear the slamming door and my stomping feet, or if she was choosing not to indulge my well-deserved tantrum.

"Well, if you must know, Genevieve won't be my best friend anymore. Her mom said you have lost your morals, and until you find them, I don't have a best friend!" I glared at her, demanding a reaction.

"Who is Genevieve?" She licked her naughty finger to turn to the next page in her magazine. She had not even looked up before responding. Her response made the crack in my heart break a bit more.

Obviously, she never listened to my answers when I talked about my day at school. They were all laced with "Genevieve this" and "Genevieve that" stories. Daddy even knew to ask for funny Genevieve stories during our Saturday breakfast routine. Momma claimed to not even know who my best friend was, and therefore, unconcerned that she was no longer speaking to me.

I stormed off to my upstairs bedroom, slammed my door and cried until I fell asleep. When I woke up, it was hours later. It was dark outside, and my stomach was growling. If it was dark out, I knew that Daddy would be home soon, if he wasn't already, from his weekly trucking route. I would talk to him. He would make me feel better and enlighten me about morals.

As I slowly crawled out of my bed, I caught a glimpse of the only photograph that I had of me and Genevieve. Her mom had invited me to join them for the town's Corn Festival celebrations. Once a year, our town's settlers were recognized and celebrated with a Corn Festival. Main Street was blocked off for a morning parade, all-day community barbecue and an evening street dance. Everyone within a twenty miles radius attended the beloved festival.

Iowa was God's corn country. North, south, east and west were corn fields that bordered every side of Normal. These fields stretched out for miles and miles beyond what the town folk could even see. I often wondered if there was anything beyond the corn. Children were described in seasonal corn measurements.

"Emma is young'un, a late spring corn," or "Tyler is a strapping lad now, definitely a ripe-for-picking fall corn."

The prominent festival offered many contests relating to corn; for example, how tall your corn stalks grew, how many corn kernels were on your cob, and a contest for the oddest shaped corn cob. The popular corn hole tournament brought in many local ringers. Everyone's favorite contest was the 4H corn recipe cookoff. The three categories included: a dessert containing corn, a drink containing corn, and a main dish containing corn. Becoming a food judge was the highest compliment that a Normal citizen could be honored with. The five lucky judges, who were considered royalty, were selected as the most popular citizens in Normal. Not only did they have the honor of sampling all the food entries, but they also cruised down Main Street as the grand marshals in the Corn Festival parade. Normal, Iowa, was very serious and very proud of their corn.

To show our pride for the farmers, a local artist created a sculpture of a friendly, grinning, nine-foot corn stalk. "Corny," as he was fondly nicknamed, stood tall at the south edge of downtown. One green arm shaped as a husk waved to everyone who cruised down Main Street. For each holiday, a city hall employee decorated him. For Christmas, he wore a big red Santa hat; for Halloween, he was often dressed as Batman; for Valentine's Day, his waving husk hand held a big red heart. Of course, during the high school's homecoming, Corny was often the victim of a senior prank. Teenagers couldn't resist decorating the phallic shaped statue. Poor Corny...

The picture was taken just as Genevieve, and I had bitten into a warm, buttery piece of corn on the cob. The yellow butter was dripping down our chins. Upon seeing that picture, all of the pain from the collapse of our friendship came pouring back. I was determined to get my best friend back. I needed to talk to Daddy. As soon as I opened my bedroom door, I heard Daddy's deep voice. When he was angry, his voice sounded like thunder.

"Rob called me over the CB to tell me that you were at Rusty Nail dancing for money. Fuck! Daisy, tell me that isn't true?" Along with the anger, there was a hint of desperation. He truly hoped the news was incorrect.

Momma's words slurred together. "Oh Benny... it was nothin'. I forgot my purse, so I needed money to pay for my drinks" - she hiccupped - "and damn, I made more than enough to pay for my drinks." - Another hiccup. - "You should be grateful, not pissed."

"Grateful? Really? How about ashamed? How about embarrassed? How about disappointed? My so-called wife is drunk at a local pub dancing for tips while my eight-year-old daughter is home alone! And you want me to be proud of you for saving money so you could get sloppy drunk? You are unreal. I don't even know you anymore."

He slammed the back door of our house. I heard our only car start up, and he drove away in it. Never did get to ask him for advice. He didn't come back all weekend.

Eight-year-old me had no idea why Daddy was so mad. Momma was right; she made lots of money and even bought me a new board game. Furthermore, like Momma, I loved dancing. I had a pink, delicate dancing ballerina inside my jewelry box. Every time I opened the lid, she would twirl around on her toes. If Momma danced like her, I'm sure she deserved every cent of the money she earned. But eight-year-old me didn't realize Momma was using a pole and wearing a lot less clothing than any ballerina wore. Her tip jar was her G-string.

When Daddy stormed off that night, his intention was to scare Momma, perhaps shock some sense into her. However, it accomplished the opposite. It fueled a fire inside her. That Saturday night, with Daddy absent, she returned to dance at Rusty Nail. She bragged to me that she earned another one hundred dollars. After that weekend, she became a regular dancer.

"What Daddy don't know won't hurt him. Plus, Uncle Freddy won't be creeping around here no more. Six years of Uncle Freddy. I wish I would have thought of this sooner," she claimed. She hid the money in a jar in the kitchen cupboard, and if I promised not to tell Daddy, she would buy me another present.

Since I didn't see anything wrong with her dancing to earn some extra money, I agreed. What eight-year-old girl doesn't want her mother to be a beautiful ballerina?

Chapter Five

1983

I stayed home sick from school. Swallowing felt like scratching two pieces of sandpaper together in my throat. I woke up from a wonderful dream where I was riding a big white unicorn through puffy white clouds. As my unicorn and I bounced from cloud to cloud, we were smiling and giggling. There were butterflies everywhere. Their wings were every color of the rainbow. But all of a sudden, my unicorn raced through a barbed wire fence, and I flew off it and landed on a cloud. The barbed wire hit me right across the neck. Even in my dream, I was holding my neck as if the barbed wire of my dream had scratched me to the bone. It was burning and sore.

Dang sore throat woke me up. I moaned a little, trying to choke out, "Momma?" It didn't come out very loud; I was positive she didn't hear me unless she had her ear pressed to my bedroom door waiting. I tried one more time. "Momma?"

My pink fuzzy slippers were waiting for me at the edge of my twin bed. I slipped them on as I crawled out of bed. As I slowly cracked open the door, I exited my safe place. After taking a minute to pee, I headed down the stairs in search of Momma.

The morning sun was trying to squeeze through the gray clouds.

Despite the heavy film in its way, the sun optimistically continued to press its rays onto the world.

"Momma?" I quietly inquired as I reached the bottom of the stairs. I didn't hear a response. It was only me and the sun creeping in. A mini cough escaped my raw throat. I needed some medicine and a bit of juice. *Where is she?*

I padded through the living room. The TV was turned off, the shades were still drawn closed, her coffee cup sat empty on the coffee table next to her usual spot on the loveseat. I headed towards the kitchen. Everything was as clean as a whistle. The sink contained no sign of the normal morning ritual. The coffee pot was on - the first sign of life.

When I reached the big kitchen window that overlooked the back-yard and driveway in front of our detached garage, I stretched up on my tiptoes to peer outside. I spotted her. Or at least her head... her hair... the back of her head was distinguishable to me inside of a brown station wagon. Her long blonde hair bobbed up and down in a repetitious pattern. The car windows were fogged up so I couldn't see all of the details clearly. It was like I was looking at a blurry photo-graph. The right side of her face was visible to me when she rolled her head back every couple of seconds as she proceeded to go up and down. Sometimes, she was smiling and other times she looked like she was making a howling noise.

When a bit of fog cleared in the wagon, I noticed a man's face come up to Momma's naked right breast. His mouth covered it. Her head rolled back, and her lips made an 'O' shape. His brown hair looked wet, and his face glistened with sweat.

He was not my father. I was only thirteen years old, but I knew what they were doing was wrong. My heart tightened in my chest. My breath caught in my sore, scratchy throat.

Wait! I recognized that dirty brown station wagon. I rode in the back seat listening to bible songs last month. "Jesus loves me, this I know, for the Bible tells me so..." I sat in the middle of the second row between Tarasue and Stella as we trucked down the highway towards

Newton Hills State Park. It was Bible camp weekend with twelve other teenagers camping, hiking, and learning about Jesus.

Chapter Six

1983

I had been looking forward to Bible Camp weekend all summer. In the front seat of his brown station wagon, Pastor Tony steered us down the road. His wife Lisa sat next to him and led us through Bible song after Bible song. Pastor Tony's hands firmly gripped the steering wheel, but he would occasionally glance in the rearview mirror to see if we were singing along. He would smile at each one of us before returning his eyes to the road. Lisa, his loving wife of ten years, wasn't wearing her seat belt, so she sat with her back resting on the passenger door. She relaxed sideways in the front seat and looked adoringly at her husband and fellow passengers. "He's got the whole world in His hands."

As each mile added onto the speedometer, we soaked it in. Our souls were fulfilled with His word. Everyone was singing, and no one cared about pitch or being on key. Our hearts pumped with purpose. It was a wonderful way to start the memorable weekend.

We slept in tents - six girls in one and six boys in the other. Pastor Tony and his wife Lisa had their own smaller tent. After an exhilarating day of hiking, Bible lessons, canoeing, fishing and swimming, we gathered around the campfire and roasted hot dogs and marshmallows.

I learned so many things that weekend in the woods, but by far the most exciting thing I learned, besides how to paddle a canoe, was how to construct a s'more. The first step was the hunt for the perfect stick. It needed to be long enough to hold over the fire and sturdy enough to hold a melting marshmallow. After the stick was selected, I poked a marshmallow onto the end of the stick and held it over the open flame until the entire marshmallow turned a nice shade of brown. Then I carefully placed the marshmallow onto one half of a graham cracker, added a piece of chocolate, and put the other half of the cracker on top. Heaven!

Around the campfire, we shared stories of how God had touched our lives. Madeline explained that after her dad died in a car accident a few years ago, she knew God was with her in that church pew. He helped her so she could be there for her mom and little brothers.

"Great example of how God gives us strength in times of need." Pastor Tony was really enjoying this deep, religious discussion. He was perched on the edge of the log near the bonfire. He had already consumed two s'mores and a bit of evidence still lingered on his bottom lip. Melted marshmallow sat crusted on his face… "Does anyone else have a story they would like to share? Raise your hand."

Tommy raised his hand tentatively. He had been fishing that afternoon. A bit of dirt was on his cheek still and stuck under his fingernails.

"Tommy, do you have a story of how God has entered your life and made your faith stronger?"

After what seemed like eternity in silence (it was about twenty seconds), Tommy slowly nodded. Tommy was new to our school, but he made friends easily and was always joking around. He had red hair, freckles and wasn't much taller than me.

"After work, my dad often stopped at the bar before coming home. He called it 'blowing off steam,' but my mom said he was up to no good. This one night when my dad came home, he was really, really angry. He cursed and threw things even before he opened the door to our house. Mom and I were watching TV in the living room. My little brother, Johnny, had just ran upstairs to put his pajamas on. When

Mom and I heard Dad outside, I quickly hollered for Johnny. Whenever Dad was in a bad way, it was my job to hide with Johnny. Hiding is what we usually did until Dad passed out. My mom suggested it. Johnny didn't come downstairs, so I hid alone behind the long curtains in our living room. When he came into the house, Dad screamed the worst curse words at Mom. I can't repeat them.

"Then I heard the sound of my dad's hand slap my mom's face. She screamed. I stayed there. I was scared. I didn't know what to do. Then I heard my little brother come down the stairs crying for Mom. He ran straight for her, but Dad grabbed him and threw him across the living room. Johnny only weighed about forty pounds, so his little, skinny body soared like a football through the air. Then, I heard my mom scream again. I don't remember much else about that night. There were sirens, red and blue lights shining. They handcuffed my dad, and he was taken away.

"My mom and I live with my mom's sister in Normal now. My Aunt Ella brought me to church. The first time that I attended Sunday school, I recognized the picture of Jesus framed on the wall. He was there with me, the night Johnny died. He was behind the curtain with me holding my hand. He kept me safe and told me that I would be all right."

Tommy's personal story sucked all the energy from his body. Tommy lowered his head as if his neck became too tired to hold it up. Silent tears escaped from his big chestnut-colored eyes and dropped onto his jeans.

A stunned silence gripped the little camp. We patiently waited to hear what Pastor Tony would say regarding Tommy's tragedy. It was incredibly quiet except for the crackle of the fire. An owl called to its mate in the distance and a few locust bugs sang their nightly song. Pastor Tony slid his fingers through his thick, wavy, brown hair. He scratched his head and glanced up to the night sky as if seeking guidance from up above with his word choice.

During the silence, I noted that Pastor Tony was wearing worn-out jeans, a gray sweatshirt and a red bandanna around his neck; not his usual church attire. He looked like a regular guy. He was a slim, healthy thirty-something-year-old.

I had been attentively listening to his weekly sermons for the past six months after Momma decided she needed to improve her life and faith. We found Pastor Tony at Our Savior's Church. He eagerly welcomed us that first Sunday after the church service. After each service, he proudly placed himself near the doorway that led to the narthex, shaking hands with the congregation as they exited. He displayed a presence of being very important and honorable standing in his white preaching robe. Only his shirt collar was visible at the top of his robe, and his shiny, brown dress shoes peeked out of the bottom.

"I'm so glad you made it today, Laura. Give Lance my best, and I hope calving goes smoothly for him this spring." We were next in line to shake hands. He eyed us up and down as we tentatively approached him. "Well, hello! Thank you for coming today. You must be new because I would've certainly remembered two pretty girls like you."

Momma simply giggled and nodded. "My daughter, Lily, and I really enjoyed your preachin'." Momma batted her big, brown eyes and smiled that million-dollar smile. Pastor Tony glanced at me for a polite, split second but as usual, Momma stole everyone's attention.

"Hello, Lily. You are a beautiful young lady." His words addressed me, but he had not taken his eyes off Momma and her curves. He asked her name, where she was from, and what brought her to Our Savior's that Sunday. Momma, in all her glory, enjoyed his undivided attention and filled his head with her version of life. I tuned out her words but noticed that their body language seemed somehow peculiar to me. I couldn't quite put my finger on it. It did not seem very Christian the way these two adults were carrying on, so I thanked him and pushed Momma out the door. She flashed him an apologetic look and a little flirtatious wave over her bare shoulder.

For a solid six months of Sundays, we frequented the same church pew at Our Savior's, allowing Daddy a chance to sleep in. He needed extra rest before he started another long week of trucking. Every Sunday, Pastor Tony would stand in front of the congregation and deliver lessons from the Bible. Honestly, I savored every word, but for completely different reasons than Momma.

During every Sunday sermon, Pastor Tony's eyes would locate Momma in the crowd of worshippers. His gaze would intensely hold hers for a bit and then slowly move to the flock. And every Sunday, Momma would purposefully be the last person to exit the sanctuary, either taking too long to collect her belongings or putting away hymnals and Bibles. As we made our way to the exit, Pastor Tony would strike up a random conversation with Momma... and me. One time, the conversation was about the weather, another time they talked about politics, and another time he asked about her favorite food. Usually, I would grow bored of their endless chatting and wander off on my own.

SITTING in a circle around the campfire, we waited again to hear what wise, Biblical words Pastor Tony would advise for sweet, sad, abused Tommy.

"Tommy, my boy, God did not allow this tragedy to happen to you. Unfortunately, evil is in every corner of the world. Everyone is tempted by evil, but when we put God at the center of our lives, He will give us strength to survive and flourish. With Him by our side, we can say 'no' to temptations and evil acts. We need to pray for those that wrong us. We must ask God to help heal the evil in their hearts and then of course heal our pain caused by the evil." We all sighed collectively and folded our hands. "Dear Lord, tonight we ask you to be with us as we all seek your guidance and strength. But Dear Lord, please place your strong, healing hand upon Tommy while he hurts. Amen."

Our group prayer didn't seem to ease the hurt and tension in Tommy. In fact, after sharing his story, his complexion was as white as a ghost and his shoulders sagged slightly lower. Since I was sitting closest to him on the makeshift log, I scooted over a couple of inches and gently draped my arm over his shoulders. He didn't react or even acknowledge my gesture, which was fine by me.

The next morning, I was the first camper to wake up in the girl's tent. I quietly gathered my toiletry items and slowly unzipped our tent door. A perfect sunrise greeted me as I exited the tent and peeked around. Our campsite was at the top of the hill. I could see the bright, yellow sun peeking up over the horizon. Songbirds quietly sang their love song as if they didn't want to wake anyone up. Perhaps they wanted to enjoy the peace of the morning. Everything was a bit damp from the lowered temperature overnight and glistened in the morning dew. Mornings were not typically something I looked forward to, but this exquisite sunrise made me smile.

I headed for the public bathroom. Our campsite was located a half mile from the toilets, so by the time I finally arrived, I rushed into the nearest stall to pee. Relief overflowed in my body. Lisa had been right; I should not have had that can of Tab just before we went to bed.

When my steady flow of urine became a thin trickle, I discovered that I was not the only camper awake. The public bathrooms consisted of the men's showers and toilets on the west side and the women's showers and toilets on the east side of the shared brick building. Through the vents in the walls, I heard a male voice on the other side of the wall in the men's bathroom.

"Ooooh… ahhh… yes… ohhh…" Weird bathroom noises. He seemed to be in pain and a bit out of breath. After a few more moans and a sigh of relief, I understood a few words: "... God, woman… amazing… need… go." I could hear some shuffling around and giggling.

I hurried to finish and rushed to the sink to wash my hands. I could hear more kissing noises and movement towards the door. I cracked open the heavy door in time to catch a glimpse of the back of a blonde woman wearing a red bandanna in her hair, walking in the opposite direction of our camp. She had a distinct walk, a confidence in her step. Her hips swayed in her denim cut-off jean shorts.

When I turned my head in the opposite direction, I witnessed a man walking towards our camping area. I saw the side of his face when he turned to glance back at the woman who was headed in the opposite direction. It was Pastor Tony. He was smiling and humming to himself. He wore the same jeans and a gray sweatshirt from the previous day. I slowly and quietly shut the heavy bathroom door. My thirteen-year-old self giggled at what I had just witnessed between two consenting adults. *Gross!* I would never understand adults. I returned to the sink to brush my teeth.

I knew what I overheard: it was sex. Momma watched *As the World Turns* every afternoon during summer break. Those actors and actresses made those exact same noises and moaned like that when they were in bed together or kissing passionately. I couldn't wait to write about this in my diary when I returned home.

Ten minutes later, as I strolled back to our campsite, I found three of my fellow campers and Pastor Tony awake, sitting at a picnic table and talking quietly as to not wake the rest of the camp. Pastor Tony sat sipping his coffee out of a mug that read, "Be careful or you will end up in my sermon."

I blushed a little at knowing that I had witnessed some 'adult actions' in the bathroom a bit earlier. I hoped Pastor Tony and Lisa would not put two and two together and realize that I was over the wall while they were doing it.

"Good morning, Lily!" Pastor Tony welcomed me when I finally reached camp. "Come join us." From his welcoming tone, I didn't sense any awareness. I put my toiletry bag next to me on the picnic table and sat next to Tommy. Not on purpose. It was the largest open space and logical place to sit. He gave me a small grin when I sat down. I returned the smile. I had manners.

"I got the new cassette by Journey. I listen to it, like, all the time on my Walkman," Tarasue explained as she stood behind Stella, French braiding her long brown hair. Tarasue and Stella were inseparable at school, so I was not surprised to see their sisterly connection in the woods.

"I can't stop singing *All Out of Love* by Air Supply. Have you heard that one?" Stella quietly sang a few lines.

Tommy' eyes locked with mine as he said, "*The Rose* by Bette Milder. There is nothing better. She sings straight from the heart." And then he turned to the group and said, "Am I right?"

Under her breath, I heard Tarasue mutter in Stella's ear, "Gag me with a spoon."

I caught the subtle look Tommy gave me, and I immediately felt my cheeks fill with redness. Pastor Tony must have noticed Tommy's glance in my direction too because he smiled at me and continued to sip his steaming hot coffee.

During that moment of silence, a tent zipper went up. Pastor Tony's wife Lisa crawled out of their two-person tent. Her brown hair was a mess. She wore a wrinkled, white WHAM t-shirt and plaid sweat-pants... and no red bandana. She yawned, stretched and strolled over to our picnic table, "Good morning, campers."

I couldn't even reply. My head was spinning as I was trying to understand what happened.

"Where is your red bandanna? It looked nice in your hair," I blurted. I couldn't contain my shock or control my thoughts. A beehive burst open in my brain; the bees were buzzing around and couldn't find an escape.

"I'm sorry. What red bandanna?" Lisa was a short brunette whose heart was as big as her huge boobs. She leaned in and gave Pastor Tony a small peck on his lips. "Good morning, honey."

Pastor Tony's face had lost its coloring. His skin became very pale. White must be the shade of guilt or shame. Last night, after Tommy revealed his story about his awful home life, his skin had turned a pasty white, and now Pastor Tony's was the same color. Always thought black was the symbol of bad, terrible things like black birds, crows, dirt, and shadows. I thought black was the color of ominous things. But this weekend, I learned that it was white.

As he tried to recover his composure, a lightbulb ignited in my head: it wasn't his wife he was feeling up in the gross, unsanitary men's room. It was someone else. Lisa had brown hair, and that woman had blonde hair...

No child wanted to have these thoughts about an adult, especially about an adult whom they looked up to and respected. I didn't know what to think, so I pushed it into the back of my mind. It was none of my business. I wanted to enjoy my weekend.

I turned my attention back to my peers who were still discussing the latest hit songs. Tarasue had finished braiding Stella's hair and was now using one of the braids as a microphone.

"Another one bites the dust! And another one gone and another one gone..." Tommy whipped out his leg and used it as an air guitar. It was still going to be a magical weekend. I would not let this new knowledge ruin my time.

When I arrived home on Sunday afternoon, I sprinted through the front door, anxious to tell Daddy about the Bible camp and request his insight on Tommy Baker. The screen door slammed behind me. I dropped my backpack in the entryway. He wasn't in the living room, so I headed for the kitchen in the back of the house.

With her back to me, Momma was washing dishes at the sink. She turned around when she heard me. "Well, hi! How was your weekend? Wanna sit and tell me all about it?" She dried her hands with the dish towel and walked towards me with her arms open ready for an embrace.

"Where did you get that? Where did you get that red bandanna?"

My feet were rooted to the floor. She enveloped me into a hug that I didn't reciprocate.

"Oh... this?" She touched her head where the red bandanna was wrapped around her blonde hair. "I don't know, but don't I look so stylish?"

Chapter Seven

1983

Several months had passed and I convinced myself that red bandannas were quite common. It could have been anyone. However, an awkward feeling sat in the pit of my stomach. Must be a coincidence. It had to be. But now I know differently.

I noticed the back bumper of the brown station wagon had a bumper sticker that read, "Remember the Ten Commandments. If you don't, the devil will remind you."

Well, if that was true, Momma was going to Hell for sure.

I couldn't stomach what I was seeing. Pastor Tony and my momma... doing forbidden acts? What were they thinking? Didn't he preach about this sort of thing? What did the Bible say about sleeping with someone else's spouse?

My sore throat was forgotten, and instead I felt nauseous. I rushed to the bathroom. After emptying the contents of my stomach, I escaped upstairs to my bedroom and threw the covers over my head. I sobbed for Daddy, who was never home enough to make the three of us feel like a real family. I mourned the loss of my innocence. I sobbed for Lisa, Pastor Tony's wife, who was also oblivious. I cried for the disappointment Momma was.

And Pastor Tony - what a disgrace! If the congregation knew, what would they think? Would they still follow him unconditionally? How would they believe what he had to say every Sunday at church? How could he proclaim God's word and tell the worshippers to follow the commandments when he was breaking one in my driveway in his dirty station wagon?

I cried so much that I wore myself out and fell back asleep. I woke up to Momma's hand on my forehead checking for a fever. I flinched and jerked away from her touch.

"Lily, I was checkin' to see if you were still alive. It's past noon. You ain't runnin' a temp. How are you feelin'?" She straightened my covers, picked up my discarded tissues.

"Fine," I snapped.

"No temp but definitely grumpy. Got it. I brought you up some orange juice and a bologna sandwich. I'll leave you to rest." She rose from my bedside and strolled out of my room, gently closing my door behind her.

From that moment forward, I referred to her as Daisy. No more sweet pet names like Momma. She didn't deserve to be my mother, Daddy's wife. She didn't deserve it for sinning with the pastor and for how she was hurting Daddy.

Chapter Eight

1988

G rowing up in a household of low income pushed me to nail down a job to supplement many teenage wishes and wants. My parents couldn't afford designer jeans or name-brand tops for my back-to-school wardrobe. If I was completely honest, there was no wardrobe. I had three pairs of hand-me-down jeans, a couple of sweaters and several T-shirts.

In a small Iowa town, teenagers had limited choices for income: babysitting, dog walking, picking beans, early morning cleaning or waitressing. And luckily for me, Kitty, the owner of Kitty's Cafe, had taken a liking to me years before I needed a part-time job. Her daughter, Tarasue, was in my grade at school and also attended the same youth group at our church.

Through our years in junior high, Tarasue politely tolerated me. I was sure Kitty encouraged, suggested, or even pushed Tarasue to include me in her social circle. She invited me to do things: go to the movies, play frisbee at the park, or join her and some other classmates at the pool. I eagerly accepted these invitations. Tarasue was the closest thing I had to a real girlfriend. I enjoyed these social outings even if I was generally ignored. I walked slightly behind the group of giggly girls. I wasn't privy to the information that they whispered in each others' ears.

When Tarasue and I were alone together, those moments were the times I cherished the most. She forgot that she was forced to spend time with me. We giggled like normal school children, watched old movies, painted our nails, braided each other's hair and made prank phone calls to boys in our class.

Tarasue and I were like step siblings who endured each other for Kitty's sake. In our case, Kitty was the stepmother. She adopted me without taking me home. She always packed me a take-home meal after I worked a night shift, simply commenting, "I didn't know if you had a chance to eat tonight. Just throw it in the fridge at home and microwave it later if you don't want it when you get home." She'd usually follow it with a wink or a squeeze of my shoulder.

Extra or unclaimed tips were collected into a jar under the counter. It didn't have anyone's name on it, but Kitty always just dumped it into my tip jar. I knew it was all charity. Kitty felt sorry for me. In the early days, I tried to refuse, but Kitty didn't take that too well. It was easier to please her and accept her generosity. Kitty wasn't a woman to reckon with.

If it was a slow evening at the cafe with not too many customers, Kitty kept me on the clock and ordered me to work on my homework in a back booth. If a customer came in then, I would take a break from my schoolwork. "Your studies are super important, Lily. A young girl that looks like you should have a mind as gorgeous as her body."

Kitty was an enormous female influence on my teenage years. Kitty celebrated when I received all A's the final semester of my junior year. It was Kitty whom I told about the football players who were caught smoking in the locker room. It was Kitty who taught me how to roll the cuffs of my jeans like all the teenagers were doing. It was Kitty who recommended books for me to read. When I needed my first bra, Kitty was the one who took me to buy it when I told her that I was uncomfortable in gym class running up and down the basketball court. Kitty was always there for me, Kitty to the rescue.

But I was not the only one who sought out Kitty for advice or a listening ear. I swear the whole town of Normal relied on her for her good home cooking and solid, honest advice. Never one to shy away from conflict, she declared the truth and offered no excuses. If someone asked for her advice, they understood that Kitty was going to give it to them straight. More times than I could count, I witnessed Kitty crossing her arms over her chest, her eyes focused on listening to the speaker while her butt sat on the cooler under the cafe's counter. Her long braids would go up and down her back as she nodded encouragement to her troubled friend. After the story was complete, I would see Kitty close her big brown eyes and consider her words before she laid out the moral lesson. Her friends didn't always like what she had to say, but everyone appreciated that she didn't pussyfoot around the truth.

Kitty's real name was Katherine. She earned the nickname "Kitty' in high school. Katherine was known for adopting and caring for stray animals. If she found an injured bird, she would not be able to leave it laying around to be sacrificed to one of its many predators. She would find an abandoned nest and gently set it in there with either a few freshly dug up worms or seeds from a flowering plant.

But her claim to fame was when her brother followed her after school one day and discovered that she had adopted twenty homeless cats. She collected each one and moved them into an abandoned home on the edge of town. She used her babysitting money to buy cat food for her adopted cats. Her sneaky brother vowed to keep her secret in exchange for a few of his household chores and, of course, fondly nicknaming her, "Here Kitty, Kitty!"

Kitty was suspended in the era she grew up in: the early 1970s. She always wore two braids on each side of her head. Her hair was a beautiful chestnut color and fell to the middle of her back. The freckles that dusted her cheeks and nose were the same chestnut color. She never wore makeup. She loved her bell-bottom pants and hippy, flowing tops. Kitty had her own style, and it matched her easy, open-minded attitude perfectly. She oozed confidence and independence.

Kitty had never been married and never wanted to be married. Kitty explained that she did not need a man to fulfill her dreams in life.

A man had provided the one thing she could not do on her own: a child. She never talked about Tarasue's father. She told Tarasue that his name was not worthy of even one sound.

"Some things are best left buried in the past for good reason. Unfortunately, he was the scum of the earth. No reason for Tarasue to know him or who he was. It will only bring more pain. His absence is a blessing."

Kitty claimed that it was for the best because she wouldn't let a man hold her back. Kitty was a nonconformist and made no excuses for the choices that she made even if several old fashioned, small town, small-minded people publicly questioned her choices. She did not hold anything against them for judging her and her situation.

"Not worth the energy. As long as I am happy with my own decisions, I am at peace. Other people's opinions will not shape who I am as a person. Remember that, Lily, believe in yourself. Value your own opinion the most."

Kitty managed her restaurant with her unique, free spirited view on life. Customers always felt at ease and at home at her cafe. If a complaint was made, no harsh words were exchanged. Kitty viewed the complaints as constructive feedback, and somehow received them with respect and appreciation. Tense issues rolled off her back. She didn't stew about things and never got visibly upset. I asked her once what her secret was.

"Kitty, do you ever get stressed out?" We were performing the closing tasks. I was wiping all the tables down, and she was balancing the till.

"Stress? Why do I need to be stressed? I don't want that bad aura around me. Fate has a way of working things out. You can't lose sleep over the little things in the universe. Everything corrects itself or will be righted in the end."

She made things seem so simple and easy. I knew it was not, but somehow Kitty possessed the ability to not let things get to her or bother her. It was her survival skill, an extremely powerful one.

For obvious selfish reasons, Daisy did not approve of my close relationship with her. "You're her charity case, Lily. She has her own daughter. Stop bothering her with all your problems."

Thankfully, I didn't give much value to Daisy's opinion anymore and continued enjoying Kitty's company while respecting her space as well. Kitty was more of a mother to me than my own blood.

Kitty eased my worries when I felt guilty about taking up her time and asking for motherly advice. "Lily, you're my chosen family. Our relationship is a choice. Remember that friendship isn't a big thing. It is a million little things."

Chapter Nine

1985

W hen I was ten years old, the movie *Fame* was all the rave. Therefore, like most girls my age, I carefully cut out the necks of my favorite sweatshirts to make a large, wide neck opening. One side would fall off my shoulder like the sexy actress in the movie. Colorful leg warmers decorated my legs over the top of my also very colorful leggings. On evenings that I would find myself alone, I would rewind the *Fame* VCR tape over and over trying to imitate her dance moves. I would crank up the volume loud to feel the beat pulse through my body. During one of my evening rehearsals, Daisy caught me practicing in the living room. She laughed when I tripped over my own two feet.

"Lily, you ain't got no rhythm. You're like your Daddy and born with two left feet. Trust me. This" - she motioned to the TV by circling the area with her hand - "ain't gonna work. You don't have what it takes."

She threw back her head and laughed again, then headed upstairs. Her laughter trailed after her. My head said she was right, but her words still stung. I hated to give up on my dream of becoming a famous dancer who was discovered in a quiet, small town in Iowa.

A short time later, I learned about jogging. Jane Fonda was

promoting women's fitness, and jogging was the new exercise fad. I didn't need rhythm or coordination to jog. After months of independent jogging, I discovered that I had a gift for endurance. I ran for miles before returning home. I loved how exercise made my body feel alive. I read about how the endorphin hormone was released when you exercised. I understood what the runner's high was. Jogging became my new hobby.

The lower half of my body became obsessed with running like a loyal, four-legged companion became excited when the four letter word, 'walk', is mentioned. Heavy panting, excited facial expression and undying devotion would explode from the walking companion. Until the promise was fulfilled, nothing else would happen. That is exactly how my legs felt about running. It was as if they were a foreign entity of my body and had a mind of their own. If my brain even flashed an idea of a possible run, my two feet become energetic and stubborn. A surge of energy erupted from my toes to my head, demanding physical activity. I never fully intended to deny them, but sometimes the surge of energy didn't have the best timing.

As I laced up my Nike white-on-white tennis shoes, the adrenaline pulsed through my veins. Running was my best friend. She was there for me no matter the weather. Not only did she answer whenever I called, she filled my soul and raised my confidence. My reward for loyalty was a lean, firm body that enjoyed the hard, steady workout. If only I could hug her, but instead, I thanked her in my head and off we went.

WHEN THE JUNIOR high Track and Field Day sign-up sheet was released, I registered for all the long-distance running events. My gym teacher approached me after collecting the sheets.

"Lily, I love your enthusiasm for Track and Field Day, but if you add up all the events you signed up for, you will be running around... eight miles in one, short afternoon. That's a bit much, honey. Is there an event I can remove for you?" She was glancing down at her collected sign-up sheets. "The three-mile run could be one and then that brings you down to five miles, which is still a bit much..." She was still contemplating.

"No! I mean, please, no." My initial, natural response came out a bit forcefully. "Mrs. Hunt, please don't remove me from the three-mile run. That is my first choice. I've been jogging on my own for years, and I'm in good shape. I'll be fine. I appreciate your concern."

Mrs. Hunt sized me up and down. She identified that I was in good, physical shape from observing me in gym class. First one down the court when we played basketball, first one across the field when we played soccer. Plus, I ran circles around most of the boys in my class.

"Are you sure, Lily? How about we make a deal: if you change your mind that afternoon, you let me know? It is supposed to be a fun day. I don't want you passing out." She ruffled my hair and sent me on my way.

On Track and Field Day, nervous energy burned in my veins. I was pumped up and more than ready. I ate carbs for lunch and drank plenty of water. The endorphins were running high.

I earned first place in all the individual races that I signed up for: three-mile run, one-mile run, eight-hundred-meter dash and four-hundred-meter dash. My relay team placed second in the four-by-four relay. I had not given in and competed in all my Track and Field Day events.

When I crossed the finish line for my three-mile run with a time of twenty minutes and thirty-one seconds, the teacher running the stop-watch couldn't believe the time that he recorded. He shook the stop-watch and glanced up and down. The next student to cross the finish line was a half-lap away. Mrs. Hunt clapped and hurried over to where I hunched over trying to catch my breath with my hands on my thighs.

"Nice work, Lily! You were right - you can run! You're a deer!" She gently patted me on the back and offered me a drink from a water bottle.

I had never completed an actual race before. Running helped me to escape and forget. I ran to get away from my life. I had to admit that I impressed myself too. *That was fun!*

The teacher controlling the stopwatch shouted in our direction, "Lily, is it? I wanna talk to you tomorrow morning before school. I'll meet you in the junior high gym. Eight sharp." I only nodded in acknowledgement since I still hadn't caught my breath. He looked familiar, but I didn't know his name. I had nothing else going on at eight o'clock tomorrow anyway. Additionally, he didn't offer an option other than accepting his proposal. He was a coach, that much I was sure of. He barked an order and didn't expect any rebuttal. Coaching 101.

Friday morning promptly at eight, I met Coach Knight - I learned his name that morning - in the gym. His attire - white short sleeve polo shirt with black shorts - screamed typical coach. Under his Minnesota Twins baseball cap, he had light brown hair. The bottom half of his legs were covered by white tube socks. His brand-new tennis shoes were white with little-to-no wear on them. He sat on the bleachers jotting down notes on his clipboard. The gym was empty except for us so he heard me crossing the gym floor.

"Lily, over here."

When I came within eight feet of him, I stopped and silently waited. I had no idea why I had been summoned here. He looked up at me when I approached. He put down his pen and did not stand. "I'm Coach Knight. I coach the high school track team. I saw you run yesterday. I was extremely impressed. Who has been working with you? Who has been training you?"

"No one. I just like to run," I answered while trying to remember the good manners that I was taught by Daddy.

He had told me a few times, "Give adults the respect that they have earned by looking them in the eye, always speak loudly enough for them to hear, and give them a firm handshake."

Shoot! I forgot the handshake.

"Well, your time in every one of your races was very impressive. I'd like to see you go out for the track team next year." He advised me to continue my training up until track season next spring and how, if I needed anything, I could call on him. "I'll see more of you in the next couple of years since I teach high school Speech. Keep up the good

43

work, Lily. You're an impressive young lady." He shook my hand and dismissed me.

Coach Knight was the first adult other than Daddy who showed a real interest in me. Over the next couple of years, we became close. I regarded him as an uncle I wished I had, and I became a regular part of his family. His wife, Susan, was as friendly and energetic as he was. They had two little boys, Luke and Zack, whom I instantly adopted as little brothers. At first, I visited Coach Knight's house for running tips or simple check-ins. Then I started babysitting their boys. Soon I was invited over for family dinners on a regular basis. During these family dinners, we would all sit around the kitchen table talking, laughing and sharing stories. This was how a family should be. It made my heart hurt that Daddy traveled so much and that we couldn't be a family like this. Daddy would love to relax around the dinner table swapping stories or jokes.

"There were two sisters. One was blonde, and one was brunette." Coach Knight decided that it was joke time. Luke and Zack had already been excused from the table and were playing a board game on the floor in the nearby living room.

With a small, teasing grin on her face, Susan interrupted him, "Not another blonde joke, Max. I can't take it." Susan had blonde hair, but she wasn't the typical blonde that was in many of his jokes. Susan graduated college with a minor in Criminal Justice. She had planned on becoming a lawyer until she found out she was pregnant with the boys. Plans were altered, and she didn't regret her choice. Susan served everything with genuine kindness, whether it was a hello or dinner. A stranger could tell that when she asked how you were doing, she really wanted to know. She was angelic, sweet, motherly and patient. I admired her in so many ways.

"Let me tell my joke. Once upon a time, there were two sisters, one was a blonde and one was a brunette. Recently, their parents had passed away and left the family farm to the two sisters. The sisters didn't know much about running a farm, but they were willing to try. One day, they noticed they only had six hundred dollars left. The brunette sister offered to head to town to buy a bull. The bull would seed their heifers and produce baby cows so they would not lose the farm. She told her blonde sister, 'I will let you know if I find a bull to buy. When I do find one, you will need to hitch the trailer to the tractor to come to town to pick up our new bull. Please bring all of the money with you.'

"The brunette sister walked to the nearest village. She searched the whole day. Just before she was about to give up, she found the perfect bull. The bull would cost $599. She needed to let her sister know to come pick it up. She walked to the post office to send her sister a telegram. She told the gentleman running the telegraph, "I need to send a telegram to my sister. Can you send her this message? *Please come to town and bring the trailer hitched to the tractor. I found a bull to buy. Please bring the money too.*

"The gentleman informed her, 'Did you know that each word costs one dollar?'

"The brunette sister did not know that, but she did know that they had only one dollar remaining, so she needed to think. A couple of minutes later, she had her answer. She was proud of herself and was confident with her choice.

"Sir, will you please send this telegraph to my sister: *comfortable?*

"The gentleman was shocked and confused. He asked the brown-haired sister, 'How is your sister going to understand to hitch up the trailer to the tractor to come to town to buy a bull, and bring the money if you only send the word *comfortable?*'

"The brunette smiled when she told the gentleman, 'My sister is blonde and a slow reader so she will read it like this: come... for ... ta... bull.'"

Coach Knight was grinning from ear to ear as he listened to us giggle and repeat the word "comfortable" out loud. The first thing I thought of was that I had to remember that one to tell Daddy when he arrived home. Now, *that* was a good dad joke.

By the time I was leaving that night, it was dark outside and had started to rain. Coach Knight kindly offered to drive me home. Normally, I jogged home, needing to stretch my legs and work off the dinner. Susan was a good cook and an even better baker. But that night,

I was tired and feeling sleepy after the heavy meal, so I accepted his generous offer.

On the short ride home in his pickup truck, we talked about the upcoming track season. It was my sophomore year, and I had even more to prove. Last spring as a freshman, I shocked everyone with my speed and endurance. No one had heard of my name until I started breaking all the school records.

"Not only is your training important, but your meals and sleep will help your focus and keep you healthy and strong. It will keep you on track. Get it? Track? On track?" He was so much like Daddy in that he thought he was funny, and he laughed the hardest at his own jokes.

I politely nodded and offered a small courtesy giggle. *Dad jokes, hahahaha...*

"I'm going to speak to your mom tonight, so she knows how important all of this is to your success." I never really shared much about my home life while I was at the Knight household. The Knights knew Daddy was a truck driver and only home on weekends while Daisy was a housewife. Therefore, I couldn't really tell him that he couldn't come into my house since he had always been so kind and generous to me. Quickly, I offered up a silent prayer to God that Daisy was either out for the night, or if she happened to be home, sober.

God heard a portion of my prayer: Mother was home and sober. She was in one of her rare good moods. She opened the front door wide for Coach Knight and me. I noticed her doe-like, brown eyes drink in Coach Knight. She must have approved of what she observed because her smile reached up to her eyes where I detected hunger. The dreaded pit formed in my stomach. She offered us both a Coke. Coach Knight and I both declined.

"That is kinda what I want to discuss with you, Mrs. Armstrong."

"Call me Daisy. All of my friends do," expressed Daisy.

I noticed as she was resting on the couch, her shorts exposed ninety-five percent of her thighs, and her white T-shirt was see-through. Furthermore, she was not wearing a bra. *Oh dear Lord...*

"Okay, Daisy, as I'm sure you are aware, Lily is a talented runner."

In actuality, Daisy was not aware of this fact at all. She verbally expressed that sports were for boys and didn't understand why I needed to run as often as I did. She had no idea but was doing a convincing job acting like she did.

"Runners should maintain a strict diet. We are hoping to improve Lily's speed this upcoming track season. I was hoping you could help us with maintaining a healthy diet for Lily. Lily is also aware of the foods and drinks she should not be consuming, but I thought that since you are the woman of the house, you could help us."

Coach Knight continued to explain examples of foods she should keep stocked in our house. Foods that would benefit my running and not hinder it. Coach Knight was doing a wonderful job, but I knew Daisy wasn't listening to a word he was saying. She was contemplating her next move.

After fifteen minutes of discussion and Daisy willingly agreeing to every one of his suggestions, she turned to me and inquired, "Lily, don't you have some homework you should be gettin' to?"

"Actually, I do. I have a history test tomorrow." I rose from my seat on one of the living room chairs across from where Daisy was perched. I expected Coach to stand up too and excuse himself, but he did not. "Coach Knight, thank you for the dinner and the ride home. I should go study now."

I excused myself and headed upstairs to my bedroom. The chatter of these two new friends started right up as I ascended the stairs. Even though Daisy wasn't dressed for visitors, I was glad she was receptive to Coach Knight and his ideas regarding my diet. My sophomore track season was going to be my most successful one yet.

Chapter Ten

1985

W hen I was a sophomore in high school, I attended my first formal dance without a date. I purchased a new dress at JCPenney with my own waitressing and babysitting income. It was a tea-length, chiffon, lilac dress that fit me perfectly. Glittering sequins circled the neckline and floral embroidered lace decorated the bodice. The skirt was layers of chiffon which accentuated my slim hips. I wore dyed-to-match quarter-inch heels. Anything more, and I'm sure I would've tripped. Delicate pearl earrings completed the look.

My own reflection in the full-length mirror that hung on the back of my bedroom door caused me to pause: a brown-haired, lean, elegant princess was staring back at me. She looked like a gorgeous girl that came to life in my imagination when Daddy recited to me his made-up fairy tales when I was a little girl. The hint of blue eye shadow and a faint, thin line of black eyeliner caused my blue eyes to pop and sparkle. They were large and mysterious. Lip gloss brushed my lips to give a little shimmer. My shoulder length brown hair contained long, spiral curls.

Daisy had been in a rare, charitable mood and had offered to apply my makeup and to style my hair. I still have the polaroid picture that Daddy snapped of Daisy putting rollers in my hair while I was perched on a stool in their bathroom. I wore her pink robe over my new dress to protect it. The picture incorrectly reflected the ideal mother doting on her teenage daughter. The photograph captured a small moment in time. Like she was always tender and sweet to me rather than cold and distant. Daddy's handwriting at the bottom of the picture read, "My two favorite flowers!"

Whenever Daddy created one of his fairy tales, the princess always landed the guy, the bad karma disappeared, and everyone lived happily-ever-after. I definitely felt like a princess standing in front of the mirror in a gorgeous dress, and I could only hope and dream that a fairy tale ending was waiting for me on this special night.

After the dance that was held at our high school a few blocks away, I decided to take a leisurely stroll home. Our neighborhood rested near the old railroad tracks that ran along the west side of town. The further west you lived, the lower your income. Every house in our low-income neighborhood looked like a first cousin to the house it neighbored. Five yards from the street and five feet from the neighboring property. The body frame and main facial structure were constructed identically, but the color and the outer upkeep distinguished each house from the other.

Across the street from our house, there was a property that was maintained with a fine-tooth comb. The mower worked out every five days whether it needed it or not. Grass clippings were collected and piled in a garbage bag. Sidewalks were edged. The trim on the house looked fresh and clean, because it was touched up on a yearly basis.

The identical home mirroring it, while it had great intentions, had grass clippings upon grass clippings layered in the lawn. Sidewalks were cracked and weeds overran it. The entire house - the white porch, white trim, white siding and white gutters - all needed a fresh coat of paint. The front steps leaned slightly to the east. The front windows needed to be cleaned. That was our house.

Just like close relatives, each house had the same genes, same possible outcomes, but each looked and acted differently due to the chemical makeup inside. Each person was born with a clean slate; our homes were built with the same kind of wood. The possibilities for the future were the same; yet with every hailstorm, blizzard or lightning strike, each human and each home weathered differently. Its outward appearance reflected the makeup inside the house.

The main reason that our house was not the best-kept house on the block was because Daddy worked away from home during the week. Since Momma wasn't an 'outdoorsy kinda gal,' the mowing happened quickly on Sundays before he headed out on the road.

When I reached the front steps to our house, I craved a few extra moments alone to collect my thoughts and memorize all of the nights' firsts. When the soft notes of the first slow dance hummed through the portable speakers, my all-time crush, Matthew, casually asked, "Lily, will you dance with me?"

I could only nod; I was too shocked to speak. He gently held my hand and guided me onto the small, gym dance floor. My heart thumped in my chest; a hundred shades of red filled my cheeks. I pinched myself in the arm before Matthew turned to place his arms around me. *Ouch! Yep, I wasn't dreaming.*

I remembered the slow song that was echoing through the gymnasium: *Saving All My Love for You* by Whitney Houston. His left hand held my right hand in a tight embrace, and his right hand rested on the small of my back as we swayed back and forth. My left hand rested on his shoulder. No words were exchanged. We both knew this was a giant, pivotal step in our friendship.

Gazing up at the bright twinkling stars that filled the quiet night sky, I settled on the front step to our house in my dress with a perma-grin on my face. I felt like Cinderella. If I removed the magical dress, I was afraid that I would return to the same old Lily, dressed in rags and waiting for my prince to rescue me. I didn't want the magic of the night to end. Slowly to see if the spell would be broken, I kicked off my shoes. *Nope, it was still real.*

Matthew had asked me to dance. My secret crush for over a year. Ever since we were partners in our freshman Biology class, butterflies would flutter in my chest when I was near him. His hand would graze over mine as he passed me the next specimen slide that we needed to investigate under the shared microscope. I feared he would notice the goosebumps that traveled up and down my arms. I could smell his freshly washed skin; the soap still lingered on his skin hours later. When it was quiet in the classroom, I could hear his steady breathing; it hypnotized me into a love trance. It was hard for me to concentrate in class sitting so close to him. And I could not logically explain what was happening.

"I thought I heard someone out here. How was the dance, Baby Girl? Everything you dreamed about?"

Daddy dropped down next to me on the small front step and draped his strong, muscular arm around me. My poofy head of hair, with all its curls still intact due to the enormous amount of hairspray that Daisy applied, rested on his shoulder. I always shared everything- hopes, dreams, newsworthy events, gossip - with Daddy, but for some reason I wanted to keep these memories to myself for a little while longer… at least until I could figure it out for myself.

"Magical." I couldn't stop the silly grin from spreading on my face. I was afraid if I said all the romantic details out loud, it wouldn't be true, or it would change it somehow. My memories and feelings from the night were that - mine. For the time being, I decided to keep it that way.

"Well, that sounds awesome. I bet you got your boogie on! Daisy went out with some friends. Wanna come in the house, and I'll make post-dance sundaes?"

He already knew the answer to that question. I was a sucker for ice cream. I jumped up and raced him into our kitchen.

Daddy's deep, hearty laugh sounded as he followed me into the house. "Hey, Cinderella, you forgot your glass slippers out here!"

I heard the door shut quietly.

MATTHEW and I became a serious item rather quickly. I knew that for me, it was because I was lonely and yearned for a close relationship with someone my age. I yearned for someone special to care for and cherish me. Matthew was sweet, shy and kind. He grew up in a big Catholic family where he felt like another mouth to feed. He enjoyed spending time at our house where it was often just the two of us.

"Your house is quiet and peaceful."

We didn't share the couch with anyone or fight over what TV program to watch. It was just the two of us, quietly enjoying each other's company.

There was a physical connection, obviously; we were teenagers with raging hormones. However, our emotional connection sparked an even larger awakening. I started to be dependent on someone other than Daddy and Kitty. We shared our thoughts, feelings, hopes and dreams. We referred to each other as boyfriend and girlfriend, but he was also my best friend. He wrote me sweet, romantic poetry and left them for me in my locker at school. I saved every single one.

POEM BY MATTHEW for his Lily:
  Love blossomed on a cool fall day
  "Please dance with me," I say
  You follow me in your dress
  I want to kiss you, I must confess
  Hold you close, I do
  These feeling are brand new
  Forever, to you I will be true
  Love you, I sure do

NORMALLY, fathers were not thrilled with their daughters dating, especially serious dating. However, Daddy was upfront and honest with Matthew from the very start. Matthew and I were going on our first official date a week after the epic homecoming dance. Our doorbell chimed the arrival of a visitor while I was completing the finishing touches on my appearance. I was wearing my favorite pair of jeans, a salmon-colored T-shirt and my white canvas shoes. My hair was pulled back in a loose ponytail. I tried to imitate my makeup from the homecoming dance; this time, Daisy had been too busy getting ready to go out herself to assist me.

Before I could descend the stairs, Daddy opened the front door.

"You must be Matthew. I'm Lily's father, Ben. Before you take Lily out, I'd like to have a few words with you."

Matthew backed out of the front door, understanding that this conversation was going to happen whether he agreed or not. Daddy exited through the front door behind Matthew and gently closed it. I tiptoed down the stairs to eavesdrop on what I was sure would be an intense conversation. I knelt below the living room window, which was cracked open enough to feel a little breeze. Daddy cleared his throat. In his husky, deep voice I heard him speak.

"Matthew, not too long ago I was a young man like you. I know the thoughts you are having when you see Lily; I know the feelings you have when you touch Lily. I know what it's like to be a young man." When Daddy paused, I noticed Matthew gulp. "And now that I have a daughter, I also know how a young lady thinks and feels. It is not the same. Not even close. If you want to date Lily, you will treat her with respect, kindness and honesty. Always. If you have trouble with this, imagine that I can see, hear and feel everything she does. And remember I can read your mind. Understand?"

I could barely see Matthew's face through the crack in the open window, but I watched his head obediently move up and down. His facial expression was stone-cold sober. He was not taking this conversation lightly.

Daddy continued, "You and I will get along great if you remember that. And her curfew is not negotiable."

I have a curfew? I didn't even know I had a curfew!

Boundaries of our relationship were established from the beginning by Daddy. As a normal teenager, I rolled my eyes and thought his protectiveness was over the top. As an adult, I was thankful Daddy set up good boundaries for my first relationship. Matthew never pushed me to do anything sexually that I wasn't ready for. He never raised his voice to me. He opened every door for me, pulled out the chair for me at any table. He was a perfect gentleman. I really couldn't have asked for a better example for a first love.

Matthew had an olive complexion. During the summer months, he was a lifeguard at the town's pool, and he tanned quickly. His skin would turn a milk chocolate color. I was a frequent visitor, lazing in a pool chair near him. Occasionally, I would sneak peeks at him while he scanned the pool for trouble. He looked so serious and professional in the lifeguard chair. *How did I get so lucky that he picked me?* He was a tan god with a prince's personality. He had hazel eyes with thick, dark eyelashes. He had a small mole above the left side of his lip, which I found super sexy. His nose was slightly crooked from breaking it as a child when he fell off the swing set. He had a scar just above his left eyebrow that he earned from a sword fight with one of his younger brothers. All of this made up the face that was my first love.

On our fifth date, I was beginning to wonder if he would ever kiss me or if I was going to have to make the first move. We pulled up next to the curb in his car. He slid the car into park but kept the engine idling. The fall temperature had begun to drop, especially in the evening.

"Lily, can I talk to you before you go into your house?"

Oh no! He was dumping me!

"Sure. I have ten minutes before my curfew. What's going on, Matthew? Is everything okay?" I pretended to be confident and not afraid of what his answer might be. I turned to face him and tried to put on my best concerned face and not my scared shitless face.

"We've been dating for a couple months now. I've enjoyed every second of the time I have spent with you. You're a dream... smart, beautiful, easy-going and ... I honestly feel like a better person when I'm with you. But..." I could feel my heart squeeze and my breath caught in my throat. *This was it! He was dumping me. 'But's' were never good!* "... I wondered if I could kiss you?"

I was so relieved that I confidently leaned over, forcefully grabbed him by his neck and pulled him closer to me. I noticed his eyes were wide open with surprise. Our young, innocent lips met, and our first kiss was everything that I had dreamed and read about in my romance novels. It felt natural and not awkward like I was afraid it might be. His lips were soft and tender. They parted slightly, and his tongue gently pushed my lips apart. He tasted like vanilla ice cream.

When our lips finally parted, I could see his white teeth in the dark. He was grinning from ear to ear.

"Well, I am glad I finally got the nerve to ask you that." He chuckled a little.

He walked me to my front door, and before I could reach the steps, he pulled me into one more sweet kiss. "Goodnight, Lily. I'll call you tomorrow."

Chapter Eleven

1986

During my junior year of high school, I was enrolled in Coach Knight's Speech 101. His lectures were interesting and maintained the whole class' attention. We would be so engrossed in what he was telling us that we would forget we were learning. He made learning fun. Anyone could tell that he loved being a teacher. His enthusiasm was contagious.

Our first required assignment was an informative speech. Our objective was to inform our audience by supplying details, facts, and real-life experiences. Coach Knight did not need to approve our topics. He wanted us to impress him with our creativity, thoroughness and uniqueness. He didn't want a generic speech about abortions, or capital punishment, or the right to bear arms. He demanded inspiration and a unique, fresh approach.

"Get creative, people. Throw caution to the wind. Take a leap. Make a stand. This is your chance to live outside the box. I wanna see what you have to say."

This speech was a quarter of our overall grade. It was the first chance of the semester to establish our grade. "Raise the flag or sink the ship," as he liked to say.

We had two weeks to research, write and rehearse our speech. For many of the students, including myself, choosing the topic was proving to be the most challenging part. I wanted to impress him and come up with something original.

My inspiration materialized one afternoon while I was on a run. I rotated between five different courses. Each one varied in length, and I chose them based on my mood, the weather and how much time I had available. On the afternoon of my great inspiration, I had selected the longest six-mile route. This path brought me to the edges of town, but it was one of the prettiest routes as well.

During the fourth mile of the route, a spectacular view of the river blessed my vision. The coursing river flowed along the east side of Normal. The route ran along the riverbed for one mile before veering back towards town. Often, I'd see wildlife collecting a drink of fresh water from the river. On that afternoon, the wind was calm, and the river was moving at a steady pace down its usual path. The sound of gushing water was very relaxing and peaceful. Mile four was my favorite.

Since there was hardly a breeze, my breathing sounded louder than usual. It could be heard more clearly without the town's constant traffic or steady hum of activity. I drew some deep breaths to slow my breathing down so I wouldn't disturb nature with my heavy panting. I didn't want to scare off any animals that I might catch a glimpse of. It was always a treat to come upon a mother deer leading her fawn to the river for a drink. I didn't want to miss my opportunity.

Suddenly, I heard rustling noises coming from a nearby patch of trees. I held my breath so I could clearly hear what was making the noise. Unfortunately, I detected right away that it was not from an animal. Two sets of heavy breathers, but I doubted their breathing was from running. The rustle of leaves followed by moaning gave it away. Probably a couple of horny teenagers. Matthew and I fooled around, but we were never desperate enough to use a bunch of trees for privacy. I kept on running hoping they wouldn't even hear the thump of my feet or my own heavy breathing.

Then, as I was trying to sneak away undetected, I heard it. *Her* name was called out at the point of climax.

"Daisy! Oh yeah... Daisy..." Not only was it my mother's name being howled, but I instantly recognized the male voice announcing the mating call. And it wasn't Daddy.

My jaw clenched, and my feet controlled what my head and heart could not. They carried me to a record setting pace and blindly led me towards home and hauled me the hell away from that river. When I reached home, I slammed the door and screamed at the top of my lungs. I dropped to my knees and cried.

How could she keep doing this? Why? And how did these men keep falling for her? Was she a witch? Did she cast a spell on them? Why was it always someone I have grown to respect and trust? Because I was home alone, I didn't bother toning down my howling and throwing things. These feelings were valid and real. I was allowed to be pissed at her for screwing him in the woods. What kind of mother did that?

IT WAS my turn to give my speech in front of my Speech 101 class. I thought I was prepared, but self-doubt crept in. I wasn't sure I could do this. My hands were shaking as I held my prepared notecards. I didn't need them. This was coming straight from my broken, disappointed heart.

"'Thou shalt not commit adultery' is one of the Ten Commandments of the Bible that is most often broken. There is no loose interpretation of that commandment. The Bible doesn't say, 'thou shalt not commit adultery unless you are unhappy... or unless it is only for one time... or unless it doesn't mean anything; it is just sex.' The Bible commands its followers not to do it.

"No one misinterprets the commandment 'thou shalt not kill' as 'thou shalt not kill unless he deserves it... or... it was only one time.' Break this commandment and the sinner goes to jail."

My gaze landed on Coach Knight. I had his full attention. Fear crept into his eyes.

"Christian and non-Christian people get married and declare wedding vows to one another. 'In sickness and in health, in good times *and bad.' The newlyweds promise to follow God's seventh command-ment, vowing to be true and loyal to their spouse."*

Normally, Coach Knight jotted down notes during a student's speech so he could back up the grade that he awarded the speech. He wasn't taking any notes. But I did witness him take a hard, deep swallow. His Adam's apple was pronounced.

"Famous people commit adultery all the time. For example, Princess Diana and Prince Charles had an enormous, televised wedding at St. Paul's Cathedral in London. The couple vowed to follow the commandment to honor the wife and honor the husband.

"Five years later and still-married Princess Diana began an affair with James Hewitt, her horseback riding instructor. After she admitted to the affair, she pointed a finger at Charles, who was also having an affair during their whole marriage to Camilla Parker. By Princess Diana outing that Charles was also guilty of cheating, does that lessen her guilt?

"Another very famous name tied to infidelity was John F. Kennedy. When he was President of the United States from 1961-1963, he had been married to Jackie Kennedy for ten years. He grew up in a large Catholic family with strong family and religious beliefs. However, rumor has it that he asked his personal assistant to schedule sex with numerous different women. He claimed he got a headache if he didn't have sex every day.

"Heaven forbid! I wonder if JFK was unaware that Tylenol had been invented in 1955. Might have helped his reputation and controlled his sex drive."

This got a lot of snickers and giggles from my classmates. Coach Knight remained silent and sober.

"Both of these very public couples had affairs after declaring their love and loyalty to their spouse. They were religious people and believed in the Bible's teachings. However, when publicly questioned about their infidelity, they blamed other people or downright lied.

"Isn't lying a sin? No one accepted responsibility for their own actions. Did they believe they were above the law? Above God? There-fore, above any punishment? Did they simply think they could down-

play their adultery by lying about it and in turn, committing another sin?

"In Iran, adultery is punished by law. This country has been criticized for stoning people to death for committing adultery. Recently, an Iranian woman who had committed adultery received ninety-nine lashes from a whip. This public and very painful punishment occurred before her trial. At her trial, she was sentenced to a public stoning for her crime. She didn't give her side of the story. Her government didn't slap her on the wrist. She lost her life for sleeping with a man that was not her husband.

"Even though this retribution was extremely harsh, we must admit to ourselves that being aware that this was a possible punishment would make you second guess your actions. Furthermore, witnessing the stoning in public versus reading about in the Sunday paper would be much more effective in making a statement. Even the best writer can't display an effective number of words that could compare to witnessing the actual event. It would make someone think twice about sleeping with another person.

"Sometimes, we need to witness something with our own eyes. It becomes real, and we are forced to have a better understanding. I would acknowledge that a physical object can be used to symbolize our emotions that we cannot see or touch. Take, for example, this beautiful, priceless, one-of-a-kind, antique watch."

I held up Mr. Knight's watch that he accidentally dropped beside my parents' bed a couple of weeks ago. I found it under the bed while I was vacuuming. His eyes opened wide with recognition. Last week, I heard him telling another track coach that he couldn't find it. "It was my grandfather's. A huge family heirloom. Probably worth thousands of dollars.".

"If you heard or read a story about this priceless antique being crushed into little pieces, it would not have the same effect as witnessing it yourself. Let this gorgeous watch symbolize the feelings and emotions that a scorned spouse or significant other would feel if cheated on and lied to. Then stomp on it like this."

I wore my heavy army boots today for this purpose. I gently set Mr.

Knight's watch on the classroom floor and brought my foot down hard on it, breaking it into millions of little pieces.

"This watch, now broken into many, many irreparable pieces, symbolizes a family broken by infidelity. No super glue or duct tape will make the watch work again. No weak apologies and blank promises will mend this broken bridge. Their hearts are broken. Their trust shattered.

"In conclusion, why do Christians study the Ten Commandments and the Bible if they are only going to obey the commandments that they feel are convenient? Why do couples publicly profess their marriage vows in a church only to break them? Our society has laws; if they are broken, the citizen must pay a fine or spend time behind bars. How are the adulterers not punished? Haven't they broken a law or committed a crime in their marriage? Sure, some lose their families or their jobs. However, the majority of the time, their sins are left unpunished. The loyal spouses who are lied to and cheated on are the ones who suffer. Their children are lost in the sea of deception. My hope is that God will seek punishment for these sinners in the afterlife since the American laws do not seek any disciplinary action."

When I returned to my assigned seat, the eyes of my classmates fell on me. I didn't care that my speech didn't really fit the requirements of the assignment or lead anywhere but for people to ponder. I was sure my grade would suffer, but I really didn't care. I wanted to make a point to Coach Knight that I knew about the affair with Daisy, and obviously I was not happy about it. I could hear the whispers of my classmates wondering what that was all about. I knew they were eating up every word.

Coach Knight was caught off guard. He paused a little too long before he spoke. The class discussion grew louder during his extended silence. He cleared his throat. "Thank you... Lily. That is all we will have time for today, but Gina Pierce, you are first tomorrow."

He rose from his desk in the back of the classroom and headed into the hall. Five minutes remained until the bell would dismiss the class. Students were looking back and forth at each other, shaking their heads, trying to figure out what was going on. Coach Knight was the type of teacher who enjoyed the company of teenagers; he enjoyed the banter and the downtime between instruction. It wasn't normal for him to retreat to the teacher's lounge before class was even over.

Gina Pierce turned around in her seat in front of me and looked directly at me. "Wow… your speech must have gotten to him. I'm not sure if mine will have that shocking of a reaction. Nice work, Lily."

She clearly misinterpreted Coach Knight's sudden departure for him being impressed. I nodded and wished her luck. The point of my speech was to hurt, shock and awe Coach Knight. I did not care if the rest of the student body misunderstood the point of my speech. I was only seeking to reach one audience member, and I succeeded.

Chapter Twelve

A large black freight train barreled down our lonely, dark, forgotten street on the edge of town. Clouds of steam rose from the smokebox. The pistons screeched as the engine roared its wake-up call to the sleepy town. Unfortunately, on this humid spring night, it was not an actual train that shrieked through town. As residents of Normal, we became accustomed to the regular trains' squeaks and rattles. Our regular train was similar to 'the little train that couldn't'. We didn't even wake up when it motored its way down the tracks. On this spring night, an angry locomotive planned to wake every resident. Mother Nature was driving the train, showing everyone her power. *I am the Queen of Lightning and Thunder. Hear me roar.*

Our two story, white cookie-cutter house shook as the storm descended on our sleepy Midwest town. The weather forecasters had not predicted how fast the rain would fall, how loud the thunder would crack, nor how strong the winds would blow.

From the comfort of my bed, I pulled back my cheap, white lace curtains around my bedroom window to peek outside. The streetlights shone down onto the road. Enormous raindrops pelted our street at a forty-degree angle. Our newly planted maple tree bent on its side, hoping its roots were strong enough to last the nasty, powerful wind gusts. Rain was racing down the gutters of the streets, searching for the nearest storm drain. Mother Nature was in a foul mood.

My small bedside alarm clock read two o'clock. The incoming spring storm woke me from my slumber. I yawned, stretched and rolled over, but the thunder rocked the house again. A few seconds later, another crackle of lightning shone through my thin curtains. As a child, Daddy taught me to count between the first flash of lightning until you heard the thunder. For each five seconds in between the lightning and thunder, it meant the storm was a mile away. If the numbers decreased, it meant the storm was moving closer.

One… Two… Three… Four… Five… Six… Seven… Eight… Nine…

A huge thunder boom rattled through the dark night sky. As I lay in my bed under my pink and white comforter, I remembered telling Daddy that the thunder sounded like God was bowling up in Heaven. *God, why are you bowling in the middle of the night?* Daddy laughed at my notion but completely agreed with me.

One… Two… Three… Four… Five… Six… Seven… Eight… Nine…

A flash of lightning followed by a rumble of thunder. According to the calculations that Daddy instructed, the eye of the storm was located less than two miles away.

I had crawled in bed at midnight because I'd been out late with Matthew. We had been dating for over two years, and we were together more often than not. We attended the new movie, *The Seventh Sign*, where we munched on buttery popcorn and Milk Duds while sharing an ice-cold Coke.

In hindsight, when I reflected back to that date night, it was a very one-sided evening. I really wanted to see that movie. Due to my excitement, I was talking non-stop all the way to the theatre. Our movie tradition included an in-depth discussion following the movie. We critiqued the movie as if we were movie critics. After seeing *The Seventh Sign*, Matthew was quieter than normal during our discussion and agreed to my opinions more readily than usual. At the time, I chalked it up to him not enjoying the movie as much as I had.

"Matthew, what did you think? Why couldn't David have possessed Abby's unborn baby's soul while still in the womb? Unborn babies have souls; they have heartbeats, so they must have souls already too."

In the movie theatre's parking lot, we were sitting in his white, two-door Ford Maverick that he recently bought used from his grand-parents. It was in good shape and had low miles. It held a lot of our secrets in it already too. Matthew hesitated to answer. He was staring out of the windshield.

"Matthew, hello? E.T. phone home?"

He shifted his teenage body to face me in the passenger seat. He was wearing his navy-blue Members Only jacket that I had given him for his birthday the year before. His acid washed jeans were compliments of my influence as well. "Sorry, Lily. That movie was intense. I'm not sure if I followed it all."

Without missing a beat, I jabbered on. "How about that dude's eyes? And why did she rent that apartment to him? Didn't she sense something was strange or ominous about him? I think she was plain hard up for money, so she did what she had to do, being pregnant and all." After being quiet for two hours in a movie theatre, I was usually very chatty and appreciated the tradition we had created to help me wind down and think through the material.

"Yeah… I agree."

"And a Catholic Father as a stalker? I don't buy it."

"Yeah… I agree."

FLASH OF LIGHTNING.

One… Two… Three… Four… Five… Six… Seven… Eight…

A boom of thunder. I decided to get out of bed and venture down-stairs to the kitchen for a glass of milk. A cold glass of milk would help to relax me. Plus, this storm was not allowing me to go back to sleep.

Flash of lightning.

One… Two… Three… Four… Five… Six… Seven… Eight…

A roar of thunder. My bedroom door squeaked as I opened it. Need to have Daddy put some grease on it. I tiptoed down the hall because I assumed my parents were still asleep. As I started to descend the stairs,

I was surprised to hear voices coming from the kitchen. Daddy's booming, deep voice was angrily interrogating Daisy. My footsteps slowed until I was near the bottom and could hear better without being seen.

"Are you sleeping with him?" He paused to give her time to answer. Her response was muted by the next delivery of the forthcoming storm.

Flash of lightning.

One... Two... Three... Four... Five... Six... Seven...

A roar of thunder.

"I cannot believe you, Daisy! Do you have any boundaries? Is there anyone you won't sleep with? Do you have morals? Do you not respect yourself enough to know what you did was completely wrong?"

"I ain't dumb, Benjamin. And I'm lonely. I love--"

Flash of lightning.

One... Two... Three... Four... Five... Six... Seven...

A roar of thunder.

Daisy's voice sounded weak and full of shame, perhaps laced with lots of alcohol. I could hardly hear her even when I held my breath to get a better listen.

"Why can't you see that you have crossed a line? He isn't just another man... if you can even call him a *man*. What were you thinking?" He slammed his hand down on what sounded like the kitchen countertop. I could hear him crying, deep, husky tears. "I can't do this anymore, Daisy. You have crossed the line. Big time."

Flash of lightning.

One... Two... Three... Four... Five... Six... Seven...

A roar of thunder.

"-- don't lecture me on who I can sleep with." Her voice was hard to understand since she wasn't speaking very loudly. "I know what happens at all those truck stops *you* visit."

"Don't go there! You have no idea what I've given up for you. And do you know you could be arrested for what you did?"

Honestly, I had to admit that I was enjoying the fact that he was standing up to her and that I didn't have to keep her adultery a secret from him anymore. However, I didn't understand why Daddy thought her whoring around was illegal... unless she was getting paid for it. Now, *that* would be a possibility that I hadn't thought of before, and it wouldn't surprise me.

Flash of lightning.

One... Two... Three... Four... Five... Six... Seven...

A roar of thunder.

The storm and Daddy's temper were escalating at the same time. His voice grew louder and angrier. "-- do this to Lily? You are so selfish! So self-centered. I can't keep covering for you anymore! I can't make excuses for you anymore. You are --"

Flash of lightning.

One... Two... Three... Four... Five... Six...

A loud crack of thunder and a thud.

Then Daisy was screaming his name.

"Ben! Ben? Ben! Honey, what's wrong?"

So many sounds to process in a short amount of time. My sleepy brain was trying to sort what I had heard. Thunder and something fell... something heavy fell... that sound came from the kitchen, not the sky. Then Daisy was screaming Daddy's name.

Daddy? A second later, I leaped off of the stairs and sprinted to the kitchen where just the light above the sink was on. The first thing I noticed was Daisy kneeling on the hard, linoleum floor next to... Daddy? He was laying on the floor with his mouth open and his eyes pleading. His hands were gripping his chest.

I hurried over to him. "Daddy? What happened? Are you okay?" I shoved Daisy off him and screamed at her, "Dial 9-1-1!" I turned back to Daddy. "What can I do? Daddy, what's going on? Are you okay? I love you!!"

His mouth closed slightly, and a silent tear rolled down his cheek just before he closed his eyes for the last time.

"Daddy, no! Daddy?" It was then that his tight grip on his lucky coin released, and the two-headed coin rolled onto the floor.

· · ·

HOURS LATER, the hospital staff hesitantly informed us that Daddy had very high blood pressure. Untreated high blood pressure caused damage over time to his arteries and prevented blood flow to his heart muscle. Any added stress or anxiety would only make the symptoms worse. It was a widowmaker heart attack, and there was nothing we could have done to save him.

This knowledge didn't help. It did not bring back Daddy.

After the hospital staff declared his time of death, we were allowed to see him. His body lay on a hard, flat, metal table in a cold, white, sterile emergency room. A flimsy white sheet covered his whole body except his head. He looked pale and very, very still. The monitors were all turned off. The only sound was my uncontrollable sobbing and Daisy's constant hiccups.

"Daisy, could you give me a few minutes alone with him?"

She looked at me with a vacancy in her eyes.

"Daisy? Leave!"

She turned around slowly, walked away and shut the hospital room door behind her.

When she was gone, I wiped my tears and bear hugged this giant of a man whom I had worshiped for eighteen years. His body wasn't cold yet, but he was becoming quite stiff. It didn't feel like him anymore. Plus, he would have returned my hug with a big squeeze.

"Daddy? Oh, God! What am I gonna do without you? You're my rock. What happened? What were you two arguing about?" A huge lump formed in my throat. Crying wouldn't bring him back, but maybe screaming would. I howled in pain. My eyes burned with red, hot tears. I could feel the weight of my sorrow resting on my shoulders. I clung to his body praying, with my whole being that this was a nightmare.

I whispered in his ear, "I am so sorry, Daddy! I love you so much! You were my sun, not her. I'll make her pay for breaking your heart."

Chapter Thirteen

1988

After Daddy died, our house became an empty shell.

During the Easter holiday, some families maintained a tradition of poking a toothpick-sized hole in a raw egg and blowing out the contents of the egg. Only a very thin outer shell remained. Life resembled a raw, empty egg without Daddy in it. Very thin, very fragile, very delicate. The slightest touch would crack it into tiny little pieces. Daisy and I had nothing, absolutely nothing to hold us together.

I was graduating high school in a month and moving away to college. Without Daddy here, it would make the transition so much easier. I would not be leaving anything behind that I loved. He was gone.

Emotional pain could trigger physical pain symptoms. I never thought it was possible, but my heart felt severed into pieces. His absence mirrored the emptiness in my heart. Every breath felt like shattered glass in my throat, every movement weighed down by inconsolable grief. My throat was dry and tight from the endless hours of crying and screaming his name. My nose was red and sore from the constant blowing and wiping. Red spider web veins surrounded my glassy eyes. The skin around my eyes was puffy. I was not a pretty crier.

No one would ever call me 'Baby Girl' again. We would never make chocolate chip pancakes together again. I'd never hear one of his silly, made-up fairy tales or stories about what he imagined when I was older. He loved to imitate my female voice - much too high and much too dramatic - but it always made me giggle, which was his number one goal.

"Oh, hi, Daddy. It's your Baby Girl calling." He would place his hand on his hip and used his other hand's thumb and index finger as a pretend phone. He paused as if future-him was responding on the other end. "No, Daddy. I'm not in love yet. No man will ever compare to you." He giggled. "It's 1993, not 1893. Dah!" Another pause. "I am graduating college this spring, Daddy." Pause. "I'll have a degree in Rocket Science, and the first thing I'm gonna buy with my enormous paycheck is a red, shiny Dodge Viper for you so you can go sixty miles per hour in four seconds." He threw his head back and imitated my giggle.

His imagination was one-of-a-kind and something that I missed terribly about him.

Following his funeral, Daisy either slept on the couch or slept in her bed all day. She would cry herself to sleep wherever she was laying. I wasn't sure if she was weeping due to guilt or if she actually missed him and wished he was still alive. I seriously questioned if she was depressed because his paycheck wouldn't be paying her bills anymore. After eighteen years of watching the 'act' that was called her life, I still didn't know what to believe. I did know that I didn't trust her one tiny bit. She was selfish; Daisy was only concerned about how everything would affect Daisy.

Over breakfast a week after he died, we were sitting down to eat one of the many casserole dishes that a thoughtful neighbor had dropped off. It was a fabulous egg bake with chunks of ham in it. Daddy loved ham.

"Anything from a pig is gnarly. The best part of the pig isn't some-thing you can eat though. It's the snort that sounds like yours, Lily." Then, he would try his best imitation of my giggle-snort. I would respond with one of my big snort laughs. Everything reminded me of him, even this ham.

Daisy was painting her freshly filed nails a crimson red in between taking bites of her breakfast.

"I know you killed him," I blurted out as she shoveled a big bite off of her plate and into her mouth.

She choked and had to spit it out. What a waste of a great bite of casserole, and she didn't actually choke.

"What? What are you talkin' about now, Lily?" She wiped off the spit around her mouth with a paper towel. "He died of a heart attack. You heard the damn doctor. How the hell could I have caused that? Please enlighten me, oh holier-than-thou Lily."

"You broke his fucking heart! You and all your whoring around. He found out it, confronted you, and it literally ripped his fucking heart into two!"

For a dramatic pause, I took a big bite of the ham egg bake to show that I was in control. My chewing was a pause for dramatic effect.

I was not weak; I was patient. I had been waiting years and years to confront her about her infidelity. Never wanted to hurt Daddy, but he was gone. I didn't need to protect him anymore. She deserved to hear what I had to say even if it wasn't pleasant. She killed him. She broke him. It was her fault.

Her big doe-like, brown eyes had always reflected the truth that she was feeling on the inside. In the years I have studied her, only her eyes betrayed her true emotions. She did not have 'lyin' eyes' like the famous Eagles hit song that claimed evil, cheating women possessed. Her big smile never left her face when we were shopping for groceries at Piggly Wiggly one afternoon, and a woman about her age under her breath muttered, "slut." Daisy kept right on smiling and even gave the woman a little nod as if to say, "I know something you don't know."

But hatred and resentment shone in her eyes.

After our house got egged, she was out the next morning scrubbing the remains off our sidewalk while she hummed Michael Jackson's *Billie Jean*. She acted like she was performing a daily chore and never even considered the reason that our house received the egging. She smiled as the neighbors walked by and the twinkle in her eye said, "If I find out who did this, I will seek my revenge the only way that I know how. Lock up your husbands."

And now, over breakfast, her big, round eyes revealed to me that she was shocked that I knew her dirty little secrets. They were wide with surprise and a bit impressed. But she was an excellent actress, her skill crafted for years and years. Quickly, she regained her composure. If you didn't know her, you wouldn't have noticed that very brief loss of emotional control. However, I'd been silently scrutinizing her for years. I noticed her subtle changes in mood. The way that her eyes glazed over when she was thinking about being somewhere else. She usually sang songs rather than hummed them when she was planning an encounter with one of her many lovers. Humming was a normal day; singing forecasted an anticipated event. I noticed how she dressed depending on her audience. She was a seasoned actress, and I was her dedicated understudy.

"Oh, Lily, always so dramatic!" She rose from our small, square kitchen table to take her dishes to the sink. She had not finished her breakfast, but I could tell she had lost her appetite.

I had struck a nerve. I wasn't going to lose my momentum.

"Daddy was a saint to stay married to you for all those years. He was way too good for you, completely out of your league. Additionally, the whole town talked about you and your whoring, but he stuck by you. I have no idea why. He must have seen something in you that was worthy of his love and devotion. Maybe he felt sorry for you? But last Friday night when he arrived home from working all week, whatever he discovered was the last straw. So, who was it? Who was the man that shoved Daddy over his breaking point, Daisy?"

Suddenly, her dishes crashed into the sink. She turned back around and faced me. Her eyes shot daggers. "Lily! You shut your damn mouth! You ain't gonna disrespect me in my own home!"

"Disrespect *you*? Really? You're going to talk to me about disrespect? This ought to be a very short lesson coming from you. My whole childhood was shaped by your lack of respect for your marriage and your family! You had sex with our church pastor and my track coach, both of who are married with families. Even Uncle Freddy! I don't know how many more men you tagged on your bedpost while you danced at the Rusty Nail. Your disrespect for our family was thrown in my face everywhere I turned! So, don't you dare tell me not to disrespect you. I've watched you for years disrespecting us with any human who had a penis."

I rose up from my designated chair at our kitchen table and stomped with a purpose towards her. I didn't intend to back down. When I was within inches of her face, I continued, "You killed my father, and long before that, you broke this family. Daddy is gone forever. He won't be back. I've had enough of you, as well. You are a whore. I hate you and plan on making you pay for the pain you caused Daddy."

We were toe-to-toe. Same height. About the same weight. We looked like sisters except for her being a blonde and me a brunette. Her brown eyes versus my blue eyes. Fury filled both of our eyes. Our jaws were clenched. Our backs were straight.

Abruptly, she slapped me hard across my left cheek. I didn't see it coming. I was too consumed with my boiling hatred for her. It burned. It stung, but I welcomed the physical pain. It helped me forget the emotional heartache that I was feeling. I slowly brought up my left hand to my tender, red cheek. I looked her straight in the eye. A small, wicked smile rose on my right, unharmed cheek. Now, we were getting somewhere. Her eyes showed a flash of regret but there was a hint of curiosity on if I'd hit her back.

"Lily, you ain't better than me. You ain't. You're just like me. I hate to break it to ya, but the same blood runs in both of our veins. For generations, it's always the same. Same blood, same sins."

She leaned back against the countertop to give us a few more inches apart. She reached for her coffee cup to take a sip. The control of our conversation was shifting. I could feel the relocation in power. I was interested in what she had to say; therefore, I was willing to relinquish partial control.

"You can sit back and judge me all you want. You can blame me. You can point your ugly little finger at me. I really don't care. You will turn out just like me; you can't fight your genes. I see the evil in you. I know what you're capable of."

She took another small sip of her coffee and continued to glare at me.

A lightbulb ignited in my brain. "Ah-ha... I figured it out... Daddy liked a project. He was always bringing home second or third hand projects. He brought you home. He must've figured he could fix you. Used, discarded, pile of crap. He was always a sucker for the needy." I knew I was hitting below the belt, but I didn't care at this point. I wasn't sure if there was a line to cross in this situation.

She shook her head at my little rant. "You ain't different from me, Lily. We're the same, you and me. People get us confused when we answer the phone because our voices are similar. I get asked if you're my sister because we look so much alike." In a hushed voice, she added, "Hell, I have even been told we kiss the same."

A smug smile crept up on her lips.

"Just because we have similar sounding voices and look related does *not* mean we are the same." I refused to accept that I was anything like her. I hated her and never wanted to be anything like her. All of a sudden, the last sentence that she uttered under her breath gripped my brain. "What did you say?"

"What part?" When she sipped her coffee, I could see her brown eyes peek over the rim of her coffee cup. She was happy and pleased with herself. She was taunting me. "The part about you and me kissing the same?"

"Yeah, that part."

I held my breath waiting to hear what would come out of her mouth next. In hindsight, this moment in my life felt like that part in the horror movie when you knew something awful was about to happen, and yet you couldn't stop watching. The viewer could see the killer outside the kitchen window, the victim heard the doorbell and went to answer the door. The axe came up... cue the scary, sinister music. Curiosity superseded common sense. The victim forgot to run. Her legs were paralyzed. She just stood there, and the horror show took control.

"How long did you think he would wait for you? You and your

teasin' him with your promises. Teasin' him with your virgin kisses and touches. A boy has needs. You think you could satisfy him? He has urges that no virgin like you could help him with."

She was on a roll. The gloves were off. She enjoyed seeing my heart ripped apart. I couldn't believe what I was hearing. I didn't know how to respond. My mouth dropped open, my eyes were wide with surprise, and my heart started to crack.

"Sorry to tell you this, Lily, but Matthew wanted me. He came to me. He wanted me, and he knew I would be able to please him. And I sure did. Time after time after time. Sometimes with my mouth, sometimes with my hand, and always with my pussy. And believe me, he enjoyed every pleasure-filled minute he spent inside of me." She looked at me like I was her prey, and she was finished chewing me up. She chewed me up and spat me out. She moved toward the sink where she rinsed out her coffee cup and dried her hands. "Now, if you don't mind, I'm gonna go shower. Need to wash off this soiled conversation."

She turned around and headed out of the kitchen.

I had become a statue, too shocked to move. My whole body had hardened.

As she was leaving the kitchen but still within earshot, I responded with only my deepest wish for her: "Karma... I don't know when or how, Daisy, but you'll get what you deserve."

Chapter Fourteen

1988

After Daisy bragged about her sexual relationship with Matthew, I needed to blow off some major steam and get my thoughts in order. I needed to separate my feelings from what I needed to do. Which sounded easy enough, but the act of separation was more difficult. I decided to go for a run. Running not only helped me relax and burn off tension, but it also helped me escape. Running was my therapy and would help clear my mind. I needed to physically distance myself from her as far as I could. As I laced up my running shoes, tears dripped out of my eyes and onto the linoleum floor. A puddle of tears collected at my feet.

Of course, the longest route was the one that I chose to run. I needed the time to comprehend all that I had learned. Each mile that my feet pounded the pavement would bring more clarity and logic.

First, I needed to break up with Matthew. But how? My initial gut reaction was to scream at him and rip out his heart like he did mine. I imagined punching him in the gut so hard that the wind was knocked out of him. Exactly how I felt at this very moment. But if I resorted to physical violence, I hurt my chances of discovering the details that I wanted him to answer. I had questions. I was deeply hurt, but I was also curious about how it happened.

How often? When? Where? Where was I? Do you love her? What were you thinking? What about the promises you made to me? How could you do this to us?

I needed to consider my options. As I turned the corner to head east, another idea occurred to me. I could repeat his behavior: I could seduce and sleep with his father... Mr. Miles was a robust, bearded man who showered only when absolutely necessary, like for church on Sundays or... I think that was it. *Oooooo gross!* Nope. That was not an option. I would suggest sleeping with Matthew's best friend, but that was me. Therefore, doing exactly what he did to me would not work at all. Additionally, giving up my virginity for revenge sounded like something Daisy would do, not me.

Another option would be to make him suffer long term. I could continue to act like I didn't know anything. Act normal; continue dating. Ask him leading questions and see where they would go. Maybe he would confess. Wasn't that a detective's job on TV crime shows? Ask questions that they knew the answers to but wanted the witness to confess and provide more details to fill in the holes of the crime. As soon as he confessed and answered my burning questions, then I would hit him... hit him hard. This alternative didn't seem like a good idea either since I was the worst actress, and I didn't have the emotional strength to pull it off.

My feet continued to lead me down my six-mile route while my heart grew heavier. I was carrying a thirty-pound stone in my chest. I needed to stop as I reached mile four. The unstoppable tears dripped from my eyes again. I slowed my pace to a fast walk so I could wipe my wet face and catch my breath. The irony was not lost on me: this was the same mile that I discovered Daisy having an affair with Coach Knight a year ago. Here I was again on the same mile thinking about her sleeping with another man. I found myself stuck in a pattern that she created.

Something was wrong with her and her loose morals. I knew what Genevieve's mom meant now. And she was right. Something happened to Daisy that made her think this was acceptable behavior. I imagined that her heart was hollow inside, black and brittle on the outside.

Was she purposely sleeping with important men in my life? My youth pastor? Then my coach and teacher? And now my boyfriend? Did she do this to punish me for some reason that seemed logical only to her? Was she jealous of my relationships with these men? Who else had she slept with that I was unaware of? How did she seduce all these men? What did she say to them to make them think this was acceptable?

I wasn't sure if I would ever discover the answers to these questions. I wasn't sure that I wanted to know everything either. My head was spinning with questions. I doubted she would ever divulge much information to me. However, maybe I could get Matthew to explain what happened between the two of them. If I approached Matthew angry and upset, he would most likely clam up. I'd have better luck getting the information that I desperately wanted if I was calm and questioned him with no judgment. Easier said than done. I needed to show more curiosity than anger. That was going to be extremely difficult. He was my first love. He was my best friend, constant companion and my person for the past two and a half years. How could he do this to us? Did he think so little of our relationship? Did I matter so little to him?

I recounted the last couple of months to see if there was a sign from Matthew that I missed. A sign of trouble. A sign that things between us had changed. A sign that he was having sex with my own mother.

Five months ago, he invited me to Thanksgiving at his family's house. His mother's side of the family was coming over for a big traditional Thanksgiving feast: turkey, mashed potatoes, stuffing and all the trimmings. The house burst at the seams with relatives. Adults and small children occupied every corner of their house. They were all Catholic and didn't believe in using birth control. Only natural planning by avoidance was the concept that they believed in and used. In my opinion, it didn't seem to work very well. Matthew's mom, Sara, had four sisters who each had five children. Not that unusual until you comprehended the ages of Saras' sisters: thirty-three, thirty-two, thirty-one, and twenty-nine. Obviously, Matthew's grandmother wasn't successful with the natural planning either. She would probably have had more children, but she died giving birth to the youngest sister.

That Thanksgiving Day, the noise level and family chaos was overwhelming to an only child. However, I would admit that all the devoted attention that I received from his younger cousins was addictive. They thought that I was the best thing since sliced bread.

"Lily, will you sit by me?" and "Lily, will you read me this book?" and "Lily, can I hold your hand?" Reflecting on that recent holiday, I recalled Matthew smiling at me over the heads of his toddler cousins. He was happy that I fit in. Nope, no trouble then.

December and January didn't hold any significance in my memory. We celebrated Christmas after he had traveled to visit family. During January, I picked up a few extra hours at Kitty's Cafe since she broke her foot slipping on the ice. Matthew became a regular at one of my tables.

In February, we celebrated Valentine's Day at my house. We decided that we would make homemade gifts to exchange. I cooked a homemade meal for Matthew as my gift to him. Daisy was in one of her rare moods: she was more than willing to help me and plan a nice, romantic dinner for our Valentine's date. We searched her recipe book together and even shopped at the grocery store together for all the ingredients I needed. I chose to make chicken parmesan, garlic bread and a tossed salad. Daddy planned on taking Daisy out for a nice dinner to leave us home alone for a while.

I set the table with two place settings, and Daisy pulled out two silver candle holders from the back of our cupboard. I had never seen them before.

"They were my mother's. They are real silver, so be careful. She only used them for special occasions while my father was still alive."

Daisy hardly ever mentioned her parents. I knew her father had a sudden and fatal heart attack when she was in high school. My grandmother had also died, but I didn't know any details of her death. I wanted to ask about my grandparents since she brought them up, but I was afraid to ruin her good mood. We still needed to prepare the meal. I didn't think I could do it all on my own. My questions about my family history remained bottled up. I would ask Daddy again sometime.

When Matthew arrived, he was wearing a navy blue, paisley tie with his white button-down shirt, khaki pants and his church shoes. My heart fluttered at the sight of him. He looked so handsome. His chiseled cheekbones, sparkling hazel eyes, and big white smile made me melt. I had chosen to wear a black lace, knee length dress that I had recently inherited from one of Matthew's aunts. She gifted it to me after Thanksgiving dinner. Her name was Mary Beth, and she was my favorite of the aunts, plus her kids were the cutest and most polite.

"I'll never be a size three again, and I hate hearing this beautiful dress weep in my closet. It wants to be worn, and it wants to have fun again! Please, say you'll save it, Lily. Give it a new life."

I giggled at the idea of her dress begging to be worn but was secretly thrilled about the generous gift. It was a gorgeous dress, and I knew I could never afford it. It fit me perfectly. The sleeves were quarter length, the neck curved perfectly around my pearl necklace. I even wore a pair of high heeled shoes.

Matthew's eyes reflected that he recognized the dress. He approved of my appearance with his big smile and a little wink. My parents ducked out as soon as he arrived, giving us strict instructions to enjoy our dinner but no 'hanky panky.' We had little over one hour to ourselves. Matthew handed me a little box wrapped in red wrapping paper. I opened it with excitement. It was a mixed tape. He labeled it, 'Valentine's Day 1989.' I inserted that cassette tape in my boom box anxious to hear what songs he had chosen.

"Happy Valentine's Day, Lily! We can't let the dress just sit here. It must dance." He had overheard Mary Beth's wishes for her beautiful dress. So, before we started eating our salads, we slow-danced in our little kitchen by candlelight. He whispered the words to the first song in my ear: "Hey, pretty baby with the high heels on. "

I stopped his singing by covering his mouth with my mouth. I could feel his hardness through my dress. He was in love with me. He wanted me. I turned him on. Everything was perfect. Nope, no trouble in February.

The rest of February and March didn't have any significance to them that I could remember. In his parked car, we became a bit more adventurous with our touching, but nothing beyond touching.

In March, I do recall that our heavy petting became insufficient for Matthew. We were cuddling on my living room couch. We were home alone. Daddy was driving his eighteen-wheeler somewhere across the United States. Daisy was… out. Fifteen minutes into our make-out session, I pulled away from Matthew's grasp, and he became slightly annoyed.

"I know you said not until we're married, Lily, but if we know we're going to get married to each other someday, then why do we need to wait? It's just sex. I don't know how much more I can take." He stood up from the couch and paced the living room. I could see the bulge in his jeans. Waiting to have sex was harder on him that it was on me, but I didn't want to be like Daisy. She gave it away to anyone and everyone. We had had this argument before. He knew this, but I could tell he needed to say his piece. Get his feelings out.

"I know, Matthew, I know. I love you, but we have to wait. Maybe we should slow down a bit so that it doesn't get this far. We can do this. It's worth the wait."

I pulled him back onto the couch. I turned on a TV show that I knew he would be interested in and would help to take his mind off me and the tempting things he wanted to do to my body.

As soon as the TV program, *In the Heat of the Night*, (ironic) came to life, Matthew began to relax next to me on the couch. He put his arm around me. He knew I was right, but physically, his body didn't agree with his mind. I understood. I wanted him too, but my desire to be unlike Daisy was more powerful than my teenage hormones.

Then I heard a noise in the kitchen behind us. Daisy cleared her throat and closed the refrigerator door. She poured something into a glass. I hadn't heard her come home. She usually came in the front door, but she must've snuck in the back door in the kitchen this time. I wondered how much of our intimate conversation she had overheard. She never brought it up to me later, so I assumed she didn't hear anything, but now in hindsight, I wondered differently. Small flicker of trouble, but nothing we hadn't already discussed or worked through before. But to Daisy, did she see a weakness in Matthew? In our relationship?

And now it was April, a week after Daddy passed away and a stick of dynamite named Daisy blew up everything that I cherished. Daddy's heart failed while having an argument about her whoring, and now she claimed to have seduced my first love. All those sweet memories of our relationship went up in smoke.

Suddenly, the optimistic section of my brain sent a signal. A white flag. A spark of hope. Maybe she was lying? Maybe she was trying to hurt me? Maybe they never slept together at all? It wouldn't be the first time.

I started to run again. That had to be it. How could I question our relationship? I knew Matthew loved me. This was just Daisy being cruel… crueler than normal, but nothing I wouldn't put past her. I had two miles to go, and then I would run straight to Matthew's open arms and tell him what she claimed. What she accused him of. He would hold me tight, tenderly pat my head, and calm me down. He would tell me that I was crazy to even consider it a possibility. We would form a plan to get away from here once we graduated and start our life together. We only had one more month left of high school. I felt terrible for letting Daisy's declaration make me doubt my relationship with Matthew.

My legs found a new pace. A pace to bring me to Matthew faster. Even my legs wanted to see Matthew, hear his promises and feel his embrace. His house was a half-mile north of our house so I would stop there before I headed home. I needed to see him and thrust this bad morning behind me.

When I reached his house, I was out of breath and needed to bend at my waist to try to catch my breath. My new track coach would have been impressed with my sprinting that last mile and a half. I pressed the doorbell. I heard the chime ring inside the house, some distant voices, and then footsteps heading for the front door. Matthew's mother, Sara, answered the door. She was holding a mixing bowl and a dish towel in her hands. She always seemed to be doing dishes or folding laundry.

"Lily? What's wrong? What are you doing here?"

My face was flushed, and I was panting, so I understood her concern.

"I came to see Matthew." I was able to sputter out a few words in between my panting. I smiled so she knew I was okay.

I hadn't seen his family since Daddy's funeral. They had sent a huge bouquet of flowers with a card that read, "We will love your daughter like she is our own. Rest in Peace, Ben." It made me cry, and I pinned the floral card onto the bulletin board in my room.

"I'm fine. Just out for a run. Is he here?"

"Well, that's strange." Her eyebrows crept down over her brown eyes, and wrinkles spread across her forehead. "Your mother called the house a little while ago asking for Matthew. She explained to him that you were very upset and to come over quickly. He ran out of the house seconds later. He must be at your house now."

Daisy called Matthew? She told him that I was upset and to come over to our house right away? It was true that I was upset the last time I saw her, but I was upset with *her*. I left my house about an hour ago. This didn't make sense.

My brain ignited another signal. This time, it was not an optimistic one. I needed to get home as fast as I could.

"Thank you, Sara! I'll head home and see if he's still there."

I turned my back and sprinted towards home. I tried not to let my mind venture to the dark places it was trying to pull me towards. I had to stay positive. There was a logical explanation for this. I needed to get home and figure it all out. I needed to see Matthew and talk with him.

A half mile was nothing to a seasoned, long distance runner. By the time I arrived home, I wasn't even winded. Eight hundred meters was a cool down for me. Matthew's car was parked next to the curb in front of our house. The driver's side door was still open. He hadn't even shut it when he got out of the car. He must have been frantic. I wondered what Daisy's exact words to him were.

Suddenly, everything seemed to happen in slow motion. My feet weighed fifty pounds. Left foot... right foot... left foot... right foot... I was in a bubble and couldn't feel the air around me or hear anything unless it was directly in front of me. Tunnel vision. I slowly shuffled up the cracked sidewalk that led to the front of our house. I advanced up the steps one at a time. My brain wouldn't allow me to go any faster. Or maybe it was my heart telling my brain that I couldn't handle what was about to happen. It was as if Father Time was trying to prolong this moment. The moment before life would throw me the most life-altering curveball.

I saw him through the screen door, his image was grainy, like a photograph out of focus. In the middle of our living room, he was standing with his backside towards me. His head and neck angled up towards the ceiling. I could see the back of his light blue T-shirt. His arms were somewhere in front of his body. I couldn't tell exactly where. His blue jeans and white underwear had dropped around his ankles, circling his white tube socks and black high top tennis shoes. His butt and thighs were bare except for a pair of hands cupping each of his butt cheeks. The two hands that had a firm grip of his butt were dainty, and the nails painted crimson red. I heard him moan, a moan of pleasure that I had only heard before when we were heavy petting, but this moan was marginally different - a hint of anguish along with pleasure.

Between his bare legs, I observed Daisy kneeling in front of Matthew. She was completely naked except for her red high heeled shoes that matched her freshly painted nails. Her blonde hair covered her face like a lioness as she stroked him up and down with her mouth. During one deep stroke, her eyes opened, and she noticed me standing just beyond the screen door, afraid to take another step, too shocked to move. Even though her mouth was maxed out in the shape of an "O", she managed to smile. In her eyes that always reflected her true feelings, I noticed she was pleased. This had been her plan.

Pity for Matthew sprouted in my heart. Of course, not because he was receiving a blow job, but because she was using him as a pawn in one of her games. He would soon be tossed aside and broken. He would be wounded by her vindictive mind. He was obviously physically enjoying every stroke, but would he be scarred by Daisy and her evil sexual advances? I didn't know if I would ever find out. I knew that he was no match, as any man was, for Daisy. He was a boy, and she used him to punish me. He was a victim. I was angry and pissed at him for being so weak; I thought our love could outlive anything. But obviously, even what I considered as strong, unbreakable love could be ruined by Daisy.

She timed it so I would walk into their passionate foreplay when I returned from my run. She had staged this. She calculated when I would return.

This repulsive game of hers was over. I needed to end it. I boldly opened the screen door. I had one move left, and it was time for it. I didn't know if I had the strength to do it. With my best poker face painted on, I calmly remarked, "Thanks for doing that for Matthew, Daisy. He has often mentioned that he wanted a blow job from an old, wrinkly lady who has a lot of experience."

She wiped her mouth after she removed it from around his enlarged penis. She didn't appreciate being called old and wrinkly but was probably ironically proud that I recognized her vast sexual experience. I would never understand this woman.

Naturally, Matthew was shocked when he recognized my voice from behind him. It took him a second or two to register that his sexual high was over - he would not be reaching climax. Furthermore, his girlfriend and best friend walked in on him receiving a blow job from her own mother. He frantically pulled up his underwear and jeans back around his waist. I caught his eye as I was ascending the stairs to my bedroom. I read many emotions on his boyish face: fear, worry, shame, hurt, sadness and regret. All were too late for him. I didn't have any words for him. No apology, no excuses or no explanations could ever ease the pain that his crushing betrayal caused me. I simply shook my head and continued up the stairs shedding, tear after silent tear.

How much more of my life could this evil woman ruin?

Chapter Fifteen

1988

I graduated from Normal High School with honors a month after Daddy's fatal heart attack. National Honors Society and fifth highest GPA in my graduating class. It was bittersweet. Successfully completing high school and moving away to college had always been a goal that Daddy and I shared for my future. Daddy explained he grew up too quickly and wanted me to enjoy young adulthood.

"Baby Girl, you got your whole life to grow up. I want you to do everything that suits your fancy. Reach for the stars. Have fun! Live your best life!"

When I paraded across our high school's wooden stage at the graduation ceremony, I reminded myself to smile upward, not out to the crowd where he should have been sitting and clapping. He watched me from Heaven; he silently cheered me on. It was not fair. I forced myself to not cry. I was strong; I was his Baby Girl. I could do this. The one parent who physically could attend the formal ceremony chose to drink herself into a stupor instead.

Furthermore, Matthew and his whole extended family attended the graduation ceremony. It was obvious that we weren't dating anymore; previously, we had been inseparable. One month ago, his family would have been my cheering section as well. His mother, Sara, caught my eye and a small, weak smile formed. I wondered what excuse Matthew had used when he told them we were no longer dating, I was sure it wasn't the truth.

Meanwhile, Daisy's grieving had taken an abrupt halt. As she cooked in the kitchen, she would sing. She pranced around in her cut-off jean shorts humming Bon Jovi's *Bad Medicine*.

A spring returned to her step. She ignored my presence in any room, or she'd simply walk out of a room if I entered it. All was fine by me. She made my skin crawl, and the sight of her caused the blood in my veins to boil. Her immaturity and shallow digs at me didn't hurt. I only stayed in Normal because I needed a roof over my head. Angry words would be wasted. I had nothing left to say to her. She killed Daddy; she seduced and stole my first love, Matthew, from me in record time. The fact that the end of my life with her in it was around the corner made living with her much easier and more tolerable.

When a runner saw the final lap mark, the pace quickened automatically. A runner became narrow-minded and goal oriented. The final lap marker beckoned me onward.

Before each race, Coach Knight would remind me, "Eyes on the prize."

I ached because Daddy was gone. Not only was he my forever cheerleader, but he was also the one person who truly loved me. The one person who treated me with kindness, love and respect. He had my back. He believed in me. I hurt because I felt alone and cheated. After he died, Matthew was my crutch, I leaned on him. Now, Daisy had managed to shatter that relationship as well.

BY MID-AUGUST, I successfully saved enough money working at Kitty's Cafe to make it financially through the first semester at college. Emotionally, I was also more than ready to go. The night before my move into the dorm, Daisy was more chipper than usual. As I finished taping up my last moving box from my childhood bedroom, I heard her getting ready to go out. She was in the bathroom down the hall. She was singing in the shower; then continued singing while she dried her long, blonde hair.

And soon enough, her high heels pounded down the hallway towards the stairs. "Lily, I'm going out. Don't wait up!" Down the wooden stairs she clobbered. She must have paused a minute to check her appearance in the entryway mirror because I heard her say to herself, "Looking fine, Mrs. Robinson!" She giggled at her little inside joke and slammed the door on her way out.

Mrs. Robinson? Another stab to my heart. She was referring to the movie, *The Graduate*, where an older woman, Mrs. Robinson, seduces a younger man. In Daisy's case, she was Mrs. Robinson, and Matthew was the young, innocent man whom she seduced. With that small reference, she confirmed that she was still seeing him.

She didn't come home that night, which was becoming her new routine. I never waited up, but I always made sure the front door was locked and the hidden key in its usual spot under the first stair of the front steps. But even in my wildest dreams I didn't imagine that she would not be home at least to say goodbye and wish me luck. She knew I was catching a ride with a fellow high school classmate that was also attending the same university. Honestly, I shouldn't have been surprised, but yet I was. Moving away to college was a huge milestone for me, and for her not to even acknowledge it truly hurt. Neither her nor Daddy had ever been to college, so Daddy stressed the goal to me.

"Baby Girl, I don't care if you study Rocket Science."

"I don't plan on becoming an aerospace engineer, Daddy."

"See, look at you, college-bound girl! You even know the real word for a rocket scientist."

I SWALLOWED a big deep breath and looked around the first floor of my childhood home. A single tear rolled down my cheek, not for her but for me as I embarked on a new journey alone. I was saying a final farewell to Daddy, too. And all the memories in this little house. His presence loomed everywhere in this house. Everywhere I looked, memories of him poured out.

The small, lower dent in the front door. One Saturday afternoon, I formulated an idea around a piece of discarded cardboard from his garage: I was going to ride it down the stairs. Hitting the front door going full speed was not part of my plan. I sprained my ankle somehow, and I was screaming in agony. Daddy heard my urgent cries for help while he was fixing something in his garage. He came running into the house.

"Lily? Where are you?"

He found me at the bottom of the stairs, holding up my left ankle, weeping uncontrollably. The ankle did really hurt, but my dreams of the greatest stair flight were shattered. My ego hurt as much as my sprained ankle. He scooped me up in his big, muscular arms and carried me into the living room where he sat down on the couch with me in his lap. He questioned me on what hurt and comforted me. We relaxed like that for fifteen minutes. My tears dried and my mood lightened. He was always my knight in shining armor.

A SMALL, light green stain on the living room ceiling was barely visible above the front window. One evening when Daisy was not home, Daddy and I had a food fight with our vegetables. I don't recall what started it, but I do remember the loud laughter and huge smiles. The little spot was from a green pea. Now, the lime green stain brought fresh tears to my eyes.

A silver picture frame rested on the fireplace mantel enclosing a picture of the three of us. It was snapped during a spontaneous weekend at Des Moines' Adventureland Park. It was one of the three family vacations that we ever enjoyed. We had finished our third ride on the newest, fastest rollercoaster, The Tornado. All three of us loved roller coaster rides; they made us giddy with screams and laughter. It was one of my favorite childhood memories. We felt like a normal family. The picture captured the genuine joy in each of our faces. Dressed in her classic Daisy-Duke shorts, a white tank top and cowboy boots, Daisy stood with her left hand on her hip, and her right hand was holding mine. I stood in the middle holding both of their hands as the glue that held our family together. My T-shirt hung on me because it was about three sizes too big. I also wore a pair of black shorts and tennis shoes. Daddy had a goofy grin frozen on his handsome face. He wore a pair of faded blue jeans and a white T-shirt with a pocket on the left peck.

In this snapshot from one moment in our lives, we all looked so much alike. You could tell we were related. Our noses were remarkably similar: the left nostril was slightly wider than the right, the end of our noses slightly turned up following a sharp slope. We all have high cheekbones and squinted when we smiled. Even Daisy and Daddy could pass as relatives rather than spouses.

It broke my heart that we wouldn't be making anymore family memories together. How I wished I could return and be that young, naive girl again thinking my parents were happy, honest, trustworthy and would live forever. The little girl who had big dreams and only wanted both of her parents there to see them come true.

I gently closed the front door behind me. Closing the door to my childhood but cherishing all the memories that I collected in this little two-story house. A rush of air escaped the front door as it closed. It was as if the house breathed out a huge, sad sigh as I finally turned my back and slowly walked away.

Chapter Sixteen

Choices shape who a person becomes. Some choices are life-altering.

Should I cheat on this exam? The teacher left the classroom, so I doubt I will get caught.

Should I steal this gorgeous necklace? The clerk is too busy flirting with that guy, so she won't be looking.

What college major should I choose?

Should I marry him?

Should we have sex just this one time? Should I keep the baby?

Anyone can understand that these are examples of substantial life choices. The threat of aversive consequences or fallout looms for poor decision making. Sometimes choices are weighed out for weeks; other times a choice is made in a matter of seconds. The decision is not made with a grain of salt, and the consequences are not trivial. Pro and con lists are created, deep discussions are shared with loved ones. Morals and standards are put to the test.

Some choices seem minuscule at the time.

Am I going to waste time carrying an umbrella if the weather only forecasts a 60% chance of rain? Nah, the umbrella stays home. It doesn't rain. The walk home is dry and peaceful. In fact, the choice to bring an umbrella or not is forgotten.

Imagine the scenario where no umbrella is carried and it downpours on the walk home. The attitude and thoughts on the way home are completely different due to being sopping wet, grumpy and irritable. Now, the choice to not bring the umbrella becomes more significant. Most likely, the next time the choice presents itself, the optional umbrella will be a given.

Dorothy, the main character on *The Wizard of Oz*, made many choices on her journey to find Oz. The only instructions that she was given was to "follow the yellow brick road." When she met up with the Scarecrow, they veered left down the yellow brick road. A few skips and songs later, the Tin Man crossed their path. But what would have happened if they had chosen to turn right? Who would have crossed their path then? Maybe turning right would have led them right to Oz, and Dorothy would have headed home for Kansas. End of the story. The simple choice between left or right would completely alter the direction of the story. She would not have learned all those life lessons skipping down the yellow brick road.

Each choice we make leads us down different paths. Sometimes, the path is not permanent, and a U-turn is allowed. U-turns are forgiveness, chances to make amends, a do-over. Choose a different life direction.

Other paths are one-way highways with no looking back. U-turns are not allowed; they are unsafe and dangerous. One-way roads are past the point of forgiveness. Blinders are on, and the driver has a firm, one-way focus. No turning back. One-way highways are unforgiving.

Other times we can make a choice that seems like a rough, gravel road. The gravel road slows you down because of the bumps and dust. The course was rockier and less traveled. The journey should be worth the wait. Patience is rewarded on a gravel road. Life slows down. Take a moment, look out the window, and ponder decisions.

All these roads - choices - shape who a person becomes. On any road, scars, bumps and scrapes are received. Choose to learn while you slow down on a gravel road, take a U-turn on a highway to make a better choice, or keep going down the one-way freeway without a chance of an exit ramp. Choices are made every day, some big and some small; sometimes they don't warrant much thought at all.

I'm not trying to make excuses for who I have become, but instead explain that I didn't start here. I was once pink with innocence. I was shiny and new. I was naive. No scars, bumps or scratches. But along my life, my road trip, the course changed me. Choices molded me. And not all the choices that affected me were my choices, but they had a sharp, strong hand in shaping whom I have become. I was a passenger down one-way and gravel roads. As the driver, I was able to determine the direction of my immediate future. As a passenger, I braced myself against permanent damage.

Not only did Daisy's infidelity permanently burn me to my very core, but her treachery also tattooed hard life lessons on my soul that shaped who I've become as an adult.

Chapter Seventeen

1988

Trying to make sense of all of the lies and cheating Daisy did kept me up at night. I couldn't help but wonder, what changed her? What made her the evil temptress she became? What dents and bruises did she receive on her life journey? Did someone hurt her? Was she abused physically or emotionally?

I couldn't accept that she was born like this. Something must have happened to make her this way. I loved to read mystery novels, and this was my real-life mystery. I wanted to unravel this mystery.

I physically distanced myself from Daisy by moving away to college, yet my heart was still back in Normal, Iowa, yearning for answers. I promised Daddy I would make her pay for all the pain she caused him. I couldn't let him down. Physically, I was distant from her, but emotionally, I was still tangled in the web of lies she weaved. I wanted freedom, and I reasoned that the only way to become free was to discover some truth, maybe just enough to help me sleep better at night.

According to Greek mythology, Medusa possessed ravishing beauty and had many suitors begging for her attention. However, Poseidon blamed her one-of-a-kind beauty for the reason he raped her in Athens' temple. Ironically, even though she was the obvious victim, she was punished for the rape and given snakes for hair. Her eyes were also given the ability to turn men into stone. Daisy was a modern Medusa. She had the seductive power to seduce men who would normally not stray, men who were happily married, men who had strong religious beliefs, and boys who knew better. However, even Medusa wasn't born seductive and venomous.

During my nights of insomnia, I tried to make sense of what Daisy did, and maybe then I could figure out why. But there were so many pieces of the puzzle missing. I needed more answers. I knew I wouldn't be able to pry the answers from her. I decided my next best option would be to question the men whom Daisy took to bed. This idea consumed me. I couldn't think of anything else. I logged a list of questions that I would ask each man if the situation presented itself. I even made a list of questions for Daddy. I still idolized him and couldn't understand why he married her and furthermore, stood by her through all of the infidelity and drama. He seemed like the biggest victim.

As I read and reread my list of questions, an idea sprouted. A little argument wrestled in my brain. A battlefield filled with soldiers firing back and forth at one another.

WHY NOT FIND these men (at least the ones that were still alive) and ask them their side of the story?

Because they would never answer your questions. They have families. They have moved on with their lives. They've forgotten Daisy Armstrong. And owe you nothing. Not a thing.

Why should they get to move on?

They made a mistake.

Over and over and over again! Why shouldn't they receive some sort of retribution for it? Why did they lead normal lives while I continued to suffer?

It was years ago. Time to move on. This isn't your battle to fight.

No, I couldn't move on. I wanted answers.

You'll cause more pain and grief to innocent people by revisiting the past. You may not like what you uncover.

I was innocent once, too. No one protected me. No one gave me a choice. It was time. It was time for these men to feel remorse.

What about their families? They didn't do anything to deserve what is coming to them.

I was one of those family members, too. Years ago, I was a victim of their infidelity and lies. I didn't ask for any of this either. I was just reacting to their actions. Cause and effect.

What you *are planning will purposely inflict emotional pain on people. Daisy and these men were selfish and didn't think of others. It wasn't directly meant to hurt you. They didn't sleep with your mother to inflict pain on anyone else. It was physical pleasure.*

I disagreed. I thought what Daisy did was on purpose. She sought out these specific men to hurt me. They were all important men in my life one way or another. She purposefully seduced them to inflict emotional pain on me. These men may have been her victims as well, but I cannot justify what they continued to do over and over again. This argument was over. I had won this battle.

Maybe the battle, but not the war. Be prepared to not like the answers you find.

I DECIDED to start with the man who would probably be the easiest find: Coach Knight. Although I already 'outed' his affair to the speech class, I didn't feel any closure. Even though he did stop seeing Daisy shortly after my speech, life moved on as if it never happened.

No one suspected anything unusual when I suddenly requested a new track coach either. My created excuse was perhaps I needed someone who would challenge me more, push me beyond my limits. The athletic director agreed, and Mrs. Hunt was assigned as my new track coach and finished my high school career with me. She received all the glory when I earned an athletic college scholarship to run track. She was the one to field all the questions from the college recruiters on my ability. She was the woman behind the track star.

Coach Knight didn't argue with the coaching change. He told Mrs. Hunt that he thought it was a good suggestion and would benefit my running. He avoided me whenever I was near. If I was walking towards him in the school hallway, he would purposely turn around and head in the opposite direction. On the track field, he kept to himself and the team members whom he worked the closest with.

Previously, Coach Knight and I were seen together often especially on the track. A couple of my track team members noticed the awkwardness between us. Walking into the locker room after practice one afternoon, I overheard them whispering.

"He is good looking. I would totally do him. Maybe they were a couple and had a nasty break up. I could totally see Lily loving all the attention he gave her."

"Nah, they were more like father-daughter, not lovers. And plus, that is gross. He's, like, super old. Ancient! At least thirty!"

As soon as they noticed that I entered the locker room, they halted their conversation and made a beeline for the door. The rumors didn't bother me, at least those kinds of rumors. Another rumor that floated around was I considered myself too good for Coach Knight. This rumor did bother me a bit. Coach Knight was a wonderful coach, and I owed him a lot in that respect. However, the fact that he had a love affair with my mother overshadowed any gratitude he had earned from me in my past.

A few weeks after my infamous speech in his Speech 101 class, Susan called our home asking me to babysit the boys, Luke and Zack. I hated lying to her, and I was not particularly good at it. Soon, I started to run out of excuses. She didn't catch on that Coach Knight was the one to split up our unique little 'family.' Eventually, she stopped calling; she probably believed the rumor about my big ego. I was sure as his wife that the rumor was an easier one to stomach than the alternative.

Thinking about Susan and her boys made me question my plan. However, Coach Knight and Daisy were to blame for ripping them away from me. I was simply exposing the truth. The truth did hurt sometimes, but it was better than living in denial and under a cloud of lies. I would be freeing Susan from the lie that their marriage was. Plus, in my heart of hearts, I knew she suspected something.

If I am honest, giving that speech and shocking him with the brutal fact that I had discovered his secret really felt good. At the time, I didn't know what to do about the knowledge I had gained. I knew that I didn't want to continue lying about it, and I wanted it to end. And I really didn't think Daisy would be listening to me about whom she could have sex with. She did what Daisy wanted to do.

The Normal High School alumni newsletter that I received each month informed me that he was still teaching Speech and coaching track at the high school. He was the featured teacher in last month's newsletter. The article read, "Coach Knight has been awarded teacher of the year twice in his twelve years of teaching. He thanks his wife, Susan, and their two sons for allowing him to heavily focus on his career goals."

Bomb! He was still in Normal, Iowa. Locating him should be relatively easy.

Christmas break was only a few weeks away. While I was home visiting - in other words, simply cohabitating under the same roof - with Daisy, I would purposefully run into Coach Knight. In the meantime, I needed to formulate a plan.

Plan A: The Knight family would come in for supper at Kitty's Cafe. I would be their waitress. Written in permanent marker on the plate under his hot beef commercial would be a message: *tell Susan the truth, or I will.*

Nah… too corny and I don't actually place the food on the plate; I deliver it to the table, so that isn't gonna work. This isn't a Lifetime movie. Need less drama, more intel.

Plan B: I would be hired as his substitute teacher and leave a huge note on the chalkboard for him when he returned: *I cheated on my wife.*

That option banked on him taking a sick day and that he wouldn't erase it before the students arrived to class. *And dah!* It was Christmas break. He was off from work. No school.

After all my brainstorming, meeting up with Coach Knight didn't go as planned. They never came into the restaurant to eat supper, and I never accidentally ran into them anywhere in town.

One week before returning to college, I stormed over to his house and knocked on the door. The lights were on in the living room, and his same silver pickup truck was parked in the driveway. When Coach Knight opened the door, his welcoming smile quickly faded away when he realized it was me. He was still terrified of the words that might escape from my mouth. Knowing I held that power over him gave me a renewed purpose. As his smile faded, mine grew. More of a smirk than a smile.

"Lily?"

It was one word. But I interpreted that one word as "Why are you here?", "What could you possibly need three years later?" and "Don't do this?" Just one word said all of that.

Then, most likely because he had opened the front door in the middle of winter and he was letting all the heat vanish out the front door, Susan came strolling down the hallway.

"Sweetheart, who is it? Don't let them stand out in the... Lily?" When she finally reached the door, she could see past Coach Knight, who was blocking the doorway with his wide frame. He had packed on a few pounds in his midsection since the days when he was coaching me. However, Susan looked the same. Maybe a few laugh lines near her eyes, but more or less, she hadn't aged. She pulled the door open wider.

"Lily, honey, come on in! It is so good to see you! Merry Christmas! Come into the kitchen. I will make some hot cocoa. We even have dessert leftovers from the holidays."

She had grabbed my forearm after yanking me through the door. I quickly kicked off my boots before I dripped all over their hallway. Physically, she hadn't changed much, and neither did her ability to talk. She chatted about how the boys would be disappointed that they missed me; they were staying at their cousin's house - Susan's sister - for a few days since school was out for holiday break. As soon as we reached the kitchen table, Coach Knight and I each chose chairs on the opposite end of the table, giving the most possible physical distance from each other.

Susan had all kinds of questions about college. I informed her about my class load and how I was enjoying my Criminal Justice classes the most. I remembered that she majored in Criminal Justice as well.

"This field of study really interests me. The law treats everything as black and white. Right and wrong. Do this, but absolutely don't do that. No room to wonder. When you do something illegal, which is also morally wrong, you are punished. You're held accountable for your actions."

"Well, good for you! Always so wonderful when someone discovers something that they are passionate about. Like my Max here" - she motioned to Coach Knight with her finger - "he loves teaching, and he loves kids. He found the perfect combination. So happy for you, Lily. Isn't that wonderful, sweetheart?" She glanced over to her husband but quickly busied herself with serving dessert. If she noticed the awkwardness between us, she wasn't letting on.

Even though it was only five degrees outside and their old home was a bit drafty, beads of sweat formed on the top of Coach Knight's forehead. He didn't trust my intentions with my surprise visit; he still remembered what I was capable of all too well. As she set a piece of cake down in front of her husband, Susan noticed her husband's flushed face but not his lack of communication.

"Sweetheart, are you feeling alright? You don't look well. Maybe you should lie down for a bit." She put her hand on his forehead to check for a raised temperature.

"No. I'm fine. Little upset stomach from dinner. I think I ate too much."

He didn't trust me alone with his wife. He wanted me to know he wasn't leaving the room as long as I was here. Fine by me. He figured I would say something to her about the affair when he wasn't around. He figured wrong.

From my coat pocket, I retrieved a small box wrapped in bright red Christmas wrapping paper. "I have a small gift for you, Susan. I

should've given it to you years ago. I'm trying to right a few wrongs."
I did not indicate that they were not my 'wrongs' to correct.

"I can't imagine what wrongs you need to correct. However, recognizing that a correction is needed is impressive, Lily. Most people would prefer to bury the secret or wrongdoing and pretend it never happened. Takes a strong person to recognize that." Susan was holding the little box but had not taken off the lid yet.

"Thank you for saying that, Susan. That's exactly how I feel."

She removed the lid from the little box. As she peered inside the box, her eyebrows rose on her innocent face in pure curiosity. She lifted the object out.

"Car keys? Wait! These are Max's truck keys that he lost a few years back. I recognize the Iowa Hawkeyes keychain. What does this mean, Lily? I don't understand."

I held her stare to see if it had resonated. A light bulb seemed to flicker, but I could tell that I needed to supply more information.

"Yes, those are Coach's old keys. Susan, do you remember where he lost those keys? Where did you pick up the truck from?" I asked her patiently.

I wanted her to put it together herself. I didn't want to have to say the words. The realization of her husband's betrayal would be easier on her coming from his mouth or her brain. I didn't glance in Coach Knight's direction, but I noticed out of the corner of my eye that he squirmed in his kitchen chair.

"His truck was parked in the alleyway behind your house. Did you steal his truck keys years ago?"

"He wasn't visiting me, Susan. I was not home. Only Daisy was."

I figured telling her Daisy was the one only one home would be enough to help her piece the puzzle together. And I was correct. The whole town knew my mother's reputation.

She gaped at her husband with confusion and concern. Her eyes darted back and forth, trying to get ahead of the information that was spewing from my mouth. "After working my supper shift at the diner, I returned home to hear the two of them in her bedroom... and yes, then I stole his truck keys."

"Max, is this true?"

Her voice cracked a bit. I could tell from her shaking tone she wanted him to deny it and tell her that I made it up. She wanted to hear a believable lie. I understood why she wanted an excuse, why she wanted it not to be the truth. The truth is often very painful. I had been in her shoes many, many times.

"There is one more thing in the bottom of the box."

Susan never received a response from Coach Knight. She glanced at me as if she forgot I was there. In a robotic motion, she again reached into the small box and brought out the broken, antique watch that I had stomped on during my speech.

"Max, this is your grandfather's old watch. You lost it about the same time as your truck keys." She looked at her husband. Tears were beginning to form in her eyes. Her eyes searched mine to find the truth "Lily?"

"I found his watch under my mother's bed. I'm sorry, Susan." My tone of voice was matter-of-fact, void of any true feeling. I took a moment to look at Coach Knight. He slouched in his chair, head down, tears rolling down his cheeks. It's never easy to see a grown man cry, but the part of my heart that blackened over the course of my childhood didn't care one bit. He deserved this. Susan deserved to know. She didn't deserve to be with someone who lied and cheated on her. It reminded me of that old saying: *You've made your bed, now you can lie in it*. And he would be laying in it alone tonight.

I figured my part in this long overdue conversation was finished. I pushed my chair away from the kitchen table. Slowly, I rose from my chair, glanced down at my untouched piece of cake. No one stopped me. They were too engrossed in figuring out what just happened. Plus, they probably wanted to continue the rest of this discussion in private. I provided the topic. They could argue the facts.

I was curious to see if Coach Knight would try to create another lie to get out of this mess with his wife. Or if he would come clean and admit it. Just a few moments earlier, Susan was impressed by me for correcting a mistake. Unfortunately, it wasn't my wrongdoing but Coach Knight's. I didn't care if their marriage survived this test or not.

Tests in a marriage can only make it stronger, and if it can't survive, then at least she'll be better off.

When I shut their front door, I could only imagine what would happen behind this closed door. I felt good about exposing the truth even if it hurt Susan, which was not my intent. I only wanted to right some wrongs that I had witnessed in my childhood.

Chapter Eighteen

1989

I knew the day would come. Nothing could prepare me for my heart's reaction. It would hurt. Seeing him again would make my heart ache. His smile would weaken my knees. His eyes, how they sparkled when he was happy, would melt all the strength I had. Even if I knew the day would come, I wasn't prepared for it.

The day was a Wednesday during Christmas break. Five days after I confronted Coach Knight. I worked a double shift at Kitty's Cafe. My feet burned. My hair was pulled up into a messy bun, and I sweated through my work T-shirt. Kitty kept the restaurant too hot. She claimed she had poor circulation so the rest of us had to suffer. Only two more hours until Kitty's Cafe closed for the day.

The tips had been decent. I was feeling upbeat about how well I did even though I was physically exhausted. As I was bringing out table seven's order of a Smoking Hot Burger, topped with pepper jack cheese, jalapeños, a tomato and lettuce with a side of homestyle french fries, and a Bet Your Ass BLT with a side salad, the Christmas bells hanging on the front door announced the entry of a new customer. I heard the signal, dropped off the meals and headed to greet the new customer. Waitress, hostess and janitor all in one.

Standing in the entryway and holding the door open for departing customers, Matthew stood in his school letterman's jacket, a pair of faded jeans and a pair of starch white sneakers. He smiled - I swear his smile reached up to his eyes - and politely nodded his head in acknowledgement when the customers leaving thanked him for holding the door. I lost my forward momentum and was awkwardly standing still with the menus dropped to my side, mouth hanging open. My heart was beating so loudly that I was sure everyone in the restaurant could hear it.

Thump... thump... thump... thump...

Then, as he let go of the glass door, he lifted his eyes up and forward. They locked with mine. His beaming smile slowly faded off his face. It was a quick subtle decrease in his smile, but I noticed it. It made my heart hurt. He still had feelings for me even though my mind warned me that this interaction we were about to have would not show any such feelings. Each of us would create a wall. Each of us would protect our heart from any future heartache. It was natural. I knew it, yet it totally sucked.

The Matthew, whom I fondly remembered from our dating before the awful, disturbing sex scene with Daisy, was wonderful, honest, caring and affectionate. Dating him was like being with my best friend and boyfriend at the same time. I never doubted we were meant for each other. I never doubted his love for me. I trusted him; I never had any reason not to. Until I couldn't anymore.

During the many sleepless nights after we broke up, I questioned everything about our relationship. Had he ever really loved me? How many times had he been with Daisy? Did he come onto her? Did he plan on breaking up with me to be with my own mother?

I concluded that he didn't plan this. It was her. "If it quacks like a duck and walks like a duck, it's a duck." She didn't have any morals. She didn't seem to care a bit about me. The more I thought about them, the more that I knew it had been all Daisy's idea. Even though I was sure it was her who initiated their sexual relationship, it didn't make Matthew any less guilty. "Takes two to tango." If anything, he was more at fault because he supposedly had genuine feelings for me. My own mother, I don't think ever had.

All these deep, dark thoughts flew through my brain in a matter of seconds as he started walking towards me.

When he was within three feet, he stopped and gently said, "Hi, Lily. Can I have a booth in the back?" He gently removed the menus from my hand since my body was still refusing to react accordingly. He motioned me with a slight nod of his head and headed to a vacant booth. All I could do was nod and follow him like a shadow. He slid down in the booth and noticed quite obviously that I was still unable to form a sentence. "Could I get a glass of ice water, Lily?"

Again, I was only able to nod my head. I walked to the counter and dumped ice in a drinking glass and walked robotically back to his booth. My brain and heart stopped communicating with each other. I was afraid if I opened my mouth, I would word vomit something I couldn't take back. Silence was the better choice.

When I set the cup of ice down in front of him, I noticed a familiar smirk in his voice. "Thanks for the ice. Could I get some water too?"

It was obvious that I was struggling with our reunion. He awarded me with one of his one-of-a-kind half smiles and blessed me with his patience.

"Oh my god! I am so sorry about that. It's been a long day." *I found my voice!* I hurriedly snatched the drinking glass and returned to the counter to grab the water gun. I filled up his glass and told myself, *Get it together, Lily!*

After a few deep breaths and a little self-pep talk, I casually returned with his complete drink order: ice and water. "Do you need a few minutes to look over the menu? The soup of the day is Chicken Tortilla… actually, it might be all gone now, but we still have some chili. It's pretty good. Kitty serves it topped with Frito's and shredded cheese. Great combo!"

I was rambling. I knew it. He knew it. Unfortunately, my rambling didn't make this moment less awkward.

"How about a piece of pecan pie? I've already had dinner with my family." His eyes remained locked with mine. He was holding the menu as if he was studying it, but he'd been coming here for years. He had the menu options memorized. He knew pecan pie was only served during Christmas break. I remembered it was his favorite.

"Of course, with one scoop of vanilla ice cream. Coming right up." I forced myself to give him a small smile and turned on my heel and walked towards the kitchen to place his order.

The restaurant was almost empty. Table seven was enjoying their meal. Table five just paid their bill, gave me a little wave as they walked out the door and left behind a healthy tip. Table eleven was having dessert, and there were a couple of regulars bellied up to the counter reminiscing about their autumn crops and drinking coffee.

I was effectively balancing the needs of these customers, but at table one sat my first love. Table one was distracting me. In the corner of my eye, I noticed he was biting the skin around his fingernails, one of his nervous habits. After I delivered his warm pecan pie with ice cream, I noticed the dark circles under his eyes. When he smiled, they were hardly visible, but my eyes were drawn to his welcoming grin and sparkle in his eyes.

He thanked me again after I dropped off his order, I nodded and stopped by table eleven to give them their bill. In a moment of silence walking from table to table, I heard a deep sigh escape Matthew's chest. This encounter was hard on him as well; lack of sleep circled his eyes.

While he savored every bite of his pie, I tried to distract myself with my evening closing chores. Mopping would wait until everyone left, so I decided to stock the dishes and cups behind the counter. I refilled the salt and pepper shakers. I refilled the napkin containers. Twenty minutes later, table seven paid their tab and made their way to the door. Matthew, our cook, Hank, and I were the last ones in the cafe. Matthew's hands folded neatly on his lap. His eyes were downcast looking at his nearly licked clean dessert plate. I set down my cleaning rag that I was using to wipe down the tables. From my apron, I pulled out my order pad and ripped out his bill. A lump formed in my throat as I remembered the first time that I waited on him years ago when we first started dating. I had signed his bill: "Thanks for coming in, hot stuff!"

His current bill contained no extra flirtatious notes.

"It was good to see you, Matthew. Thanks for stopping in." I placed his tab carefully down on the edge of his table. Before I could pull my hand away, Matthew swiftly placed his hand on top of mine. A bolt of an electric shock shot through me when I felt his touch after an absence of eight months. I hated how my body betrayed me. I couldn't and shouldn't feel anything for him.

"Lily, I am so sorry. From the bottom of my heart, I'm sorry." His voice was low. It had a slight tremble to it. I could tell this conversation was extremely hard on him as well. "Never in a million years did I intend to ever hurt you. I wanted you to know that I take full responsibility for my actions. I only hope someday you'll forgive me." He lifted his sweaty palm and returned it to his lap as if to gesture that his confession and apology was complete. His letting go of my hand symbolized my heart's release.

A single tear rolled down my cheek, and I finally exhaled a deep breath after holding it while I listened to his heartfelt confession. Part of me wanted to scream at him. The same part was still angry at him and wanted to tell him sex made him weak, wanted to tell him to screw off and that I didn't plan on forgiving him anytime soon. *Don't hold your breath!*

But the forgiving, human part of me acknowledged he was no match for Daisy and her seduction skills. She anchored her sights on him. He had no chance of escape. The same sentimental part also remembered him fondly as my first love and best friend. He knew me as well as I knew myself.

What I was about to say would haunt or heal us both in our future relationships. I would keep my response short, honest and to the point. I chose my words carefully.

"Matthew, you were no match for Daisy. I'm sorry I didn't see what she was planning to do to you… to us… to our relationship. She wanted to hurt me by using and manipulating you. I don't blame you. You did break my heart, but I am okay now." I awarded him one more small smile, turned my back and walked away.

"Happy New Year, Lily."

His sad, quiet voice barely reached my ears and caused another lump to form in my throat. There was no going back. I would never forget that memory of him and my mother in the living room. There was no future for us. I could not say I forgave him yet. I wouldn't say those words until they were completely true. This was good, appropriate closure for two high school sweethearts.

Chapter Nineteen

1989

Returning to my freshman college dorm room was refreshing after my hectic holiday at home. All my worldly possessions, which honestly wasn't much, surrounded me. My clothing and shoes were organized neatly in my small closet. My typewriter, notepads, array of pens and pencils, journals, a boom box, and a few pieces of jewelry from Daddy and Matthew. The twin bed and desk that were both bolted to the floor were not mine. Even though I could pack up my possessions in a couple boxes, this small space was home. This twelve-by-nineteen-feet space was where I felt safe and relaxed now.

My roommate decided not to return after the holiday break, so I had the small, rectangle shaped room to myself. It was for the best. Meredith was a mousy, reserved, frown-faced introvert. Her lack of personality didn't help me make any friends or venture out of this dorm room. We simply co-existed together. We shared the fewest amount of words possible on a given day. Having her not return in January wasn't much different than when she was here. It was as quiet and lonely as before. Just as I liked it, like how it had always been. Alone. Independent.

After getting unpacked and settled, I plopped down on my bed with my journal. Feeling pleased with my conversation with Susan Knight, I checked off Coach Knight's name on my list of men whom my mother seduced. The conversation did not answer any of my burning questions, yet I was pleased. He hadn't told his wife, and he deeply regretted the affair. Maybe that was enough. It felt like closure. I was not sure what would become of their marriage, and honestly, I didn't really care. I did know Susan deserved to know the truth, and Coach Knight should have to answer for his infidelity.

Seeing Matthew and hearing him say how awful he felt helped with my closure mission as well. Even before seeing him, I knew that he would regret this affair with Daisy. I knew him as well as he knew himself. I was glad for him that I was able to free him of some guilt. Still a good, ol' Catholic boy.

Next up on the homemade list due to pure curiosity was Pastor Tony. I had more questions under his name, besides Daddy's, than anyone else. I didn't understand how a man of God could be so easily tempted by sins of the flesh. He lectured about infidelity during his sermons all the time, yet he personally couldn't deny the temptation in the end. His love affair with my mother seemed to be a very heated, physical relationship. I had caught them several times sneaking around even after I first discovered their affair at Bible camp. They referred to their relationship as 'Bible Study.' When they talked to each other on the phone, I could hear Daisy giggle in response to whatever he said on the other end of the phone. "Amen."

Before I knew what was happening during their weekly 'Bible Study' sessions, I would open the front door and welcome Pastor Tony into our home and embrace him with a hug. I respected him and viewed him as a chosen disciple of God, an honest and truthful man who taught a large portion of our small town how to show God's wonderful influence through our dealings with others. He was an affectionate man who hugged, shook hands or touched the shoulders of his congregation members. Because he was a pastor, no one seemed alarmed by his physical touching or thought it was odd. Maybe people thought he had some kind of physical connection or healing power from God, so they simply allowed it.

After I discovered Daisy and Pastor Tony's affair, I refused to attend church with her. Still in bed fifteen minutes before the church service was to start, Daisy struggled to pull off my covers and get me to accompany her to church. My response was only mumbles and burying my head under the covers.

"Lily, I don't understand. Last week you were pullin' me out of the door for fear we were gonna be late. And now this Sunday you refuse. These teenage years are gonna be tough if your mood changes so drastically all the time."

I didn't have the words to confront her with my knowledge. She even tried to enlist Pastor Tony by asking him to discuss my attendance over ice cream.

To begin my search for Pastor Tony, I dialed up our old church, Our Savior's, while I was home for Christmas break. I figured I would begin there and see if they possessed any relevant information to help me find him.

"Hello, Maggie! My name is Lily. I am wondering if you are able to help me."

"I sure will if I can," Maggie, who introduced herself as Our Saviors' receptionist, cheerfully responded on the other end of the phone. I didn't recognize the friendly, high pitched voice or her name, but then again, that didn't seem out of the ordinary since I hadn't attended that church for over six years.

"I attended Our Savior's when I was a child and wanted to reconnect with Pastor Tony Shade. I was hoping you could tell me what church he transferred to after he resigned from Our Savior's." None of that was a lie. I did want to reconnect with him but only to punish him for his sins. And I attended when I was a child, but not after I discovered my mother screwing him in the driveway. It didn't seem necessary or helpful to disclose all of that information to a complete stranger over the phone whom I wanted to help me.

"Oh, sure. He left here and has transferred a few different times over the years. I do keep track of that because we receive a lot of calls about previous clergy. Something I started on my own."

I could read between the lines: Maggie was proud of herself and her grand tracking idea.

"Great thinking, Maggie!" I stroked her ego. I understood how this game was played. *I give you what you want, and you'll give me what I want.*

"Thanks! Now, let me check…" I heard some papers being shuffled around. "I thought I remembered something about him moving to Nebraska and then onto Minnesota. And I was right! Here it is…" She was reading from her notes. "Pastor Tony Shade in Irving, Nebraska, and the church was called Cornerstone. He was there for three years before he transferred to Canby, Minnesota. I believe he is still there. The church's name is Holy Cross. I have a phone number for that church if that would be helpful to you."

Thank my lucky stars that Maggie was an excellent information collector. Too bad, I didn't need her help tracking down any other men from the church.

"Wow! That would be most helpful, Maggie." In my psychology class, we learned that using people's names often in conversation not only helps you to remember their name but also shows respect and consideration for the conversation you are involved in. All that money on my courses was paying off already!

After she rattled off the phone number, I thanked her and hung up. That was easier than I thought it was going to be.

Lying flat on my stomach on my pink comforter, I contemplated my next move. I needed to verify he was still in Canby, which by pure luck was only a thirty-five-minute drive from my college town. It was almost as if I was meant to find him. My lucky stars seemed to be aligning.

After a quick, long distance call to verify that he was the current pastor at Canby's Holy Cross, I decided that the following Sunday would be the perfect time to dress in my Sunday best and get back to church. It reminded me of how I thought about a race: calculate it in sections, complete a section and then figure out the next one. Always keeping my eye on the prize.

. . .

HOLY CROSS HAD A LARGE CONGREGATION, so I could sit comfortably in the back pew and go unnoticed. I remember when I was a child listening to him preach. He had the same effect on his flock now. They laughed at his bad jokes or preacher puns.

"How does Moses make his coffee? He-brews it!"

The congregation members absorbed his words. He had a gift, even I could admit to that. He reeled them in, held their attention and filled their spiritual bucket. From the last two rows of the church, I was able to witness how full the collection plate got by the time it reached the back. It was heavy with their hard-earned money. Pastor Tony was successfully seducing his congregation.

Every Sunday for six weeks, I attended church with Pastor Tony in the realm of the sanctuary. I will admit that a few times I had forgotten my true reason for visiting and was consumed by his sermon. His ability to draw everyone in still held true years later.

"James was a servant of God, my friends. He is telling us through his letter that we must resist temptations. We must be strong and ask God to help guide us.

"My people, God wants you to come to Him for help with your temptations, and do not doubt His ability to save you. He will be there for you. You must admit your sin and seek His forgiveness. You must hold strong to your faith." He raised up his arms towards the roof of the sanctuary and tilted his back. "Lord, save me from all evil temptations." He kept his arms in the air but faced his congregation with wide eyes. "People, say it with me 'Lord, please save me!'"

And they did. Even the young children who normally didn't pay close attention during the sermon, only the music, raised their hands and roared, "Save me!"

After the first Sunday service I attended, I walked around downtown Canby. I came across a hometown diner a few blocks from the church. Many church members were walking down Main Street as I was and headed into the diner to continue discussing the sermon topic. I followed the flock and found myself sitting in a corner booth listening to friends and neighbors greet each other as if they hadn't seen each other in years. They exchanged pats on the back, firm handshakes, a few hugs and kisses on the cheek. Canby's citizens acted like one big happy family. It reminded me of Kitty's Cafe back home in Normal, Iowa.

While I was busy eavesdropping, the waitress strolled over to my corner booth. "Howdy, darlin'! Well, ain't you a pretty little thing! And new to these here parts. My name is Flo. What can I start ya off with to wet your whistle?"

Her hair grabbed my attention first: it was a bright red, red like fresh cherry stains. Later, after our friendship blossomed, I learned that she dyed it herself and chose the color because she thought the color's name was funny: Flaming Hot Diva. Her hair was styled like Marilyn Monroe, except instead of a knockout blonde, Flo was a feisty red head. Layers and layers of hairspray froze that style in place. Flo and her hair wouldn't be safe near any open flame. To add to the 1950s bombshell image, Flo had thick, fake eyelashes accenting the heavy streak of baby blue eyeshadow. Flo was a middle-aged, short, apple-shaped woman who wore her light blue and white waitress uniform tight and her lipstick bright red. She was always cracking gum in the right side of her mouth. She greeted everyone who walked in the front door of Canby Your Diner with a big smile and a "hello, darlin'!"

After six weeks of regular weekly conversations, it was confession time for Flo. "My real name ain't Flo, darlin'. It's Pam, but I thought Flo would fit my role here at the diner better. Have you ever seen that funny old sitcom, *Alice*? Flo is the name of the blonde, feisty waitress. She always makes me laugh. She smacks her gum and has some darn tootin' witty comments, so I thought to myself, 'why the hell not?' Everybody knows my real name around these here parts anyway, but they play along. It's fun. Plus, it's just a name tag. I'm playin' a part when I put on this apron and nametag.

"See Andy over there…"

She used her elbow to gesture to a large robust man in his fifties who wore bib overalls everyday as well as a dusty, sweat-ringed 'John Deere' green mesh hat. Yes, I recognized Andy; he was here every Sunday too when I stopped in for breakfast.

"Well, he pretends that the damn bank didn't repossess his tractor last week and that his farm is gettin' foreclosed on. And as his good ole friends, we all pretend that we ain't know anythin' about that. And see Ernie, his pal to his right? Well, Ernie has got a problem with the bottle... if you know what I mean." She cupped her hand around an imaginary jug of booze, touched her thumb to her red lips, and gulped some pretend alcohol. "He pretends he ain't drank a bottle of whiskey every stinkin' day, and we, his good ole friends, pretend we ain't noticed him slurrin' his words... if you know what I mean."

I glanced over at Ernie. He was a very tall, slender man who, if you erased the wrinkles, the wiry hair in his nose and ears, and perhaps gave his teeth a thorough cleaning, would pass for a good looking, older gentleman.

"You do a lot of pretending around here, Flo. As soon as you punch in on the timeclock and pin your 'Flo' name tag onto your uniform, you become someone else. Then, as you work your entire waitressing shift, you pretend to care about your customers - so called friends - by ignoring the pain in their lives."

Flo and I often had these deep discussions. We didn't always see eye-to-eye, but I enjoyed hearing her unique perspective on anything. She was a lively, unique character. She was always quick with a smile and a sought-after opinion. My Sunday breakfast stops after church became a weekly event that I looked forward to. The food was above average, but the spirited banter was what kept me coming back each week. Flo was the closest thing I had to a friend.

"Don't you think dealing with the truth would be better than all this pretending? Isn't acting - which is a form of lying - exhausting?"

She shook her head at me but smiled brightly. "Oh darlin,' you are just a pretty, young thing. You got all these strong ideals and morals. Hell, you ain't even been scarred by the world yet. When you get old like me, pretendin' can be a way to show a friend some needed kind-ness. We old folks have learned that all the frettin' and worryin' ain't gonna do nobody no good. It will take care of itself... if you know what I mean." She was holding a pot of coffee. "Want a refill, darlin'?"

"Only if you tell me if you are really from the south? The southern drawl... is that part of Flo or Pam?" I tilted my head to get a good look at 'Flo' to see her natural reaction. But she was a great actress. If Canby had a theater, Flo played the lead.

"Oh darlin', sometimes you ain't need to know the whole darn truth. Wonderin' and daydreamin' is fun if you can keep your head out of them there clouds. Does it honestly matter to you one way or the other?"

She poured coffee into my cup thinking that that was enough of an answer. Yet, I still didn't know what she was referring to. I did know I liked her and her Sunday morning banter. I didn't care if she was faking the accent or not. I didn't care if her name was Flo or Pam. She was very entertaining and always truthful, as much as a person could be who went by a fake name and possibly fake accent.

She moved onto another table and gave them her awarding-winning smile and a little wink. Even if she wasn't from the south, she did a great job of adding little characteristics to her 'Flo' personality. I could see from the pleased customers at nearby tables that they were sucked into her unique charm as well. No one cared that she was using a fake accent or name; they appreciated how caring and sweet she was. She was also an attentive waitress.

"Order up!" I heard the greasy, overworked cook holler from the kitchen.

I prayed it was my eggs benedict. My stomach was growling, and the coffee was making me a bit shaky. I witnessed Flo grabbing a plate from the kitchen pick-up window, and she waltzed in my direction.

"Smells like heaven and looks spankin' good, darlin'." She deposited my warm breakfast plate down in front of me. Steam was rising from my hot fresh eggs covered in hollandaise sauce. "Need anything else, you just holler."

She turned to walk in the other direction as I responded, "One more question for you, Flo." She twirled right back around. Her big green eyes were filled with interest. "You seem to know everyone here: Ernie, Andy and the Townsend family in the corner. What do you know about Pastor Tony from Holy Cross?"

Her eyes sprang open even more. She looked curiously at me,

wondering where that question came from. I could tell by the way she licked her lips that she did want to tell me something.

"For the past few months, I have been attending church where he preaches. He is a great preacher, interesting sermons. But if there was something to know about him, I am sure you would be the one to ask."

I was buttering her up. I knew she liked to feel as if she was in the know. She was proud of the town gossip she knew. It was a hobby for her. She was wonderful at collecting information, a lot like Maggie. People seemed to want to tell her their troubles. Unfortunately for them though, she wasn't very good at keeping it a secret. I was counting on this major personality flaw to be my personal gain.

She turned her head from side to side to see if anyone at the nearby tables was listening. Everyone was too engrossed in their own table conversations to pay any attention to ours.

"Darlin', that man doesn't amount to a hill of beans." She had lowered her voice a couple of octaves and leaned over the chair across from me to talk quieter. "What knowledge I know about that dirty, vile man would even shock a lap-dancin', kinky-sex-addicted, disease-carryin' hooker." She looked around, making sure no one had overheard her. "Problem is that the majority of the folks around these parts think that he is holier than thou. They regard him as a mighty fine preacher, a bona fide healer. So, when a rumor comes a-barrelin'-in, even if it's true, they darn sweep it under the goddamn church rug... if you know what I mean."

She straightened up and smoothed out her apron. She wanted to put a halt to this conversation. I was far from finished, though. I needed to hear what she knew. I would verify its truthfulness later. As I said before, Flo was great at collecting information; however, the knowledge she gained tended to grow like a weed in her garden. Just a little sun and water, and it was sure to grow.

"Wow... I can't even begin to imagine what he did. You can't leave me hanging, Flo." I took a bite of my warm, steaming breakfast so she would know that I was all ears, mouth full so I wouldn't be interrupting her. I didn't want to appear too interested.

"Another day, darlin'. I ain't gettin' paid to sit around and spill gossip. Oh man, I would like a job like that though. Plus, I got some ole friends to feed."

Her words said she needed to get back to work, but I knew she would stand around and gossip all day if she could, but she was right. The little diner was filling up with the regular Sunday morning crowd. I would be patient. She wanted to spill as much as I wanted to listen.

Chapter Twenty

1989

I struggled to concentrate during my college classes that following week. My mind wandered a lot during lectures trying to imagine what Pastor Tony did that could make even gossipy Flo all tongue-tied. When Sunday morning rolled around, I was running on adrenaline and caffeine. I needed some sleep and answers. I felt anxious to talk to Flo again. I didn't want to appear too eager, but I had to know what she was holding back. It baffled me that she was fine and willing to discuss men that were in the same room with us, only forty to fifty feet away, yet when I asked her about Pastor Tony who obviously was not even physically present in the diner, she started to whisper and look around in fear of being overheard. It was as if she was scared of what might happen if someone overheard us talking about him. What could cause her to be so frightened? What were the rumors about? I couldn't imagine what Flo knew that would stop her mouth from flapping. I was determined to find out.

As I selected my clothes for my Sunday morning ritual, I chose an outfit that would give the appearance of innocence, trustworthiness and honesty. I wore a white lace dress that I purchased at a secondhand store. It was delicate and fit my curves well. To hide my hourglass figure though, I threw on a jean jacket.

Inheriting my mother's looks was a blessing and a curse. As a blessing, I could honestly say that I looked good in a paper bag. Not trying to be conceited, just honest. Shopping for clothes was easy, but I captured no joy in retail therapy. The curse was that my good looks often attracted unwanted male attention. So, shopping at a secondhand store was the most frequent choice for me. I wasn't picky, and visiting the mall, which seemed to be a teenage pick-up zone, wasn't where I wanted to be. When I found this dress a couple of months ago, it was a perfect fit and would give me the look of innocence that I desperately missed.

I stuck my fake pearl earrings into my pierced ears, slipped on a pair of my favorite cowboy boots, and grabbed my purse. My stomach was in knots. I wondered how I would be able to sit patiently in the back of the sanctuary when all I wanted to do was interrogate Flo.

Surprisingly, the sermon held my attention. It was a gospel reading, so everyone in the church stood.

"Friends, please take out your Bibles and follow along with me. Matthew, chapter 4:1-11." Pastor Tony paused as the congregation members pulled out the pew bibles and shuffled to the right page in the Bible. As soon as he felt the majority of the people were ready, he began reading straight from the Bible. His voice was smooth and inviting. I didn't want to follow along; I wanted to watch and observe him.

Soft church bells rang on cue as he bowed his head for full effect. After a brief pause, Pastor Tony looked up at his congregation and addressed them, "This is the Gospel of the Lord."

Everyone responded with, "Praise to you, Lord Jesus Christ." A hush fell over the Sunday morning crowd as we sat down to intently listen to Pastor Tony's interpretation of the gospel. *This ought to be good.*

Over the six months I had been attending his services, I watched him engage with his congregation. And just like when I was a child, he had everyone in the palm of his hand. Not only did he have a charismatic personality, but he was also a nice looking older man. Even under his preacher's robe, his trim frame was obvious.

As I looked around the front of the church, I noticed his wife Lisa sitting in the front row. That was her usual spot. She stared up ador-ingly at her husband, almost as if she was worshiping her husband and not the Lord. From my view of her side profile, she had a permanent smile painted on her face. She nodded her head at all the appropriate spots in his sermon. Her actions looked more robotic than simple agreement or understanding.

Sitting to her left was a teenage girl holding an infant who couldn't be more than a few weeks old. The baby was swaddled in a yellow and green receiving blanket. My eyes were drawn to the teenage girl who looked about sixteen. Her face didn't have that motherly glow or swollen cheeks from eating for two. In fact, her cheekbones sunk in, and large, dark rings circled her eyes. Young mothers lacked sleep for obvious reasons, but the combination of her dark circles, sunken cheeks and the blank expression on her face made her seem more depressed or scared, rather than exhausted and overwhelmed. Her jet-black hair - an obvious self-dye job - accented her very pale, almost translucent skin. Her eyes were focused downward at the baby, which she was holding like a football. Her back was hunched over the baby with protectiveness. From my view in the back row, she seemed sad and lonely.

I was getting sidetracked again. Needed to focus on what Pastor Tony was rambling about today.

"So, my good people, Satan will tempt you. He will offer you everything you could have ever wanted. He will sugarcoat his offers, making them almost too good to resist. But remember 1 Corinthians 10:13: 'No temptation has overtaken you except what is common to mankind. And God is faithful; he will not let you be tempted beyond what you can bear. But when you are tempted, he will also provide a way out so that you can endure it.'

"God is telling us that life will not be easy. Tough choices will be made, but through those choices, you and God will see what you are made of." He paused a minute to take a drink from his glass that was hidden in the podium he spoke from. When he set it down, the sanc-tuary was still silently waiting for his conclusion.

"Take a look at dear, sweet Lucy sitting next to my wonderful wife, Lisa." He pointed to the front row where they were sitting.

Lisa basked in the attention. She could have been a politician's wife for how much she enjoyed it. She ate it up. She sat up straighter and even slightly turned her head towards the congregation to give a little nod in case there was someone who didn't know who she was.

But Lucy, the young teenage mother, turned fifty shades of red. She was apprehensive about being the center of his sermon. She did not want any attention drawn to her.

"The devil tempted Lucy. She fell victim to his evil ways, but God provided her a way out. God introduced Lucy to my beautiful, generous wife Lisa. Lisa discovered her plight and wanted to help her - a pregnant, helpless young girl. We became her saving grace. She is now part of our family, and we will help her raise her beautiful baby. She was abandoned by her family due to their own shame, judgment and misunderstanding. Shouldn't this beautiful young woman and her innocent child deserve another chance to follow the righteous path into God's forgiving arms?"

The body language in the front row caught my attention again. Even from the back row, I could sense the difference. Lisa's frozen smile seemed to have altered a bit; however, I couldn't put my finger on what changed. She was still smiling, but it was definitely more forced.

Lucy's demeanor had also changed. The color of her cheeks changed from crimson red to a shiny shade of peach. She was sitting up straighter, and a sweet smile formed on her lips. The baby was held tight in her skinny pale arms. It was a large shift of attitude from when he first pointed her out to the congregation. If I didn't know better, I would say she was flattered by the words Pastor Tony used to describe her. She almost seemed to perk up when she figured out why he was bringing her up in his discussion.

I always departed the church early to keep my anonymity. I didn't want to be noticed until I was ready. Timing was crucial. When I got to the diner, it was almost full. Flo motioned for me to sit at a reserved table near the back.

"I saved this one for you, darlin'." She pulled out the seat at my table. It was a typical busy Sunday morning at the diner. Since I didn't intend to leave until Flo and I had our chat, I brought a book along with me to read after I consumed my breakfast. I didn't think Flo would mind me taking up one of the tables, as I knew that she was as anxious to talk as I was to listen.

While I waited for my order, my mind wandered back to the teenager, Lucy, sitting in the same pew as Pastor Tony's wife. I couldn't quite put my finger on it, but something seemed abnormal in the front pew. Maybe it was the body language; Lisa had been slightly turned away from Lucy in the pew, her back to her. There had been about six feet between the two of them. Her body language didn't seem to portray Lisa's interest in 'saving' Lucy. Maybe Lucy and the baby had overstayed their welcome. Maybe Lisa was tired of her house guests, but now after Pastor Tony announced it to the whole congregation, she felt pressure to keep her opinion to herself.

And then there was Lucy's body language as well. Initially, Lucy was hunched over the baby. Maybe subconsciously shielding it from Lisa. Maybe trying to protect it from everyone around her. Her eyes were cast downward the entire time as if she didn't want to make eye contact with anyone. Maybe she didn't want to be seen or heard. Maybe she felt judged. Both women heard the same words spoken by Pastor Tony, but their responses were completely different.

Before I realized it, I had daydreamed long enough for the breakfast rush to dissipate, and Flo had started the clean-up process by sweeping the floor. My biscuits and gravy settled in my stomach while my third cup of coffee made me feel anxious and a bit jittery. I decided to sip my water. As I was about to open my book, Flo pulled out the chair across from me at my little table.

"Thanks for waitin', darlin'. That was a heapin' lot of hungry townsfolk." She sat down in the vacant chair with a cup of coffee and a blueberry muffin. I noticed her nametag and apron had been removed, but the southern accent remained. Maybe it was real.

"You do such a great job, Flo. I have a couple years of waitressing experience under my belt, but you would run circles around me." I was impressed by how she never seemed overwhelmed or short with anyone. Always the same Flo every Sunday - friendly, open, honest, and hard-working.

"Oh darlin', you are either too sweet or too easy to impress." She giggled and waved off my compliment. "Luckily, I enjoy my job, and these folk are my family." Through previous conversations, Flo informed me that she was married and had one grown son who had joined the army. She was very proud of them both.

"Flo, I have been dying all week for you to tell me the gossip about Pastor Tony. It must be something dark if you were so worried about someone overhearing us."

The diner had two other customers still - leftovers from the break-fast rush who were still enjoying their coffee.

"That is part of it, darlin'. But the main reason is that it has somethin' to do with my best friend, Molly. It is an awful sad story. Are you sure you wanna hear it?"

I hadn't more than lifted my chin to nod when Flo started spilling the story that cast Pastor Tony into an even darker light.

Chapter Twenty-One

FLO -1989

"Molly has darn-near been my best friend for over twenty years ever since I moved to these here parts from Alabama. We met when our babies, my boy Spencer and her oldest daughter Grace, were enrolled in nursery school together. Them two were like peas in a pod! Got along like Mickey and Minnie...like Batman and Robin...like Donny and Marie. And so did me and Molly.

"God only blessed me with my sweet Spencer, but Molly had two more babies: Mallory and Lucille. Three girls who were all two years apart. She was a busy momma. But we stayed thick as thieves.

"And then Molly and her man ran into some marriage troubles. Mainly on the account of her bein' busy with the girls and him workin' all the time. They darn-near grew apart. I ain't makin' excuses for her - just tellin' ya like I seen it.

"Molly was an active church goer. She was always volunteerin' for one committee or another. Always helpin' others. She was lonely, and he was appreciative of all her help. Now, I am talkin' about the devil himself, Pastor Tony. He was new to Holy Cross, and Molly oversaw his welcomin' committee, if you know what I mean.

"She even kept the relationship a secret from me 'til it darn-near blew up in her pretty little face. She came over to my place all cryin' and upset one night. Said she couldn't stand the guilt and shame anymore. She broke it off with Pastor Tony, but he didn't take it well. He hadn't seen it comin' and didn't want to lose Molly. Said he would leave his wife and marry her if she would be patient. But Molly didn't want none of that. She still loved Earl and wanted to work on the marriage. She told Pastor Tony she didn't love him. It was more of an infatuation, and the spark was gone, as far as she was concerned.

"He got all fired up and yelled awful things at her. Nothin' you would expect a pastor to be sayin'. 'You are gonna go to hell anyway' and 'I was tryin' to save your soul' and 'I will punish you for this, Molly' and 'You are gonna regret this.' She brushed off all the hurtful things that he said as the outbursts of a scorned lover. It was a secret affair, but he didn't like bein' rejected at all in secret either.

"Unfortunately, he was true to his word: he punished her. At first, it was subtle things that didn't add up to anythin' until you pieced it all together. First, a dead rat was rottin' on her front step. Peculiar, but Molly ain't think anythin' of it until it happened every mornin' for the next week. The followin' week they started receivin' middle-of-the-night phone calls. The call would wake up the whole darn family. No one on the other end of the phone ever said anythin', but the calls happened every night for a week straight. Again, she didn't put the pieces together, plus they didn't know who the intended target was. Havin' teenage daughters, the family assumed it was one of their so-called friends doin' a little horseplay.

"And then the next week, Molly was headin' to work and noticed one of her front tires was flat. The cap to the valve stem was sittin' next to the tire. Earl couldn't find a hole or a puncture in the tire, which seemed very strange. That meant someone sat next to her car and manually let the air out of her tire. That would take a darn tootin' long time! The next mornin' as she got to her car, she noticed a back tire was flat and again the cap to the tire stem was layin' next to the tire again. The intended victim was obvious now. Molly knew without a doubt that Pastor Tony was behind the flat tires and most likely the other pranks.

"Finally, he hit a nerve, and she damn near had enough. She

decided that she needed to pay him a visit. On her lunch break, she sped over to Holy Cross. She stomped into his office in the back of the church and demanded that he stopped this nonsense at once.

"She told me that she had never before seen the sinister smile that crept up on his face - it was filled with pure evil. A shiver traveled down her spine. He simply replied, "Ok," and asked her to shut his office door when she left. She was so relieved. She truly thought he would leave her alone. She was partially right. He didn't flatten her tires again, prank call her home, or leave dead animals on her doorstep.

"Things returned back to normal except she stopped attendin' Holy Cross. She didn't want to keep seein' him preachin' God's good word every Sunday. Earl never attended church, so he didn't give a rat's ass. But Mallory and Lucille made many friends in the youth group, so they continued their involvement at Holy Cross.

"About six months later, Molly found a used pregnancy test in the garbage of her girls' shared bathroom. Thank goodness it read negative, but that still meant a serious talk with her daughters. Since Grace was away at college, the next logical choice would be her eighteen-year-old, Mallory. Mallory was simply appalled at the idea of sex before marriage. Definitely wasn't from Mallory.

"That left Lucille...her baby. Her sweet, introverted, baby Lucille. She was only sixteen at the time, but Molly did notice that Lucille was more aloof lately. She chalked it up to bein' a teenager. She didn't seem interested in boys. Never went on dates, so Molly was obviously concerned. She decided to be more cautious this time when she talked to her youngest daughter about sex, especially casual sex.

"At the end of the day, everyone in the house was gettin' ready for bed. Earl had his sleep ap device on and was breathin' deeply. Mallory was brushin' her teeth in the shared bathroom. And Lucille had just crawled into her bed with a book. Molly told me that she brought the test stick into Lucille's room with her and simply stated, 'We need to talk, Luce.'

"The fatal flaw of a fair-skinned beauty is her pale complexion. Instantly, Lucille's cheeks turned violet. Molly explained how sex was an intimate act to be shared by two people who were in love. It should never be taken lightly.

"Lucille stayed stone-faced and simply nodded. Molly asked who the young man was, but Lucille's lips were sealed. Molly felt good about the conversation with Lucille and figured Lucille needed some time before confidin' in her. Molly was a patient woman. Maybe too patient. Her patience was a downfall in this situation.

"Molly watched Lucille with a protective eye. Most everythin' she witnessed could be chalked up to teenager behavior: mood swings, growin' independence, slammin' doors, endless phone conversations, and more mature clothin' choices. Nothin' waved a huge danger flag.

"A month later, she was pickin' up dirty clothes from Lucille's room and noticed a very lacy, very black and very expensive pair of lingerie hidden under her bed. Normal teenage boys cannot afford to buy their girlfriends such fancy undergarments. Molly grew genuinely concerned. It was time to put some pressure on Lucille and get some information.

"At dinner that evenin', Molly noticed Lucille had bags and dark circles under her eyes. She also seemed a bit paler than normal if that could even be possible. Molly asked her if she was feeling alright.

"'I'm tired, Mom. No need for the third degree. Geez.' Lucille's sassy comment even caused Mallory to roll her eyes at Lucille.

"'As if, Luce. She asked you one question. Don't be such a rag.' Mallory was the daughter that always spoke her mind; she inherited her straightforwardness from her momma.

"Earl just stared down at his plate of tater tot hotdish, eatin' in silence, wishin' he was finished so he could go watch the game. For Earl, livin' in a house full of girls meant there was always a game to watch.

"Lucille's comment didn't deter Molly from questionin' Lucille further at bedtime. When she knocked on her closed bedroom door, she peeked her head in just as Lucille announced into the phone, 'I gotta go.'

"'Who was that?'

"'No one.'

"'No one, as in a boy? Maybe the same boy who bought you the way too sexy undergarments?' Molly wasn't one for beatin' around the bush. More accurate reactions and quicker results was her motto.

"Lucille did blush, of course, but this time she was defensive. 'Snooping around my private stuff, huh? I should have known better than to trust you to leave my stuff alone.'

"'Yes, Lucille, you are right. I looked in your room, but only because you won't help me understand what is going on with you. Furthermore, a sixteen-year-old girl shouldn't be wearing anything like that! Secondly, how did a young man afford them?'

"'Who says he is young?' Lucille fired back. Now, it was her turn to shock her mother.

"'What do you mean by that, Lucille?' Molly grew more concerned. 'This young' - she couldn't help herself because she couldn't imagine anything else - 'man could be arrested if he is over eighteen years old. Additionally, you are too young for a serious rela-tionship, Lucille.'

"'He said you would freak out. Don't worry about me. I'm in love, and he will take care of me no matter what. He even said so. His love is patient. His love is kind. 1 Peter 4:8 says, 'Above all, love each other deeply, because love covers over a multitude of sins.'

"The Bible verse Lucille recited frightened Molly. But she wasn't sure why. She was too shocked to keep discussin' love and sex with Lucille. She told her that they would finish their conversation the next day.

"Molly wanted to figure out what Lucille meant by quotin' that verse. Molly had a hard time sleepin' that night, but she did figure out a couple of things from their conversation:

"One, Lucille thought she was in love. Two, he wasn't a boy from her school or class. Three, he was someone who quoted Bible verses often and helped Lucille learn the ones that best applied to their situa-tion. Maybe someone from Holy Cross' youth group?

"Four, they were having sex often enough that she had to take a pregnancy test. And five, he had enough money to spend on sexy lingerie.

"That next Sunday afternoon, Molly was completin' one of her weekend chores: cleanin' the bathrooms. Her arms were full of the cleanin' products. She had finished the master bath, so she was makin' her way to the girls' bathroom. The door was partly ajar, and the light was on. She was about to push it open with her hip when she noticed Lucille admirin' herself in the mirror. She had always been naturally slim, flat chested, pale skin and dark hair. But when Molly looked at Lucille's reflection in the mirror, she was startled by what she saw.

"Lucille's breasts had filled out. Her nipples - if I can say that without offendin' you - were large and dark brown. However, what startled Molly the most was that Lucille's always flat stomach was not flat anymore. Lucille's midsection had a slight but noticeable bulge to it.

"In these few short seconds, Molly's brain flashed all the warnin' signals: the pregnancy test, lingerie, full breasts, belly bump. It all added up to only one conclusion: Lucille was pregnant.

"This realization made her arms go limp, and she dropped all of her cleanin' supplies onto the floor. The loud crash startled Lucille, and she noticed her mom starin' at her outside her bathroom door.

"The rest of the day, Molly begged and pleaded with Lucille to open up to her about the relationship. No name was given. She told her mom that they were in love. She didn't need to worry. Her 'man' promised to take care of them both. He had plans and money to make it all happen.

"Molly appreciated Lucille's positivity, but she asked her some basic questions: who would take care of the baby while she was in school? What about cheer? Where were they gonna live? How would they pay for all the baby supplies, formula, diapers, clothing, etc.? Babies were a lot of work and not cheap.

"Lucille did seem concerned after her mom brought up these ques- tions. At the end of the day, to wrap up their discussion, Molly informed Lucille that she would have three days to divulge the name of the baby's father. These three days allowed the young man a chance to tell his parents before Molly took the matter into her own hands. Again, my Molly, she was a patient woman.

"Molly felt she was only bein' fair. She didn't want to be the one to tell another family that they were soon-to-be grandparents. But after three days, Lucille would still not reveal any information. A tiny smile formed on Lucille's lips when Molly threatened to tell the boy's parents before he was able.

"The next day, while Lucille was at school, Molly combed through her room. No more privacy bullshit! She was a detective on a mission. She knew where Lucille hid her secret treasures - under her bed in a shoebox.

"The only treasures in the box were from grade school: a fake ring from a gumball machine, a note from a boy, a lucky penny and a painted rock. Nothin' to help Molly discover the baby's father. She dusted Lucille's bedside table. She returned some books from Lucille's floor onto her bookshelf when she noticed a red, hardcover book. It did not have a title on the spine. She opened up the cover to see a personal note written inside:

"*Lucy - I love you, doll, with all of my heart. Together forever and never to part.*

"Very sweet note, but for some reason, a chill shot up her spine. She couldn't quite put her finger on it. She placed the book back on the shelf and finished dustin' Lucille's room.

"When Molly finally parked her caboose down later to eat a quick lunch, a light bulb shattered inside her brain! She remembered where she had read that love verse before. Her tummy felt queasy. She was glad she had only taken one bitty bite of her peanut butter and pickle sandwich. She hesitantly walked to the den where her personal books were stored on a bookshelf. She had never been a big fan of poetry. Always felt it was rather cheesy, but she did have one book of poetry that she had received as a gift.

"She found the hardcover book among others on the bookshelf. She opened the front cover and read in his beautiful cursive handwriting:

"*Molly - I love you, doll, with all of my heart. Together forever and never to part.*

"She had received the book of poetry from Pastor Tony during their affair. She sprinted to the bathroom and threw up what little content she had in her stomach."

Chapter Twenty-Two

1989

I couldn't believe my ears! Pastor Tony was the father of that teenage girl's baby. She sat in the front row with his wife, as if it was completely normal. That was why Lisa seemed upset when Pastor Tony brought their names up in his sermon. Maybe she even knew he was the father. He made the rest of the congregation believe that Lisa and himself were saving this teenager and her baby from homelessness.

He had told everyone that Lisa was rescuing Lucy from her family who abandoned her since they discovered her unwanted pregnancy. Pastor Tony had continued to explain how generous his wife was to welcome her into their home, as if they were one big happy family.

Wow... wow... I was in shock. Flo had finally paused to allow this information to sink in. "Wow, Flo. I had no idea. Your poor friend, Molly. I don't even know what to say!"

I was not lying; this was more than I had imagined. This was huge. He had an affair with another member of his church, which alone was terms for dismissal, and then seduced his mistress' daughter, who was underage, which meant jail time. He was a pedophile.

Flo wasn't finished telling me Molly's story.

"See, I darn near told you that I had a doozy of a story. But I ain't finished. Believe me when I tell ya that Molly was more upset than a hyena in heat on a hot summer day!

"That very day she discovered the book of poetry, she stormed over to Holy Cross to confront him. Again, he was alone in his office. Probably workin' on his weekend sermon. She burst into his office screamin' and yellin' profanity at him. He pushed himself away from his desk, crossed his legs, and calmly stared at her. He darn near acted like he was watchin' a live variety show. He didn't say a darn word, didn't react at all. She couldn't believe he could just sit back and look at her. His pastoral training must have covered handlin' distraught, angry, momentarily insane people.

"Finally, she screamed at him, 'What do you have to say for yourself, Tony? I am calling the police when I leave here. Do you have anything to say for yourself? How could you do this to a child?'

"Her hands were on her hips. Her cheeks were flushed with the anger that pulsed through her body. Her heart rate was sky-high.

"He took his sweet, old time respondin'. I think he knew all along that this exact moment would present itself. He didn't need to think about what to say; he had rehearsed it. He knew she would want answers before callin' the authorities. He knew her well. He knew she'd think she had the upper hand. But he also knew that she was wrong.

"'Oh, dear, Molly, please have a seat...'

"He acted like her stormin' into his office was a regular visit and she hadn't just screamed profanity at him. He motioned to her to take one of the vacant seats.

"'I didn't come here to sit and have a little chat, Tony. I came here to tell you that your game is over. Your life - it is over! I am going to the police.' Molly glared at him. Hate oozed out of her pores. My sweet friend, who had never physically harmed another person in her life, wanted to erase the confidence and smugness of this horrible man's face by usin' her very own two hands.

"'Suit yourself, Molly, but you won't phone the authorities. And do you know how I know this? You love your daughter. You don't want her precious name and innocent face splashed across the newspapers and the evening news. And believe me, it will be a tidal wave of destruction. Her name would be a household name, and all because her mother was a incompetent whore who raised a daughter with loose morals and poor judgment. That is what people would believe, you know? Lucy loves and adores me and will defend our relationship to the press if I asked her to. Do you want to tear your sweet, little family through brutal and very public scrutiny? And what about Lucy? And what about the baby? Do you want to put an innocent baby through such turmoil and judgment?'

"'Molly fought the urge to throw up. He had thought this through. He was partially right, but she didn't want him to be. Her next words to Pastor Tony did not come across with as much conviction as she initially felt when she entered the church building.

"'We are strong. We would get through this together as a family. I don't care what other people think. And Lucille is too young to know better. You seduced and brainwashed an innocent child! That is what people will talk about! How could you do this?"

"'I told you that you would regret breaking it off with me. You regret it, don't you, Molly?"

"'You did this to get back at me?' She couldn't believe it. He was blaming her for his seduction of her daughter. 'You are completely out of your mind if you think I am to blame for your madness!'

"'Oh, Molly, but you are. If you hadn't broken off our nearly perfect, sex-filled affair, I would never have found my sweet, willing-to-do-anything-to-please-me Lucy, made her fall in love with me, and then taught her to fuck like I fucked you."

"Molly instinctively lunged across his desk to hit him, scratch his eyes out, punch him, or perhaps kill him. She wasn't sure. She was a ball of fury. He had crossed the line. He darted out of her reach and laughed at her feeble attempt to cause him physical harm. In a deep, stern voice, he demanded, 'Molly, sit down. Now, whore!'

"His stern tone of voice unnerved her. Yes, she was angry and pantin' from her botched attempt to harm him, but she obeyed. There was somethin' evil and commandin' in his voice. Sometimes during their affair he would bark commands at her to complete kinky sexual acts. At the time and in the heat of the moment, she willingly obeyed. But now, when he used the same disciplinary voice, it wasn't sexy; it was frightenin'. And she had every right to be scared.

"'Thank you, Molly, for being willing to have this conversation like two mature adults.'

"He interpreted her sittin' down as being compliant, when in reality her knees were shakin', and she didn't want to pass out in his office for fear of what he would do to her body while she was unconscious. She hadn't realized how psychotic he was until then. There were small, obsessive warning signs when they were sneakin' around, but nothin' that would have shown her that this was where they would be in six months time. Nothin' could have prepared her or warned her for this hell she was livin' in.

"'Now, maybe we can talk reasonably.' He drew a deep breath and settled back down in his big, black office chair. The shift of control rotated to the wicked. He considered himself powerful behind his big desk, this shield.

"'After you rejected me, Molly, I was devastated by your dismissal. You were my muse. I am man enough to admit that I didn't take your rejection well. I was heartbroken and hurt, but then Lucy caught my eye at youth group. Lucy was a sponge, bright and cheerful. She was like a mini-you except even better. She was naive, innocent and timid. She was like a shiny new penny. I had to make her mine, and it wasn't hard. The attraction was mutual. You don't need to hear all of our dirty little secrets. Just know that I will not lose Lucy or the baby. You need to come to terms with that right away.'

"'You can't be serious? Do you know how crazy you sound? You knocked up a teenage girl. You had sex with a minor; that's illegal no matter if you think you are in love or not. I will not sit here and let you steal Lucille away from her family, her future. You are disturbed, Tony, very sick. If I wasn't so repulsed by you right now, I might pity you. Something is legitimately wrong with you if you think any of this is okay.'

"'I never said this relationship is ideal. This was not my choice. I wanted you, Molly, but since I can't have you, Lucy will be your replacement. Plus, the baby will bring so much joy to Lisa. She has never been able to have a child of her own. We will be one big, happy family.'

"Molly stood up. She had heard enough of his crazy talk. ' You are a monster. Good luck in jail, Tony.'

"'Sit your ass down, Molly. I am not finished!' His voice was filled with insane intensity. Molly wasn't sure why, but she paused and turned around to hear what more he could possibly have to say. His pupils were completely dilated, as if he was high or possessed.

"'Do you remember how we met? Here at Holy Cross? You spear-headed my grand welcome, but I am referring to when you sought me for professional advice, guidance. You wanted to get something off your chest. You wanted your sins forgiven. You wanted me to tell you that God would forgive you. Do you remember that day, Molly?'

"Oh, how my girl, Molly, wished she could turn back time and erase a lot of things. She told me she knew exactly what he was refer-ring to. She remembered that day very clearly. She regretted several events of that day - if only she wished she could press a huge delete key.

"'I'll jog your memory. You came rushing into my office, right here, all flustered. You claimed you did something unforgivable. Tears streamed down your face. You were a hot mess.

"'I couldn't wait to hear what terrible, nasty sins such a gorgeous, voluptuous woman could have accomplished. Unfortunately for me, it was not as interesting and sexy as I had hoped. I was extremely disap-pointed. Didn't peg you for an over-reactor. But I patiently listened to your long, boring story. Do you remember now what story I am talking about?'

"Molly couldn't even nod her head. She remembered, she regret-ted, and he knew the worst thing she had ever done in her career, the second worst thing she had done her whole life besides having the affair with him. She did not agree that she overreacted.

"'Well, how do you think Brian Evers would feel to know that you threw away the one piece of evidence that might have gotten him a 'not guilty' verdict rather than 'guilty'?' He put his feet up on his oak desk, tipped back his office chair. He was wearing brown loafers with his freshly pressed khaki pants. He was comfortable, showing how little concern he felt about Molly's earlier threat to call the police. 'I'll be sure to mention that to the police as well. We will be in jail together, Molly. Maybe Brian Evers will be released to murder more innocent, fresh people since you illegally destroyed evidence in his murder trial.'

"'What do you want, Tony? You've obviously thought this through.' Molly didn't want to lose her job as a paralegal. She loved her job, every aspect of it. Daily, she sensed that she was making the community a better place.

"'Let us let Lucy decide. I am a reasonable man.' His definition of reasonable must have been insane!"

Chapter Twenty-Three

FLO - 1989

"When Molly escaped his office, her whole world began crumblin' around her. One moment she had everything, and the next moment everything that she loved and cherished was bein' ripped from her. She told me she had a dream that all the people and things she cherished were lined up on the side of a steep cliff: her husband, each of her three children, her job as a paralegal, and her values. And one by one, they were shoved off the side of the cliff and crashed onto the harsh, unforgiving ground below, breaking into unrecognizable bits and pieces.

"The saddest part was that Molly was the one thrustin' each one of them over the edge. She was to blame for her family members and morals takin' a skydive to their death. She had to confess everything to Earl. She hadn't even told him about Lucille being pregnant yet. Everything was blowin' up around her so fast. She had a love affair with Pastor Tony months ago. It was the ripple effect of her downward spiral. She was about to lose her job, her husband, her daughter, all in a matter of seconds. She had to come clean to them all. She would pay the consequences. She felt she deserved to lose everything. It was time to do what was right.

"She didn't regret destroyin' the evidence in the Brian Evers murder trial. She knew what she did was illegal and against everything she was taught, but she knew, without a shadow of a doubt, from readin' the case files, that he was guilty of murderin' those people. The evidence that she destroyed would have cast a small shadow of doubt to the jury. She had seen things like this happen before in cases she assisted with. Jurors never wanted to award a guilty verdict unless they were one hundred percent sure. After they served their time on the jury, they didn't want to lose any sleep worryin' if they did the right thing. Anything that made them question, that gave them the opportunity to deliver a non-guilty or hung jury verdict. She could not and would not let anything hold back Brian Evers from servin' his much-deserved jail time.

"But she regretted the day she ran sobbin' into Pastor Tony's office. The guilt had been eatin' her alive. She needed a man of God, a man of principle to help her deal with her guilt, and if at all possible, advise her that she performed the proper response. Selfishly, she wanted to be absolved of her sin.

"He translated Bible verses about doing the right thing even if others would not agree. He listened to her for over an hour. He held her when she cried and invited her back the followin' week. She departed his church office feelin' understood, accepted and validated.

"It hardly seemed possible that it was the same two people in that memory as the one in his church office only moments ago. Even Molly had to admit what a wonderful actor he was. She had no idea that that confession would lead them down this narrow path. Her Lucille was payin' the price for Molly's sin. It wasn't fair. Molly had no idea what to do.

"Earl was surprisingly very understandin' and forgivin' about the affair. In the last few months, he admitted that he had strayed outside of their marriage too. They both agreed to seek counseling and work harder on their marriage; however, they needed to focus on their youngest daughter.

"They agreed that they could not simply force Lucille to stop seein' Tony. That might drive her further into his arms. They tried to reason with her and made future plans to expose Tony. Unfortunately, before any of that could happen, Lucille had some complications with her pregnancy and was forced to go on bedrest. Before they knew what was happening, Lucy was serving her doctor-prescribed bed rest at Pastor Tony's house.

"To make a very long story short, they confronted Pastor Tony and Lisa and demanded that they return their underage daughter to them. They were at their wit's end. They threatened to go to the authorities and tell them she had been kidnapped if Lucille didn't come home at once.

"Surprisingly, Pastor Tony and Lisa told them that they would persuade Lucille to return home after the weekend. Molly and Earl were relieved that they had talked some sense into them.

"Their relief was short-lived because the very next day during the Sunday church service, Pastor Tony and Lisa informed the entire congregation how Molly and Earl refused to accept their daughter's surprise pregnancy and kicked her out of their family home. To make matters worse, a young man from Lucille's youth group admitted publicly that he was the father of her baby.

"That godforsaken man and his loins have blown up a storm in our little town. I would love for that man to get what he has a-comin' to him. You young folks call it karma."

Chapter Twenty-Four

1989

W hen I returned to my dorm room later that afternoon, my heart ached in my chest for Molly and her family. I'd never even met them, but this family came so alive in Flo's story that I had forgotten that I didn't know them. I had observed Lucy in the front row at church, and now I understood what events placed her there. I couldn't fathom why Pastor Tony's wife Lisa allowed her husband's lover and their child to take up residence in her home. According to Flo's story, when Molly and Earl confronted Pastor Tony in his home, Lisa silently and obediently stood by his side. Seemed very odd and quite disturbing.

Flo was absolutely right. I couldn't believe what a horrendous man Pastor Tony had developed into. The tragedy that she reported to me about her friends was more than I had bargained for. And there was no way I could allow this appalling information to sit idly in my lap. I needed to brainstorm the facts. I needed to do something. I just didn't know what yet. Again, I hoped my criminal justice classes would be beneficial.

Pastor Tony was a pedophile that was getting away with it by blackmailing the child's family. Molly and her family didn't want to be ostracized by their small town. They had a lot to lose as well as losing their youngest daughter. Furthermore, I'm sure they didn't want to cause Lucy any more heartache. They were in a state of shock, and therefore, unable to move forward and accomplish what needed to be done. He was so much worse than the simple adulterer that I thought he was. I needed a 'smoking gun,' as they say in investigations, to bring him down. I needed to sort a few things out.

As I sat down at my small dorm room desk to create a thorough list of questions that I had, my phone rang. I didn't have many friends, so I figured it was a wrong number, and I let my answering machine pick it up. When the answering machine sounded, the anonymous caller hung up, and the phone rang again. I decided to answer it this time.

"Hello?"

"Hello. Is this Lily Armstrong?" the deep, serious male voice on the other end of the phone formally asked. The voice sounded familiar, but I couldn't place it.

"Yes. Who is asking?"

"Hi, Lily. It's Sergeant Mallone. Will you please come down to your dormitory lobby? I am here and need to speak with you."

I have never been in any trouble with the authorities, but during my childhood, Daisy often had.

Sergeant Mallone was from Normal, Iowa. He had been compassionate and gracious to Daisy and me. If he witnessed her stumbling home after a late night at Rusty Nail, Officer Mallone - as he was known previously before his promotion - would offer her a safe ride home. Often on these late nights, he would find me asleep on the couch when he carried Daisy in. He would gently nudge me awake and ask me to get up so he could set Daisy down on the couch. He didn't think it was appropriate to enter her bedroom. He was a man of strict principles and high morals.

When I left Normal and headed to college, I didn't even say goodbye. I had forgotten all about his kindness and generosity toward me when I was a child. I was glad I was getting the chance.

Of course, I assumed right away that it was about her and took no time making my way down to the lobby. *What has she done now? How bad can it be for Sergeant Mallone to drive all the way here?*

144

As I made my way down the long hallway to the lobby, I caught sight of him. Sergeant Mallone was a tall, slender, dark-skinned man with a mound of black, coarse hair on the top of his head. I would guess that he was 6'5" tall, and if wet, he would weigh maybe one hundred and eighty pounds. His slender build made me assume that because of his busy, crazy work schedule, he had little time to enjoy the pleasure of good fattening food. He was wearing a black blazer over his white T-shirt - which reminded me of Don Johnson's 1980s style, except I doubted Sergeant Mallone owned a pastel blazer - and a pair of loose Wrangler jeans where his shiny, official police badge hung on his belt. As I approached him, I observed that he was looking down at his small black notepad, a typical accessory of a detective. His thick, wiry mustache needed a good trim. The hairs were growing over his upper lip. Seconds later, he noticed me approaching him.

"Lily Armstrong?" He looked up from his notepad, and while waiting for my answer he shut the cover and placed it inside his blazer. Just like on TV. I nodded. "You may not remember me, but I am Sergeant Mallone from Normal."

"Hi, Sergeant Mallone. Of course, I remember you. I am glad you are here. I wanted to thank you for all the kindness you showed me while I was growing up. I never properly thanked you." I extended my right hand to shake his.

He smiled slightly and firmly shook my hand. "No thanks required. I was doing my job, and you were a sweet kid who deserved better. And that is why I am here now. Lily, it's your mom."

"Yes, I assumed. What kind of trouble did she get into now?"

"She isn't in any trouble, Lily. She had a stroke and is currently in the hospital. I wanted to come tell you myself and offer you a ride back home if you wanted to visit her."

WE CONVERSED most of the way to the hospital. He asked me questions to fill in the gaps of his perceived timeline of my life. I welcomed the distraction. I wasn't sure how to feel about Daisy being in the hospital. I didn't know what I was feeling about the whole situation.

Was I sad? Was I worried about her? Did I truly care if she lived or died?

When I arrived at the small-town hospital a few hours later, Daisy had been unconscious for approximately two days. Forty-eight hours. The hospital staff had trouble locating the next of kin - me - since Daisy and I weren't in regular contact, plus we had no other immediate family to check with. Sergeant Mallone said he always kept track of my where-bouts as I grew up. He was aware of my regular job at the local restaurant, so he questioned Kitty, the owner. She told him where I was going to college and even gave him my phone number to call.

I was Daisy's first visitor. The only noises filling her small room were her hospital monitors that beeped repeatedly. This redundant noise showed the hospital staff that her body had not given up yet. The annoying beeps made my skin crawl as if they were counting the seconds, I stood there... watching her.

Beep... beep... beep... beep... beep...

I'd been home over the Christmas holiday a few months ago, but we hardly made eye contact, had a conversation or were even in the same room for more than a few minutes together. On Christmas Eve, we both volunteered to work shifts since no one else wanted to work the holiday. I waitressed at the cafe and Daisy pole-danced at Rusty Nail. What a wonderful way to say, "Merry Christmas," with strangers at greasy, sweaty local establishments. Eye contact was strained because I subconsciously blamed her for Daddy's death and everything awful from my childhood. Avoiding eye contact or even glancing in her direction was a simple way of ignoring the pain.

Laying there in the hospital bed even with tubes coming out of her nose and an IV stuck in her wrist, she looked relaxed. It was almost as if she was sleeping. Her long blonde hair was in a loose braid off to the side of her pillow. I examined her, her eyes were closed, and no heavy makeup was caked on her eyelids. Her skin was clean and shiny from soap. As if someone had knowledge of her preferences, she was dressed in a pale pink gown and covered up to her armpits with a soft, white blanket. Her arms had been placed carefully at her sides.

I'd never witnessed her laying so still or so peacefully. In this hospital bed, she reminded me of Sleeping Beauty. There was no pain expressed on her lips or forehead. She didn't look greasy or exhausted. In fact, she didn't look like Daisy at all. Normally if I did see her sleeping, it was because she was passed out and snoring on the living room couch. Rough night at the Rusty Nail. One arm would be draped over her eyes, shielding her from the morning sunlight entering through the front windows. One leg would be thrown over the back of the couch while the other one landed on a couch cushion. Her clothes would be wrinkled, and she might or might not have her shoes still on her feet.

Suspended in the doorway of her hospital room, my feet didn't seem to know what to do. My eyes couldn't register what they were seeing to tell my brain what to do. I stood frozen in the doorway. Suddenly, a nurse tenderly touched my shoulder, and I jumped.

"Sorry to startle you, honey. Are you, her daughter?" I nodded in response. "I've been taking care of your mom during my last couple of shifts. I braided her hair. Not sure if she normally does that, but when a patient lies in bed for too long, her hair mats up in the back. The doctors don't wanna deal with it and suggest cutting it to get it out of the way. Or it breaks off in clumps. Her blonde hair was just too beautiful, so I figured I could help her take care of it, then no one would cut it off. Her golden hair reminded me of that fairytale, Rapunzel. Always a favorite of mine, maybe because I'm envious of long straight hair. Just beautiful. And I'm Nurse Jenny by the way." She was a chatterbox. I wasn't sure if she even took a breath the whole time she talked while checking Daisy's monitors, the IV, and the charts. I was still a statue in the hospital room doorway. I had only slightly moved to the left to allow her to pass through the small doorway.

"You look just like her, you know, except for the hair. Yours is beautiful too though. Chestnut brown. Reminds me of caramel. Ooooo… and that makes me hungry. A sundae with chocolate and caramel sounds good. Can I get you anything? We don't have ice cream, but I could grab you water, coffee, or a muffin? What's your name again?"

Nurse Jenny was perched next to Daisy on the rolling stool, taking her pulse. On the top of her head, her black hair was twisted into a tight bun. Little daisies decorated her hot pink scrubs - ironic. This petite ball of energy made my head spin.

"Lily. My name is Lily. A cup of coffee would be fabulous." I slowly took a few tentative steps into the cold hospital room. I dropped my purse on the visitor's chair that was placed along the wall near the bed.

"Sure thing, Lily. A cup of coffee coming right up. I'll be right back." She jotted down something on Daisy's chart and skipped out of the room.

After a few more steps, I was standing next to Daisy's bed. As I studied her relaxed face, I noticed a scar above her left eyebrow. I never noticed it before. I wonder as a child if she fell off her bike or got a rock thrown at her. I have scars from both. Of course, Daddy had been the one to ice my injuries and wipe away my tears. Daisy had not been known to have a nurturing bone in her body. Whenever that 'bone' was evident, it was hard to believe and wasn't readily accepted. So unfortunately, as the years progressed, she nurtured me less and less.

It felt strange to stare at her, and she could not do anything to stop it. I was invading her privacy, which she typically protected with an iron fist. Her body was on display, and I was silently gawking at her. I decided to sit down in the visitor's chair. Maybe that would help.

Nurse Jenny came bouncing back into the room with my coffee. Luckily, it had a lid on it, or I'd be afraid she would have spilled coffee all the way down the hallway.

"I didn't know if you preferred cream or sugar, so I grabbed a few of each. You seem like a cream girl to me if I took a gander. We are limited in our flavors so I grabbed what I could fit in my pockets." After she handed me the warm disposable coffee cup, she retrieved the sugar and cream packets from her scrubs and dumped them on the end table next to my chair. "I need to see my other patients now, but Dr. Opland will be in soon to answer any questions you might have about your mom and her condition. Lily and Daisy? Huh... Just got that! If you have a daughter someday, you should name her Rose, Tulip or maybe Dandelion? You would have a whole bouquet of gorgeous flowers in your family. Don't tell me that your grandmother's name was a flower too?" She talked so fast that I wasn't sure she wasn't expecting a response from me. She graced me with a playful wink and bounced out of the room.

Nurse Jenny couldn't know this, but my grandmother from my mother's side was named after a flower too. Her name was Iris. I never met her because Daisy told me she died a long time ago.

As a garden of flowers, harmonious growth wasn't possible. We were too different, each one beautiful and unique but carriers of meanings that couldn't be reconciled. I don't know if the Armstrong women grew to embody the meanings of our names, but in our mismatched little garden, a daisy had begun to wilt.

Chapter Twenty-Five

1989

After what seemed like more than an hour of eyeballing Daisy, glancing around the room, and staring out the big picture window, a good-looking man in his early 50s wearing a white doctor coat paused outside Daisy's hospital room door. He was wearing blue scrubs under his flawless white lab coat, white tennis shoes and a stethoscope around his neck. He had intense sky-blue eyes, thinning hair, a dark, thick mustache and very white teeth with a small dimple on his left cheek. I also noticed a shiny gold band on his left ring finger. If Daisy was conscious, I could imagine her claiming that she was gonna 'tap that' regardless of the wedding ring or not. That image of her and how she could embarrass me so easily with her inappropriate comments caused a smile to break out across my face, which felt awkward and totally inappropriate due to the timing and my current location. Against my better judgment, a little giggle escaped my throat.

Dr. Opland glanced up from Daisy's chart and caught my eye. He must have heard my sudden burst of laughter and saw me looking like a cat who swallowed the canary. *I am a complete idiot!* He hung the chart back up on the hook just outside of her hospital room. He strolled casually into the room.

"Hi. You must be Daisy's daughter. I'm Dr. Opland." He extended his right hand out and firmly shook mine. I felt like a young child who was caught doing something wrong. I could only nod to affirm that I was Daisy's daughter. "Your mother was brought to the ER on Monday. She was unconscious and appeared to have suffered a major stroke." He filled me in on the details of her health, but most of the medical terminology was lost on my ears. *Daisy had a stroke? A coma?*

"I'm afraid that this type of heart defect is genetic, meaning that it is inherited within your DNA when you are born. This type of heart defect is not caused by a lifestyle but by the cells within your chemical makeup. However, it can and should be medically treated. With that being said, while you are here visiting your mother, I highly recommend that you consider some genetic testing. Her condition could have been treatable if it had been diagnosed early enough. Have any members of your mother's family ever died of a heart attack or suffered from a stroke?" His sparkling blue eyes showed genuine concern. His polite bedside manner made me want to disclose everything - details of my life which had nothing to do with Daisy's current health. *How long do you have, doc?* The details of Daisy's stroke had been delivered so calmly that I didn't even feel like I had been given any bad news.

"I'm not sure. Daisy and I are not close. She hardly ever mentioned her immediate family. But strangely enough, my dad died of a heart attack a few months ago. He was brought here to this hospital, in fact. I also believe my grandfather - Daisy's father - died of some type of heart problem. However, I don't know any more than that."

"I'm sorry to hear about your father. What was his name? Was there an autopsy done to determine his cause of death? Besides just a heart attack, I mean." He retrieved a ballpoint pen and a small tablet from the inside pocket of his lab coat and looked at me for the requested information.

"His name was Ben Armstrong. He died on April 15. And I'm not sure about the autopsy results."

Dr. Opland jotted down that information on a small notepad. "I would definitely like to order some tests on your heart, Lily. If we discover anything, we can discuss treatment options with you. You won't have to go through what your mother is going through. I will have one of the nurses inform you about what tests are needed, and perhaps we can schedule an appointment sooner rather than later."

After Dr. Opland left me alone with Daisy, his shocking news started to sink in. Both of my parents had heart defects. Daddy died because of his abnormality. My mother was lying unconscious in a hospital bed because of her defect. The odds of my heart not inheriting a defect seemed extremely low. Math was not my strong suit, but my high school Math teacher would've calculated my odds at having no heart defect at a low percentage. If my heart didn't feel heavy before, it definitely weighed a ton now.

Chapter Twenty-Six

1989

D aisy's condition remained the same throughout the next week. I continued to be her only visitor. Her hospital monitors continued to make the same constant set of beeps. Nurse Jenny educated me about my heart test procedures, the possible medication, and the possible surgeries if something was found wrong with my heart. There were lots of options if we found anything wrong. There were lots of possibilities. The medical staff must have agreed that the odds were not in my favor because hardly ever did anyone mention 'if' or 'maybe.' So, I reluctantly started to accept my obvious fate as well. Modern medicine and early detection were to be thanked and appreciated. However, I still didn't feel very lucky.

The tests weren't too scary or painful as long as I allowed many long needles to puncture my skin and answered endless questions about my family's health history. Waiting for the results was by far the worst. Sitting in a hospital visitor's chair every day, staring at what could be inevitable and wondering if I'd be lying there unconscious in a few years too, now *that* was painful. Never in my life had I ever wanted more to be nothing like Daisy, and now more than ever, I wanted to be the polar opposite.

"Some medical researchers believe that even when a loved one is unconscious, like in a coma, he or she is still able to hear you." Bouncing Nurse Jenny woke me from my daydream and private pity party. She was doing her routine check on Daisy's vitals. "You should try speaking out loud to your mom. Tell her how much you love her. Tell her how much you want her to pull through. Tell her some anecdotes from your childhood. You're supposed to use her name a lot. Daisy... Daisy... Daisy... Who knows what will jolt her consciousness? Anything is worth a shot, right?" She gave me a big smile for some encouragement. She motioned towards Daisy with her head.

"Now? No, I don't know what to say." Nurse Jenny wasn't going to be anywhere near Daisy's hospital room if I was gonna 'talk' to her. Nurse Jenny would be shocked to her sweet, innocent core by the word vomit that would explode out of my mouth. Nope, I was completely content staying silent and daydreaming.

"Well, you could start by reading a book to her or you could even sing. Are you a singer? You should be a singer with your good looks." Nurse Jenny never waited for an actual answer. She kept on talking. "Imagine your fan club! Young hormonal boys would be buying your records left and right. Teenage girls would envy you, think that you are amazing but then hate you for being so awesome and gorgeous. Girls! We are just crazy! Speak and act one way but think totally differently. Maybe you could write a song about that!" She had no idea. It was as if she was reading my mind.

"Thanks, Jenny. I'll think about it." I was doing exactly what she said 'us girls' do: say one thing but think the opposite. She was smarter than I was giving her credit for.

"Well, good! Our loved ones should always know how we feel about them. Right? I mean I am sure that there are things you wish you could say to her if you knew she could hear you. Maybe something about the last time you were together that you forgot to say... or something silly you haven't told her yet... or maybe something about..."

Oh my god! I tuned her out. She didn't even need another human to have a conversation with - she could do it all by herself. This woman must talk in her sleep.

I started to daydream about what I could possibly say to Daisy. A one-sided conversation might be ideal for our relationship - if you can call it a relationship.

I would start by telling her about how disappointing she was as a mother. She didn't even have a maternal bone in her body. I could bring up some facts I knew about her infidelities. Tell her what I knew about the current Pastor Tony. And of course, wrap up the conversation with how I completely blamed her for Daddy's death. Maybe Nurse Jenny was right. It might feel good to release some of my bottled-up feelings from my childhood. Wow, this chatterbox might have a valid point.

"... and who knows, maybe she'll wake up and will remember your conversation word for word." She shrugged her shoulders as if to say, 'who knows.' "Well, gotta go check on Larry next door. Holler, if you need anything, Lily."

Bouncing Nurse Jenny left the room, and I sighed in relief. She meant well, but lordy she was windy. The silence was welcoming. I glanced at Daisy. Her blank facial expressions were the same, her arms were by her sides. Her monitors beeped in a steady rhythm.

DURING THE DAYLIGHT HOURS, I rested quietly in the visitor's chair either sipping coffee or water. I watched Daisy with curious eyes. Noticed her even breathing. Thought about how helpless she seemed. Thought about how I wished it was Daddy laying there instead of her, fighting for his second chance. I had more dreams and wishes to share with him. I had more memories that I wanted to make with him. I would talk to him if he was lying there uncon-scious. Looking at Daisy, I felt empty. I didn't have anything I wanted to share with her. There were too many unkind words, too many hurtful memories and too many disappointments to fake real feelings.

After a bland hospital cafeteria supper that consisted of green Jell-O, runny mashed potatoes and a slice of slightly warm turkey breast, I decided to call it a day and returned to our family home. Daddy had been gone for almost a year now. It seemed like just yesterday I heard him holler at me as I opened the front door after working a shift at the cafe.

"Baby Girl, is that you? There's a bowl of ice cream in here screaming your name. Come in the kitchen!" He knew he would get my attention with ice cream. I still noticed him everywhere in this house: a triangle-shaped grease stain on the couch where he dropped a hot pizza slice, the green pea stain on the ceiling as a result of a food fight, the stairs where he held me as I cried about my failed sledding attempt, and the sage green phone on the wall that he would call me on every Wednesday night while he was away trucking.

Daisy had changed a few things since Daddy died and I moved to college. For example, she purchased a new entry way rug that was very bright and floral. Daddy hated floral print. He said flowers were created by God to be outside.

"Would you like it if I parked my truck in the living room, Daisy? Hell no! And I know that, so keep the damn flowers outside too." She never seemed to mind and laughed at his ridiculous comparison. I will give her credit for having a soft spot for Daddy and loved to tease him. His laughter was contagious. We both worked hard to hear his booming, deep laugh.

She also added a new picture to the mantel. Next to the picture of the three of us at Adventureland was a black and white photograph in a silver frame. The picture was taken of two young, dark-haired boys, who were mirror images of one another except that the one on the right was older. A blonde girl stood in the middle holding both of their hands. Each boy was wearing a pair of shorts and a button-down shirt. Because the photo was black and white, I assumed that they had matching outfits on. Their haircuts were military short. Standing in front of a small maple tree, both boys were squinting at the camera as if the sun was in their eyes. The girl, who must have been a teenager, captivated the attention of anyone looking at the picture. She had shoulder-length, light-colored hair. She was wearing a light-colored spaghetti strap sundress. She beamed at the camera. Happy, content and full of life.

Finally, my intense studying of the photograph lit a spark - this captivating, gorgeous teenage girl was Daisy. I don't ever remember seeing photos of her or Daddy as children. But as soon as I realized it was her, there was no denying it. I wonder where it came from, and why, if she had it all this time, did she finally choose to display it now? And even more importantly, who were these two boys she was holding hands with?

I grabbed the silver picture frame and decided to open the frame to see if the back of the photo could answer my questions. In cursive writing, I read, 'Daisy and the boys - Dupe TX 1967.' The teenager was Daisy, but no names were supplied for the two younger boys. In 1967, Mother would've been fifteen years old.

Dupe, Texas? Never heard of it. Was she there on vacation? Did she live there as a child? Was she visiting someone, and they took this picture with her? But they must have been significant to her for Daisy to have framed the picture and placed it on the mantel next to our family picture. Obviously, who they were was the biggest question, but also, what was the significance to the timing of displaying it? Did she just get it? Did something happen to one of these boys that made Daisy want to remember them?

And with Daisy in a coma, she wasn't going to be answering any questions. Thank goodness I enjoyed a good mystery. Nothing like the present time to snoop around the house and see if I could find more surprises.

Chapter Twenty-Seven

1989

With my life being on a slight holding pattern - my college classes were giving me a temporary pardon while I was home with Daisy, and I had no roommate or boyfriend to worry about - I figured that now would be the perfect time to dig into my secretive family history. My investigative search began in the living room. Since I found the mysterious photograph in there, it seemed likely I would find more. As I opened drawer after drawer and paged through several old photo albums from my childhood, I thought about my lack of knowledge of my parents' lives before I was born. Realizing how little I knew made me feel very self-centered.

I remember that I asked for their childhood stories and asked if I had any grandparents, aunts, uncles, and/or cousins. Eventually, I stopped inquiring about distant relatives and family stories since I would receive the same resistance.

"What about Uncle Freddy? Is he really my uncle?"

"Hell no! He thinks he earned himself a title, so we gave him one." Daisy's response to my innocent question really caused a spike in her blood pressure.

In third grade, I was assigned a project to create my family tree. I had never heard of my ancestors' names before. I was beyond curious to know more. I recall a frightened look that passed between Daisy and Daddy when I was completing this project. It was as if they were eager to tell me more, but for some reason they would not disclose more than the assignment needed. I'm not sure if the information that they reluctantly gave me was even truthful.

Basically, this was the limited information that I was led to believe: Daisy grew up in a small town. She refused to disclose the name of the town. Her parents' names were Iris and William. They were no longer living. She had a little brother whom she only discussed if it was a happy childhood story about him.

Daddy told me he lived in an orphanage for as long as he could remember. Occasionally, he would mention a story about siblings, but I never was sure if he was referring to his own or Daisy's. Sometimes, I got the feeling that Daddy adopted Daisy's memories of her family as his own. Maybe it was less painful. As soon as he turned eighteen, he ventured out on his own. He never talked about his childhood in the orphanage.

"It's too sad and very painful. I don't live in the past. Only the present. I look forward to the future." But Daddy often asked Daisy to recount stories of her family and younger brother. Stories of a little boy that he had never met made Daddy's smile reach his eyes. His eyes would glisten with happy tears. At the completion of Daisy's story, he often would retreat to his bedroom for a bit. It seemed like a strange reaction to a narrative about a young boy that he had never met, but I never questioned it. I imagined that Daddy wished that Daisy's little brother was actually his own younger brother and that he had stories to tell about them growing up together. Adventures that two mischievous young boys created.

The living room search turned up nothing of interest. However, I did locate an old photo of Daddy that I decided to remove from the photo album and save for myself. He was so handsome in the picture, wearing the only button-down shirt that he owned with a navy blue tie that I had given him as a gift. I remember taking this picture of him after one of my school choir concerts. I expressed to him that if I had to get all dressed up, he had to too. He looked so sharp, even Daisy

159

admitted how handsome he looked. She laid a quick, rare peck on his cheek before we headed to my school. I only remember this because they never showed any affection towards one another. I thought to myself, *Even Momma thinks he looks dapper.*

Since the contents of the living room were not cooperating with my investigation, I decided the kitchen might be the next possible room. Plus, I was starving. After throwing a couple pieces of wheat toast in the toaster, I started snooping around. She attached her bills to the side of the refrigerator with magnets. Nothing of interest except she was overdue on her phone bill.

When my toast popped up, I slapped some peanut butter on each slice and continued with my so-far fruitless hunt. It is complicated to search for something when you don't know exactly what you're looking for. No wonder there are so many cold cases in crime. Some clues will only make sense as soon as you uncover the truth. That is why they say, 'Hindsight is 20/20.' During my criminal investigation classes, I learned that if something seems out of character or unusual, it might be part of the puzzle that will help uncover more facts later. Therefore, the unpaid phone bill in itself wasn't anything too special, but it was noteworthy in the sense that all the other bills were up-to-date and paid. I decided to set it aside for now and perhaps later it would lead me somewhere.

On the front side of the beat-up refrigerator hung an old, crumpled-but-now-flattened drawing that I created as a kid. I wondered where she found it after all these years. I removed the magnet that was holding it in place and studied my artwork.

It was a picture of our white house outlined with a black crayon. It leaned a bit to the left. I had drawn a few colorful flowers near the front steps. On the front side of our house, standing in our green grass, three stick figures stood. I had drawn arrows to each one: 'me,' 'Daddy,' and 'Momma.' In my portrait, Daddy and I were holding hands and smiling. Stick-figure Momma stood off to the side, and no smile was drawn on her face - a straight crayon line symbolized her mouth. When I flipped the drawing over, my childlike handwriting read: "Lily, age 6." How sad that even at that young age I had already grasped the lack of closeness with Daisy. It struck me as odd that she chose now to display it. I didn't remember ever seeing it before. I returned it back to the fridge. Maybe Daisy was getting sentimental. Maybe she was lonely after Daddy died, and I had moved out. She had always been hard to read and rather impersonal. She pushed people away, but maybe she regretted her behavior.

On a cupboard shelf next to the cereal, I discovered her tip bank. Even when I was younger, an old, empty coffee can stored her dancing tips. Same coffee can in a new location. When I was a kid, she hid it in the upper cupboard above the refrigerator. She figured that I was too short to reach up there, and Daddy was too lazy to go searching for anything. Now that she lived alone, it was stored in the cupboard with other groceries behind the actual can of coffee. *Very clever, Daisy.* I peeked in it just like I did as a child and tried to imagine how much money was in there. I used to imagine all the candy that I would buy if it was all my money: Twizzlers, bubble gum, Laffy Taffy and of course my favorite, Hershey's with almonds.

As a budding adult, I envisioned depositing it into my bank account and not having to worry about bills for a couple of months. And why did she have all this money and still not pay her phone bill?

Chapter Twenty-Eight

1989

The sage green wall-mounted phone woke me from my little catnap on the couch. I did not plan on answering it - I assumed the phone call was for Daisy anyway. After I wiped a small amount of drool from the corner of my mouth, I stretched my arms out above my head and sat up to contemplate my evening plans. The answering machine picked up on the fifth ring.

"It's Daisy. You know what to do," her voice barked to the caller. *Beeeeeep...*

"Lily, it is Dr. Opland. Would you please give me a call when-"

I jumped up from the couch and sprinted to the kitchen to grab the receiver off the kitchen wall.

"Sorry about that, Dr. Opland. I didn't hear the phone ring." *Why did I feel the need to lie to him?* I'm not sure. Maybe I am a bit like Daisy after all.

"Oh, hi, Lily. Good, I am glad I was able to reach you. I had a message at the nurse's station for you to come see me in my office, but I was notified that you haven't been to the hospital today to see your mother. I have some... interesting news regarding your test results from last week. I wondered if you would be able to come to my office to discuss it with me."

"Today? Now? This afternoon?" First of all, I was shocked that he took the time out of his busy schedule to make the phone call himself. I was also surprised that he was still willing to see me today. It was already three o'clock. "I can be there in twenty minutes from Normal." The hospital, where Daisy was being cared for and Dr. Opland worked at, was located in the neighboring town of Madison.

"This afternoon would be perfect. I will be here catching up on my charts. When you arrive, check in with Nurse Jenny, and she will escort you to my office."

Wow, it must be some awful news if he would wait around for me to show up. Honestly, I was going to take the day off visiting Daisy at the hospital, but I was very curious to hear the 'interesting news.' *Interesting* was the word that he chose to use. Not *bad* or *extraordinary* or even *heartbreaking*. I had already reached the conclusion that since both of my parents possessed heart defects, I was destined to, too. Maybe in my case it would be even worse since both suffered heart-related issues. Or maybe the word 'interesting' meant 'remarkable', as in a miracle. No problems were discovered. That would be *interesting*!

I quickly ran a brush through my long hair, swished around some mouthwash and drew a deep breath. I headed for the door. Here we go. Was anyone ever ready to hear their own death sentence?

WHEN I ARRIVED at Daisy's room, she was alone. Medically, she was still the same: no brain activity and no response to voices or physical touch. However, she would be disappointed to know that physically, the coma was erasing her natural beauty. The shine in her hair lost its luster while dusty gray sprinkled her roots. Her skin paled without vitamin D to color it. Her weight loss caused her cheekbones to become more pronounced even without a smile in sight. Her already slender arms stuck out of her sides like two twigs. Previously, I asked Nurse Jenny about teeth brushing when a person is in a coma.

"I do that for her. It probably isn't as thorough as a dentist would like, but we do the best we can. We even have a saliva ejector now." She beamed proudly.

"A *what*?"

"A saliva ejector to suck out the excess water, toothpaste and saliva in her mouth. Before, it was a total nightmare! We were always nervous about a patient choking on their own spit. I wonder, who invented it? Probably a retired dentist thinking 'you know what would have made my job so much easier? A tool to suck out the saliva.' He was just discussing it over his morning coffee with his retired friends and BAM! He's a millionaire! He was already well-off because he had his own practice, and he sold it for a good chunk of change. Lucky damn dentist!" Her hands moved the entire time her mouth moved. It was as if they were in a race against each other.

"Jenny, you have a very active imagination." Her need to fill all silent space with chatter often exhausted me. After three weeks with no one else to talk to, I looked forward to hearing what this crazy nurse would come up with next.

"Funny you should say that because my granny used to tell me that all the time. I should have used my 'gift to gab' in my career. I could have been on the radio. Talking to all my listeners. Telling them about the weather and local news. Or maybe even a talk show host! But I love to help people too and meet new friends." As she was taking Daisy's pulse, she reached over with her free hand and squeezed my arm. "I need to check on Larry next door before I show you to Dr. Opland's office. Give me a couple minutes, honey. Larry just had his first bowel movement in five days."

Daisy's teeth were being taken care of, so hopefully she wouldn't lose those. As a kid, I remember more than a few times her saying, "I might have drawn the short straw in this life, but damn I am grateful for my raging good looks." I knew she would be devastated if she woke up with rotten teeth, defined wrinkles and gray hair.

I dropped my purse and coat in the visitor's chair, really just *my* chair since no one else had been visiting. Since I was alone with Daisy, I decided to give Nurse Jenny's advice a whirl before seeing Dr. Opland.

"Hey, Daisy... It's me, Lily. A huge, hairy spider crawled up your sleeve. Do you want me to slap it?" I started with something that would normally get a reaction from her. Nothing. The beep of her monitors stayed consistent.

"Just kidding. However, you do look like shit. You better wake up and do something with yourself." Nothing. No eyelid movement or quickening heartbeat. "I found a photograph at home that you framed and placed on the mantel next to our family picture. The young teenage girl bears a striking resemblance to you, but who are the two boys in the picture? Curiosity got the best of me, so I looked at the back of the picture. Someone had written 'the boys.' Who are they? Should I let them know you're in the hospital?"

Nurse Jenny cleared her throat, which startled me from my conversation. "Nicely done. I wondered if you ever talked to her. You never know. Keep it up...but later. Dr. Opland wants to see you now." She gestured with her head that I should follow her. "She's not going anywhere. Stay put, Daisy. We will be right back." Jenny chuckled at her own little joke that made fun of Daisy's condition. What we didn't notice as we walked out the door but discovered later when they reviewed her vital stats was that Daisy's pulse quickened just before I left the room with Nurse Jenny.

Dr. Opland's office was located in the opposite end of the building, top floor, big corner office. Very impressive office space for a small-town doctor. Nurse Jenny tapped politely on his partially open door. His back was to us as he looked out the huge picture window that over-looked the river and rows and rows of corn. He was speaking into his handheld recorder. He clicked it off.

As he turned around to face us, he softly said to me, "Thanks for coming to see me so quickly, Lily. Have a seat." He indicated to a pair of chairs that sat opposite his office chair. His large oak desk was located between us. He took a seat in his big, black, leather office chair that screamed, 'I am important. I know stuff.'

Nurse Jenny squeezed my shoulder, and she excused herself from the room. The door softly closed behind her. I sat down, crossed my legs, took a few deep breaths, and told myself I could handle whatever news he was about to deliver. He opened a file that was on top of his massive oak desk. He must be a little bit obsessive about right angles and being organized because there was not an object out of place on his desk.

"Lily, let me begin by saying that I am pleased that we performed these tests on your heart. I'd like to take a moment to praise this amazing organ: the heart. We take it for granted. Your heart wants to please the body and perform at top level every day. Your heart works every second of every day of your life. That is a lot of pressure. I have great admiration for the heart... obviously.

"And your heart, Lily, I am pleased to inform you, is nearly perfect. Not a defect, murmur, or any signs of stress to it at all." A huge breath of air escaped my body. I didn't even realize that I was holding it in. Dr. Opland paused for a moment to let this good news sink in. He smiled before he started again. "However, I have some other news, Lily."

Oh no, I knew it! My heart was fine, but I had cancer! I had months to live! Or maybe I had an alien growing in my body! Or maybe I was pregnant even though I was a virgin! All these crazy thoughts consumed me, and the panic returned.

"Don't panic, Lily. You are not dying. Let me explain." He must've been able to read my mind or maybe witnessed the terrified expression on my face. "As I'm sure you are aware, having both parents with a heart defect made the chances of your heart not having one very rare. First, no defects, holes, blockage or a heart murmur were revealed in the test results. All exceptionally good news.

"Of course, we were overjoyed for you and could've stopped there, but I was very curious as to how that happened when the odds were extremely low. I searched for the answers in the facts regarding your dad's death. He died from a thoracic aortic aneurysm. This is a hereditary heart condition, meaning that he inherited this condition from one or both of his parents. It can be treated if diagnosed in time. There is medication and/or surgery that can correct it. Unfortunately, in your father's case, as you are well aware of, it was too late.

"Oddly enough, your mother has the same exact defect in her heart. She had to also inherit her condition from one or both of her parents. The fact that both of your parents had issues with their heart completely perplexed me since your heart did not show any signs of stress to it. Your heart escaped a strong, hereditary trait when the odds were very much against you. I decided to investigate all the medical records for both of your parents to discover a reasonable explanation. And there was one… a reasonable explanation.

"Let me explain. Your mother, Daisy, has type O blood, and your father, Ben, also had type O blood. To you, that may mean very little, but the part that causes instant alarm to a medical professional is your blood type, Lily. You are B-negative" He paused to see if the information he supplied would spark a light bulb in my brain.

I knew my blood type; I knew it was rare, but I wasn't sure what it had to do with my heart and my parents' blood types.

Dr. Opland cleared his throat. "Lily… I am sorry to be the one to divulge this sensitive information to you, but the man that you called your father, Ben, was not your biological father. He couldn't medically be. The reason I knew this right away is because both of your parents have type O blood. When two people have the same type O blood, their children would automatically have the same blood type, type O."

The only response that I was capable of was a few rapid eye blinks and a blank expression. Daddy was not my daddy? How was that possible? Had he known? Dr. Opland must be wrong. How accurate were these tests? How could this be possible? Who was my biological father then? God, let it not be one of the random men at the bar.

Dr. Opland was not only a thorough doctor and researcher, but he was very observant as well. He must have noticed my skin color change or perhaps my mouth starting to water because before I even realized what was happening, he had raced around his desk with his nearly empty garbage can just as everything in my stomach decided to erupt from my body. After my stomach contents were displayed at the bottom of his garbage can, Dr. Opland grabbed a bottle of water from his office refrigerator. He also handed me a towel, which I used to wipe the sweat from my sticky forehead and the spit from around my mouth. After what seemed like hours, I regained my composure and a few tears escaped from the corner of my eyes.

"I'm so sorry about that, Dr. Opland. I am completely embarrassed." My eyes were downcast, and I felt like a child again. I hadn't seen that coming at all. I'd never had such a physical reaction to emotional pain.

"Don't worry about it, Lily. It's completely normal to react that way when you receive news that you are unprepared for. I didn't know how to tell you any other way. Obviously, you had no idea."

"Correct. No one told me differently. I guess I never came right out and asked. But I believed with my whole heart that he was my biological father." My throat hurt from throwing up, so I finished my water. Tears were rolling down my cheeks. I had no control over my emotions. My heart felt broken.

"This revelation makes a lot more sense to me as a medical professional and explains how your heart is in such great shape and escaped a near fatal verdict. I was very concerned before we had the results that we would be unable to help you. So, I had to discover a logical, medical reason. Daisy's blood type is O, which is nothing special but when the second parent also has the same type O blood, then their children would be born with the same blood type. This only happens with type O blood. Research shows for you to be B-negative, one of your parents would need to have an AB blood type.

"I requested a DNA test to see if we can one hundred percent confirm that your biological mother is Daisy. I should know more soon regarding those results. I believe we will find that she is your biological mother, but since we had no idea that Ben was not your biological father, I decided you can never be too sure of anything.

"Again, Lily, I'm sorry. I hope you and your mother can have a conversation about this misunderstanding one day." He stood up from behind his desk and held out his hand. I read that gesture as a signal that our meeting was finished.

"Thank you, Dr. Opland. I appreciate your concern for me and the great care you are giving my mother." I accepted his handshake. Mine was not steady, and tears continued to fall from my blue eyes.

Leaving his office and heading home was a complete blur. I wasn't about to visit Daisy. I was more than upset about her lying to me. I needed to go home and process this shocking new information. The one person whom I had loved unconditionally with my whole heart was not my actual father. We were not related. We did not share DNA. My heart wouldn't accept that he might have had knowledge of this fact. He couldn't have lied to me for eighteen years!

If he wasn't my biological father, then who was? The possibilities, unfortunately, seemed endless. She met so many men at the Rusty Nail, but all of that was after I was born. I needed to dig deeper. Maybe the key to unlocking this mystery lay in Dupe, Texas.

Chapter Twenty-Nine

1989

Unfortunately, when I arrived home from visiting Dr. Opland's office where I learned Daddy wasn't my biological father, a half bottle of Captain Morgan taunted me from the liquor cabinet. With a splash of Diet Coke, Captain Morgan drowned my sorrows for the rest of the evening. My investigative work would have to wait for another day. My broken heart required me to numb it slightly.

When I woke the next morning in my childhood bedroom, my head thumped with regret; however, my heart ached even more. I couldn't believe this was really my life. The father whom I loved and adored my whole life wasn't actually my blood relative. Yet, he was the one person who made me feel loved, valued and cherished. We didn't even share the same DNA. I didn't understand how the one human I felt the most connected to my entire life was not who I believed he was. We weren't connected by blood; he was as much my father as the mailman.

My wounded, fragile heart - with no physical defect detected according to Dr. Opland - wanted to believe that Daddy didn't know. That Daisy deceived him, too. That he believed with his whole heart that I was his actual "Baby Girl." I knew he loved me as his own. She must have seduced him and claimed that the baby she was carrying was his. It was the only thing that made sense. She was manipulative, and he was easily sold. In my heart, I knew Daddy - he was an honest, trustworthy man who genuinely cared about me.

My head, unfortunately, didn't completely agree. *Hey Heart, I get what you are feeling, but logically the facts don't add up.* Daddy always told me that I was too smart for my 'britches.' And my head was saying that something was going on here. Biology doesn't lie. Dr. Opland would not have informed me if the facts weren't there. Just ironic that neither adult that was involved could verify this new knowledge. My brain hurt thinking about the fraud. How could I not have known? Were there clues that I missed?

Basic facts are taught to young children - Mom, Dad, no, yes. All facts are compiled with more knowledge. This basic life knowledge is a lot like math. If a student can't master addition, multiplication would cause a struggle. Learn the basics of life, and then when confronted with new information, a child can sort and add information to the current foundation. As a child, I was taught, "This is a rock." I stored that information and didn't question that fact. "That is a rock." Around two years of age, the man pointed to himself and said, "Daddy." As a child, I didn't question him. I called him, "Daddy." Questioning even the simplest facts doesn't occur at this age of learning and categorizing knowledge. He called himself "Daddy"; therefore, he was.

I wondered as Daisy rested on her hard, thin hospital mattress in her profound, deep sleep if she dreamed about me and Daddy. I wonder if she wished things had turned out differently. *Does she dream about my biological father? Did she love him? Did he die? If not, where is he? Does he know about me? Is he alive somewhere searching for me?* Maybe she never told him that she was pregnant and that was why she was able to keep her secret for so long.

I wondered if Daddy knew he wasn't my real father. Was he fine with it? Why did he go along with it? Did he just go along with Daisy's story because she was blackmailing him for some reason? Did he love her so much he was willing to lie about something this big? And obviously, if Daddy was not my actual father, then who was?

This confusing, crazy nonsense conversation was giving my headache a new sense of urgency. I desperately needed some answers and some aspirin.

DAISY'S BEDROOM. She had to have hidden things in here. Kept her secrets close to her so they were able to remain just that - secrets. When I opened her bedroom door, the first thing I noticed was that she had pushed their two twin beds together to make one big bed. Growing up, I inquired why they didn't sleep in one big bed together like my friends' parents did and the parents on the TV shows that we watched did. Their random answers ranged from "your dad snores" to "Mommy kicks me in her sleep" to "we just sleep better apart." Now a young adult armed with my newly gained knowledge, those excuses screamed lame and questionable. Maybe it was another clue. Maybe it actually meant something more.

Next to each side of the bed were the nightstands Daddy had made in his garage years ago. It was obvious what side of the bed that Daisy slept on - the right side, because it had many signs of life: a lamp, lotion, an alarm clock, a romance novel, and a fingernail clipper. She had purchased a new pink and white floral comforter. There were numerous throw pillows decorating the head of the bed. Another thing Daddy hated: throw pillows. My eyes scanned the room for anything else new or out of the ordinary. On the dresser near the bedroom closet, another new black and white picture sat. I had never seen this photograph before. The black and white photo showed the same two little boys. I again opened the back of the picture frame to see if there were any more clues written on it. This time in cursive writing was 'the boys. 566 S. Prairie Drive, Dupe, Texas.' A whole address? *Jackpot!* I deposited the photograph in my pocket to save for further investigation. I placed the empty frame back on her dresser and continued searching her room.

No more obvious items were on display, so digging would be necessary. The search under her bed produced a lot of dust bunnies, a comb, an empty overnight bag, one dirty sock and a used tissue. As I sat on the side of her bed and slid the overnight bag back under her bed with my foot, I noticed the drawer of her nightstand was slightly ajar. Daddy built it with a lock on it, because Daisy insisted that she had private things that needed locking up. I remember the conversation when she requested him to make her one.

"Ben, I have things that are for my brown eyes only. Private things. A lady needs some bit of privacy in her own home." Her eyebrows gave a little signal that he should know what she was talking about. I noticed him catching on. I didn't know what he was catching onto at the time. I simply recall when we were building it in his garage that he swore a lot under his breath about what a pain putting a lock in was going to be.

The drawer was propped open and not locked. Those private things weren't going to be so private anymore. I yanked on the handle to reveal its contents. There were stacks of different size notebooks. On the front cover of each notebook written in Daisy's handwriting was 'Daisy's Private Journal' and a year. There were so many. *I hit Mother's mother lode!*

On top of the pile rested the journal of the current year. 1989. Maybe she wrote something in it recently that would help me discover who these two little boys were and why all of a sudden, she was displaying their pictures throughout the house. I grabbed "Daisy's Thoughts 1989." I fluffed up Daisy's new throw pillows and made myself comfortable on her bed. Part of me felt guilty for going through her personal effects, but the other part of me was beyond curious to understand the brain of the woman who gave birth to me. I couldn't use the word 'raised' because Daddy did the heavy lifting of raising me. She was physically present in my life. Plus, the same, very curious part argued that she didn't leave me much choice by lying to me my entire life. No, I was right, and I deserved to know.

When I cracked open the first page, I recognized her delicate, cursive handwriting, the same handwriting from the back of the pictures. The first page read,

Dear Diary -

Your purpose seems lame and meaningless. I need help. I need a

friend. Yet I waste my time with you. The only one who'll listen. Are you real in another reality? In this other reality, would you be able to get me out of a jam? Loan me some money? Offer advice? Or give a fuck? Who knows. Maybe I'll never know.

- Daisy

Chapter Thirty

*J*anuary 1, 1989
    Dear Michelle Pfeiffer -
    I figured I would give you a real human name - Diary seemed lame and pointless - and then maybe this wouldn't feel like a gigantic waste of my time. Writing to someone who never answers me back! I am a lonely loser.

    Happy Fucking New Year! I worked at Rusty Nail last night and made lousy tips. My regular, John B - can't tell you his last name because of a confidentiality agreement that we were forced to sign at work - told me my tits aren't as perky as they used to be. He even suggested that I was losing my looks. I didn't make him hard anymore. Can you believe the nerve of that drunk?

    Maybe he is right...what do I do now? Everyone I have ever loved has abandoned me! I have no reason to live! I should have listened to H. He knew this would happen. He told me I was too good for it, but I never listened. He believed in the good in me. But I never saw it. Now look at me! Sagging tits, losing my looks and all alone. I am a hot mess. Very attractive.

    I ain't gonna make any resolutions this New Year. I can't seem to keep them anyway. Like the year I tried to give up drinking - that didn't work! Like the year I gave up men - that lasted one day! Like the year I gave up swearing and said things like "son of a nutcracker" instead. It was funny though when three-year-old Lily started saying it!

Nope, no New Year resolutions for me. Gonna stay the same fucked-up loser I was and always will be.

D

January 10, 1989

Dear Bruce Willis -

You are a prick! All men are pricks! They all abandoned me... Father, Little H, T, Tony, Max and H. Why do I love the ones who always leave me?!?!?

Speaking of pricks, this one is a cactus: Lily. She was home for the holiday break. I can't stand to look at her. She has his eyes - piercing blue. She reminds me of all the things that have been taken from me. That I can't have. That I lost. She is to blame for my life being such a mess. Why can't I lose her?

She is the reason I have lost these men! Shit - Max literally told me that he was breaking it off because it was too difficult on him being Lily's coach and teacher. Are you kidding me? You bark orders at her and teach her a little lesson at school! What does that have to do with fucking me? Nothing!

T - I don't know where we would be if it weren't for Lily. Maybe we would be together. We would have found a way to work it out despite all the odds. I know he loved me. Yes, she is completely to blame for that man not being in my life.

Tony, well shit - that sick bastard was obsessed with her! And she was like a baby when I was seeing him. All he would talk about was her: her smile, her budding breasts and her ass. It was rather gross and annoying. Not sorry that one is over, but if it wasn't for Lily, we might have had a chance. But as soon as she started grabbing his attention, he never noticed me. Yep, if she wasn't around, I could have kept his eyes from wandering.

Lily... Lily... Lily... I sense a theme.

D

January 12, 1989
Dear Bruce Willis -

I need to retract my statement... Lily isn't to blame. I am. I know that. I was just mad because the holidays were a complete disaster. Without H here, I can't seem to say the right thing, do the right thing. I am only half without him.

She left, and it wasn't on good terms. I am not sure why I care. We were never close. But now with everyone gone, part of me wants to save the one relationship I have. But is it a relationship? Blood, maybe... but is that enough?

D

January 15, 1989
Dear Matthew Jackson -

I had too much to drink last night after my shift. Trixie and I sat at the bar and emptied bottle after bottle. When I got home, I called Dupe looking for T. He has the same phone number he did years ago. Directory Assistance gave it to me. I called him... When he answered, I hung up. What would I say? What the hell was I thinking? I have completely lost my mind without H. He would never have let me make that call. I can't make that mistake again. That bridge is broken, and I can't go back.

D

January 18, 1989
Dear Magnum PI-

Do you know how much I resent her? Do you wanna know how much I blame her for this? One hundred percent! If it wasn't for her, I would be living with a man I loved and adored. Instead of settling for this life of lies!

D

January 30, 1989
Dear Madonna -
I had a dream last night about Little H. This time though, I ripped him out of her grasp and saved him. He came to live with us. We were one big happy family. There was no harbored guilt or hiding. We were together. All three of us. I woke up feeling like he was here with me. Maybe he is... maybe he doesn't blame me for not saving him. Maybe he understands I was a kid, too. Maybe he is trying to tell me something. I wish I could go back to my dream.

'Livin' on a Prayer,' Madonna. Although that isn't completely true because I stopped believing in God a long time ago. He gave up on me, so I stopped believing in Him.

D

February 1, 1989
Dear Matthew J. Fox-
Do I feel I am to blame for his untimely death? No and yes. First of all, since the time he signed up for this life, I have tried to make him happy. I wanted him to feel loved and cherished. Yes, I have my own demons, so I was not always the picture-perfect wife.

However, I did give him Lily, whom he absolutely one hundred percent - my mother always used to say, "One hundred percent!" - adored from head to toe. It amazes me the bond that those two had. Sometimes, they would just look at each other and laugh. They had their inside jokes, own language, and an unbreakable bond. Yes, I was jealous. Hell, the brat came out of my va-jay-jay and worshipped the ground he walked on. Totally unfair, except he gave up everything to be with us. I guess he did deserve every extra hug, kiss and wave. I think the family I gave him helped give meaning and life to his years. Without me and Lily, he would've been a grumpy old trucker with no home to return to.

But yes, I feel terrible that we were fighting when his ticker gave

178

out. What horrible timing! And I never got to see forgiveness in his eyes. He looked scared and shocked. Maybe it was the pain or the realization that he was dying just like Daddy did. He died in Lily's arms, the one he loved the most. He was an amazing father. I am sorry that I never did anything to deserve him. Maybe this was Karma paying me back for all my sins. I hate Karma. She always seems to find me.

D

February 2, 1989
Dear Brooke Shields -
I stayed home sick today. Rusty Nail didn't seem too shaken up about it. And I never miss work. But I felt crappy all day. Must have caught something from one of my regulars. Damn John B and his nasty hygiene… Can hardly get off the couch…

I found some old pictures of the boys in a box that we had stored in the attic. Made my heart happy to see their little smiling faces. I decided to frame a couple. I need to remember them. They deserve to be remembered and not forgotten.

D

February 15, 1989
Dear Eddie Murphy -
I stayed home sick from work for five days. That has never happened. I still felt under the weather when I went back, but I needed the money. I still haven't paid my phone bill from when I called T. Shoot! I shouldn't have done that. When I got the bill, I noticed I called him a lot when I was drunk - which I'll admit is most every night. I wonder what I said, or if I said anything. Did he say anything? I think I would remember something if we talked.

I wonder if he got into trouble from Mrs. A. Wonder if she wondered who was calling at all hours of the night. Dang! I shouldn't have ever looked up his number.

H, you should've stopped me!

D

Chapter Thirty-One

1989

W hen discovering new, shocking information, your brain processes the new knowledge slowly in bits and pieces. Primarily, you work through the strongest emotion first: anger, self-pity, happiness, fear or sadness. You may focus on how the information made you feel. Or you can focus on how the information made someone else feel. You tend to feel empathy or sympathy for someone else.

For example, if a co-worker informs you that he received a promotion, initially, a sense of happiness for him and his hard-earned reward may erupt as your reaction. However, if that was a promotion that you were in line for as well, self-pity and rejection may also surface. You have conflicting emotions battling in your body: you are happy and proud of your friend; however, you feel you should have received that promotion, so you feel angry and disappointed for yourself. Outwardly, you managed to push out a strained smile, firmly patted your co-worker on the back and congratulated him on his well-deserved success while your heart slowly cracked in defeat.

In my case, after reading Daisy's journal from 1989, profound sadness emerged as my initial emotion. Sadness for the mother I didn't know, sadness for how lonely she seemed to be, and sadness for the mother-daughter relationship we would never possess. Sadness for her conflicting hatred towards me. I dropped her 1989 journal down on my lap as I still sat cross-legged on her new comforter. I closed it and started to cry. The tears rolled down my cheeks. Sobs escaped my throat. Some of the noises coming from my mouth sounded like an injured animal.

The woman I knew for eighteen years didn't betray that she was unhappy or regretful. The Daisy who existed in my childhood memories appeared cold, unfeeling and unapologetic. I had no idea that there were several layers of emotion to this woman I lived with. I witnessed her massive mood swings, of course. She never expressed how unhappy she was. In her diary, she seemed human and vulnerable, while in real life she was disengaged and frigid. She never disclosed any emotion that would indicate that she didn't love the life she led. She was so closed off emotionally that I assumed she had no strong feelings about anything. She expressed that she thought it was lame to keep writing down her feelings to someone that wasn't helping her after all these years. But wow, it did help me uncover a different side of her.

After about fifteen minutes of a good, hard cry for my raw cluelessness and surprising but strong sympathy for the woman who was my mother, I felt overwhelmingly curious. What else didn't I know about her? A lot, apparently. Her journal proved that I didn't know her at all. I simply thought she was a terrible mother and repetitious adulterer. By simply reading one recent journal from earlier this year, I realized that there was much more to Daisy. Obviously, she was an angry woman who continued to blame other people for the wrongs in her own life. Her feelings towards me conflicted daily. Additionally, her journal indicated secrets that might help me realize why she became this cold, unemotional woman. Maybe by understanding her, I could 'like' her a bit. That might be pushing it, but miracles happen every day.

The next thing that I needed to process were all the names or initials I didn't recognize: H, Little H and T. She created her own code for important people in her life. She had a dream about Little H. From her journal entry it sounds like something dreadful happened to him, and Daisy was unable to save him from whatever happened. They were children at the time. However, in her dream, she was able to save him. Saved him from another woman? Where was he now? What happened to him? Why does Mother feel she was to blame? What was the relationship with Little H? How did she know him? Did she mean to save him from physical harm or emotional harm?

The man she referred to as 'T'. She recently called his home phone number in Dupe, Texas. According to this journal, Daisy had a history and 'people' in Dupe, Texas. I had never heard of that town before or her other life. Now, the unpaid phone bill became an important piece of the puzzle. I would wager good money that T's number was listed on there. Calling him and asking a few questions might answer some of these initial questions I was making a list of. However, in another journal entry, she blamed me for their relationship dissolving. I didn't know who 'T' was, and to my knowledge I had never been to Texas, so I wasn't sure how I was to blame. I decided to hold off on making that call for now. Figuring out how he fit into this mystery before the call was made might be more beneficial to my desired outcome.

Daisy referenced another man as 'H'. According to her diary he 'left' around the same time as Daddy died. No wonder she felt lost and all alone. H was obviously important to her as much as Daddy was. But why did she keep him away from us? He must have been a good influence on her since she sought him for advice. Who was he to her? Her writing didn't indicate a sexual relationship, more like an advisor and friend. Seems strange that after all of these years I hadn't met him. Maybe the letter H stood for husband? And she was referring to Daddy?

I had more questions than answers after reading her journal. First fact that I did know was that she resented me for her failed relationships with many men. Secondly, somehow three important men had left her life and broke her heart. I decided to dive back into her messed up brain and read 1988's journal.

Chapter Thirty-Two

*J*anuary 1, 1988
  Dear Diary,
  Happy freakin' New Year! I worked at Rusty Nail to ring in the New Year, and the tips were fabulous-o! Rusty served some free champagne for an hour, so that helped. I walked home after a few after-work cocktails to find Lily and Matthew making out on the living room couch. I cleared my throat.

  "Oh, my! Shoot! I better get home. Hi, Daisy. Bye, Lily. I will call you tomorrow." Matthew, Lily's boytoy, was all flustered. Good to know I could do that to men of all ages. But the hard-on that he was sporting was a direct result of Lily and her teasing. Poor kid. He couldn't even walk normally to get to the front door. He was gonna explode if they didn't screw soon.

  I giggled and stumbled upstairs to my bedroom. One thing that Lily did not learn from me was how to satisfy and please a man. She thought he was happy just cuddling with her on the couch, watching her drama-filled TV shows, and sharing their feelings. Oh, Lily, you have so much to learn.

D

January 5, 1988
Dear Diary,

Boytoy was over again. I swear they can't be apart. I noticed him looking me up and down before I left for my shift at Rusty Nail. His eyes traveled up my long legs to my thighs that were squeezed in my tight black skirt and then to my bare waist and then to my tight, white, fuzzy crop top sweater that was barely covering my breasts. Then his gaze finally found my dark brown eyes that were twinkling with his secret - I was staring right back at him. I raised one eyebrow as a sneaky smile crept up on my lips.

His face instantly turned three shades of red. He quickly looked away and directed his focus on whatever Lily was rambling on about. I choked out a small giggle. All men were alike and motivated by sex. It felt great to know I could turn the heads of boys half my age. He was still a boy.

Chalk one up for Daisy! Yep, I still got it!

D

January 15, 1988
Dear Diary,

Ben is home for the weekend. I love my Saturday mornings when he takes over 'family duties.' It ain't like I actually do much while he is away; Lily tends to most of the household chores. But I can tell that she enjoys it. With her Walkman covering her ears, she sings and dances in our living room while she vacuums or dusts.

On Saturdays, I normally sleep until noon or purposely stay in bed reading magazines, but for some reason this morning, the smell of fresh pancakes woke me from my beauty sleep. My neglected, empty stomach started to growl and wouldn't let me go back to sleep. I dragged my sleepy, hungover ass out of bed and made my way downstairs. Yeah, the sober train had left the station.

Ben and Lily didn't hear me descending the stairs because they were deep in conversation. My bare feet paused a few feet from the kitchen so I could hear what they were discussing. It was Ben's deep voice that I heard first.

"You are doing the right thing, Lily, by waiting. I know it isn't easy. It's hard on both of you, but you don't want to end up pregnant. And then what? Give up all your dreams? No more college? Raise the baby here? In this house?

"In high school, I knew a girl that got pregnant, kept the baby and her whole life changed. She changed. And not for the better. She's not the same girl." He paused to take a bite of his pancake and kept talking with his mouth full, one of my pet peeves. "Matthew is a great guy, Lily. You both can wait. Sex is great - don't get me wrong, but a baby is forever."

"I know you're right, Daddy. Matthew keeps asking. He says he's fine with my constant rejection, but sometimes I don't wanna say no either. I know it's definitely harder for him. So glad I can talk to you about this."

I couldn't see them from where I stopped in the living room, but I'm sure she either beamed her big cheesy smile at him or gave him a sweet little squeeze.

I slowly and quietly crept back upstairs to my bedroom. I avoided the creaky spots on the stairs and crawled back into bed. I lost my appetite.

D

January 29, 1988
Dear Diary,

I know I am evil. I can feel it. It creaks in my bones. It courses through my veins. Evil is the fuel that drives me.

Everyone has two voices in their head, a positive and a negative voice. You have your optimist voice of reason. The kind, calm, logical voice. She is your cheerleader who is always encouraging you, often claiming, "You can do it." She builds up your confidence level. I call her Benny, named after Ben because he always knows what to say to get me 'off the cliff.' Without Ben in my life and Benny in my head, I might have become an axe murderer a long time ago. I think I turned out pretty good, considering.

However, the other pessimist voice who is more evil is loudly echoing his opinions in my brain. I fondly nicknamed him Lucifer. He makes me laugh. He is twisted. He has a great sense of humor. We get along well. Lucifer is sarcastic and sinister. He never takes any blame. It is always someone's fault.

As the years and heartaches hardened me, Lucifer became more popular in my head. He was the one who I listened to and tended to side with. Benny was still there, but her voice has become more of a whisper.

D

February 7, 1988
Dear Diary,
Ben cornered me this past weekend asking me about how I was doing. We were both home and alone with no Lily. It felt odd. She has been our focus, attention, and the one thing we had in common all of these years. Now, she was creating a life of her own. We were alone on a Saturday night wondering if this was it. Would we ever find true happiness? Can we move on now? Do we still need to continue living a lie?

Okay, to be honest, Ben was asking those questions. He is the romantic, thoughtful one. Things - mainly men - have hardened me. This is it for me. I have no dreams of a happier, fuller life than this. And I told him so.

"Daisy, what happened to you? Where is that sweet, strong, passionate girl who I grew up with? You can't be that hardened, can you?"

"H-"

"Don't call me that."

"Ben, men did this to me. Filling me with their BS and giving me false opportunities to dream only to be shattered by their constant lies. I am realistic while you, pal, are still dreamy and innocent. We ain't

getting any further down the road of success. This is it. We chose this life, and we are stuck living it."

I finished my gin and tonic, my mother's favorite drink. Reminded me of my teenage years - the lime and the stale smell of alcohol.

Ben wasn't alarmed by my honest, harsh sense of reality. He was used to it.

"Daisy, you blame everyone else for the choices that you have made. Have you ever considered who the common denominator is? You, Daisy. You have made these choices. You have been the driving force behind your decline in happiness. It makes me sad to see you this way. It truly does. But you have no one to blame but yourself.

"I am not saying all of your previous lovers haven't hurt you, but you allowed them to. You put yourself in bad, toxic relationships. Many of these errors in judgment, that I was aware of, were married men. Isn't that a huge red flag? The guy can't commit. He is already promised to someone else. Maybe even dedicated to a family. But you waltz in and think either:

a) you can change all that, or

b) you have no respect for relationships, and you didn't intend for it to go too far. You prefer when they are not available to commit to you, because you don't want commitment. You want someone to blame for breaking your heart."

He shifted himself on the opposite side of the sofa and turned his body towards me. I continued to stare at the TV. I knew him well. He wanted me to open up. He wanted me to confide in him. He wanted me to break down and tell him he was right. Tell him how lonely I was. How sorry I was for being a shitty mother to Lily. How sorry I was for not holding up my end of the bargain. He wanted to see me surrender to these feelings that he thought I possessed. He gave me too much credit.

His words hurt - I ain't gonna lie. If I thought about the truth behind them, I would know he was right, but instead, I grabbed my empty glass and returned his condemning stare. Alcohol was loyal and would stuff those feelings back down. I stood up and said, "Fuck you."

D

February 14, 1988
Dear Diary,

Ben must have felt remorseful after our harsh conversation last weekend. When he called home from the road, he asked me to take Valentine's Day off from work - Valentine's Day wasn't a big night for strippers, anyway. He was gonna take me out for a nice, quiet dinner. Going out for dinner was a luxury that we didn't indulge in very often.

I took great care in choosing my outfit, making sure it was Ben-approved. I chose one of my ole churchgoing outfits from when I was trying to save my soul. Unfortunately, I dug my grave deeper to Hell when I met Tony. I painfully forced that guilty thought out of my head. I wasn't about to let the sins of my past ruin a perfectly good evening.

I wore a pair of black, straight dress pants that had a permanent pleat at the front of each leg. I chose a white peasant blouse and a red blazer. If I was going on an actual date, I would have worn a black bra under the blouse to hint where the night was going to lead. But for Ben, I chose a white bra and a white camisole as well. I was dressed like a real, proper lady - even I was impressed with the results. As I glanced at my reflection in the bathroom mirror, the ghost of my mother was staring back at me. Goosebumps traveled up and down my spine. I looked a lot like her before Father died and she became an alcoholic.

For Valentine's Day, Lily planned to prepare a homemade dinner for her boytoy. Since my dinner date established my good mood, I generously offered to assist her. We planned, grocery shopped, and prepared the meal together. I actually enjoyed spending time with her. It was a rarity.

Ben and I enjoyed a nice dinner at a little town south of Normal called Hartford. We both enjoyed pretending to be an average, loving couple. We chit-chatted about the latest news regarding our country and some gossip about famous people. We didn't have common friends or family that we could share gossip about, so we indulged in people we have never met. Conversation was light and enjoyable. The steaks were lean and mouthwatering.

When we arrived home, Lily and boytoy were done with their candlelight supper. The kitchen was spotless, and they were cuddling on the couch while watching Cheers. For the last fifteen minutes of the sitcom, Ben and I relaxed in the living room with them.

When the show was over, boytoy stood up and started making his way to the front door. Ben and I said our goodbyes as well while Lily escorted him to the door. Ben headed upstairs to get ready for bed, and I made my way into the kitchen for a glass of water. My prime rib steak had been very salty, and I needed a glass of water to wash it down.

A couple of minutes later after some loud lip smacking, I overheard boytoy comment, "Your parents are unusual. Not lovey-dovey or anything. Kinda like a couple of good buddies."

It was then that I realized they thought I retreated upstairs to bed when Ben did. They were so caught up in each other that they didn't realize I had walked to the kitchen and was currently in the very next room.

"You have no idea. I don't even try to understand their odd, unhealthy relationship. My dad is a saint to stay married to her. I have no idea what he ever saw in her, and why he continues to stick around.

"I can't even count the number of men she has cheated on him with. When I was a kid, I swear a new man was 'visiting' her every month. She must have thought I was a complete idiot for believing the excuses that she gave me for why the mailman delivered the mail into her bedroom. And then there was strange Uncle Freddy, who wasn't really my uncle. He stopped over at the end of every month to spend quality time with Daisy."

During Lily's dramatic little description of my life, her tone of voice became edgy and upset.

"That can't be true, Lily." Boytoy was attempting to calm her back down and comfort her. "I am sorry I brought it up. I know you don't like to talk about her." More lip smacking...

I had nowhere to go. I could choose to make my presence known or I could be patient. I could save this 'stab' and use it to my advantage at a later date.

I continued to sip my water. An idea started to formulate in my *head. I waited quietly in the dark kitchen until I heard their quiet good-byes, the front door shut, deadbolt locked, followed by Lily going upstairs to her bedroom.*

D

February 15, 1988
Dear Diary,
I do better each day when I have a goal in mind - a task to complete. I am excited for this new mission. Look out. It's gonna be a doozy! Lucifer supports me one hundred percent.

D

February 17, 1988
Dear Diary,
When a hunter stalks its prey, patience is a must. Without it, you will not succeed. A hunter must also understand the prey. Know what they are interested in, what makes them tick, where they hide, what they like and of course, what their weaknesses are. Collecting this knowledge is vital for hunting success.

D

February 18, 1988
Dear Diary,
Deja vu - after writing that last passage down on paper, T's name sprung to mind. Did he do this same thing to me, nineteen years ago? My obvious weaknesses were that I was young and naive. I was also vulnerable and sad from my father's passing.

He watched me daily from across the shared driveway. He knew my daily routine. He asked for my help knowing I wouldn't say no. I was eager to please. Yearned to feel needed and appreciated. He knew things were difficult at home. He could hear my mom yelling.

He preyed on my weaknesses. I was playing the role of an adult, yet

191

I hadn't even hit puberty. I had adult responsibilities, hormones that I didn't understand and was completely naive. However hard that reality hurt to finally realize, this realization didn't hold a candle to how powerful I felt turning the tables. Now, I was the hunter studying my prey. Once the student - now the teacher.

Hunting.

D

February 19, 1988
Dear Diary,

In order to understand my prey, I read Lily's journal. She wrote her thoughts down in an old, red three-ringed binder from school. It was labeled Chemistry; she was more creative than I thought. But her thoughts were fucking boring! From hearing birds outside her window as she described it: 'notifying me that my favorite season, Spring, was on its way' to how terrible the school lunch was: 'last week's leftover meat morphed into today's meatloaf.'

I tried to leaf through it to find anything of interest. Finally, I figured out her pattern. When she wrote about him, she used a red pen. The weather, cafeteria food and other rants were written in black ink. Red was reserved for boytoy.

D

February 20, 1988
Dear Diary,

Most boring read of my life! After pages and pages of mindless passages and falling asleep while reading it, I collected what information I needed: they haven't had sex yet. He really wants to, but she claims she wants to wait. She didn't want to be like me and "hand it over to whoever comes knocking." Those are her words.

They are gonna come back to haunt you, Lily.

D

February 25, 1988
Dear Diary,

Around three thirty this afternoon, the doorbell rang. On his way home from school, boytoy spontaneously stopped over to see Lily. Lily wasn't home yet. Being the welcoming person I am, I invited him in, explaining he could simply wait for her in the living room. He followed me in the door. A thin white T-shirt with no bra covered the top half of my body while the bottom half consisted of a pair of hot pink workout tights, my favorite brightly colored leg warmers and my white tennis shoes. No panty lines. My skin glistened with sweat earned from my Buns of Steel workout.

Being the wonderful hostess that I am, I grabbed us both a glass of water from the kitchen and joined him in the living room. He was sitting on our couch looking painfully uncomfortable. When I handed him the glass of water, his eyes were level with my pride and joy - my tits. I noticed he looked straight at my hardened nipples through my see-through shirt. I didn't cover them up - that would suggest I was ashamed. No, instead I told him, "I wasn't expecting company."

By arching my back, I pushed them out a bit further so he could get a better look. His face turned three shades of red, but his eyes stayed on my nipples.

I sat down on the couch right next to him. His body tensed up, and his back straightened as well. I had invaded his personal space. The only muscle that moved was his growing hard-on in his jeans. Gently, I placed my hand on his inner thigh. His eyes left my chest and reached my eyes. His eyes contained both a look of fear and yearning in them. I held his steady gaze and moistened my lips with my tongue. I knew I was tearing this boy's hormones to shreds, but boy, it was fun!

Seconds into our moment, I faintly heard Lily on the front steps making her way into the house. I smoothly and swiftly rose from my place on the couch and started for the stairs. My first step on the stairs matched Lily's opening of the front door. From the corner of my eye, I noticed that boytoy stayed seated on the couch - probably because of his healthy cramp in his pants - but gave his girl a big, cheesy grin.

Game on. Actually, that was just a pre-game warm-up.

D

March 1, 1988

Dear Diary,

My research was complete, or at least, all that I was going to discover from Lily's writing. The rest of my information gathering would include my observations. After "working" for Tony for years, my ability to read men was spot on.

For example, while I was shopping at Piggly Wiggly yesterday to get a few necessities, the young male cashier, Clark, was completely ogling me - mainly, my perky bosom. After my ten-second observation of him, I concluded that:

a) he was a twenty-year-old virgin,

b) he was currently growing an erection as he was calculating my bill - the pleats in his tan Docker pants were losing their crease - and

c) I was about to make this young man's day.

As I opened my wallet to retrieve my cash, I granted him a good, long glance down the front of my v-neck shirt at my cleavage. I bent over to search for the sixteen cents that I needed for change. As I was still leaning forward, I stared at him, he didn't look away - not like most timid virgins might. This Piggly Wiggly clerk was bold and planned on taking full advantage of every free peek he could get. I provided him a flirtatious little wink and licked my lips that were coated in bubble gum lip gloss. My tongue sealed the deal. Clark needed to glance away and busy himself with double bagging my groceries. His erection was completely obvious.

A flirtatious little giggle escaped my moistened lips. I handed Clark my correct change.

He whispered, "Sure appreciate the tip." His smile projected over-confidence.

Again, a giggle escaped, but this time it was completely genuine. Clark surprised me. Maybe his black, thin-framed glasses were fake and part of his costume like his super-ego, Superman. Either way, he definitely deserved the hand job I performed on him in the employee bathroom a few minutes later.

Boytoy was a few years younger than Clark, also a virgin and not as confident. He could never look me in the eye. Shoot, he still called Ben, 'sir'. Ben is no 'sir.' And he often addressed me as Ms. Daisy, which I completely hated. Made me feel like an old, decrepit lady. He was so polite and respectful. He would be harder to break, but Clark was a good test for my skills.

Go Superman!

D

April 14, 1988
Dear Diary,

Things are heating up with boytoy. Last night while the teenage lovebirds were saying good night on the front step, I patiently waited around the corner of the house in the driveway. My heart skipped a beat when I finally heard the front door close. Time to pounce on my prey. When he finally descended the steps and started down the side-walk for home, he turned right into me as I smoked a long lady finger. I startled him a bit, which was my intent. Caught him off guard. I offered him my cigarette. He shook his head and informed me that he needed to get home. I told him I needed some fresh air so I would walk him part of the way. A look of surprise lit up his face, but he didn't argue with me.

After walking half a block, I abruptly stopped, forcefully grabbed his wrist, and confidently pulled him to me. The nearby streetlight was unlit, and trees blocked the homeowner's view of us on the sidewalk. He was only a few inches taller than me, so I craned my neck just a little as I breathed into his face and pressed his fit, muscular body to mine. Tonight, he was wearing a pair of unforgivable gray sweatpants so his "excitement" was easier to detect. Because of the elastic waist-band, I easily slid my available hand down the front of his pants. He didn't fight me off. He didn't try to kiss me. He didn't even seem surprised. I stroked him under the moonlight. He began to pant a bit and kept his eyes shut. It was less than five minutes before he came. When he was finished, he opened his eyes. I witnessed a bit of shame but plenty of relief. I wiped my hands on my shirt and reached up and pulled his open mouth in for a deep, passionate kiss. He wasn't ready for that and pushed me away gently.

"Well, you are welcome, Matthew. Anytime I can 'help' you out, just let me know." I turned seductively away and swayed my hips a bit extra as I headed the opposite way.

Score one for Daisy!

D

April 16, 1988
Dear Diary,

Last night was the worst of my life! My Ben died! How could he leave me just like that? What am I gonna do without him? It wasn't supposed to be like this! I can't do this alone! He promised he would always be here! And in the blink of an eye, he is gone! My heart aches for him. He was my other half! He meant more to me than anyone or anything!

D

April 17, 1988
Dear Diary,

I need to tell you that it was all my fault that he died. We were fighting... or rather, he was yelling at me again. I always seemed to disappoint him. I was never good enough or smart enough for him. I should've never tricked him into this life. He deserved much better. He deserved to be loved and cherished. He was a good man. Too good for me! Too good for this life.

D

April 20, 1988
Dear Diary,

Without him, I am not whole. He was the reason I kept going. He was the reason I thought I could be better. How can I cry for days on end?

Being sober is just too hard...

D

April 25, 1988
Dear Diary,

Well, that little bitch really did it this time. She pushed me and pushed me, so I hissed out the truth about me and Matthew. I ain't ashamed. Proud, actually. I didn't know if I could pull it off, but men are all alike. Even if their head and heart is pure and genuine, their penis is the decisive vote.

Her face revealed it all. I crushed her. My words broke her heart. Her sapphire blue eyes reflected her hatred for me. She deserved it - she was blaming me for Ben's death! What a little bitch! It is one thing to feel guilty about the fight Ben and I had that night right before he died, but she ain't got no right to blame me. Everything is her fault! If it wasn't for her, we would have never been in Normal, Iowa, in the first place. If it wasn't for her, we would have never had Karma following us down every long, lonely road to nowhere.

But the best retribution occurred about an hour later. I telephoned her boytoy. I rambled on and on about how Lily was very upset, and I didn't know what to do. He offered to come over right away, like I knew he would.

When he arrived, she wasn't home from her run yet, so I shed some expected tears and allowed him to console me. Honestly, it felt great to be wrapped up in his big muscular arms. He patted my back and told me everything was going to be alright.

As I was lifting my head from his chest, my lucky high heels proved my point - perfect height for kissing. My wet lips pressed onto his. The sudden kiss was full of passion, and most importantly, he didn't pull away. When we came up for air, I heard him quietly moan. Because this was not my first rodeo, I knew I didn't have any time to lose.

I quickly removed all my clothing right there in the living room

197

except for my lucky red high-heeled shoes. His chest was rising and falling at quick intervals; his nostril opened wide, seeking more air. Boytoy's panting was faint but obvious. From the look in his eyes, I could tell he was very curious about what was about to happen. I don't think his body would allow him to protest. He wanted this to happen, too.

I unbuttoned his jeans and tugged them down to the floor. As I was pulling down his tighty whities, his panting grew heavier and more excited. This poor kid was about to burst. I placed my hand on the 'heart' of his manhood and cupped it. His throat let out a soft, uncontrollable moan. I was going to enjoy giving boytoy his first blow job.

About three minutes into the act, Lily opened the front door. Boytoy was within thirty seconds of climax. Poor kid. To my disappointment, she did not appear appalled or devastated. She acted like she had walked in on us doing a puzzle at the kitchen table, not in the middle of the most intimate act of two lovers. Boytoy's noodle went instantly limp. And my purpose was fulfilled.

D

April 30, 1988
Dear Diary,
After a few drinks tonight, I came home and passed out on the couch. When I woke up, I couldn't stop crying. Ben is gone! Way too early! Way too young! It should've been me.

D

May 15, 1988
Dear Diary,
One benefit to my shenanigans with Matthew is that it opened up new doors. Rather than meeting drunk, dirty, old men at Rusty Nail, now I was finding hot, young, fit bodies at the local park where the younger generation tended to hang out. A few of my regular hookups started calling me, "Mrs. Robinson."

Boytoy and Lily obviously called it quits after our love fest. Her running began to increase along with her cold shoulder. Fine by me! If she didn't talk, then I didn't have to hear how unhappy and disappointed she was in me. The silent treatment was a godsend.

D

August 30, 1988
Dear Diary,

It has been a fun, busy summer. Many 'gentlemen callers' have knocked on my door. These young lads were good for the soul at making me fill the void of having no one to love or call my own. They stroked my deflated ego while I stroked their eager noodles! Ha ha ha! Seriously, very literal reference.

Lily moved out. Her absence didn't make much of a difference in our shared life. It was quiet and lonely while she was here, and it's quiet and lonely now that she is gone. What irks me the most is that she is the reason we have this life, the reason everyone has been so unhappy, the reason we struggle, the reason I've become who I am.

D

Chapter Thirty-Three

1989

I knew it! She was nothing but pure evil. She purposely seduced Matthew and made it almost impossible for him to resist her. Daisy was the serpent in the Bible when Eve is tempted by the serpent to eat from the very tree that God specifically told Adam and Eve not to eat from.

Matthew completely knew right from wrong but like the serpent, Daisy was relentless. I have unfortunately watched her in action and know that men find her irresistible. Not only was she blessed with a beautiful, curvy body, but she also possessed an abundance of seduction techniques that no man (or boy) could resist. And even worse yet was that she recognized her power over them. I am sure she didn't feel any guilt for what she did to Matthew. She viewed it as a game and that she won the game.

How could a mother even consider doing this? What was her true motivation? Revenge on her daughter? Because I somehow unknowingly ruined her life by being born?

I almost...almost felt sorry for Matthew - who she nicknamed "boytoy" in her passages. He was a pawn for her. Nothing more than a chess piece she used to win her own sick and twisted game against her very own daughter. He was vulnerable, only by the fact that his hormones were raging in his body. He inserted himself in those situations alone with her. I had informed him of story after story about how awful she was, how manipulative, and how sneaky. But unfortunately, he learned the hard way - on his own.

I also learned that Daddy was aware of her infidelity and seemed to understand her need to see other men while he was away. Their marriage was like no other I had witnessed or read about. They considered their marriage 'open' which was very hippie-like. However, he knew she was targeting unavailable men. And he simply scolded her! That was not the Daddy I remembered. Maybe he was exhausted by her demons and wild ways and just resorted to scolding her now and then. If what she wrote in her journal was accurate, I was extremely disappointed in Daddy for not sticking up for himself and their 'marriage.' I could never allow anyone to lie and cheat on me like he allowed Daisy to do in their relationship.

Before I could stew too long about the evil that was Daisy, I received a phone call from Dr. Opland. After five weeks in a coma, Mother needed to be transferred to Normal's nursing home facility. Dr. Opland explained that the healing of a brain was extremely complicated and oftentimes very unpredictable.

"For example, when a patient breaks his arm, we can estimate the approximate amount of time that it will take to heal depending on the patient's age, health and the location of the break. For each patient with a broken arm, similar medical procedures are performed, similar treatments are advised, and similar healing takes place in the body. Science and history have proven to show us how to correctly heal a broken bone or torn muscle. However, a patient's brain is unlike any other part of the body. Each person's brain reacts and heals differently. There is no predictable pattern. Recovery and return to normal functioning all depend on the cause of the brain injury and the symptoms that brought on the injury. It will not fully mend like any other bodily injury. Pardon the pun: but the brain has a mind of its own." Dr. Opland chuckled a bit at his own joke.

"If you describe what the brain is to a child, the easiest way might be to characterize it as a big sensitive blob of matter surrounded by live wires of electricity. And in Daisy's case, we can assume that either some of her wires got crossed or worse yet, severed. There is no magic time frame that I can give you, Lily. There is no set pattern of recovery for the brain. I cannot make any promises as to when and if your mother will recover from her injury.

"And unfortunately, we haven't seen any signs of medical improvement to warrant her staying at this hospital under our watchful eye. I'm sorry, Lily, that I don't have better news." Dr. Opland did all he could do for her, I comprehended that. I wasn't sure how much I cared now though. However, if she were able, she would probably consider him just another man that disappointed her and broke her heart.

He explained that she was in a vegetative state, which meant that she didn't respond to any outside stimuli. She hadn't opened her eyes, which some coma patients eventually do in their early stages. When asked to respond by squeezing or blinking, she didn't move. While there had been spikes in her vitals at different times, nothing seemed to indicate that she was still in there. There was no pattern to the raised levels.

Daisy was transferred to Normal's small nursing home on a Friday. The hospital staff assured me that the nursing home staff would take good care of her and get her settled in. I decided to take the weekend off from visiting her. My emotions were completely conflicted, so I easily accepted their advice and let the staff take care of her. I telephoned Kitty at the cafe to see if she needed any help over the weekend.

"Oh honey, you are an absolute angel! I'd love to have the weekend off. Me and Tarasue wanna head to Des Moines for some girl time. When can you come in?"

I picked up four weekend shifts. I could use the money. Our medical insurance would take care of Daisy in the nursing home for the meantime, but I didn't know how I would pay the mortgage and any other outstanding bills that she might have. She might lose the house and her car if I returned to college full-time. Both of our futures were at a standstill.

Since Kitty was like my surrogate mother, I knew that she was worried about me and my well-being. I wasn't surprised that she knew about Daisy's stroke and inquired how I was coping with the whole mess. "You know, honey, I'm here for you anytime or anything. You can always lean on me. I love you like one of my own."

"I know, Kitty, and I really appreciate your love and support. Right now, all I want and need is to be distracted for a while and obviously earn some money."

Thinking about unpaid bills reminded me of her unpaid phone bill with all the calls to Dupe, Texas. So, after I returned home from my Friday shift, I retrieved it from the fridge where I left it. I highlighted a total of twelve phone calls dialed to the same number in Dupe, Texas. I assumed from reading her diary that this phone number was owned by the man that she referred to as 'T'. It was too late to call him now, plus I wasn't really sure what I'd say. Maybe my head would be clearer in the morning to make the call. I was mostly concerned with what colossal secrets 'T' shared with Daisy. But did I want to know? Could my sanity and heart take another secret? What more could Daisy be hiding?

Either way, I wasn't going to uncover the necessary answers that I so desperately wanted. I would only make myself even more crazy by dwelling on the unknown. This wasn't going to be one of the black and white issues that could be resolved easily. I would need to accept that. I might never understand why she did what she did, but I was at least gonna try until I couldn't anymore. The 'why' might always be locked within her, but the 'what' could be discovered with some investigation. My childhood bed welcomed me, and I crawled under the covers.

WHEN I WOKE up after a troubled night of sleep, I decided to gather more intel before I made the phone call to the person Daisy referenced as T. I didn't want to say something that would jeopardize what he might be willing to share with me. He was one of the only people remaining who might have some honest insight into Daisy and what made her become the person she was today. If I didn't ask the right questions, I might hurt my chances of finding the truth. I wasn't ready to do that.

Reading another one of her diaries seemed like the logical next step, but honestly, I needed to be willing to push my own limits. First shock was delivered by Dr. Opland that Daddy wasn't my biological father. After discovering on a cheap piece of lined paper that my own mother detested and blamed me for the awful life she was leading, I wasn't very eager to read much more. That life-altering secret was more than I had bargained for when I started snooping through Daisy's things. Then, to add more salt to the wound, her next journal detailed her seduction of my one and only love, Matthew. Seriously, can you blame me? It was as if I was just standing with my hands behind my back and getting punched in the face. Did I want to submit myself to that again? I wasn't sure how much more my heart could take. The last year of my life had already been one of numerous, extreme heart aches: Daddy's sudden death, breaking up with Matthew after discovering he was sexually involved with my own mother and now the questionable history of my DNA. But then again, how much worse could it get? Could my heart withstand the breakage Mother could inflict on me from her simple words written on paper? My heart might be physically strong, but emotionally, could I suffer another blow?

We were about to find out.

Chapter Thirty-Four

J anuary 1, 1986
    Dear Diary,
        This is the year that I am making changes. I am sick of every-thing being about Lily. Ben only cares about her and what she thinks.

This marriage is a fraud, and I am tired of it. I have tried over and over to make this situation work. But no more. No more New Year's resolutions to make and break only a few weeks later. This year is about me.

D

January 10, 1986
Dear Diary,
I am so glad I decided to make that resolution: 1986, the year of me! Because I figured out today how to start it! Coach Knight - another man that is all about Lily. We bumped into each other at the grocery store.

I helped him find the nutmeg. He had no idea what it was. He looked lost in the produce aisle. I steered him to the spices, where I intentionally dropped the little spice, bent over, and gave him a good look right up my short skirt. Lucky for him, all my underwear was dirty. There were definite sparks. His cheeks were a nice shade of pink, and I noticed he needed to lean into his cart to walk down the aisle. He used it a bit like a crutch! Ha!

I am sure I can turn his head to my direction easily enough. After all, I have been making men do what I want for ages. But I need to make this interesting and fun. The married ones are eager to please and enjoy the attention, but sometimes too easy to seduce since they are so desperate. Coach Knight, you are my bunny and I am the coyote. This will be fun.

I am sure you will be cheering my name soon, rather than my daughter's!

D

January 11, 1986

Dear Diary,

It was conference night at school. Normally, this type of event holds no interest for me at all. However, there is a new stake in the game. So, when I informed Lily that I planned on meeting with her teachers, she flew off the handle and begged me not to go. She would do anything, she said.

"Well, charming daughter, if I embarrass you that much, then I must go and make sure that everyone knows that I am indeed your mother." She must have known she wasn't going to change my mind, so she asked me if I would at least change clothes. Oh, hell no! I grabbed my purse and added a new coat of red lipstick. I strutted out of the house in my thigh high black boots, short black leather shirt, and a fuzzy, pink V-neck sweater that showed off that my bra was about two cups too small. I had not realized that I was going to enjoy this adventure so much.

When I arrived at the high school, the hallways were rather deserted. However, I had only intended on visiting Coach Knight and didn't need an audience for this interaction. After looking over the school map, I found his classroom: A11. He was alone reading the *local newspaper at his desk. I think I startled him a bit. I am sure the school had a record of my flawless no attendance policy.*

I slid down into the hard, wooden chair on the opposite side of his desk. I think he needed to distract himself from my presence because he got right down to school business. Lily was an excellent student, attentive listener, wonderful participant, and smart as a whiz. Blah blah blah... then he continued with how much he enjoyed coaching her on the track team as well. I tried to listen attentively - like he praised Lily for doing - and nodded in all the right places. I was bored stiff. I was more interested in Coach Knight and how attentive he could be.

"I am sure you are aware that I recruited Lily for the track team when she was in grade school." He raised his bushy brown eyebrows as if I should know this fact, but I did not. I tried to be the least involved in Lily's affairs as possible.

"Of course, I knew that. Lily mentions you all the time. Coach Knight this... Coach Knight that... it is like you are famous or something." I flirtatiously batted my eyelashes at him.

"Well, great! I didn't want to come off inappropriately fascinated by your daughter, but I am. Fascinated, that is. She is extremely talented and highly intelligent. I have enjoyed getting to know her and watching her grow up. Again, sorry if that came out creepy. I just wanted to compliment you on a job well done. You and your husband have done a wonderful job raising Lily." Coach Knight's praises would have normally given a typical mother a warm, proud heart; however, for me, that compliment about Lily added more fuel to my fire. I was going to turn this man to Team Daisy sooner than later.

D

March 20, 1986
Dear Diary,
Things are finally heating up. Lily was invited to Coach Knight's house for dinner, and to my luck, Coach Knight drove her home afterwards. I was dressed for the spontaneous visit: no bra and my favorite worn out t-shirt.

After Lily excused herself and retreated to her bedroom to work on her homework, the temperature in the living room peaked. Coach Knight tried to talk about Lily's running and what I could do as the woman of the house to help, but his eyes were hungry, and I could tell he was a bit distracted. I have seen this look often at Rusty Nail. These were the men who were neglected at home and starved for attention. They were able and ever so willing to please. I decided it would only benefit me more if I teased him for a while longer.

D

April 20, 1986
Dear Diary,
Soon, Coach Knight surrendered to me and my devilish ways - my endless teasing, flirting and taunting had worked. He gave in to his desires way too easily and quickly. My customers at Rusty Nail had much more stamina than Coach did.

He surprisingly showed up on my doorstep two days after I wore my crop top to Lily's first sophomore track meet. I jumped up and down when I noticed my cheering for her caused him to look in my direction. After his stare lingered seconds too long, I awarded him a flirtatious wink and blew him a kiss. I'm sure other parents in the crowd were shocked by my sudden appearance along with my visible excitement. I'm sure they assumed I was drunk and simply excited about Lily winning yet another damn race. They couldn't be more wrong.

Two days after Lily earned three first-place medals for running circles on that track, her coach decided to pay me a little visit. Unfortunately for him, I was nursing a nasty hangover and was still lazing on our couch. After he aggressively rang the doorbell three times, I hollered.

"Geez! I'm coming! Don't get your panties in a wad!" When I yanked the door open, Coach stood nervous as a hooker in church on a hot July day. Right away, I apologized for my rude remarks and invited him into our living room.

"I have coffee or water, Coach. Would you like a cup?"

"No… no.. I'm fine. And call me Max. I'm not truly certain what I'm doing here. Well, I know why I'm here, but I'm not certain how I got here. Actually, that is incorrect too. I drove here, that's how I got here. But I shouldn't be here. I just couldn't get you out of my head. I'm sure you get this all the time… admirers just showing up unannounced at your doorstep. You're amazing, gorgeous and so free." He paused long enough that his voice of reason - his own Benny - must have been heard inside of his head. "Gosh… I should go. I shouldn't be here, Mrs. Armstrong." He was very flustered and uncomfortable, that much was completely obvious.

I had to make a split-second decision. I could have him - I won - or I could tell him to go. I could admit that I taunted and teased him because I wanted him here, or I could send him on his way knowing that I won. Lucifer surprisingly agreed with Benny to let him go. The challenge was over, and I wasn't that interested in him anymore anyway.

But this time, I didn't listen to either voice. I reached out and grabbed his hand as he was turning away.

"Don't go. Let's have some fun, Max."

D

May 2, 1986
Dear Diary,
Because I work evenings at the Rusty Nail and Max teaches during the day, our extracurricular activities occur during his planning period at school. He sneaks over to our house as soon as the third period ends, rips off my clothes and ravishes my body. And by fifth period, he returns to school, and I go about my day.

D

May 29, 1986
Dear Diary,
I'll admit that now that the challenge is over, I'm rather bored with

this thick, easy-to-please, ordinary man. The sex is fine, but what he could do for me any man at Rusty Nail could accomplish.

D

June 1, 1986

Dear Diary,

Even though in my youth I believed that I wanted a normal family, husband and several kids, I recognized that that fact had changed. I was hardened by all my experiences and was not cut out for a normal, boring, one-man relationship. How did I know this? Did I not learn anything from Tony's lies and deception and now Max's possessiveness and neediness?

After a few weeks of 'rolling in the hay' - as he referred to it - Max asked me to quit my job at the Rusty Nail. He didn't appreciate me working there with all the low lifes of the town. Ironic, since Tony preferred me working there to identify clientele.

"You're being ridiculous, Max. You're married to another woman and me to another man. I don't think you should be concerned with my virtues. You sure weren't concerned about my virtues ten minutes ago."

This little argument with him was kinda fun. I knew he truly cared for me and not just for sex. He wanted to talk and get to know each other better. I think he thought we were dating. But honestly, his over-protectiveness was getting on my nerves. Never had I been told what I can and cannot do with my adult body. "Daisy, I am serious. You should quit working there."

"That's a hard 'no.' I make excellent money, and I like my job."

"I'll pay you whatever you make there to supplement your income. Then you can stop because you won't need it anymore." He thought, just like all other men, that he had all the answers. He could solve my problems, even though I didn't have any.

"So, I'll be your 'kept mistress.' Wow, Max! I feel very special."

"It isn't like that! I want to see you do better than the Rusty Nail is all."

And he thought paying me to be 'on-call' for our afternoon bangs was better than drinking for free, hanging with my friends and taking off my clothes in a bar. We have a difference in opinion.

D

September 3, 1986
Dear Diary,

Max surprised me this evening. He knew I wasn't scheduled at Rusty Nail, Ben was away at work, and Lily was waitressing at the cafe. He arrived with a bouquet of daisies - real original - a bottle of my favorite wine and assorted chocolates. He claimed it was our six-month anniversary. Dear Lord, this man is a sap! But I ate it up. No one had ever treated me like a girlfriend. Honestly, in most of my past relationships, I felt like more of a hooker. With Tony, we were always banging quickly and roughly. Max was tender and sweet. Which was completely not my type. I couldn't let this continue. What if he wanted to leave his wife and kids for me? Oh, hell no! I have to end this!

During the heat of the moment, we lost his truck keys somewhere in the house. We couldn't find them anywhere. He used our home phone to call his wife to come pick him up. His excuse for being here was that he was helping Lily with edits on her speech. He parked in the alley, so he met her by his pickup when she came with the extra set of keys. No questions asked. It is incredibly sad how much these women trust their men.

D

September 10, 1986
Dear Diary,

I truly planned on telling Max it was over, but sex got in the way. And yesterday afternoon's sex was extraordinary. Not sure why he was holding back. We met at the river for a little picnic. One thing led to another, and we were making animal noises in the weeds. It was hot and sexy!

Anyway, it is no excuse, but damn! I am glad I kept him around for that!

D

September 20, 1986
Dear Diary,
The nerve! That sap of a man broke up with me! I know we aren't keeping score, but he had the nerve to tell me that it was for the best. We were both married with families. He needed to focus on his family and his job.

"I'm so sorry, Daisy. It's hard for me to call this relationship a mistake because I had real strong feelings for you, but it was a mistake to act on those feelings. We need to forget each other and act like we never meant anything to each other. I need to continue to be in Lily's life as her coach, not her mother's lover. She is important to me, and I hope you understand that."

Seriously, was this man for real? Good riddance! I can't believe another man put Lily before me again! Whatever!

D

September 22, 1986
Dear Diary,
Lily has been acting strange. Stranger and colder toward me than normal. I can't quite put my finger on it, but I can sense it. She claims she is preoccupied with her schoolwork. She does take school very seriously, but she doesn't have any problems with her grades. Reminds me of myself when I was younger and thought I had the world at my fingertips.

D

October 5, 1986
Dear Diary,

Do you believe in Karma? I sure do! And she hates me. She is like Mother Nature, all bossy and selfish. When she wants someone to listen, she will throw a thunderstorm of a tantrum. Karma has never been a friend to me. She has crushed my dreams. She has burnt bridges. Karma has sabotaged anything good that might have ever developed in my life.

What Karma has taught me is that if she gives you a gift, you will pay the price if you accept what she offers. Kinda like working with the devil. Here are some examples of how Karma has controlled my life:

1. *"Yo Daisy, wanna finally meet the man of your dreams? Here he is, and he is crazier than you."*
2. *Before that: "Here, Daisy, enjoy this house for your family. But wait! You will need to give up your dignity and self-respect for it!"*
3. *Travel back in my memory a little further: "Hey, Daisy! Your husband loves his job fixing things. But wait! This lonely, creepy old man is here to violate you."*
4. *Travel even further back: "Hey, Daisy! Remember this tender, sweet man who was married with three children. Wait! Here is a heart attack and he is gone."*

Yeah, Karma is a bitch.

D

Chapter Thirty-Five

1989

The first time that Daisy reacted to her surroundings while she was in her coma, no one even noticed it. Her vitals spiked, but by the time anyone discovered the elevation, we didn't know what triggered it so there was no way to know if she was reacting to stimuli or some type of healing was occurring in her damaged brain. I would figure out later after careful examination of recalling daily events that the initial vital spike occurred after the first conversation that I tried to have with Daisy informing her that I found her diaries. The next reaction didn't come until weeks later after she had been transferred to the nursing home, Cornbelt Nursing Care.

I was sitting in my usual spot in the stiff visitor's chair in the corner of her room. I did my best to make it as comfortable as possible by using a few pillows from home to give the chair some padding. I brought an old blanket from home as well. It was an ugly, green afghan that I found in the back of the hallway closet. It clearly needed a good washing before I brought it into the nursing home; it smelled musty and a bit like limes. I figured if it got lost, no one would miss the ugly thing. But then again, who would steal it?

I was curled up in my converted chair reading a novel. I must have dozed off a bit when I heard a familiar voice.

"Sorry to disturb you, Lily. I just got off work and wanted to visit my favorite patient in her new digs." It was Nurse Jenny from the hospital. It was hard for me to admit, but it was nice to see a familiar, friendly face. Nurse Jenny had been wonderful to me as well as to Daisy. With her big smile and outgoing attitude, she made the day brighter.

"Hi, Jenny. Thanks for coming by." I yawned and stretched out of my little chair.

Nurse Jenny approached Daisy's bed, grabbed a hold of her veiny hand and gave it a gentle little squeeze. "Hey, there, Daisy. You're looking good. Wanted to bounce over and say hello. Everyone at the hospital in Madison misses you." She glanced in my direction and gave me a little wink. "I can tell Lily is taking good care of you. She is worried about you, Daisy. You should sit up and give her some hell. I bet you are good at that as a mother."

Nurse Jenny took her nursing oath to help and serve others to her very core. She was off work and still checking in on past patients. This truly was her passion in life. She was devoted to caring for others. I hoped one day that I loved my profession as much as she loved hers.

"Lily, you honestly look like crap." *Ahhhh... Nurse Jenny, so good of you to visit.* Her blunt form of honesty made me smile. She knew I appreciated it. We got to know each other after five weeks in the hospital.

A big grin spread across my make-up free face. "Ummm... thanks?"

She burst out into her unique, hearty laugh. She was still holding Daisy's hand, but there was no visual reaction coming from Daisy.

"You do, Lily. You are a pretty, young thing, but even you young-sters need sleep and healthy food. What is the last healthy thing you ate? A carrot?" No one ever answered her questions. She didn't give anyone a chance. "You need a good home-cooked meal that includes all four food groups. And Cheetos isn't one of them." She knew my weakness: Cheetos and ice cream. We previously had a lively banter about Cheetos being a dairy option. I knew what I was doing, but it had been slightly amusing watching her get all worked up about it.

She patted Daisy's limp hand one last time before she released her grasp. She directed all of her focused attention on me. "I have tomorrow off. I will cook a well-balanced meal for you. You come over at five. I won't take no for an answer." She grabbed the pen and tablet that I had sitting next to me and jotted down her home address. "I will see you tomorrow night at five."

When she exited the room, I could only smile. She was a feisty, petite ball of energy. Nurse Jenny was not someone to argue with, not because she was scary but because she was relentless and never stopped talking long enough for someone to get a word in. She could talk her way out of a sticky situation, just because the other person would become exhausted or tired of her constant chatter. But over the last five weeks while Mother was in a coma, I had usually welcomed her energy and positive attitude. She seemed to grow stronger and louder by every interaction she had. Her energy grew from other people; it was a snowball effect.

"Well, Daisy, I guess I have dinner plans tomorrow night, so don't wait up."

It had gotten dark outside. Time to head home. I wasn't sure why I felt the need to sit with her each day. Maybe I needed to contact my college and get back to classes.

WHEN I RETURNED the next morning to visit Daisy, I decided I would follow through with Nurse Jenny's advice and 'talk' to her. The nurses at the nursing home checked on her less frequently than the hospital nurses. It would give me more time to muster up the nerve to spill everything out without being interrupted. When I entered her room, the first thing I noticed was the faint smell of urine which a huge dose of Lysol was trying to disguise and the fact that Daisy was not in her bed. Daisy was not in her room.

Standing in the doorway, my brain couldn't process her sudden absence. While my brain tried to comprehend what my eyes were interpreting, my size seven feet would not move. *Did she die? Did someone move her back to the hospital? What happened? Where is she? Even her bedding is stripped. Did she finally wake up and simply walk out?*

A nursing staff member who was pushing another older resident in a squeaky wheelchair noticed my internal struggle in the doorway of Daisy's room.

"Hey, you there." I turned my head around to the direction of her stern, raspy voice. She paused only for a moment to tell me what happened. "Daisy wet herself, so Beatrice took her down the hall for a quick hose down. She will be back shortly." With that odd and quick explanation, she continued her trip down the long hallway.

The male resident who sat hunched over in his wheelchair moaned and quietly mumbled under his breath, "My body is a car, and the exhaust keeps backfiring."

The grumpy nurse, who seemed to have a soft spot for him, giggled and commented, "Mr. Horner, you are a rare one!"

I breathed a sigh of relief. Nothing happened to her. She was still alive... if you wanna call what state her body was in *alive*. Why did I care? I hated her, and it was obvious she detested me as well. Yet, I was not ready to say goodbye. This little scare proved that I had unresolved issues that I needed to get off my chest. I decided to get myself settled into my little cove in the corner of the room that Daisy now called home. Everything was white: white walls, white mattress, white lamp shade next to her bed, white blinds and white curtains.

White lies.

"HI, Daisy. Honestly, I am rather glad you don't open your eyes or respond at all to what is happening around you. Your coma makes having a conversation with you much easier and actually more enjoyable. It comes as no surprise to you that we have never been close. I never wanted to have a heart-to-heart with you. I always preferred Daddy. I am not sure why you always held me at a distance. You never wanted to get too close to me, physically or emotionally. I have no idea what I ever did to you to make you hate me so much." I brought a thermos filled with cold water, so I drew a long pull from it. I don't know why I felt so nervous about having this conversation with her. It wasn't like she was going to bolt awake and argue with me. I did some research on my own at the local library. If she ever did wake up, it would most likely happen in stages. Research was also questionable about whether she would actually remember what she heard while she was in the coma.

My nervousness could be chalked up to me always avoiding these deep, dark feelings about Daisy. Once I said it out loud, it was 'out there' - no take-backs. It is easier to stuff these unkind feelings deep down, never to see the light of day. The people I grew up with around Normal never mentioned Daisy or asked me about her. They knew it was a taboo topic. When I started college, that was new territory. My rehearsed response was, "I grew up in Normal, Iowa. My dad died, and my mom and I aren't close." Simple, short and honest.

As I took a few minutes to regain my composure, wipe the few surprise tears that leaked from my eyes and gain back the momentum, I continued talking out loud to the shell of Daisy's body.

"You're an enormous disappointment as a mother. Not only were you never there for me emotionally, but you have also never shown me a bit of interest, love or respect. You're an ice queen with a hollow heart. I remember drawing you pictures to hang on our refrigerator, and you hardly gave them a glance before I discovered them crumpled up in the trash. You never attended my sporting events, my choir concerts or even planned a birthday party for me. You were emotionally turned off as a mother. It's as if there is a parent switch on you, and your switch was permanently off. Every young girl needs and wants her mother's love and affection. You were supposed to be my first best friend. Other friends from school relied on their mothers for advice for everything from boys to homework. I knew I was on my own. You were either too busy or completely uninterested. You let me down."

I wasn't sure where all these pent-up feelings were coming from. I had always considered her indifference normal, my reality. I accepted it because I acknowledged there was nothing, I could do about it. Was I happy about it? Obviously not.

"I'm not sure why I keep torturing myself by visiting you every day. I'm a glutton for punishment, I guess. Still hoping after all of these years that you'll confirm that you love me, apologize for all the wrongs, or even grab me in a big bear hug." And then the animal noises escaped from my throat again. I'd never cried this much my whole life as I had this past year.

"I've located your very personal and - might I add - disturbing reflections about your life and everyone in it. Maybe I'll finally discover who you are. Yes, Daisy, you heard me right: I found your diaries. What an enlightening read. You didn't hide them very well. But then again, I'm sure you had no idea that you were gonna have a massive stroke, end up in a coma while your sketchy life that you have done such a good job at hiding would now be on full display." I wasn't sure if it was my imagination, or did the right side of her face twitch?

"Keeping the fact that Daddy was not my biological father from me was cruel and selfish. How could you do that? Who is my father? Do you even know? I can't believe you would withhold that information from me! I would like to believe you had a good reason, but unfortunately, I am probably giving you way too much credit. Maybe I'll find out the truth in your journals. Your secrets and deception are no longer safe. I plan on exploring everything that makes Daisy Armstrong tick. Wish me luck."

I decided this was enough honesty for one day. I was full on crying now and didn't feel she deserved to witness my tears even in a state of unconsciousness. She caused them, but I wasn't going to allow her to tear me apart like this in a public setting. By being honest, I had to open my heart to reveal my pain. It had been sealed shut where Daisy was concerned for so long. A tiny crack opened, and I wanted to go home and super glue it back together.

Chapter Thirty-Six

1989

The clock struck loudly - it was decision time for me and the future. Administration at the college contacted me via phone and letter asking me to inform them about my intentions. Meanwhile, I had been collecting Daisy's bills and calculating what I needed financially to hold onto my current life. If I wanted to continue with my future plans - my college career - I needed to consider selling my childhood home and Daisy's car in order to pay for the nursing home and medical bills. Our situation looked bleak.

Following my one-sided conversation with Daisy, I was fried. I was exhausted by the diarrhea of feelings that I had bottled up and vomited out of my mouth. Quality alone time was necessary to sort through my life that was cracking bit by bit. My daily visits to Daisy halted while I collected my thoughts and feelings. I picked up some shifts at Kitty's Cafe, called the college administration office and discussed my return, and of course entertained myself with her diaries.

The next diary that I read was labeled, 'My dedication to 1987.' It more or less contained ramblings about how awful her life was, how everyone else was to blame and how she wished she could go back in time to change everything. She hated everything Lily-related, and literally wished that I had never been born. Nothing new. I learned nothing of significance, nothing she had not already complained about in her other diaries.

I no longer harbored any guilt about invading Daisy's privacy. She admitted to doing the exact same thing to me when she was collecting information for her seduction of Matthew. Like mother, like daughter, I guess. She found my private thoughts and used them against me. I did feel, however, that my reasoning was more appropriate - she simply wanted revenge. My snooping was to gather information regarding my life and the secrets my own mother chose to hide from me, while she snooped and gathered information to ruin a perfectly innocent, youthful relationship that was just budding into something magical and possibly long-lasting.

I had a difficult time dealing with that revelation. She researched, plotted and then completely destroyed another innocent person to punish me - for what, I still couldn't quite grasp. She was jealous of the attention that I received from other people, mainly men. To ruin my relationship with another teenager, she was willing to ruin her own reputation. Okay, that might be a bit of an exaggeration. She managed to ruin her reputation around Normal long before I even started dating Matthew.

People whispered about her, blatantly stared at her as she walked by and some even pointed their 'shame' fingers. I heard them whispering. I was aware of what they were saying about her and also about me as her daughter. I was the town whore's daughter. They wondered about me and my morals as well. "The apple never falls far from the tree."

However, I never added any fuel to the fire. I was quiet, polite and kept my head down. I gave them no reason to gossip about me. Daisy gave them enough material to work with for the both of us.

Some of the rumors that ran through the streets of Normal were legitimate. Not only was she a regular employee at the town's notorious strip club, but she also was often seen on the outskirts of town meeting up with men - some married, some customers of the bar.

Perhaps doing extra dances or favors for them in their truck beds, behind a barn or even in the corn fields. Daisy seemed to have no boundaries when it came to sex and whom she would practice it with.

Getting to know her through her private writings painted a colorful, more accurate picture that she was in fact worthy of all the finger-pointing and gossiping. People put the obvious puzzle pieces together. Conclusions were established, and unfortunately Daisy did nothing to prove them wrong. She simply did exactly what she wanted to do with no concern for others. She didn't care who she hurt along the way. If she was emotionally or physically pleased, that was all that mattered to her.

In her self-destructive wake, Daddy and I were the ones to suffer. Of course, I heard the whispers around town and the name calling. I suffered because people assumed that I was like her since I looked like her and carried the same DNA. I was judged, tried and hung before I could even grow up and make my own decisions. At the top of the suffering list, though, was Daddy. He was the one who still believed that she was deep down a good person, worthy of his love and devotion. He encouraged her to be better, try harder and believe in herself. Daddy was her loyal, constant cheerleader.

He was gone now, and I couldn't do it. Not anymore. Seeing into her soul like I was able to do from reading her journals made me realize how broken and blackened her heart really was. I wasn't even sure she was worth saving or fighting for. I read her diaries lately due to pure curiosity. I wanted to see if I could discover what made her tick, where her life took a hard turn.

While I was learning more about Daisy, I was also discovering things about myself. When Daddy died of his sudden fatal heart attack, his death shook me to my core. Physically, it felt like a broken bone. Piercing pain shot up and down my body. Instant tears poured out of my blue eyes. My breath caught in my throat. Physical weakness took over my limbs. My heart ached, knowing I would never be able to see the love and adoration for me in his eyes again. It was a grief like no other I had ever felt. I literally felt out of control of my emotions and purely reacted with vulnerability and a broken heart. He was my world and wouldn't be here to share it with me. The grief that consumed me was normal and textbook.

A different type of grief can happen over the course of a long period of time. Grief doesn't have any rules as to when it will take place and how long a stage lasts. Psychologists believe there are five stages of grief: denial, anger, bargaining, depression and acceptance. Grief doesn't only happen with death. It can be any type of loss. For example: a loss of a job, a loss of a loved one, a loss of normalcy, or a loss of a relationship.

I experienced a long drawn-out grief with my mother-daughter relationship with Daisy. When I was a young child, she performed the necessary motherly tasks of reading a book, changing diapers and feeding me with a spoon. Somewhere along the way, she lost her nurturing instinct, or perhaps I became more aware of her weaknesses as a mother. I am still trying to discover what happened. Preferably, I'd like to believe that it was that something happened to her ability rather than that I did something so wicked to make her stop loving me. It was obvious to me through her journals that she detested everything about me, but she did struggle with the guilt of not loving me. There was a bit of a human quality in her.

Honestly, maybe my innocence and youth clouded my childhood memories and feelings. The first stage of grief is denial. But a child wouldn't know the difference, would not understand completely what was happening. I denied anything was wrong. A child would simply compare other mother-daughter relationships by simple observations: "my mommy doesn't like to hold my hand" or "my mommy never tells me that she loves me."

My childhood denial created excuses for the lack of motherly behavior. "My mommy doesn't hold my hand or tell me that she loves me all the time because I am a big girl and don't need her to hold my hand. Plus, I know she loves me." Denying that there is even a problem; denying that things are different. **Denial.**

As a child, I started to act out as I became aware of her lack of attention and love. My first best friend abruptly ended our friendship because Daisy was sleeping with men other than her own husband, and the whole town noticed it. That wasn't the first time her life choices affected my relationships, but it was the first time I was actually angry. I was angry that my mother couldn't be like all the other mothers. I started to realize that she wasn't someone I could be proud of. I started to realize that it was better that she didn't walk me to school, hold my hand or accompany me to the park. Even though I realized these harsh facts, I was still upset.

Not long after Genevieve informed me that our friendship was over, Daisy hadn't returned home after going out with her friends. I struggled to stay awake on the couch waiting for her to arrive home safely. I had fallen asleep and woke up to the morning sunshine peeking through the living room windows. No sign of her. That wasn't the first time she had left me home alone as a young child - legally too young to be home alone - but it was the first time my worry was lessened by my intense anger.

That morning as I was brushing my teeth, I heard the front door open and her high heels stumble in the house. She giggled when she tripped, and soon, I heard her fall onto the same couch I had waited on for her all night. When I came down the stairs, I saw her lying on the couch without a care in the world. Oblivious to everyone around her. Especially me. She was already passed out on the couch. Usually, I would remove her shoes, place a pillow under her head and cover her with a blanket; however, this time my teeth were clenched, my nostrils flared with air, and my heartbeat heavily in my chest.

I ripped out every page of Daisy's latest *Cosmopolitan* magazine that I had collected from our mailbox the afternoon before. She loved her juicy magazine filled with articles on how to please your man, how to put the right amount of makeup on your eyelids and how to land the perfect job. All BS! I wanted her to know I was mad. I didn't hide my destruction; I left it right next to her as she was passed out on the couch. **Anger.**

My bargaining phase began when Daisy started dragging me to church to see Pastor Tony. In Bible School, we were taught to talk to

God, pray to him. He was always listening. I prayed and prayed again and prayed again.

"Dear God, if you'll make Daisy love me, I promise to never say a swear word ever again." Or "Dear God, if you make Daisy stop flirting with Pastor Tony and just love only Daddy, I'll take out the garbage every night without complaining." Or "Dear God, if you can make my mother like Tarasue's mom, Kitty, I'll never stop believing in you."

In this grief stage, it is often common to make promises to a higher power hoping that someone else had the power to intervene. My prayers were raised in the hope that God could make changes in Daisy. I was desperate and wanted my childhood to be filled with love, trust and honesty. **Bargaining.**

When I reflect back on my subconscious grieving about the lack of a mother-daughter relationship, I recognize that depression arrived as soon as I accepted that God couldn't change Daisy. Even though He beckoned her to His church, He was unable to control her immoral thoughts and desires. God had no more control over Daisy than Daddy or I did. I needed to accept that Daisy could only change if she wanted to, and that even though God cleared a straight path for her to follow Him, Daisy's normal patterns of behavior and low morals won. Accepting that I would never have a normal, healthy relationship with Daisy crushed my hope. Without hope, I was depressed and gave up. I abandoned the notion of ever having a normal, healthy relationship with her. **Depression and acceptance.**

FOR SEVEN DAYS, I didn't visit her at the nursing home. I had given her a piece of my mind and my heart the last time I saw her. Now, I needed a little break from feeling so raw and vulnerable. Additionally, I wasn't sure if I believed Nurse Jenny, that Daisy could hear me while she was in the coma. Perhaps I got all upset for nothing except to get it off my chest.

During my time away, Kitty scheduled me to waitress at the cafe. It was good to get my mind off my troubles. The tips would help ease the burden of the mounting medical bills. In fact, one particular evening really formed a dent.

Weeknights were filled with the regulars coming in for their routine night off from cooking. Customers loved to tell me why they were eating out on a weeknight. It seemed like they needed an excuse. That evening, I heard the best excuse from Ava Jean, who owned a flower shop in Normal.

"I bought a hundred dollars in groceries today, but when I got home, all I had was ingredients." Ava Jean and her husband Kelvin were Tuesday night regulars. If they didn't come into the cafe on a Tuesday night for supper, Kitty would have called the local sheriff so he could pay their farm a visit to make sure they were okay.

That Tuesday dinner shift was like any other Tuesday on the calendar. The restaurant buzzed with constant chatter. Aromas from Hank's cooking awakened many taste buds. The same regulars filled the cafe, ordering their same dinners. The same friends enjoyed each other's company and shared stories about the weather and town gossip.

The shift flowed like clockwork. No spills, no broken glass, no fires. Nothing out of the ordinary. Until five minutes past seven when a very tall, thin, well-dressed gentleman walked in. The only reason I noticed the time was because Ava Jean and Kelvin always paid their dinner bill at seven o'clock so they could be home in their matching La-Z-Y Boy recliners in time to watch their favorite TV show, *The Wonder Years*, which started at half past seven.

As the gentleman dressed in a long tan overcoat pulled the door handle, the door chimes rang to announce the entrance of a new guest. I made my way over to the door with a menu.

"Hi. Welcome to Kitty's Cafe. Would you like a table or a booth?" I politely greeted the newest customer. His overcoat was covering up his light blue button-down shirt and black dress pants. He appeared dressed for a church service. He looked vaguely familiar, but I couldn't put my finger on where I had seen him before. He seemed a bit lost and out of sorts. At the sound of my voice, his aging facial expression reflected confusion or perhaps wonder. His mouth formed an 'O' shape, and his shockingly blue eyes widened in surprise. Even his eyebrows rose slightly.

As he tried to regain his composure, he cleared his throat and answered, "A booth would be my preference." His voice was deep and hearty, like a heavy smoker. Just by his response, I could tell he was a man who chose his words carefully. Normally, if a man who was a perfect stranger stared at me as intensely and firmly as he was, goosebumps and warning signals would have flared up. But neither of those alert signals even transmitted. However, I noticed his blue eyes seemed to be enlarged perhaps because he was high or in some state of shock. I didn't know which, but honestly, at the time, I didn't care.

I guided him to booth three and laid the menu down on the table where a party of one would normally choose to sit on - the side facing the door. Unless they were hiding from someone, then they would choose not to face the door. He sat down in front of the carefully placed menu. Good, not hiding from anyone.

"The soup of the day is chicken noodle, and Kitty made her famous Prairie Melody Pie. I will grab you some water and come back for your order." He held my eye during my entire spiel; he did not waver.

In self-defense class, we were taught to hold your aggressor's gaze so that you don't show signs of vulnerability or fear. The majority of the time, the attacker becomes intimated and looks away - ultimately, then they will not attack.

This man didn't look away. His wide blue eyes continued to stare at me. I figured I better warn Kitty that we might have a little trouble with this customer if his high wore off or whatever was agitating him reached a striking mark.

"Kitty, just a heads up, that dude in booth number three is either on a great trip or something crawled up his butt. He is a bit off. Seems harmless but thought I would give you a heads up." Kitty was balancing her business checkbook at the counter while I started to put ice and water in one of our restaurant glasses that looked like glass but were actually plastic.

Dressed in her usual attire of bell-bottoms and floral blouse, she glanced nonchalantly towards his booth. "Oh darling, just be your regular, charming self. You will win him right over from the dark side. You could charm a snake charmer. But just in case he is immune to your witchery, I will keep my eye on him, darling." She flashed me one of her famous winks and ushered me with a slight nod of her head back out onto the cafe floor.

If I was being honest, I wasn't really worried about him, but it was always good to know someone had my back. Plus, I had been wrong about people before. This would not be the first time that I misjudged someone and was fooled by their actions or intentions.

I gently placed the glass of ice water in front of him, presenting him with one of my fill-your-face kind of smiles before I inquired, "Have you decided what you are hungry for? If not, the BLT and chicken fried steak are a couple of my favorites." My focused smile stayed plastered across my face. Who knows, maybe he only needed someone, even a stranger, to show him some kindness and he would feel better. Maybe his pained expression would lessen. Maybe Kitty was right.

Before he answered, he peeked quickly at the menu, but I don't think he even read a word on the page. "A piece of the recommended Prairie Melody Pie with some vanilla ice cream would be fabulous. And a small cup of coffee if the pot is still on. Please." He attempted to smile and for a second the shocked, troubled look on his face eased. He was a goodlooking man in his fifties with gray strands glittering on his full head of hair. When he tried to smile, I again noticed his piercing, blue eyes. They reminded me of marbles, very unique.

"Good choice. And yes, we still have coffee. I will get you a cup while I warm up the pie." I removed the menu from the table, gave him a slight nod, turned on my heel and headed to place his order with the kitchen.

"I'm sorry, Miss, but I didn't get your name."

I heard him ask for my name as I was headed the other way, so I turned my head slightly to answer him. "Lily. And I will be right back with your coffee."

I heard him mumble my first name under his breath. He mumbled it again. And then out of nowhere, the dreaded goosebumps rose on my forearms. The hairs on my arms were standing straight up. Where did that come from? It was the way he said my name... as if my first name completed a deep, dark mystery for him - my first name was the answer to his riddle. My first name was the missing puzzle piece. It was eerie.

By nine o'clock when Kitty's Cafe closed, I initiated the closing tasks. I disinfected the tabletops, refilled the salt and pepper shakers, restocked the shelves and collected my tips. Booth number three was the last booth that received my attention. The strange man had snuck out the front door while I was serving another set of customers their meal. I thought nothing of his quiet departure except that if he stiffed me, it would come directly out of my paycheck. Previously, when I noticed he was gone, I glanced over to that booth and noticed a couple of bills under his coffee cup. I was relieved. A piece of pie and a cup of coffee didn't cost much, but I still needed all the money I could get. Plus, it was the principle of being stiffed.

He departed before I could drop off his bill, which totaled two dollars and five cents for the pie and coffee. I picked up his empty coffee cup and pie plate, which was practically licked clean - he must have agreed with me that Kitty's pies were fabulous - and placed them on my waitress tray.

Out of the corner of my eye, I caught Benjamin Franklin's face smiling back at me. And it took a minute to process. George Washington was normally the president to bless my tip jar but Benjamin - never! And there were two of him.

The strange man, whom I judged as high or in a state of shock, left me two hundred dollars for his tab of two dollars and five cents. Even though he exited the cafe over an hour ago, my head quickly jerked to the door to see if he was still around and could explain this enormous amount of money. Of course, it was only me and Hank left in the cafe at closing time. No piercing blue eyes were staring back at me through the big picture window. I was left with no answers. My perception of this stranger went from frightening and fearful, to sad and lonely, to generous and mysterious. My character judgment was completely off.

No matter why this man thought he should leave me this huge

amount of money, I did not feel worthy. I had judged him and awarded him no special attention except that I was leerier and more suspicious of him. Kitty was never going to believe this. I hardly could either. The fashionably dressed man, who stared at me as if I was a ghost or something, gifted me with the biggest tip I had ever received and left without an explanation.

My life was currently filled with mystery everywhere I turned.

Chapter Thirty-Seven

January 1, 1971

Dear Diary,

So many late-night moves. So many small towns. So many harsh words. So many times, I wanted to run away. So many regrets. So little sleep.

And to top off my negative attitude, I can't find my 1970 journal anywhere! Not sure if we forgot it during one of our rushed middle-of-the-night moves, because we couldn't pay rent - again. Not sure if it was thrown out in the trash. Not sure if it was abandoned in Montana, Idaho or Colorado. A lot of things I'm not sure of these days.

One thing that I do know for sure is that whoever finds it - one of our previous landlords or the next tenant - is gonna get more than she bargained for when she picks up an innocent looking notebook to take a quick gander at what its contents might be. I am sure my reader was appalled by what has happened to my once happy, typical life. I'm sure my honest, unfiltered words shocked her.

"Who is this poor author of such terrible circumstances? Where is she now? How did her life flip over - like a turtle stuck on its back that can't get back on his feet? Why did everything keep snowballing out of *control for her? Where was God when they needed Him to show them an ounce of His grace and peace?"*

I am sure my reader wonders how broken a young girl can get before she crumbles. Perhaps my reader wonders how this little, sad family came to be. Three misfits just trying to survive in the world. Perhaps she wonders if we'll ever catch a break. Will we ever be happy? What does fate have planned for us next? Can we stoop any lower? And can we beg louder? Where were we going to end up next?

Believe me, dear reader, I'm wondering the same things.

D

January 10, 1971
Dear Diary,
Spontaneously, we liked to choose the towns that we lived in based on the welcome sign that announces the town's name. For example, when we reached the southeast corner of Montana, we came across a town named Broadus. The welcoming sign at the beginning of the town's main road read, 'Welcome to Broadus! We know what 'brought-us', but what brought you?' So clever! Ben loved repeating this phrase over and over as we idled into the little town and scoped out the prospects.

"Know what brought us to Broadus?
"Bad freakin' luck!
"Know what brought us to Broadus, Montana?
"A long, boring, bumpy road from Nowhere, Utah.
"What?
"Seriously, I am not kidding you! That was the name of the town we used to live in!" Ben was carrying on a simple, crazy-sounding conversation with himself. He even laughed at his own jokes. It reminded me of the Three Stooges. Nonsense conversation. I was too tired to participate. I let him enjoy his simple-minded banter with himself. We didn't have much to our name, but he managed to maintain his sense of humor.

We found a small room with an attached bathroom at the Broadus

Inn. Ben worked his magic with the owner by offering to work for room and board. Since we didn't have much money, Ben offered his handyman skills for free if we could stay for free. Mr. Patrick seemed very keen on the idea of receiving help around the rundown inn. Some of the tasks that fell into Ben's lap were repairing leaky faucets, oiling squeaky doors, shoveling snow after an overnight surprise dusting, and rewiring the heating units in a few rooms. Ben was in Heaven! He loved to tinker and get things working properly again. It was an exceptional arrangement that we knew would not last forever, so we felt grateful.

Ben and the owner, Mr. Patrick, became fast friends. Ben always managed to make a new friend wherever we stayed. He was gifted with hands that could repair anything and gifted with his friend-making skills.

I, on the other hand, was busy night and day taking care of my needy, fussy six-month-old baby. She literally and figuratively sucked the life out of me. I was breastfeeding her, and she was always hungry. Nursing was not my choice. This decision was based on necessity since we had no extra money to buy formula. I was very skeptical of the whole natural custom. It felt strange and uncomfortable.

Of course, being a man and of little parenting knowledge, Ben voiced his unrequested opinion.

"Daisy, God created the wonder that is you and blessed you with this sweet child. You have all the ways to take care of her. You are her mother, and your body automatically knows that it must produce breast milk to carry for its offspring. As her parents, we need to keep her safe, happy, healthy and clean. But only you can give our baby the nutrients that she needs to live. That is a miracle, Daisy. A true miracle."

"Oh, my god... what has gotten into you? Puke. You breastfeed her, then."

D

January 11, 1971
Dear Diary,

Mr. Patrick knocked on our room door one afternoon while Ben was completing one of his assigned duties. I peeked through the peephole in the door. Mr. Patrick was dressed in his usual attire: white baggy T-shirt, bib overalls, and a baseball cap with a big sweat ring around it. I spoke loudly through the door that I was feeding the baby and was not ready for visitors.

"Daisy? I just stopped by to let you know that my wife would be willing to help you out with yer baby if you ever needed a break. We have two grown boys. She has a wee bit of experience if you ever needed advice."

"Thank you, Mr. Patrick. I appreciate the offer. I might take her up on that sometime." My childhood manners reminded me that I should open the door to speak to him, but I wasn't about to open the door even slightly because I was topless. It was easier to feed the baby without a shirt on. Breastfeeding was not a comfortable or natural feeling for me. When she was hungry, I would pray she would latch on so she would quiet down. Then, I would nap as well.

D

January 13, 1971

Dear Diary,

I mentioned to Ben that Mr. Patrick had stopped by the other afternoon to offer up his wife's babysitting services if we ever needed it. "As your wife, don't ever volunteer me for anything. I hate when couples do that!"

Ben didn't give a courtesy laugh or anything. He looked confused. "Mr. Patrick's wife died several years ago. He told me she drowned in their own bathtub. It was very tragic and sudden."

"What? No, he said she offered to help and something about them raising two boys of their own, so they had experience. You must have heard him wrong. He was probably talking about someone else."

"No, I am pretty sure he was talking about his own wife, Daisy. I asked him if he was married, and he told me the sad story. Maybe it was you who heard him incorrectly."

Hmmm... I wasn't sure now. He was speaking to me through the door, but that was a lot of information to totally misinterpret. Whatever... I guess I didn't have a free babysitter after all.

D

January 20, 1971
Dear Diary,

Again, during the baby's afternoon feeding, a knock rapped on the door to our room. I decided to not even respond to it this time. The baby was falling asleep as she was nursing. Soon, I could take a nap as well... if the knocking didn't wake her.

After the last knock, I heard the key turn in the door lock. Oops! Ben must have decided to knock and annoy me rather than simply getting his freakin' key out of his pocket. If this baby fell asleep like I was hoping, I would quietly give him my dirtiest, annoyed look for being so lazy and bothersome.

Surprisingly, it was not Ben using his room key but Mr. Patrick. Obviously, since he owned the inn, he would possess a master key to all the inn rooms. I was not prepared to see anyone other than Ben coming through the doorway. I gasped and tried to cover myself up as I lay shirtless on the bed with the baby at my breast. Mr. Patrick didn't show any signs of recognizing that he was doing something wrong by entering our room without our permission. He quietly shut the door and turned the deadbolt.

Shocked and unable to process why this man entered our room, I quietly inquired, "Mr. Patrick, I am sorry, but now is not a good time. I am nursing the baby to sleep. Can you come back later?"

He never looked at me or even in my direction. He did not acknowledge that I was speaking to him. His body language suggested that he was in a trance of some kind. Like he was sleepwalking during the day. He plopped down on the edge of the bed and started to unlace his work boots.

"Mr. Patrick? Are you okay?"

He was starting to freak me out a little. Through the snapback of his old Ford cap, his bald spot peeked out. Sweat rings circled under his armpits and soaked through his white T-shirt. His bib overalls were grimy and dirty. After his boots were removed, he removed his hat. The hair on top of his head was patchy, as if he pulled it out in clumps of rage. The strands that remained were long and oily. Random bald spots dotted the top of his head.

I was unsure if Mr. Patrick's brain registered where he was. He seemed lost and confused. Maybe he thought he was in his own room. I slyly slid off the right side of the bed and placed the baby on the pile of blankets folded on the floor. I quickly slipped my sweatshirt over the top of my head. But just as my head popped out of the neck hole of my sweatshirt, Mr. Patrick reached over and violently grabbed me around the waist, forcing me back onto the bed. I panicked and screamed, "What are you doing?"

He silenced me by quickly wrapping a dish towel around my mouth and tied it behind my head. My hands were fighting him off at the waist where I could feel his nakedness. As soon as my mouth was covered, he swiftly tossed me face down on the bed and tied my hands behind my back. Never in my life had I prepared for this. I had no idea that it all could happen in a matter of seconds. I had not reacted quickly enough.

Tears streamed down my cheeks as Mr. Patrick tugged off my pants and underwear. I rolled my head to the right side and saw the baby sleeping softly on her cloud of blankets without a care in the world. She had no idea her mother was being violently raped a few feet away.

After stroking himself hard, Mr. Patrick penetrated me again and again with his ugliness. He grunted and panted but never uttered an intelligible word. When he finished, he lifted himself off me and robotically started to get dressed.

My whole body ached from the weight of this robust man on top of me, and my lady parts bled from being brutally assaulted. My tears had turned into sobs now. With the dishcloth still covering my mouth, my sobbing was muffled and coming more from my throat.

"Stop that now, hussie. I let you and yer man live here for free. This is the least you can do for me." He finally acknowledged me but wouldn't look me in the eye. He was fully dressed and getting a drink

from the bathroom sink. "You will not say a word about this to yer man. You will accept me whenever I come to you. Got that, hussie?" When I didn't answer him but sobbed more, he rushed over to me and raised his arm as if to strike. He asked again. "You hear me, hussie?"

I frantically nodded.

Never in my wildest, darkest dreams had I imagined that this mouse of a man could be this cruel and heartless. When we met him a few weeks ago, I commented to Ben that he reminded me of cranky Archie Bunker from All in the Family, *except Mr. Patrick appeared weaker and quieter.*

"Now, lay still, and I will remove the bands around yer wrists. You won't scream or cry out. Got that, hussie? No one will come for you anyway. Yer man is busy working." He calmly untied my wrists and put the rope back in his pocket. "Get dressed, hussie. Remember, if you tell anyone, you will have nowhere to sleep again. Stuck in yer car with yer man and yer baby."

I understood Mr. Patrick: sexual favors for a roof over our heads. This hussie got it.

I needed to write this down even though it was very painful. I needed to remember why to not let my guard down. I never wanted to feel this vulnerable and hurt again.

D

January 21, 1971

Dear Diary,

You are my secret keeper! I didn't tell Ben, only you. When he got home from running errands for Mr. Patrick, he was happy and chipper. He even brought me a burger and french fries from the local restaurant. I couldn't tell him; he would kill Mr. Patrick and then we would be on the run again, but this time for murder!

Ben gave up so much for me! He was taking care of me and our baby by doing the best he could. I needed to suck it up and keep the door locked whenever Ben was gone. I needed to be more careful. I could be strong again. I had to do this for Ben.

D

January 30, 1971
Dear Diary,

For ten days, I never saw or heard Mr. Patrick around the motel. Ben noticed that I was a bit edgy. He offered more than usual to help with the baby. I appreciated it but didn't know what to do with myself since I didn't want to be alone in case Mr. Patrick attacked me again. So, I flipped through a magazine while they played or took a bubble bath while they napped.

When Ben left to check in with Mr. Patrick for chores to do around the motel, I would instantly deadbolt and chain the door. I have never been so scared before, and we have been through so much already. But this was a different type of fear and higher level of desperation.

D

February 7, 1971
Dear Diary,
I'm glad I haven't told Ben.

He came home today so excited to tell me about the history that he discovered about our new 'hometown'. Ben's energy and positivity has always been contagious. Even on a bad day, Ben could cheer Winnie the Pooh's Eeyore.

"Daisy, I knew there would be a good history to this town." His conversation started even before the door closed. He removed his jacket and reached for the baby. "I could feel it. It is named after a cowboy named Oscar Broaddus, who built that little log cabin we noticed on our first day in town. It was built in 1886. Can you believe it is still standing? It is part of the historical society now. Anyway, Oscar was a bona-fide cowboy. He settled in his area next to the river and invited his family and friends to join him. After he settled down and got married, he had ten kids. Can you imagine? I wonder if any of them still live around here?"

D

February 14, 1971

Dear Diary,

Valentine's Day has never held a fondness in my heart before. T has been my only love interest, and it only lasted for a couple of months one summer. On the other hand, Ben has always been a bit of a heart-breaker. In junior high, his female classmates would leave him secret gifts in his school desk or in his locker. Any girl that got up the nerve to telephone him or vocalize her affections, he would kindly acknowledge but never commit. By the time he was in high school, he had a reputa-tion for being a player. He didn't do it on purpose; he just never had true, deep feelings for any of them yet. So, he flirted with and admired them all.

He learned something from all the admiration that he received: he knew how to make someone else feel special. And this year, he showed me how it felt to be loved. By the time I had woken up, he had already rushed to the corner gas station and purchased us each a donut with white frosting and candy heart sprinkles. I had a piping-hot hot cocoa on my bedside nightstand.

And to top it off, I didn't wake to a hungry, whiny baby. Sitting in the small accent chair in our motel room, Ben was holding and snug-gling the baby who he had dressed in a hot pink outfit. She adored him. Never seemed to whine or claw at him. So even though she was usually screeching for her morning nurse, she was cooing and playing with the buttons on his shirt. Ben was magic.

"Happy Valentine's Day, 'husband'," I softly muttered as I started to sit up in one of the room's double beds.

"Good morning, sleepyhead! And Happy Valentine's Day. Lily and I wanted to let you sleep in. You have been struggling a bit lately, and we wanted to give you the gift of sleep. Right, Baby Girl?" Ben wore his button up nightshirt that had been Father's. It was still a bit too big, but it suited him.

"Well, thanks. I appreciate it. I haven't been sleeping well. I am worried. Do you think we need to move on? We have been here for a

month and a half, Ben. I am afraid we need to think about our next adventure."

Ben loved Broadus, Montana. He loved the distant view of mountains, the small river that ran near town, and of course, the fresh air. Additionally, he thoroughly enjoyed his work. He loved to work with his hands. He loved being able to fix something that was broken and make it new again. I knew his answer before he voiced it so I remained steadfast in my resolve to persuade him.

"Ben, we need to do what is best for Lily. I think it is time to hit the road. I know you love it here, but I'm sure we can find another town for you to explore. We need to keep one step ahead of them. We don't know what would happen if we were discovered. I don't want that to happen."

"I know you are right, but I'm afraid we will never get this lucky again. Room and board for free as long as I repair the little things that Mr. Patrick needs fixing. He has been so good to us! I hate to say goodbye."

If only he knew that Mr. Patrick broke me, and I needed fixing too.

"I know, Ben. But it is for the best." I gathered the baby from him for her morning nurse. That was Ben's cue to hop in the shower so he could start his day of handyman work. I draped the green afghan over Lily as she latched on.

Ben would come around to my suggestion. He knew I was right. All of this has been hard; no decision has been made lightly. We're a team. We were in this together.

D

February 17, 1971

Dear Diary,

I am ashamed to admit that I let my guard down, and the very second, I did, Mr. Patrick found that small opening. Ben took the baby to play at the park while I surrendered to a much-needed nap. She was teething, so I had been getting little sleep while I tried to soothe her. Obviously, Ben was up in the middle of the night too since we were in the small room altogether, but he tolerated the lack of sleep much better than I did. I got cranky and short. Never much fun to be around.

As soon as I laid my head on the pillow, sleep came easily. A half hour later, I was jarred awake by Mr. Patrick flipping me onto my stomach so he could tie up my wrists. "No!" My natural response was to fight him off. I kicked and wiggled to try to get away from him. His two-hundred-pound frame easily overwhelmed me. He was already naked and tugging off my pants.

"Hussie, yer rent is due. Just lay still and quit yer hollering. No one is gonna hear you or care for that matter." He tied the same dish towel around my mouth. And I did what I was told.

When he was finished and dressed back in his white T-shirt and bib overalls, he slapped my butt before removing the rope from my wrists. My sobbing loudly echoed in my head, so I couldn't totally hear every-thing he muttered, "... leaving that gag in yer mouth because I don't wanna hear you complain." He left our room before I had even moved on the bed.

D

February 18, 1971
Dear Diary,

After Ben and the baby returned from playing at the park, I finally informed Ben why we had to move that very night. He was utterly shocked. It wasn't that he didn't believe me - he just couldn't imagine that someone could be so evil. He wanted to hurt Mr. Patrick. He couldn't believe I didn't tell him after the first time it happened. Ben punched a hole in the wall near the door. I didn't get after him - that was an acceptable reaction. We packed up what little belongings we had and escaped in the middle of the night.

If it weren't for Ben, my view regarding all mankind would be shat-tered. He was the good that I knew was possible. I cried the whole nine hours until we finally found the next town we would stay in. Mission Lake, Colorado.

D

March 1, 1971
Dear Diary,
Ben said he chose Mission Lake because he was on a mission to make a good life for our little family.

Mission Lake is beautiful! Mountains everywhere. If it snows, some days it melts by sunset. My kind of snow! Ben is happy; he found a job at a local resort as a tour guide. He takes visitors cross country skiing in the winter and hiking in the spring, if we still live here by then. I work at the same resort taking reservations for visitors who are vacationing here and want tours. The manager allows me to bring the baby to work with me, and she plays behind the desk in a playpen.

D

April 2, 1971
Dear Diary,
Life in Mission Lake was fine, but expensive. We pulled one of our middle of the night escapes when we couldn't pay our overdue hotel bill.

D

April 15, 1971
Dear Diary,
Cosmopolitan *magazine diagnosed me. After having a baby, many women experience disturbing thoughts and feelings. Your hormones are all out of whack, so you have crazy thoughts of harming your baby and yourself. A mother feels detached from her baby and helpless. It is caused by postpartum depression.*

Of course, the rape by Mr. Patrick caused me to feel even more depressed, but it made sense now why I never referred to the baby by her name. I was detaching myself from her. Sure, I performed normal motherly duties, but I didn't want to get too close. I was withholding my love. I know this for a fact now, but it didn't make it any easier. I still looked at her and felt nothing.

D

May 5, 1971
Dear Diary,
We have been on our own for a year and a half now. No support, no steady income, no friends or family. I didn't think it would be this hard, but it is. We weren't ready to be on our own - all alone in the world. And the world is harsh.
Our old beater of a car broke down near a town named Normal, Iowa. Ironic since nothing in our life has been 'normal' for quite some time. Ben, always the optimist, read it as a sign.
"This is it, Daisy! This is our do-over! This town is gonna be the key to making our lives whole again. I can feel it!"
"If that is true, then the town should be called Miracle, Iowa or Do-Over, Iowa. Not Normal. Everyone living in this town probably leads normal lives and has normal families with normal drama. We, my friend, are anything but normal. We are going to stick out like a crusty wart on a bare naked, backend of a nun."
"Another good reason to stay here: we will appear normal to everyone. A young couple just starting out. I am sure we can do this, Daisy. I can feel it. It is another sign from God. Furthermore, no one will be looking for us in Iowa."
We were normal once. We could do it again.

D

June 30, 1971
Dear Diary,
Sorry, it has been so long, but we have been busy. Busy arguing, busy fighting and busy being stressed out! Summer in Iowa is hot and humid. And downright awful without a fan or window air conditioner. The mosquitos are something to be reckoned with!

Thanks to Ben and his naivety, people in Normal were beyond generous when we first arrived. Sweet Ben viewed the world as half full... always. He could discover the silver lining in anything. And I wanted him to stay that way. If he changed and became hardened by this world, then our sacrifices would be for nothing. I didn't have much, but I did have the power to help him stay sweet and innocent.

That first night when we arrived in Normal, we were at a low, vulnerable point. I would like to say that was our lowest point, but that would be a lie. We each had one bag of clothing - maybe a week's worth - and every article needed to spend some quality time on the inside of a washing machine. Our car, the one roof we had depended on, broke down. We were hungry, tired and desperate. As we were creeping down the main street in search of another one of God's signs to point us in the right direction, we heard a high-pitched voice holler from the opposite side of the street.

"Hey, kids! You look a bit lost." The older woman was slipping her mail into the post office's drop box. "I'm Faith. Do you have supper plans?" Ben and I looked at each other in complete disbelief. We turned back to her and shook our heads. "Great! I have a lasagna in the oven back home and no one to eat with. Come on. Follow me."

Faith...yep, believe me, when I tell you that Ben had a heyday with her name and the coincidence that she was the one to invite us to her home for a free meal. He nudged me with his bony elbow and raised his eyebrows at me as we followed her.

"Told you so," he whispered.

Faith told us that she was sixty-five years young. Her husband had passed away, and her children had all moved out of state. It didn't take a rocket scientist to realize that not only was Faith kind and generous, but she was also lonely.

When we arrived at her two-story immaculately clean home, she ushered us right in. "Make yourselves at home in the family room. I will go check on supper."

As soon as she was out of earshot and in the kitchen, Ben turned to me as I was getting the baby out of her cheap, random stroller that we found next to someone's trash cans in our last 'hometown'.

"I told you. Have a little faith, I said. Holy crap! Can you believe it? When she said her name, I had to pinch myself to make sure I was awake." He spun around in the elegant living room with his arms open wide. When he stopped, he announced, "Let me do the talking, Daisy. You keep busy with Lily. Alright?"

And talk he did! He invented an elaborate, sob story of how we became homeless and - he used these exact words - 'our mode of transportation' died. Faith listened and listened and refilled our supper plates. In Iowa, we learned that it was supper, not dinner. Dinner was noon, or lunch time.

Lily was an angel that first night at Faith's home. It was as if she could sense this was a test and we needed her to be on her best behavior.

After we filled our bellies, Faith took Lily from my arms and offered to bathe her in the kitchen sink while Ben and I got settled in her guest room.

"Don't refuse me or my generosity. You kids need a break and some kindness. Tomorrow, we will get your things from your heap-of-crap car. I have an idea or two we can discuss after a good night's sleep. Now, go!" As soon as she dismissed us, she looked at Lily and purred, "Miss Lily, you and I are gonna do some splashing in my sink."

The baby smiled up at Faith with her big gray-blue eyes like they were old friends.

D

July 1, 1971
Dear Diary,
Faith did restore our faith. Or at least for a little while for me. The next day after meeting Faith on Normal's Main Street, she informed us that she was aware of a small, empty house that we could live in. She did not own it, but her brother did, and the house had recently been abandoned by tenants that couldn't make rent (hmmm... sounds familiar). Frederick, Faith's younger brother, owned several rental properties. His main occupation was being a landlord. After we collected

over belongings from ole Betty the Buick, Faith would bring us to meet her brother at the house. We were in awe of this kind, older lady and the generosity that she was showing to perfect strangers.

Faith's brother Frederick was not at all what we were expecting after spending time with her. Ben and I both assumed he would be as wonderful, friendly and approachable as Faith. While Faith had time-less beauty and flawless skin, Frederick's comb-over didn't fool anyone. Not only had he missed the personality gene in his family, but he also didn't possess anything that added up to good looks either. Even his teeth were nasty. They were not visible when he smiled, because he never smiled. We only saw them as he was barking orders on how to maintain his house, our rental.

The little, white two-story house was more than we could have ever hoped for. Luckily for us, the previous tenants rushed out so quickly (been there done that) that we also inherited many household necessi-ties: pots and pans, a few dishes and unmatched silverware, two twin beds with sheets and a few odds and ends toiletries. The house itself screamed, "I need TLC!" but I knew Ben could handle and would enjoy the task.

That very first week after we claimed its residency, we polished the floors, so they shone, hammered nails to mend broken trim and rearranged the hand-me-down furnishings to make it feel like home. Faith stopped by unannounced a few times and seemed quite impressed by our hard work. Each visit, she brought us housewarming gifts: a toaster, a used crib and a beautiful painting that I admired previously in her home. That first night we met Faith, I complimented the picture hanging on her dining room wall.

"The vibrant colors make me feel happy and warm inside. I can almost imagine the little girl smiling at her brother (that's who the figures looked like to me) as they enjoy all the fireflies flying around them in that field. It is as if they are in a dream." Just that simple inter-pretation brought the painting into our home.

"My late husband loved this unique painting. He picked it out, and I know he would have loved you as well, Daisy."

Old men normally do.

D

July 15, 1971
Dear Diary,

A week after we moved in, Ben landed a great paying job as a truck driver. He would start the following week if he passed his CDL test. CDL stands for Commercial Driving License. Because he truly felt our luck was turning around, Ben's happiness was uncontainable. If I am honest, his optimism poured over into my heart as well. It was hard to not be affected by his charm and positive outlook. It was contagious. So, while summer weather seized this small town, smiles emerged on our faces. Grabbing a silver spoon from the silverware drawer, we danced and sang in our kitchen listening to "Lola" by the Kinks. Lily was almost one year old now, so she bounced on her wobbly, stubby legs to the beat of the music.

We were happy. Relieved, content and grateful.

D

July 21, 1971
Dear Diary,

It was officially the hottest day of summer, and on the flat plains in Iowa, there was no breeze, only scorning hot sunrays. I opened the windows, praying for a little relief to cool off the hot box of a house we lived in.

Rap... rap... rap...

A hard beat of knuckles pounded on our front door. After living in Broadus, I learned to lock my doors even in a small town in Iowa. You can never be too careful. Being a rape victim was not gonna happen to me again. I was in charge of who touched my body.

When I answered the door, a sweaty, bloated Frederick was hovering in denim jeans and white wife-beater T-shirt with obvious light yellow sweat circles under his arms. He looked completely miser-able in this heat.

"Hi, Frederick. I'd invite you in, but our house is hotter than it is

outside today. Literally a little oven in here." I was fanning my face with a piece of mail that I picked up off the little inherited table by the front door.

"Faith is dead. She died." Frederick blurted out the awful news of his sister's passing as if he was blurting out an answer on a game show. Quick and forceful, with no emotion.

"Oh, Frederick! I'm so sorry. Poor Faith! What happened?"

"She ain't gonna be paying your rent no more, so you gotta or get out."

I'm not the most sentimental person anyway, but Frederick's personality and lack of sentiment made me look saintly. He showed no emotion, pain or sorrow when he delivered the news of his sister's sudden death. And immediately forecasted that his generosity was due to her good grace. Frederick obviously did not share the same feelings towards our housing arrangement. Faith had previously approached me with an idea that would spare Ben's ego. She would cover half of the rent.

"Just tell Ben that the rent is fifty dollars, and I'll cover the other half with my brother. You guys get yourselves back on your feet, and we'll discuss our arrangement again in six months." When Faith set her mind to something, she didn't want any arguing.

I wholeheartedly agreed with our little secret because I knew Ben would want to pay the full amount, even though we would hardly be able to afford it. He already thought Faith was overly generous, and he was worried about taking her for granted. This seemed like a simple plan. Now, she was gone. I know for a fact we can't afford one hundred dollars a month just yet. I was still home with the baby every day, and Ben was driving a truck each week. We were saving up for repairs for Betty the Buick.

I had to come up with the money somehow. What could I sell? I tried to rack my brain for a craft or a recipe that I could create that people would be willing to pay for. Nah-dah. I was talentless.

"Rent is due next week. I will be back then." Frederick delivered the news of his upcoming return and the death of his sweet, older sister with the same monotone in his voice. He abruptly turned to walk away.

"Frederick, wait! Can you tell me how or when she died, at least?"

He spun back around to face me. His eyes were darting to everything but me. "This morning. Poisoning."

D

July 25, 1971

Dear Diary,

The whole town of Normal attended Faith's funeral. She was rather famous in this small town. Her friends described her using phrases like, 'Iowa small town charm,' 'generous to a fault,' 'always willing to lend a hand,' 'not afraid of hard work,' and 'saw the good in everyone.' Tears rolled down nearly everyone's cheeks. Faith was, in fact, not poisoned; not sure where Frederick came up with that idea, but she died peacefully in her sleep. No foul play was suspected. Such a relief because I couldn't imagine anyone wanting to harm her.

D

July 30, 1971

Dear Diary,

Frederick showed up to collect the rent. I still had not formulated a plan to pay for the other half that Ben didn't know about. I was going to do my best to stall Frederick. I had to! We weren't gonna get this lucky again. Even cynical me knew that!

When I opened the screen door to invite Frederick in for a glass of water, he shook his head back and forth a few too many times to be considered a normal response. "No, just here for the money. No Faith, so you pay the full amount. I ain't dumb. I can count."

As usual, he would not look me in the eye. His eyes darted all around but would not focus on me. I had been too distracted to notice, but now I saw he was 'a little slow to start the race'. As soon as he announced he wasn't dumb, I realized Frederick was what a doctor would label as cognitively low.

A light bulb ignited! I would use his disability to arrange for the rest of the rent we owed him. I would trick him.

"Frederick, come in for a second while I get your money." I ushered him through the screen door with a sweep of my hand. "Come on. It'll just take a second." He reluctantly entered our home, his rental. He looked around the living room.

"Hey! That is Faith's picture. Not yours. You stole it." He pointed to the beautiful, firefly artwork hanging on our wall. His voice was edgy, and he started to appear agitated. I needed to de-escalate this situation and fast.

To say I am proud of myself would not be a true statement. To say I am proud of myself for keeping a roof over our heads would be more accurate. I did what any talentless, poor, desperate woman would do in my shoes.

D

August 5, 1971
Dear Diary,
Here we are, orphaned, alone and hungry. Yet, she coos and begs for attention. When Ben is away, I hardly pay her any attention. For a damn baby, she is smart because she stopped crying for me to come for her. She has learned not to be needy when only I am around. The weekends when Ben is home, she turns on the charm, and he showers her with his love and attention. Leaving me as usual - alone, depressed and despising them. What a great life this has turned out to be!

D

August 30, 1971
Dear Diary,
Frederick paid his monthly visit today. He isn't even remotely polite about what he wants now. Literally pockets the fifty dollars from Ben and pulls my hand into the bedroom where he demands I undress for him.

250

"Sexier!"

What have I done? If I could come up with the money a different way, I wonder if he would understand that this is over. Or would he demand sexual favors anyway? He is smart enough to know when to collect the rent, but I'm not sure if he understands that I'm not enjoying this. He probably doesn't care.

D

September 5, 1971

Dear Diary,

When I look at her, I remember him. Him with his gorgeous, gray-blue eyes and his gentle, calm manner. Him with his soft, tender touch. Him with his broken promises and bitter betrayal welcoming her *into his strong embrace. Him…everything reminds me of him. Before him, life was mundane and bland. Before him, I had not known physical pleasure or a man's touch. Before him, my life had promise and opportunities. How was I to know that his love - even though a bit fleeting - would change the course of my life?*

Of course, when I look at this baby, my thoughts become hardened and spiteful. She is my constant reminder of my poor choices. I can hardly stand to look at her.

D

251

Chapter Thirty-Eight

1989

W hen something becomes ordinary or routine in everyday life, desensitization takes place. The first time that marijuana was inhaled, nerves were on high alert. Anxious looks over the shoulder. Concerned with other people's opinions. Guilt about participating in an illegal activity. After several inhales and additional experiences later, consideration of the whole event received nonchalant attention. Worries about people's opinion and guilt for inhaling an illegal substance were no longer a big deal.

I was beginning to feel this way about Daisy's diaries. Any new shocking information I gathered from one didn't astound me like the first few incidents had. Initially, a crack seemed to emerge in my heart - I ached for the loss of innocence. In the last diary I read, Daisy was raped repeatedly by a much older man, Mr. Patrick. She trusted him. In the beginning, she felt no fear or apprehension about him. He ripped her innocence and trust; he shredded her naivety. Since I read her journals out of order, I needed to remind myself that she was only seventeen or eighteen years old at the time. I was beginning to discover what had made her jaded and desensitized to sex. The sad pieces of her lonely existence molded together.

During my infant years, Daddy and Daisy bounced around from

town to town finding low-income housing and low-paying jobs to make ends meet. They were running from something that I had yet to discover from her writings. I wondered if it was something I should be fearful of as well.

I remembered Uncle Freddy - Daisy referred to him as Frederick in her journals - from my childhood. He came around and visited Daisy when Daddy wasn't around. He was an odd man, never very friendly or talkative. I'm not sure why they both referred to him as an 'uncle' when we were not related to him. In her diaries, she explained that she had sex with him once a month for half of the rent of our house. Her diaries were revealing so much.

Besides the stories that Daisy told about her little brother, I had only heard one story of another possible relative. Daddy told me the story once after he had had a few too many whiskeys. We were sitting in two plastic lawn chairs next to the side of the garage, where earlier Daddy had changed the oil on our push lawn mower. Spring had finally arrived in Iowa. Sunshine and vitamin D had been greatly missed. It was a calm, slightly warmer than normal evening. Only a few bugs had woken up from their long winter nap. Bunnies frolicked on the lawn. Birds chirped from the treetops. Everyone, including me and Daddy, were enjoying the long-awaited change in weather.

Daddy was celebrating with whiskey. Every time he refilled his whiskey glass, he brought me a popsicle. It was a win-win.

"Don't ever take someone you love for granted, Baby Girl. You hear me?" His words sounded like cursive writing; they flowed and slurred together. "I had a little br..." He paused for a minute as if searching for a word. "... friend named Henry. People told us all the time that we looked so much like each other. But he was younger and six inches shorter than me. We didn't see it. We were a couple of kids." A single tear rolled down his cheek. I only noticed it because he raised his greasy hand to wipe it away. "Anyway, I loved that kid. He didn't say much, but he was always happy and easy to please. A joy to be around."

Even though I was only eight years old when he told me this story, I realized the significance of the moment because Daddy never talked about his past. It was as if he didn't have one. In my silence, I took notes of the details that his alcohol-induced loose lips were providing.

"This two-headed coin was his." Daddy showed me a shiny copper coin that he pulled out of his pocket. "Father... his father gave it to him on his birthday. Told him it would bring him luck wherever he was. Henry rubbed his lucky coin all the time and made many wishes on it. He believed his father.

"On the day he died, Henry was rubbing his lucky coin between his fingers. It had become a rather nervous habit. Hurtful words were being shouted, and Henry wished and wished that he was anywhere but there. Suddenly, his mother jerked the arm that he was holding the coin in, and in that quick moment the coin flew out of his little fingers and rolled onto the pavement. Henry didn't have a chance to retrieve it. His mother tossed his little body into the front seat of her car, and the car roared away with Henry in it.

"Henry died that day without his lucky coin. But I found it in the driveway. Every time I hold it, I think about him. Today is his birthday. He would've been twenty-one today. And you would have really loved Henry, and he would've adored you as well, Baby Girl. You remind me of him a great deal."

This conversation entered my mind when I thought about my parents' past lives, and it felt like this was a piece of the puzzle. But I didn't know where the piece fit.

AFTER MY SHOWER, as I was getting ready for my shift at Kitty's Cafe, thoughts of my own mother being used and abused by a man invaded my mind. *I am gonna need to see a therapist soon.* Conflicting emotions about Daisy were battling in both my heart and mind. She may have been a shitty mother to me and an unfaithful wife to Daddy, but I was beginning to understand that there were reasons for it. She was messed up, and no matter what happened, she spiraled deeper and deeper down a rabbit hole. She was unable to love us properly because she didn't respect or love herself enough to start with.

Deep into my own internal dialogue, I didn't notice as I walked into the cafe that my big tipper was waiting in the same booth, booth number three. Magically, Kitty appeared beside me and whispered quietly in my ear, "He has been here for a half an hour. He asked specifically for you, and only you, and a glass of water. That's him, right?" Kitty had been just as shocked about the two-hundred-dollar tip as I was but also pleased that I was the sole recipient of such generosity.

"Yes, that's him." From under the counter, I grabbed a black work apron. Expertly, I tied the apron around my waist, grabbed a blank order pad and a couple of pens for my apron pockets. "He isn't local. I wonder what he's doing back here only a few days later."

"Are you implying that it isn't for my mouth-watering Prairie Melody Pie? Well, there's only one way to find out." She nudged me with her bony hip and grabbed an order from the kitchen window before Hank could even yell, "Order up."

She was correct, of course, but I felt uneasy about talking to him. What if he expected something from me after giving me such a huge tip? I wasn't that kind of girl, that was for sure. And I had no problem telling him that. With Daisy's journal from 1971 fresh in my mind, I would make sure that I was not taken advantage of.

However, my gut instinct advised me that that wasn't why he was here again. He dressed like a gentleman - that was my first impression of him. He took care of his appearance, his eyes were kind, and his smile was genuine. I didn't get the creepy vibe from him. Yet, there was something that I couldn't put my finger on.

As I approached his booth with a menu, he looked up from his local newspaper and kindly smiled at me. He carefully folded the paper back into his proper creases.

"Hello again, Miss Lily." His voice was deep and raspy, but his words were slow and deliberate. If I had to guess, I would bet money that he was well-educated.

"Hello there. First of all, I would like to properly thank you for the extremely generous tip you gifted me a few days ago. I am not sure why you did it, but it was very much appreciated and unexpected."

"You are welcome, Lily. I expect nothing from you in return but exceptional customer service and a gracious smile. What do you recommend today for lunch?" He got right down to business. I was relieved.

"Hank's chicken pot pie is legendary in this town, but if that sounds too heavy for a lunchtime meal, my all-time favorite is the BLT and french fries." I retrieved my order pad and a pen from my apron pocket. I appreciated his candor and his calm demeanor. I had been lied to enough in my life - even little white lies were not appreciated. With my order pad and pen in hand, I glanced up as he was intently observing me. His gaze was focused and questioning - not a typical 'checking out the goods' glance. Goosebumps...

"I am sorry if my focused attention on you is making you uncomfortable." My non-poker face must have shown the slight alarm caused by his intent gaze. *Damn it.* "You remind me of someone from my past. The similarities are uncanny. I am sorry to be so forthcoming. As you grow older like me, you realize beating around the bush is a waste of time and effort." He sipped his water. "The objective of my visit to Normal, Iowa, entails a search for a woman. Her name, when I was acquainted with her, was Daisy. If my intuition serves me correctly, you are also familiar with this woman."

His eyes yearned for me to positively acknowledge his inquiry, to confirm the relationship and, I was sure, to inform him of her whereabouts. Instead, his honesty encountered silence and created a barrier. I did my best to strum up a poker face. I didn't know this stranger - he appeared harmless, kind and well spoken, but his intentions were not clear. Additionally, in complete honesty, Daisy's track record with the opposite sex consisted only of trouble. Inviting more trouble into our complicated lives seemed disastrous.

"Let me apologize again. I am often told that my blunt honesty can be somewhat unsettling." Again with the mind reading or my lack of a poker face. *Damn it.* "I realize you don't know me from Adam." He chuckled at his own private joke.

It was my turn to match his straightforwardness.

"Sir, you're correct in acknowledging that I have no idea who you are and what you think you'll learn from me. But I'm simply your waitress here at Kitty's Cafe. I will deliver your food order with a smile. I will refill your drinks as requested. However, my job doesn't include being your friend or being someone who will answer your probing questions. You requested good service. I will give that to you because I am good at my job, but not because you blessed me with your generosity. I'm sorry - I cannot be bought."

My frankness erased the friendly smile from his thin lips. However, it didn't create the shock and uncertainty I had intended and assumed was earned. Our altercation stalled as we both stared at each other. I only wanted his food order - he only wanted answers that he predicted he wouldn't receive.

"Checkmate, Lily. I respect your confidence and honesty. My intent was not to build a giant impediment between us. I apologize." His response appeared genuine, but his facial expressions revealed his grave disappointment. "I would like the Hefty Heifer Burger with all the trimmings please as well as another glass of water."

I nodded to confirm his order, collected the menu, and turned on my heel as I jotted down his lunch order. I didn't want to be affected by his inquiries into Daisy's location, but I was.

Chapter Thirty-Nine

J anuary 1, 1983
    Dear Diary,
    Will this be the year I can get my shit together? Probably not,
but why not give it a shot.

D

February 1, 1983
Dear Diary,
Something pulled me to church. Maybe it was thoughts of reuniting
with Little H. I decided one church service couldn't hurt. Lily was
curious as well.

D

March 1, 1983
Dear Diary,
When I first noticed Tony at church, I only chalked him up as a
challenge. He was married AND a pastor. If I could turn his head in

my direction, I had real sexual superpowers! I am not even sure if initially I was attracted to him. It was more about the chase.

We flirted for about a month before I decided to try to see him outside of Sunday morning church service. I volunteered to serve food at a congregation member's funeral. I didn't know this elderly member, but I figured I might get an opportunity to talk more in depth with Tony. I was right.

After the service and the fellowship meal, the other volunteers and I started the cleanup process. I was taking out the trash to the dumpster behind the church when Tony suddenly appeared from around the corner. He claimed that he was taking out trash too from his office, but I observed that his garbage bag was far from full.

We chatted like we usually do, nothing too serious. However, it was clear that there was an electric spark between us. A magnetic pull. At one point, I noticed his gaze slowly take in my curvy body. Men are always appreciating my body, but this time was different. It was as if he was taking notes, savoring every inch with his eyes. He looked hungry.

D

June 15, 1983
Dear Diary,

I never dreamed of becoming a stripper, you know. It was not a life goal. You might not believe this, but in high school, I planned on pursuing a college education in Public Communications. I dreamt of becoming a journalist. How naive I was to the world only a few short years ago.

But here I am in Normal, Iowa, working as a stripper for the last couple of years at Rusty Nail. Initially, I applied for the opening as a bartender. I figured since I like to drink and could mix myself a decent cocktail, why not do it for other people and make some money! They offered me the job on the spot.

However, a few days later I discovered that I wasn't hired for my cocktail mixing skills. The owner, Rusty, wanted me up on the stage. He offered me a 'promotion' to a stripper even before I was taught how to make an old-fashioned.

I didn't mind. I appreciated the compliment. My whole adult life, men have thrown themselves at me. I was used to the attention that my stunning looks received. However, I was nervous about removing all my clothes for an audience. Sure, I was no virgin but still, this was many, many strangers staring at all of my body parts on full display.

Rusty's full-time gal Trixie gave me my first piece of advice.

"Pretend it is only one guy. Stare at him as if no one else is in the room. Then blink and stare at the next guy until you blink and look away again. It helps for the first couple of weeks, I promise. Then you'll get into a routine, and forget your tits are on display. You can choose your own music. I like to change my routine every night so I don't get bored doing the same thing. I make up dance routines for each song on my rotation. It becomes quite fun to do. I am sure you will be a pro. What do you think your first stripper song will be? Mine was 'You Shook Me All Night Long' by ACDC."

Trixie was sweet and extremely naive. I know she meant well, but I was feeling overwhelmed and nervous.

"Maybe you could pretend like you are shy for the first couple of weeks. The guys will go wild for that, especially if one of them can get you to remove something. It's like you're a virgin all over again. Be a tease."

D

June 20, 1983

Dear Diary,

I wasn't sure if Tony was aware that I was employed at Rusty Nail. So I decided during one of his visits to perform one of my dance routines for him. For obvious reasons, I did not have a pole in my bedroom, so I adjusted some of my alluring moves.

His reaction still blows me away. He was thrilled! He admitted that he heard I worked there when he first met me at church. He asked other congregation members about me. He had no idea that I was so talented. He begged me to dance for him again.

"It will cost you!" I teased him.

D

August 1, 1983
Dear Diary,

Morally - if I had real morals - I should feel guilty about sleeping with married men. But I have been doing it since I was a teenager, so I can blame it on that I don't know any better.

Seducing men, especially married men, is easy. They are so starved for attention that as soon as I bat an eye at them, they become interested. They yearn to feel desirable and free. I give them that with no strings attached. I don't want a single, unattached, free-and-willing-to-commit guy. I couldn't handle them coming around, sleeping over and being in my business. Nope, married men are better. I please them, make them feel desired and then I send them back to their wives. No promises. No rings. No commitment. Just how I like it.

I chose Ben. I chose this life. I was young and naive. I thought I could be happy with my pretend family. And now I live with my choice and make the best of it. Really, what choice do I have now?

I have encouraged Ben to move on, but he won't hear of it. He says he agreed to this life, and he isn't about to leave Lily. Ever.

There it is again - Lily. All comes down to Lily. No wonder I envy her. She has no idea what sacrifices we made for her. It is all about Lily.

D

August 3, 1983
Dear Diary,

Due to our secret relationship, I can't telephone Tony too often or people will suspect something is going on between the two of us. He needs to be especially careful, since he is a pastor of a small-town *church. I have used many excuses to call him: "I have a question about my faith. Is the pastor available?" or "I am not sure how God would view this thought that I have. Is the pastor available to talk?", and "Sorry to bother you, Lisa, but is Pastor Tony home? My car won't start and my husband is out of town until this weekend." Believe me, I am a good actress - maybe even great, but after a while, I don't even want to play the mistress part.*

"Is Tony there? I need him and his six inches. Could you send him to my bedroom right away?" But I don't. I don't think that would go over very well.

This was the internal conversation that was taking place in my brain when the doorbell rang. As I opened the door, there stood my dream man. He was dressed in a police officer uniform that was obviously not his. The sleeves were too short, the hat came over his eyes, and his pants were too tight. But he grinned and tipped his hat to me.

"Hello, miss. You are in a bit of trouble. I need to come into your home and perform a thorough search."

I could roleplay this part! My hand covered my O-shaped mouth, and I remarked, "Oh dear me, Officer. Is there a problem?" Both of us smiled so big that you would think our lips were going to split.

We are made for each other.

D

August 15, 1983
Dear Diary,
Summer Bible Camp - never attended one myself as a kid - but Lily was so excited to go. Sending my kid camping with my lover and his wife felt a bit odd. I brought her to the church parking lot to drop her off. She lugged her sleeping bag and her overnight bag that she insisted on packing herself, towards the group of kids waiting to pile in the chaperones' cars. She was so awkward standing there. I felt sorry for her... a bit. She didn't fit in, and it was obvious.

I watched Tony throw Lily's luggage into the back of his station wagon or as we fondly nicknamed it, 'Tony's Shaggin' Wagon'. She climbed into the same back seat where we screwed last week. Ironic. She turned and reluctantly waved goodbye to me.

Tony treated me like I was any other congregation member, any other parent dropping off their kid for camp, any other woman standing in the parking lot as he and his devoted wife drove away with our precious children. I felt his eyes lingering longer on my ass in his favorite pair of shorts. I caught him gazing at my breasts in my tight red tank top.

He was conversing with the group of parents who were standing in the parking lot. He made his way to me. He shook my hand while he slyly passed me a little note that I am keeping forever.

"Come to Camp! Saturday at 8 am. Meet me in the men's shower so I can clean you. XXOO-T"

Now, I have something to look forward to! I was going to be home alone this weekend. Lily was at camp; Ben was picking up a weekend route since Lily wasn't going to be around. And believe me, Ben and I could use a break from one another. We have been bickering all the time lately. He is getting on my nerves. He always went along with my crazy ideas ever since he was a teenager. But lately, he voiced some strong opinions. Especially on how I should be raising Lily, how I should act, and who I am spending my time with. All sorts of opinions on my life! Did I ask him to care so much?

When offered a little adventure at camp in a public restroom with a married pastor, of course, I nodded my head. Ben wasn't here to tell me what to do, and plus, I'm a consenting adult… a very consenting adult.

D

August 20, 1983
Dear Diary,
Honestly, I don't care what people think of me. I know the truth, and they don't. People around this town judge me, say I am a whore, a cheating whore. They see me with a man that isn't my husband and assume we are having an affair. These judgmental people question my morals, look at me as if I am wearing a scarlet letter on my sweater.

The men that I've been seen with aren't being judged like me. Other men are envious of what they are able to get away with. These other men only wish they had me as their arm candy, while their naive, clueless wife sat at home. I can see their envy in their squinting eyes and sly smile.

The women - they are fearful that I will steal their men. These women are afraid that they've seen me before - perhaps at a dinner party, another local establishment getting too friendly with their husbands. All women fear me: I'm the woman who is willing to flaunt her assets and use them to her advantage. They fear me, but they are also jealous. They see my power and envy it.

I understand and respect their stares. I deserve every snicker, every jealous stare. I deserve it because I know how to use my power. However, I am not the one guilty of cheating. Look at your men, ladies. They are cheating, not me.

D

August 25, 1983
Dear Diary,
He understands me. He understands what I want before I have to ask. I sense he can look deep into my soul. His love is magical. Perhaps he can communicate with Lucifer in my brain. Maybe he is a mind reader.

He guides me with his tender touch. Begging me to please him. Feel his love. Physically, I feel it between my legs. Furthermore, I feel love in my soul.

I have only felt this way once before. I was just a girl then. Now, I understand love and its requirements from each party involved. As a woman, Tony brings out the best in me. I never want to stop feeling this way!

D

September 1, 1983

Dear Diary,

Lily is refusing to attend Tony's church. She won't get out of bed on Sunday mornings. She was my excuse to Ben why I was suddenly so Christian-like. But a few weeks after Bible Camp, she started to refuse. First, she didn't feel good. Then she overslept. Then she flat out ignored me.

Even Tony is concerned about her absence. He keeps asking about her. Even offered to talk to her himself. I appreciated his concern, but I told him I could handle it. Ben didn't care whether or not Lily attended church. He was suspicious of my attending church. I am sure deep down he knew but didn't want to talk about it. Plus, I wouldn't have listened. Tony is my dream man! Everything I have always wanted.

D

September 3, 1983
Dear Diary,

After school, Tony stopped by the house and took Lily to get ice cream. He told me it was fine - no one would be suspicious. He did this all the time with other troubled kids of our congregation. No one will suspect anything.

Lily seemed reluctant to go but finally agreed. She can't refuse ice cream. I watched them pull out of the driveway imagining what it would be like if the three of us were a family. I wondered if I could be 'normal'. I wondered if I could be a 'normal' wife and mother. Live with one man for the rest of my life. I think that with Tony as my husband, I could. I truly hope it wasn't just the sneaking around and the secrets that kept the spark in our relationship.

When Lily returned home, she looked ill. I asked her how much ice cream she had because she looked like she was gonna throw up. She didn't laugh at my small attempt at humor. She turned and ran upstairs to the bathroom. I looked back to Tony's station wagon from our front door, and from the front seat I saw Tony shrug his shoulders. He waved goodbye and backed out of the driveway.

Lily never came down for supper. After a long time in the bath-

room, I heard her shut her bedroom door. I figured she was doing homework. Since I had the night off of work, I decided to make her a little supper and bring it up to her in her room. Maybe she'd tell me about how her little ice cream date went.

She was fast asleep at seven o'clock when I peeked in her room. Maybe she really didn't feel good. But there were lots of discarded tissues on the floor next to her bed. She looked like she'd been crying. Poor thing - now I felt bad, but at least she was resting now.

I picked up the garbage, shut her drapes and just tidied up her room a bit. I never did this type of thing. Wow! Maybe I could be a good mother after all.

D

September 5, 1983
Dear Diary,
When Ben came home for the weekend, he told me he could tell Lily was upset about something. "She seems off. Did something happen this week?"

I'm sure Ben is aware of my love affair with Tony, although we never talk about it. It's the one good thing about our relationship that works for the both of us. We know there are indiscretions on both sides of the marriage. But why change something that works? It is not broken, so what is there to fix?

We may have jumped quickly into this situation years ago, and for the most part, everything has gone in our favor after a rocky first few years. Ben found a job that he loves, and it gives him the freedom to live as he chooses for five days a week.

If I'm honest, I want a normal family life. I want to love and adore my husband. I want an equal partner. I want someone I look forward to spending time with. I don't want to settle. I want my husband to be my best friend. All of these things describe Ben except that he is not my lover or my best friend. If he was my best friend, I would never keep these secrets from him.

Selfishly, I want it all. Tony could be it. I do love and adore him.

We talk and share a lot about ourselves, our thoughts, and our feel-ings. I just need to share these feelings with him to see if we are on the same page with the future of our relationship. I have never had these feelings for anyone since T. I am nervous about putting myself out there.

D

September 10, 1983
Dear Diary,

No, I haven't approached that topic with Tony yet. I'm having my doubts.

The other day before sex I asked him to tell me a fantasy of his - he already filled mine by wearing a police officer uniform for me. He paused a bit before he admitted that he would enjoy watching me have sex with another person.

"Really? It wouldn't bother you at all? Even if I enjoyed it?"

"No. Not at all. I am confident enough to understand that you would be performing for me and my pleasure. Is this something you would consider? I have been thinking a lot about it." He kissed me hard on the mouth, and when he pulled back, he had a twinkle in his eye and a smirk on his face. This devilish look was something about him that I found incredibly sexy. It was very hard to say 'no' to that look. And I didn't.

D

October 2, 1983
Dear Diary,

When I opened the front door, Tony held a box all wrapped up with a pretty bow on it for me. Normally, I would refuse a gift from a man that I was seeing, but honestly, I was super curious. And I really loved this man. We seemed to be on the same wavelength sexually and mentally. We both liked it rough and quick. We seemed in sync.

I tore open the box and revealed a hair coloring kit under the wrapping paper. Huh? I was hoping for some jewelry. But a brunette hair coloring kit? This was not expected. I had no idea what to say.

He said tomorrow night he wanted to wash my hair in the shower, dye my hair himself, and then we could role play.

D

October 3, 1983
Dear Diary,

Before Tony arrived, I took great care in my appearance. I soaked in a long hot bubble bath, shaved my legs and painted my nails. I wore a few of his favorites: high heel strappy sandals, my tight white jeans with no underwear, and my soft deep V-neck blue tank top. It was obvious that my effort was well appreciated when he finally arrived. He hungrily looked me up and down when I answered the door. I could tell by his smile that he was pleased.

After the front door slammed closed, he laid a deep, wet kiss on my freshly moistened lips. "Do you have the box?"

"Yes, of course. Are we doing it right away? I've never been a brunette before. Will it wash out?" I was already kicking off my shoes and trying to unbutton his pinstriped, button-down shirt.

"It says it'll fade with each wash. It should be back to normal in a few weeks." He was running his long, lean fingers through my long blonde - for a little while longer - hair.

"Before we take care of my hair, I wanna take care of you." I bent down and unzipped his trousers. He was hard and ready for me as I kneeled before him, taking him in my mouth.

That pleasant exchange didn't take long, so we were in the kitchen eating some appetizers that I made for us: crackers with spreadable cheese and a half of a green olive on top. I tried to tease him about how different I would be if my hair was a brunette.

"Maybe I'll cut it too! Go for a totally different look." I pulled up my long hair into a shoulder-length bob to give him a taste of what I would look like with shorter hair.

"No! Absolutely not!" His sharp, quick response took me off guard,

and my shocked facial expression must have shown it. "I mean, no, I love your long hair. I just thought this might be adventurous. But don't cut it, darling." He came over to me and started to caress my head and play with my hair. Suddenly, he pulled on it quite forcefully. My neck responded with a quick jerk. "Do you hear me, bitch?"

"I hear you, master." I knew the correct response when he became dominant. I do whatever he commands. I could tell by just calling him 'master' that he was aroused again. I decided the harsh tone that he used earlier deserved a little punishment: teasing. I removed my top, looked at him with my pouty lip, and put my head under the sink to get my naturally blonde hair wet.

He opened the hair coloring kit box and started to apply the product to my hair as soon as I shut off the water. He massaged it in gently as he pressed his body up against my back side. He was totally aroused, and I had no idea what was so sexy about this process except that I knew he liked it when I bent over and touched my ankles.

Since we were in the kitchen and never made it to the bathroom shower, I never saw myself in the mirror when he was finished with the application, and we rinsed it off. He was obviously very pleased with the results. We ended up on the kitchen counter, up against the refrigerator and eventually on the hard, cold kitchen floor. As he was climaxing, I swore I heard him whisper very softly, "Lily…" But I wasn't positive. It was hard to differentiate when we were both out of breath and breathing rather heavily.

After we finished, I grabbed the uneaten appetizers and a couple of beers. We sat naked on the kitchen floor and had a little picnic.

Following a big chug of my beer, I said, "Tony, I swore I heard you call out 'Lily' while we were doing it." It was a statement, but it came out more like a question.

He didn't apologize. He didn't look appalled by the question. He didn't seem surprised at all, in fact. He just continued to nibble on our snacks without responding.

"So, did you? Seems pretty awkward that you would say my daughter's name while we were doing it." I could feel my blood pressure starting to rise, as if I already knew what he was going to say. Part of *me wanted to take back my question. My pride wanted to slap him already.*

"Daisy, I'm aware of what your name is. We have been screwing for over eight months now. I was well aware of the fact that I said Lily. I was role playing like we often do." He tossed another decorated cracker into his mouth.

Alarms sounded in my head, but again my stubborn pride needed to speak.

"You were pretending that I was my thirteen-year-old daughter, Lily? You were pretending to fuck my daughter? You were imagining her, while doing me?"

Even as the words poured out of my mouth, I couldn't believe it. Even as loose as my morals were, I was totally appalled. She is thirteen years old. She doesn't even wear a bra every day. She probably doesn't know much about sex yet. And here, a grown man was fantasizing about her. I stood up and crossed my arms across my bare chest.

"Seriously, Daisy, this is where you draw the line? You invited a strange woman whom we just met to join us in the backseat of my car. You blew me in the sanctuary of my church. You had no problem 'servicing' my college friend when he was in town. But when I simply create in my head an image of someone besides you lying breathless beneath me, you draw a line? Do you realize how bizarre that is? Do you even realize with your hair-colored brown that you look just like her?"

I touched my hair. I had forgotten in the heat of the moment.

I sprinted to the bathroom on the main floor, flipped on the light switch, and looked in the mirror. Damn! He was right. With my darkened hair I could pass as Lily's twin or sister. Shit! Was this his plan when he gave me the hair coloring kit?

Sending a jolt through my body, I suddenly heard Tony right behind me. "See, I told you. It isn't my fault that I called her name. You look just like her." He raised his hand to play with my hair, and I batted it away. Not many things turned me off, but comparing me to Lily - yep, big turn off!

D

November 1, 1983
Dear Diary,

For our weekly 'Bible Study,' Tony invited me to join him at his house. For obvious reasons, I had never stepped foot inside his home before. Normally, we met at my house, the church, at a park or some-times a shady hotel. I was anxious to see how he lived. Since I had started to imagine Tony and I as a couple, I wanted to put some details into my daydreams.

I chose my outfit carefully: a pair of tight white jeans, my favorite green tank top that fit my breasts perfectly, a black, oversized jean jacket and a pair of high heel black strappy sandals. A pair of hoop earrings decorated my earlobes.

I pulled up to the address that he provided me. The house was a two-story, colonial style, white home in a high-class neighborhood. They lived on the opposite side of town - the good neighborhood. Iowa had not suffered its first snowfall yet so the yard was still very green and freshly cut. A black iron gate surrounded the yard and home. The home was very intimidating with its big black columns standing at the front. I felt completely out of place. My stomach did a few nervous flips as I started up the sidewalk that led to the front door. The welcome mat on the large, cement porch read, "Welcome, all God's children".

I felt like a complete phony. I was one of God's children, but I was here to perform some sexual acts with my married lover and possibly another stranger to please the man I loved. Everything about this felt wrong. I wish I would've listened to my gut.

As I was about to lose my nerve and turn around and head back home, the big, black, heavy front door creaked open. To add more guilt and regret to my already sinful heart, my big brown eyes stared straight into Tony's wife Lisa's dull, hazel eyes. She was at least five inches shorter than me. Her straight brunette hair was perfectly styled and trimmed. Just like their yard: perfect and nothing out of place. During church services, I had observed her from a distance; however, we had never been this close before. She appeared very impassive.

I was expecting surprise to register on her face, but instead she politely invited me into their home. "Welcome. Come in, Daisy." She stepped to the side to allow me through the doorway.

Due to the shock of the entire situation, I simply did as I was told. I was sure my face reflected the shock and guilt I felt. As soon as I was through the doorway, I heard the big, black, heavy door shut and the dead bolt lock in place. I gulped a large wad of saliva.

If I was smarter or quicker, I would have listened to the warning alarms sounding inside my head. They were immensely powerful and were sending a tension headache my way. However, instead of running the other way, I smiled at Lisa as she offered me a glass of wine or whiskey. We had paused at the well-stocked liquor cabinet about twenty feet into the house. She was unsure of my preference. I accepted the whiskey, neat. I needed something to calm my nerves and quiet the loud voices screaming in my head.

I obediently followed Lisa down the long hallway that led to the back of the house.

Click, click, click… the heels of her sensible shoes echoed. I followed her like a stray dog down a dark alley. I was sure I would be ambushed soon.

Lisa was dressed in her usual church attire that I observed every Sunday as she sat faithfully in the front pew: black, small heel pumps, a red pencil skirt that ended just below her knees and a matching red blazer. Delicate pearl earrings and a pearl necklace completed her perfection. She probably owned this same outfit in a rainbow of colors. Honestly, she looked like a model from a 1960s catalog. Always dressed in formal attire, perfectly blended makeup and not a hair out of place. I was envious of how she pulled it all off every Sunday, and now I witnessed her in her home still presenting herself perfectly.

The long hallway led to the back of the house and into the kitchen. She stopped abruptly in front of a tall pantry door and pulled it open. It was an actual door that led into a hidden room. Alarms were sounding again in my head! I ducked my head and followed her in.

"Daisy…welcome!" I heard his familiar voice before I saw him. My eyes were trying to adjust to the dim lighting after exiting the

bright kitchen. He was seated in a room that I would describe as an old-fashioned parlor.

Tony was seated on a red velvet couch. His bare legs were crossed, and he was wearing only a black and red, silk smoking jacket. If I hadn't been so apprehensive, I would have totally been turned on. He looked powerful, assertive and sexy. In one hand, he held a rocks glass filled with an amber-colored liquor. The other was holding a lit cigar.

Against the back wall, a fully stocked bar stood. Lisa was already fixing herself a drink. A large mirror hung behind the gorgeous, black marble bar. I could see her heart-shaped face reflecting in the mirror. Her expression was blank, unreadable. As if this was just another day in her life, just another room in a pastor's house. I also caught a glimpse of myself. My brown eyes were wide open looking frightened and alert.

In front of the bar were three vacant stools. There were no windows in this room, so three lamps with low wattage were being used for light. A thin red silk cloth hung over each lamp, giving the room a pinkish haze.

"Come sit, Daisy, while Lisa prepares herself a cocktail." He persuasively patted the seat next to him on the red velvet couch. Again, I can only explain that I was so shocked that refusing to do as I was told didn't even enter my mind. This was the man whom I loved and adored so I trusted him, even if all my protective alarms were loudly ringing. I sat down next to him and took a big swig of my stiff drink.

When Lisa finished with her cocktail, she strolled towards us and took a seat in one of the chairs that sat opposite the couch. She was completely naked. She was only wearing her pearl earrings and pearl necklace. She crossed her legs and took a lady-like sip from her glass.

I think my mouth dropped to the floor, or at least it felt like it. What the hell was going on? I could no longer contain my shock and fear. I looked at Tony, "Tony?"

"Daisy, finish your whiskey, and I will gladly explain." I don't know if I even understand it, but this man has some invisible power over people. He can get people to do as he wants - even if you don't want to. I polished off my drink. I held the empty drink glass towards naked Lisa and asked if I could have another one.

Tony explained that everything that happened in this room will stay in this room. The events will never be discussed outside of these walls. I was free to leave right now, but if I didn't leave, I was agreeing to everything that was about to happen. I was not allowed to leave until Tony approved it.

"Daisy, you are my inspiration for this one-of-a-kind room. It is you and your enthusiastic sexuality that inspired me to create this grand idea. Daisy, do you want to stay?"

I looked him right in the eye. Eight months with this gorgeous, kind, sexy man. Did I want to throw it all away for some unknown sexual acts that I'm sure wouldn't kill me? My heart beat loudly in my chest. I was taking deep breaths to try to slow it down. My brain, which didn't seem to be working since the front door opened and Lisa invited me in, decided to finally break through the cobwebs and yelled, "Run!"

Lisa appeared with my second drink, a little fuller this time. I downed it in one shot and replied, "I'll stay."

A large toothy grin filled his face. My response pleased Tony.

When I handed Lisa my empty glass, I noticed she was smiling as well. However, I had never seen that smile. It seemed off - evil, odd. At first, when I saw her at the door, she seemed like one of Tony's servants doing as she was told. But her smile made me question who was in charge.

And believe me, for the next twelve hours in the red-haze room, I discovered who was the boss. It was definitely not me.

Twelve hours later, I was given back my clothes, a glass of water and allowed to leave. When the front door opened and I stepped back in the world, the sun was bright and hurt my eyes that seemed to adjust permanently to the dark of that room. I was exhausted, sore and famished. I hurried home.

I opened the door to our home as Lily had slid her backpack on and was heading out the door to school. She looked up at me as I entered. She was only thirteen, but she knew that if I was getting home at eight in the morning, I was up to no good. Her eyes showed her *disapproval. She shook her head and walked past me out the door without saying a word.*

Believe me, Lily, I'm ashamed of myself as well.

D

November 18, 1983

Dear Diary,

Not only am I to entertain the Room visitors, but Tony also demanded that I recruit them from Rusty Nail. He suggested that during my private dances I should hint at more possibilities.

This man who I envisioned as my future husband is now my pimp.

D

December 20, 1983

Dear Diary,

I've learned a lot about myself in the Room. I am not allowed to discuss who has visited the room or what we do in that room. The Room has changed me. I will never be the same, I know that now. At first, the changes seemed subtle, but now when I look back, it was huge and fast.

At first, I learned that different things pleasured me. Things that normal society would be totally appalled by. Tony and Lisa are masters at hosting this room. New ideas are slowly introduced. So subtle that you don't even realize what you are doing is wrong until it is too late. But unfortunately, the Room doesn't allow for a cleanse or forgiveness of sins. The Room is a point of no return.

My dreams as a future wife to Tony have been erased. I clearly understand what I was to him in our relationship. He was grooming me. Lisa was the hostess, and I was the entertainer. All our former adventures and sharing of fantasies led me to this hell. Tony only partly opened up to me while I was a wide-open door.

Tony explained to me that I was everyone's fantasy. I couldn't be one man's wife - I need to be shared.

"You're the ultimate fantasy for men and women. Men want to dominate you, and women want to be you. You can be everything to everyone. Never limit yourself to one man or woman. You can be so much more."

D

December 30, 1983
Dear Diary,

He broke me. He used me. He stole all my hope. He played with my heart and my body in order to manipulate me into believing he wanted a future with me. He is a master of manipulation. I could never claim that I wasn't a willing participant after everything that has happened. No one would believe me. Furthermore, no one would care.

D

Chapter Forty

January 1, 1984
> *Dear Diary,*
> *Tonight, I will write about her: Karma. I dream about her* *often.*

Karma with her emerald green eyes purposefully winked to prove to me that this was all for her amusement. Her ploy reminds me of the game, Battleship, *except my ship was enormous and easy to sink. Any letter, number combination would hit my battleship.*

"B12."

"Hit."

"D6."

"Hit." It did not matter the combination because the result was always the same. Karma does not play a game that she cannot win. She always wins.

Her shocking emerald green eyes are too large for her sharp-edged face. She is underweight and always hungry; therefore, every facial bone is defined and sharp. In the middle of her pale white face sits a pointy, slightly upturned nose, followed by her thin, pale, pink lips that surrounded her nicotine-stained teeth. At the top of her smaller-than-

normal head rests a mop of stringy, bright orange hair. If she was miniature size, she would resemble an evil Irish Leprechaun.

This is the woman who haunts my dreams. She is the woman I see whenever I close my eyes after that bitter taste of resentment fills my mouth. Karma lurks in the shadows, always waiting for her chance to laugh in my face.

Earlier in the Room, as the men celebrated the new year, I squeezed my eyes shut to block out the one sense I could control from my surroundings. Under my eyelids, I saw her... laughing. Throwing her orange, stringy head of head back and slapping her thigh as if my pain and suffering filled her soul with pure enjoyment and satisfaction. To Karma, my failure was pure entertainment. She got off on watching me suffer for any good deed that came my way.

D

Chapter Forty-One

January 15, 1984

Dear Diary,

So, when I looked up the definition of Karma, it literally was like a slap in the face. I don't deserve all Karmas' retaliation. Maybe it is passed down through generations, in order to "right" the universe. Thanks, Father!

Webster told me that Karma results from actions. I wonder if Karma has an expiration date.

D

April 15, 1984

Dear Diary,

Things seemed normal, or as normal as they are when you are summoned to the Room several times a week. I was getting used to different partners, different moves, different requests. Almost nothing shocked me anymore.

I vowed and even signed an official-looking document stating that I would never discuss who or what happened in that Room. I have no intention of not keeping that promise. I have pleasured men of political power in that room. I have shared spit with their wives and mistresses if they came along. I have performed 'circus acts,' if requested. Occasionally, I was given a generous tip for my services, outside of my normal pay.

But after five months of working in the Room, I reached my limit. For the guests, I was mixing strong cocktails behind the bar dressed as Lisa was during my first time: pearls and high-heeled shoes. Lisa was delivering my well-made drinks to the businessmen who were relaxing and conversing on the red velvet couches. There were six distinguished men visiting. The room was filled with their cigar smoke and deep, hearty laughs. The alcohol was lifting any unease that they might have been feeling.

Suddenly I heard the heavy deadbolt turn, and the secret door opened. Tony was leading three reluctant teenage girls into the Room. The tallest, most confident teenager had long, flowing blonde hair. Her friend walking reluctantly next to her had short, stylish brown hair and was of Asian descent. The last girl's hair was jet black, which was a sharp contrast to her very pale complexion. The innocent expressions on their youthful faces were similar to my reaction to this room five months before: scared, apprehensive and shocked.

I take that back!

Two girls were scared, apprehensive and shocked. The blonde bombshell appeared aroused and excited. She didn't seem innocent or surprised. She appeared confident. She had been here before. From my quick read and observations of her, she was the leader of the pack. She must've talked her two naive friends into joining her. Tony's hands were placed on the small of the two girls' backs, gently guiding them into the Room, the point of no return.

The voices of the older men seated on the couches dropped an octave at the appearance of the young guests. One man removed his suit jacket and nodded in acknowledgement to the veteran of the teenagers. She must have been his personal request.

The brunette girl standing next to her shed a single tear. That would be her final natural instinct if she was able to survive this room. Tony whispered something in her ear that I am sure informed her that

that type of emotion was not allowed. She nodded in response and inhaled a deep breath.

After months of 'entertaining' with Lisa, I became knowledgeable of her mannerisms. We have never talked about what is happening; everything between us had been nonverbal. With the entrance of the new young girls, I noticed her back stiffened.

Because we were both in love with Tony in our own sick ways, we seemed to accept him and his odd, abnormal, kinky sexual desires. We accepted whatever he would offer us for attention. Honestly, as I write this, I think Lisa and I are very much alike: we both believed Tony was our knight in shining armor. He was everything we wanted. He was good looking, romantic and attentive. Those qualities are what hooked us. As soon as we were suckered in, he slowly introduced his deranged side, and Lisa and I are weak women. We had become accustomed to his attention and love. At first, what he asked of us was not too out of the ordinary for lovers; however, with each request, he brought us one step closer to the real 'Tony' and this room that encompassed his deep, dark fantasies.

To help solidify and escalate his power in the church and in the community, we were performing sexual acts with other men of power for Tony. It amazes me that other pillars of our and nearby communities also shared the same sick hunger and bizarre desires as Tony. He fulfilled their desires and kept their secrets while they helped him rise untouchable in society.

By the end of each evening, the men were satisfied, happy and relaxed. Lisa and I were robotic. We completed what was expected of us. Our physical acts were nothing more than that to us.

But Tony's new recruits would be deeply scarred. The young blonde, who I eventually learned was named Isabella, seemed to enjoy and acknowledge the strong, sexual power she had over these men. But she was young and naive and didn't realize that it would not last. Too soon, she would realize her power fades every time she gives herself to them. She loses a fraction of her power every time she enters this room. She will eventually become resentful of Tony and how he stole her youth and innocence. But like me, it will be too late. I was seduced as a *child by an older man who knew better and then discarded me just as quickly. These scars run deep.*

The other two girls looked physically sick, like they might throw up what little contents their stomachs held. Hopefully, they weren't virgins before this momentous night.

The brown-haired one seemed to be in a state of shock. She 'accepted' everyone that requested something of her. I wasn't sure if it was out of fear or indifference. She was staring blankly at the opposite wall as she sat naked on one of the red couches. There was a man resting on each side of her smoking their cigars. They were unsympathetic to her catatonic state.

She reminds me of my younger self. She is the reason I never went back.

D

May 1, 1983
Dear Diary,
I'm not sure why, but I documented a list of names that Tony and the Room demanded that I never breathe a word of. I am going to keep it locked in my dresser. Most of these men went by a nickname in the Room, but many times I recognized them from the newspaper or local news. If I saw one of them outside of Tony's home, I would never acknowledge them. Not even with a nod, a glance or a polite "hello". Nothing. Ever.

I did see some of them around town. A couple of these men even attended church with their wives and children. Yes, I was told that I must still attend church regularly. It would have looked odd or questionable if I suddenly stopped. People might notice my absence. I truly doubt that. I think it was just another way for Tony to control me.

I did everything Tony and Lisa requested of me for five months while I was seeing Tony and became a regular entertainer in the Room. I was paid well for my services and silence. I felt hollow inside, so it was easy to follow their rules.

... Until the young brunette participated in the room. She was a

broken, naive, younger version of me. She cleared the fog of sins that Tony had created. I learned her name was Ivy. Ivy Just.

When I didn't return Tony or Lisa's phone calls that requested my attendance in the Room, I received numerous home visits.

I finally opened the door to Lisa, who was pounding with her now-red fist on my front door. I told her I was never coming back, but don't worry, I would not breathe a word to anyone. This is the longest conversation we had ever had. For some reason, she simply nodded and left my home. No heated argument or physical bullying. It was almost as if she wished she could escape the Room with me.

D

Chapter Forty-Two

1989

Daisy's dark secret grabbed my soul and squeezed it tight. The Room haunted my sleep. After reading Daisy's 1983 and 1984 journals, I suffered many sleepless nights on the count of nightmares waking me in the middle of the night. I couldn't keep this ominous secret to myself any longer. I needed to confide in someone, but it had to be someone I trusted. This newly acquired information was going to eat me up inside. It was so much bigger than me. I needed to talk to someone who would give me honest and healthy advice. Someone who I respected as well. The only person I could imagine talking to right now was Kitty.

I hated to burden her again with more of my troubles. She had already seen me through so much turmoil as a teenager: many disappointments with Daisy, Daddy's sudden death, and even my painful breakup with Matthew. Kitty always hugged me, patted my back and purred, "Everything will be alright," into my ear. Kitty was my anchor.

She was my solid ground, always there when I needed her. I needed her again.

The clock indicated it was thirty minutes after one. My daydreaming consumed a large chunk of my day along with Captain Morgan's hangover that I suffered from last night's too many refills.

Maybe if I finished the bottle, I would quit drinking. Haha! *Good one, Lily!* I almost sounded like my mother.

When I reluctantly walked into Kitty's Cafe, I found her perched at the lunch counter balancing her business checkbook. The Cafe smelled of grease from one too many hamburgers frying in the kitchen, but the decor welcomed everyone. It had a personal feel to it since Kitty decorated the walls with pictures of different 1960s albums from some of her favorite bands. The booths lining the wall were red, and the floors were black and white checked. The swinging door to the kitchen was covered in bumper stickers that people either donated from their travels or Kitty found amusing. The tabletops and kitchen counter, which was on the opposite side of the restaurant, were white with black and white speckles in it. The customer side of the counter was lined by circular, red stools with no backs on them. These were normally occupied by the local farmers who came to the cafe to compare crop stories and take a little break from their hard work in the fields.

The door chimed my arrival. Kitty's face lit up when she identified me stepping in.

"Hey, Lily! Are you hungry? I can have Hank whip up your favorite: a Bet Your Ass BLT and french fries." Kitty's menu reflected her quick wit and humor. She meant no one any offense; she just thought laughing was more important than anything else. Numerous times, Kitty offered me her advice.

"Girl, you have to be able to laugh at yourself. Quit taking life so seriously. I know you have lots going on at home, but make sure you don't let it steal your humor. Smiling and laughing are so important for the soul. As soon as you stop laughing, you grow old. Stay young, Lily."

I had not ventured into the cafe looking to eat, but the mention of food caused my stomach to grumble. "That would be great. I didn't realize I was hungry."

I plopped down next to Kitty at the counter and removed my jacket. Hank obediently nodded from the kitchen window that he overheard the late lunch order.

"Girl, you are carrying around some nasty aura." She waved her arms around the air above my head as if she could push the aura away. "What is going on? Lily, talk to me." She pushed her checkbook and adding machine away, rose from her seat and poured me a Coke.

The cafe was empty, probably just cleared out after the lunch rush. I knew I could talk to Kitty, but Hank was a male and I didn't know him very well. What if he was a previous visitor of the Room or a friend of Pastor Tony's? I needed to be discreet and careful. I could feel the importance of the information that I had locked up inside of me. Kitty noticed my eyes shifting from her to Hank and to the front door. This amazing woman had another skill besides being a great listener and advice giver: the ability to read people. Small body movements caught her attention. She absorbed the words, body language and anything between the lines.

"I need to put my feet up a bit. Let's move our conversation to the back booth." As Kitty locked up her checkbook and put the adding machine under the counter, she directed her attention to the kitchen. "Hank, give me a holler when our favorite employee's BLT and fries are finished. I will come get it. Then take the afternoon off. Us ladies can handle any late lunchers." We collected our drinks and got comfortable in the semi-private back booth. Kitty decided to talk my ear off while we waited for my BLT.

"Did I tell you Tarasue decided to major in Nursing? Yep! Makes her momma proud! Both my girls make me proud." She gave me a little wink; she considered me one of her girls, even though she gave birth to only one daughter. "Did you confirm your major declaration yet? Criminal Justice - you are gonna be a star, Lily! I just know it. Maybe you will get to meet Jon and Poncho from *CHIPs*. They are so dreamy." She rested her chin on her hands and closed her eyes to picture her favorite actors.

"Kitty, seriously? They are actors; not real cops." I giggled at her comment. She had the biggest crush on Poncho.

"Well, then maybe the show could hire you to give them legal advice. You could help them with their story lines and make sure they are accurate and realistic. That would be rad!"

She knew how to lighten my mood and make my grin stretch from ear to ear. "Kitty, you are nuts! I am not going to major in Criminal Justice so I can be an advisor on a TV show. I want to solve real crimes, help real people seek justice."

In the middle of me trying to convince her that Poncho was simply hired by MGM, we heard Hank holler, "Order up! And I am out of here. You two have a good afternoon." And Hank was out the front door. He didn't need to be told twice to take the afternoon off.

"All right, girl, we're alone. You eat and then tell me whatever is on your mind. It can't be as bad as your pretty face is making it seem."

After I chewed and swallowed two bites of my sandwich, I summarized what I read in Daisy's 1983 diary. I noticed that the first time I mentioned Pastor Tony's name, Kitty's face lost a little color, but I kept going with the details of the Room and the things Daisy described doing in there.

"I don't know what to do. I mean, I know what I should do, but I am scared. These are some serious accusations. This is huge, Kitty, tell me what to do." By now, I was crying and begging her to do what she was so wonderful at - give me advice and boss me around.

She didn't answer me right away. She sipped her water and rubbed the temples on her forehead.

"Wow, Lily... this is heavy. I had no idea that this is what was behind your troubled expression. I need to think about this. I need some time to process it all."

"I know. This is so awful and involves so many members of this town and nearby towns. It will crush these people and their families. I am not sure if it's worth sharing after all these years."

Kitty stood up, came over to my side of the booth and held me while I shed new tears.

"Kitty, that isn't everything." I swallowed hard and looked her in the eye. She was caught off guard and appeared afraid of what more information I had to tell her. "Over Christmas break, I tracked down Pastor Tony. He has a new church, not far from where I go to college."

"Please don't tell me he opened another Room."

"Not that I know of. But he did conceive a child with a sixteen-year-old member of his congregation and is blackmailing her family to keep their mouths shut. Kitty, he is a monster."

"How do you know all of this, Lily? How do you know it is true?"

I explained to her how I met Flo at the town's local restaurant and that it was Flo's best friend's daughter who had his baby. I could tell she was stunned and appalled by my latest news, even more so than the Room. I found both equally disgusting but felt completely awful for the innocent teenage girl, Lucy, who became a pawn in his game of revenge.

"Lily, I need more than water. I will be right back." I didn't know Kitty to be much of a drinker, but desperate times call for desperate measures. But instead of going to the kitchen to grab a bottle of liquor, she walked to the front door and locked it. She turned the sign over to announce that the cafe was closed.

I finished my BLT while I waited for Kitty to return. When she sat back down, she offered me a cigarette from her Marlboro pack. I shook my head, never could choke one down. She lit up her Marlboro and took a few long drags. I absently nibbled on my french fries while I waited for her to share her thoughts. She always thought before she spoke - she chose her words carefully. She prided herself on using the right words, not more words. In another life, I could imagine her being a great therapist.

It was my turn to be shocked and appalled.

"Lily, what I am about to tell you cannot leave this room. This needs to stay between us until we, as a team, figure out our next steps." She paused to take another inhale of her nicotine that seemed to be calming her nerves. She obviously was the absolute right person to confide in. Kitty would help me with a plan. She would know the right thing to do. "I can trust you, can't I, Lily?"

"For sure, Kitty! I would hide a dead body for you."

She giggled a bit which helped to break the tension. "Very good to know."

"Seriously, Kitty, you are more of a mother to me than Daisy. I would do anything for you. We are a team. You can count on me."

"Pastor Tony... Anthony... he was my stepbrother." She paused to let the revelation sink in. As she took another drag of her cigarette, my brain started to catch up and grasp this startling fact.

"What? I don't understand. How did I never know this? The same Pastor Tony with the Room and the baby with the teenager?"

"His father and my mother were married for a few painful, dramatic years. Anthony lived with us after his biological mother suddenly passed away. Her family would not take him. We didn't know why, but I have my suspicions. My stepfather was a good, kind man. He wanted to do what was right - they both did.

"Before he moved in, I heard my stepfather and my mother discussing Anthony many, many times. He had been in trouble at his last school. After each truancy, his defiance of rules grew. First, he cheated on a math test. Then he rigged all the fire alarms to go off at the same time and finally, hid in the girls' locker room after volleyball practice. Stuffed in a locker, he silently watched the girls change clothes.

"My mother worried about us being the same age under the same roof. We were both fourteen years old. She never shared her worries or concerns about Anthony with me, only behind closed doors with my stepfather. I overheard bits and pieces through the paper-thin walls of our home.

"Instantly, after meeting Anthony, I knew something was off with him. My gut instinct warned me. His Cheshire smile held a hidden meaning, or maybe it was the twisted twinkle in his eye that was not from happiness or joy.

"We literally had just opened the front door to his arrival and already I felt like his prey. His head tilted to the side when he looked me over. Up and down. Back up to my face. The look that I read on his face was approval. Unfortunately, at fourteen years old, you don't know to trust your instincts fully yet. You listen to the rules laid out by your parents, the school, and law enforcement. 'Don't be silly. He is a harmless boy. Just give him a chance.' You assume they know best.

"He was sneaky. And he lied about even the smallest things. It was as if he just wanted to see what he could get away with. He hid my mother's jewelry all the time, making her feel like she was being extremely forgetful. She would search the entire house looking for her wedding ring in a true panic. And then suddenly the next day, she discovered it in her jewelry box where she always kept it. It had not been there the day before. But I could see his shifty eyes and his wicked smile. I knew he did it just to torment her. He enjoyed the control over her weakness.

"They brought him to see a therapist once, who chalked up his odd behavior to his own mother's sudden death and being ripped from the only home, school and town that he knew. The doctor prescribed some anxiety medications which seemed to mellow him down a bit. But his evilness couldn't be controlled by medication. It was in his soul.

"Then he became obsessed with our church. He had never been to a church service before, and he was completely in awe of our pastor. I remember him making strange comments like, 'Pastor Abraham possesses God's powers. God speaks to him and controls his words. God can make people do anything He wills them to do.' My stepfather tried to explain to him that God wasn't like that. God is love, not possession and control over another person. Believing in God is a wonderful choice that a person can make. He doesn't make us believe Him. We chose to.

"But Anthony did not listen. He had a mind of his own. Eventually, my stepfather and mother figured his current obsession with religion would not do him any harm, so they welcomed it. And the more he studied the Bible, the sooner he would see the true meaning of God. He would be better for it if he came to his own understanding.

"As time passed, I simply viewed Anthony as a strange, nerdy, obsessive boy. Even though we lived under the same roof, we didn't interact much since we had different interests and friends. He had lived with us for months by this time. I paid him little attention, and he started to blend in as time went on.

"But then one Friday night, I was relaxing in my bedroom reading. My mother and stepfather were at another couple's house playing cards. Anthony stumbled into my bedroom but carefully shut my bedroom door. I thought I heard the door lock. I glanced up at him. He had never been in my room before. This was my private space. As he looked around at the posters on my walls, I asked him, 'What are you doing in here, Anthony?' He never answered me and didn't even acknowledge that he heard my question. 'Hello? Earth to Anthony! Get out of my room!' He seemed dizzy or something. He acted like he was in a trance walking around my room, touching things and ignoring me.

"It was then that I noticed he had an erection pushing from the inside of his sweatpants. It was hard not to notice when he reached the side of my bed, and his fingers traced my alarm clock and lamp. He was within inches of me. Before I knew what was happening, he was undressed and on top of me ripping my pajamas off of me. I tried to fight him off, but I was no match for him. Another one of his obsessions after moving in with us became lifting weights. He was strong, muscular and intimidating. I tried to scream, but he stuffed a dirty tube sock in my mouth. It was all over in a matter of minutes. But before he exited my body, he warned me not to tell anyone.

"'No one will believe you over me. You sneak out of the house at night to serve your many boyfriends. It will be your word, a word of a whore, over my word, the word of a church choir boy. Don't even try it, or I will come back. Again and again and again.' Then he penetrated me one last time before he stood up next to my twin bed and put his sweatshirt and sweatpants back on.

"I didn't tell anyone, except my parents eventually because I had to. This is the first time I have discussed it in eighteen years. I was so ashamed and terrified of him. I kept my head down and tried to act normal. Until I couldn't act normal anymore..."

Her voice trailed off at the last part. Somewhere in the middle of her story, I reached across and held onto the hand that she was not smoking with. Tears rolled down both of our faces. I didn't know what information to process first. This man who seduced Daisy into many, many sexual acts with many, many different partners then bore a child with a young teenage girl that he seduced as well, started this deviant sexual nature as a teenage boy himself. What made someone like this? This man was so much worse than I ever thought.

"Kitty, I am so so sorry. I had no idea. I just didn't know what to do. I didn't have any idea that you knew Tony at all."

"I ran away from California when I was seventeen years old. I needed to get as far away as I could. I couldn't be anywhere near him. He was evil. I left and didn't tell anyone where I was. Normal, Iowa, sounded like the perfect town to start fresh.

"Lily, I was pregnant."

My eyes searched hers. Pregnant? At seventeen? Why run away from home if you are pregnant and only seventeen? Unless you are running from something... or someone?

"Oh, no... Was the baby Tony's?" I saw the painful answer in her eyes even before she responded. My heart broke for her.

"Yes, and I don't want Tarasue to know. She must not know that that vile, disturbed man is biologically tied to her. Understand, Lily? It would break her. This is the reason I fled. This is the reason I have tried to protect her from him for years. When he showed up here in Normal a few years ago, I thought he had figured it out: that Tarasue was his daughter. He didn't, but he did want to scare me a bit by showing me that I could not escape him. It worked." I had never in all my years of knowing Kitty seen her this vulnerable and simply crushed. She was weeping uncontrollably. The smoking had ceased. I slid over to her side of the booth and wrapped my arms around her and shared her deep sorrow.

Chapter Forty-Three

1989

Following Kitty's confession that Pastor Tony was her stepbrother, we both decided to keep our shared secrets to ourselves a little longer while we brainstormed a plan. Thankfully, Kitty agreed with me that we couldn't simply let this terrible, abusive man get away with years of torment to his silent, defensive victims. Kitty wanted me to check Daisy's notes for additional clues and of course to look for the list Daisy created with the names of his men.

"If we could verify what your mother claimed to have happened, we might even be able to follow up with charges against him. He could serve some serious time."

My homework included investigating Daisy more. We didn't have any real reason not to believe her writings, but as a character witness, she was sketchy. While she was in a coma, she was obviously unreliable.

Kitty and I agreed that we could not wait to inform Flo. She needed to tell Molly.

It was time to call Flo. We had been in touch a couple of times since Daisy's stroke. I called her at home as soon as I returned home from visiting Kitty. If I was lucky, Flo would have the night off from waitressing and be lounging around at home with her husband.

I was in luck. Her familiar southern drawl, that I missed so much, answered the phone on the fourth ring.

"Hi, Flo! It's me, Lily."

"Lily! Hi there, sweet thin'! I was just talkin' about you. Are your ears-a-ringin'?" She giggled her one-of-a-kind giggle. "How are you, darlin'? Comin' home to me anytime soon? I could use some face time with my Lily." If Kitty was like a mother to me, Flo was like a grandmother.

"Do you have a few minutes, Flo? And can you sit down?" I cleared my throat; it was feeling awfully dry. This was not information that should be revealed over the phone. I wish I could see her face and give her a hug.

"Oh, darlin', you have me nervous. What in tarnations could be so terrible that I gotta sit down? Spill it, Lily, before you give ole Flo a heart attack - oh! That is so insensitive of me with all you are goin' through. Scratch that, will ya? I am so sorry. My mouth has no filter some days. I am sorry. Go ahead, Lily. I am listenin'."

"It's okay, Flo. Don't worry about it. No harm done. But listen to me for a minute, will you?" I paused for a couple of seconds where I imagined her nodding her head in agreement. "It is about Pastor Tony. I have new information."

"What has that son of a bitch done? How can one evil man wreck so much havoc on one tri-state area? I swear, if I could get away with it, I would darn near run him over myself! I know lots of people would thank me."

I summarized the strongest facts from Daisy's diary regarding the Room and the fact that he had minors involved. I did not mention yet that Kitty was his stepsister - it didn't seem relevant yet. The purpose of my phone call was to keep Flo 'in the know' and to assure her that I was still determined to make him pay for his awful, devilish choices and sexually abusive influence.

When I was finished, I heard Flo take a sharp breath. Then there was a long silence. I tried to imagine what she was doing on the other end of the phone. Probably finally taking my advice and sitting down. I waited patiently with the phone pressed to my ear. The information needed to settle and the shock to subside, so she could process all that I had told her. A weak sob escaped her throat.

"Pam?" I purposefully spoke her real, God-given name to gain her attention and prove that we shared secrets and that I kept my promises as well. "I'm so sorry I had to tell you this over the phone, but I couldn't wait any longer. I just discovered all of this myself. I'm trying to figure out the next step so we don't screw this up. He needs to be punished."

After she blew her nose and sniffled, her confidence spoke volumes. "Oh, Lily, darlin' this is good news. That son of a bitch is gonna fry! I can already smell his burnt skin! Time for a barbeque!" I could imagine her kicking her husband's chair to get his attention. "Honey, light up the grill. We are havin' us some steaks for supper to celebrate!"

Chapter Forty-Four

1989

I t was time to reunite with Daisy at the Cornbelt Nursing Care facility. I had been avoiding her. My feelings of heartache, shock and pain had lessened a small fraction. Mentally stronger. Confiding in Kitty and discovering a shared desire had eased my sense of dread and loneliness. For some reason, even with Daisy lying in a coma, I still feared my sudden, intense heartbreak that I couldn't control whenever I was near her. Even though years had passed since we shared a heart-warming connection - or at least what my naive heart believed we once did - seeing her each time evoked a continual, secret yearning for her acceptance. I still wanted and yearned for the love of my mother. I still hoped that someday she would grab me and pull me into a tight embrace and whisper in my ear the love she felt for me.

Recognizing that I still harbored those emotions proved to me how pathetic that wish was. Time after time she demonstrated the complete opposite. Time after time she had treated our relationship with abso-lutely no interest. Time after time she voiced her dislike and disgust for anything 'Lily-related'. An instinctive psychological longing to be loved by your own biological mother could be the only reasonable explanation for why I continued with the internal struggle. A physical tightness squeezed my lungs and made it difficult to breathe. While my body battled against an unseen force, my brain rolled its eyes in annoyance of my weak, vulnerable heart.

My weak side squeezing my heart was what guilted me into visiting Daisy again. I didn't extend much attention or care to my physical appearance. I ran a brush through my long brown hair, grabbed a clean sweatshirt from my pile of freshly washed clothes and headed for the door. When I opened the door, I heard birds chirping, neighbors working in their yards, car doors shutting and engines roaring to life. Spring was peeking out from behind winter. Earth's creatures were happy about her appearance even though meteorologists only predicted a short two-day higher than normal temperature rise. Living in the Midwest taught the citizens to take advantage of any amount of glorious, pleasant weather. Midwesterners knew the likelihood of snow or rain was highly possible after a perfect springlike day.

I decided after being influenced by the neighborhood buzz to walk to the nursing home. It wasn't as if I needed to be there at any certain time or stay too long. Time seemed to stand still in those Lysol-smelling walls. But outside in Normal, the world was waking up and stretching its winter-white arms and was bound and determined to enjoy Mother Nature's gift of sunshine and warmth.

My long lean legs ached when they reached the sidewalk and begged for a faster pace. I had been neglecting my body since returning to Normal after Daisy's stroke. My daily runs ceased. The neglect was not purposeful; I enjoyed running. I loved the endorphins it produced, I loved the fresh air filling my lungs, I loved how my body felt, and I loved the freedom of running. As the flashbacks filled my head, my legs naturally began a slow jog. I wasn't dressed for a regular run, but a short jog in my worn-out sneakers was doable and just what I needed. An uncontrolled smile crept on my face. *Thank you, Mother Nature!*

By the time I reached the nursing home on the opposite end of town, my body felt good. A little out of breath, but good. I smiled at the receptionist at the front desk and gave her a polite head nod. Everyone at the facility knew who I was. Not only did I look a lot like Daisy, but it also was a small town. People talked. The receptionist, dressed in the assigned - color-coded yellow for non-medical personnel

- nursing facility scrubs, did not return my smile or head nod. Odd but not unusual. The grimace on her pudgy, round face appeared apprehensive. Kinda like she was surprised to see me. I would accept her response since it had been a week. I deserved it.

I continued to stroll down the hallway towards Daisy's current residency. Lysol and urine filled my nostrils. Nope didn't miss that. I noticed a bit of a commotion at the end of the corridor, near Daisy's room. The disturbance included clapping, giggling and cheering. I had never witnessed such positive, boisterous noises in this building before. I wondered what was going on.

One of the male nurses named Scott, whom I honestly thought was mute because I have never heard him speak, noticed me approaching Daisy's room. He leaned on the doorway just outside of her room. His smile evaporated into a look of concern similar to the receptionist's expression. He quickly disappeared into Daisy's room. He shushed the room, and I overheard him explain to the group gathered, "She's here. The daughter."

As I rounded the corner of the doorway to her room, I was not at all prepared for what I witnessed: surrounded by four female nurses and Scott lay Daisy in her nursing home bed with her doe-like, brown eyes wide open.

The grumpy old nurse, who announced recently that Daisy had wet herself, approached me first. The leader of the pack.

"We was gonna call ya. I came in to change her beddin', and she was sittin' there all awake. Scared the shit out of me!" Her nursing friends giggled from behind her. I couldn't remember her name, and her required name tag was not pinned to her assigned blue nursing home scrubs - blue was the code for medical staff. "We already phoned the doc who said she would hightail it over here. Damn near miracle, if you is askin'." Grumpy turned to her friends. "Come y'all. Let's leave these fine ladies alone to get reacquainted."

As the nurses made their way out the door, Daisy and I simply stared at each other. There was no mother-daughter moment of joyful screams or big bear hugs. There wasn't even a crack of a smile or a single tear sliding down a cheek. Our relationship was not the makings of a Hallmark movie. I knew I was the last person she wanted to see when she woke up from a lengthy slumber. Furthermore, she knew that being with her was the last place I wanted to be. Yet, for months I played the role of the devoted, loving daughter. I visited often. I asked questions about her care, and I thanked the staff for all their help. A few people even witnessed me talking to her in a hushed whisper. No one inquired about our relationship before the coma, except for Bouncing Nurse Jenny. When she paused for a moment between her many drawn-out stories, she would ask me personal questions regarding Daisy:

"Is she married or divorced?"

"What does she do for a living?"

"Were you two close?"

When people inquire about your day - "How are you doing today?" - they are not expecting a deep, long answer. They are expecting a response as simple as, "Good. How are you?" Even though it's a probing question, no one expects a response like, "Shitty! My father, the only person who truly loved me, suddenly died last year. Further-more, I recently discovered he was not actually my biological father. My mother, the town's whore, is lying in a nursing home because she is in a coma after suffering from a stroke. I'm her only living relative, and even though we hate each other, I'm the only one who can take care of her. So yep, shitty sums it up. Aren't you glad you asked?"

As we continued to stare at each other in silence, my brain fired all these thoughts.

Now, what? I couldn't return to college for the summer semester. Would she move home and I had to help bathe her and wipe her butt? How would she afford to keep the house? How could she pay her bills if I went back to college? How would I mentally handle this? Would she ever talk, walk or feed herself? Was it a good thing she was awake? Or would it have been easier if she would have just died?

"Well, this is a twist I had not been expecting today. Good morn-ing, Daisy."

I forced myself to enter her room and head for what was designated as my chair. Her curious eyes followed me across the room. She was alert, more than I imagined she would be when and if she ever woke up. The silence was uncomfortable, mainly because I was the only one who could speak, so the pressure was on me. But I didn't want to be wasteful with my words. *Choose them wisely.*

"Your eyes are open, obviously. But can you hear and understand what is going on?"

I looked at her for any slight feedback that her fragile brain had processed my question. I received only a blank stare. I was sure she had many questions but didn't know how to formulate a question. If I had control over anything in regards to her sudden consciousness, I decided it would be information. Yes, it was petty and downright cruel, especially considering she was handicapped.

Before I could feel any more guilt - which wasn't much - Dr. Murphy entered the room slightly out of breath.

"Wow. I heard but needed to see it with my own two eyes. Hi, Daisy." Dr. Murphy reached out and squeezed Daisy's hand. From what I gathered, Daisy was only able to open her eyes; it didn't appear she had any control of her body and its movements. "It's nice to officially meet you. I'm Dr. Murphy here at Cornbelt Nursing Care. You've been here for about a month now. Do you understand what I am telling you? Blink once for no and twice for yes."

Are you kidding me right now? If she doesn't understand, she won't blink at all. Does this doctor have credentials? While I was thinking what a joke this doctor was, she began to take Daisy's pulse and used her stethoscope to listen to her heart. The only response from Daisy was a blank stare. Her eyes darted from me to the doctor then back again to me. She appeared overwhelmed and confused. "It's okay, Daisy. It's a lot to process right now. Each day, you will show us signs of improvement. I'm sure of it."

To me, Dr. Murphy said, "She is a bit agitated right now. I think we need to keep her stimuli to a minimum until we can get her heart rate under control. I could give you ten minutes of alone time, and then I would want to run some evaluations on her and get her relaxed. Will that be enough time?" She suggested I could come back later to visit longer.

"No problem at all." I forced one of my sweet smiles onto my face. "That would be wonderful. Thank you."

"Sure. I need to check on another patient and will be back in about ten minutes." She turned to Daisy again and grinned. "Welcome back, Daisy."

Ten minutes.

Chapter Forty-Five

1989

K*arma is a bitch, but so is she.*
Yet, I calmly and patiently remained seated beside her, embracing the silence and wanting to remember every aspect of this quiet moment. I wanted to get it just right. It might be the last time I sit next to her. Trying to think of the perfect words, I gently held her right hand with both of my hands and rubbed the large vein that extended from her thumb to her wrist. If a stranger walked by and randomly looked into her room, they would assume that they witnessed a tender moment between two women who appeared extremely close. I stared down at her aging, pale hands. Hands showed the first signs of aging. Her hands looked one hundred years old. Her slender, bony hands endured a lot of self-inflicted suffering. Age spots, freckles and lots and lots of wrinkles. No fancy rings decorated her slender fingers. A nursing home bracelet that labeled her by name, birthdate and room number circled her thin wrist. Her nails were trimmed short. No visible cuticle. No need for polish or even filing. Those hands weren't going anywhere.

Her hospital bed was slightly elevated. No IV cords hung from her veins. The white hospital sheets were tucked tightly around her small frame as she took up a minimal amount of space in the twin sized bed. Two pillows supported her head.

She had lost weight since she began her residence at the nursing home. She had always been thin; took care of herself and never over-indulged in treats or snacks. "Once on the lips, forever on your hips" was one of her coined sayings. The weight loss made her look fragile and weak laying in her bed. Her face that once captivated men of every age contained wrinkles and many brown age spots earned from the sun. Her smile - that hadn't gleamed often in my direction - was set in a permanent scowl. Her eyes were still deep brown, but now sadness, worry and concern lined them. Between her eyes sat her small, perfectly proportioned nose. Her slim, long neck held up her once head-turning face that was framed by her wavy, blonde hair that landed just below her shoulder blades. Her hair that hadn't been styled lately fanned across her pillow. The nursing home provided a professional hair stylist to wash and style her hair once a week. I knew she would complain about what a 'piss-poor' job the minimum wage hair stylist did if she could complain, talk. But she couldn't.

Her neck bones and its veins stuck out, almost like it could be easily snapped and then her head would roll to the side, lifeless. Her perky size-C rack was supported by her slim hips and long, lean legs. She had been a knockout, and she knew it. She used her physical beauty to her advantage whenever she could. In her youth, all of these features gifted her with runway model looks. But as she lay helplessly in her nursing home bed, a stranger would have no idea what a beauty she once was.

She smelled like an old person; maybe it was the oil on the aging skin or perhaps aging pores secreting decades of toxic chemicals that had entered her body. Maybe odors were sins escaping through her pores. The worse the stench given off perhaps symbolized the worse the sins? *Interesting thought.* Among the old lady smell, a hint of lavender lingered from the laundry soap that was used to wash her hospital gown. In her youth she smelled like cheap grocery store perfume. The kind that lingered after she already strutted out of the room. Roses, lilacs and rosemary.

Inhale slowly, exhale slowly. I took a few deep breaths to relax myself. Years of meditation taught me techniques to calm myself. By relaxing my body and my mind, I would be able to muster up the right words that I needed to formulate.

I glanced around the room. No crayon-colored pictures lined her basic white walls. No 'Get Well Soon' balloons floated in the sanitized air. No bouquet of flowers blessed the room with its fragrance. No personal effects were displayed. Her faded pink robe that had seen better years hung from a hook on the back of the bathroom door.

Her room contained a large picture window that overlooked the resident park and allowed a great amount of natural light into the room. The park was quiet except for the aggressive black birds fighting over the tiny left-over seeds in the popular bird feeder. The television displayed the popular game show, *The Price is Right*. I muted it. Bob Barker smiled as he welcomed to the stage the winner of the karaoke machine. Young, pregnant Carrie bid one dollar to win her trip onto the stage.

My eyes settled back on her. Honestly, she looked tired - not like she had been sleeping for months - and ready to die. I wondered what she was thinking. *Why is Lily here? Why is she not talking? What does she want now?*

I wondered if my little whispered words would help. Push her over the edge. Break her heart. Maybe it would be the nail in the coffin.

As I stood up from my chair seated next to her hospital bed, I gently leaned over. My nose buried in her unwashed, wavy hair as I moved closer so I could whisper in her ear. I felt her body immediately stiffen. She didn't appreciate me in her personal space. She wanted to push me away, but her frail body wouldn't cooperate. My coffee-stained breath whispered in her ear, telling her what I'd discovered.

"I found your precious, very disturbing diaries, Daisy. I discovered that Daddy was not my biological father. Thanks for that pain. I'm curious to know if he knew this little fact that you harbored. I also uncovered that you bedded over half the men in the town. You seduced Matthew and Coach Knight simply to hurt me. Now, it's my turn to drive a stake into your heart...that is, if you even have one. I'm going to publish all those names from the Room. Yep, that will put a big red target on your back. I will take great pleasure in watching you squirm. You can't stop me even if you wanted to.

"Furthermore, I intend to leave you here in this nursing home to rot. Laying in your own piss and shit. You are right - I am like you. Get some rest, Mother, because you look like crap."

Her body tensed up. Her eyelids closed very forcefully. She bit her dry, pale lips, leaving indents. One single tear rolled down her cheek.

Blink twice if you understand.

Blink. Blink.

Chapter Forty-Six

1989

"Daisy, are you in any physical pain?" One blink. "Daisy, do you want the TV on?" Two blinks.

"Daisy, do you want to watch *As the World Turns*?" Two blinks.

Daisy had been responding to the nursing staff's questions for over a week. She blinked twice for yes and once for no. The resident doctor Dr. Murphy informed me it was only a matter of time before she was able to communicate verbally.

"She is quite the spitfire, your mother. You can tell what exactly she is thinking by her facial expression and her big brown, curious eyes. She wants to talk. She has so much more life to live. However, she will need someone to look after her for a while though after she is discharged from here. I'm not sure she will be able to live alone."

"You're discharging her?"

"Sorry, no, not yet. I didn't mean to startle you. Of course, she needs additional tests completed, and Dr. Opland said he would personally come examine her to make sure there was nothing but her healing brain holding her back from recovering fully. But all signs are positive. Lily, your mom is coming back to you. It's truly a miracle!"

Dr. Murphy, whom I did not respect fully yet like I did Dr. Opland, previously visited Daisy only a few times before the 'great awakening'.

She was a little overzealous about caring for Daisy now that she was making history. Being the official medical staff at a small-town nursing home facility usually entailed calling the time of death, examining a resident after a hard fall out of a wheelchair, and perhaps investigating charges of neglect by her staff. I was sure having a comatose patient wake up didn't happen too often. Over half of her patients didn't talk, and the half that did communicate often didn't make much sense. A large portion of Dr. Murphy's job was time dealing with the resident's family members. Addressing their concerns and answering their questions.

When I left Dr. Murphy's office and headed towards Daisy's room, reality started to sink in. My feet became heavier and slower. She would recover and leave this facility. Each day, the nursing staff tested her physical strength and assisted her with exercise. However, she was not fully recovered from lying in a bed for almost three months. She was weak and would obviously need someone to help her around the house. And all fingers were pointing in my direction even though that was the last place Daisy or myself wanted me to be. I took a deep breath.

When I entered Daisy's room, the facility's speech therapist stood next to her bed holding up flashcards of letters. They advised me that they would start small and build on her knowledge. Each brain injury was different, and a starting ground needed to be established. Daisy answered simple yes or no questions with corresponding blinks. Yesterday, the therapist showed her numbers one through nine to see if she could match the number of fingers to the flashcard. She succeeded until number six. Using both hands at the same time proved to be more of a struggle.

I paused in the doorway so I would not interrupt them. Additionally, I was also curious as to how much Daisy comprehended. Of course, on top of my curiosity was how much she remembered of the conversations I had with her while she was unconscious. Did she want to answer my questions? Was she interested to know how much I had read? I wondered if it was killing her not to defend herself and tell me more lies to get me off track. I didn't know how much more patience I had. I remembered a Bible lesson under Pastor Tony's direction regarding patience.

"When you pray to God for patience, He doesn't just give you patience. He gives you opportunities to *be* patient." I acknowledged that was what God was doing now. I believed in His ways of teaching, but that didn't mean I had to like it.

Daisy's speech therapist finally concluded, "... great job today, Daisy! I will be back tomorrow to continue where we left off." She collected her flashcards and other supplies and meandered her way towards me blocking her only exit. "She did well today. Improving every day. You are welcome to ask her some simple yes or no questions. I should not be the only one to grill her."

The speech therapist closely resembled the sweet, short, old lady from the scary, iconic movie, *Poltergeist.* A cryptic smile played on my lips imagining this sweet speech therapist saying, "Y'all mind hanging back? You're jamming my frequency." On the top of her head, her dark black hair was twisted into a bun and provided two more inches to her five-feet-tall stature. Her clothing included a long black skirt and a multi-colored tunic that was almost as long as her skirt. I wondered if she could not only get Daisy to speak but also rid Daisy of demons as well. Dr. Murphy told me that miracles happen every day.

It was comical to me that people assumed Daisy and I wanted to speak to one another when in fact, since Daddy died, we had limited our conversation to about one hundred words a week unless we were arguing. I knew she was not worth the effort that I might put forth, and she didn't seem to care if she communicated with me as well.

After the speech therapist or perhaps the eccentric medium vacated the room, I slowly maneuvered my way to my chair.

Squeak... squeak... speak...

Just like in the movie, *Poltergeist,* the speech therapist's - the medium's - shoes marked her path down the long corridor. I couldn't contain my giggle. The squeaking eventually faded away.

I did not greet Daisy or exhibit her any polite interest. Our mother-daughter relationship never consisted of fake gestures or unnecessary small talk. Silence was welcomed by both of us. Meaningless chatter would not be wasted between us.

After I broke the news about Pastor Tony to Flo, she immediately darted over to her best friend Molly's house to reveal to her what discovery I had unearthed in Normal. As Flo described it to me, "Rivers and rivers of tears were shed, darlin'. Never seen so much pain pourin' out of one person's face!"

But the greatest news of all was that Molly, who worked at a lawyer's office as a paralegal, had a wealth of legal advice at her disposal. Her boss asked her to dig up as much factual evidence she could and direct the investigators. He was sure she had a strong case: blackmailing, sex with a minor and sex for hire. Fame, fortune and the front page of tabloids flashed in that lawyer's eyes. Cha-ching!

Following my heart-to-heart with Kitty and disclosing the latest news to Flo, I had decided that it was time for me to move on - get back to college and my own life. Daisy and her immoral character have sucked out more than she deserved. I was finished picking up the pieces and discovering harsh truths. This was the last time I would visit Cornbelt's Nursing Home. The last time I would see Daisy.

The decision to not have a relationship with my own mother would not be a popular one, but it was the right decision for me. It was not made lightly. I couldn't control her actions. I could only control how I reacted to them. I made peace with my decision. It was time to let go. It was time to move on. Forgiveness didn't equal a relationship. Forgiveness meant peace for myself and letting go. Healing couldn't happen without trust.

Before I could formulate my departing words, I heard a different set of footsteps echo in the hallway. The squeaky *Poltergeist* shoes of the speech therapist vanished. Daisy's nursing home room was located at the end of a long, tiled hallway. The noises from the nearby rooms and the long corridor echoed into Daisy's room, which was more than often quiet. I regularly sat and listened to the comings and goings of the visitors in the other nursing home rooms.

At first, the new footsteps were quieter down the hall. It sounded like dress shoes, but not high heels. The heels of the shoes clicked on the hard, linoleum floor. A man or a woman in flats. They were pronounced steps; perhaps the newest visitor had big feet. The footsteps continued to grow louder.

Suddenly, the owner of the pronounced footsteps of the big feet halted. Only a few steps outside of Daisy's nursing room door, the toes of the dress shoes pointed into the room. I noticed the shoes first, and I was right - brown Oxfords, probably a size twelve, belonging to a man. They were polished and shiny.

As my inquisitive eyes traveled up the khaki dress pants of the man standing outside the doorway, I recognized the combination of the squeaky-clean shoes and perfectly ironed slacks. The light blue dress shirt and tan overcoat were the final piece of the puzzle. My gray-blue eyes reached the familiar face of my biggest tipper. His gray, wiry eyebrows jetted upward to create deep wrinkles in his forehead. Tears sprang from his sad, gray-blue eyes that were keenly locked on Daisy. His body released a mild sob as his journey came to an end.

Then, I faintly heard a familiar, extremely weak, female voice. She hadn't spoken in months while unconscious in the hospital bed, and yet managed to softly whisper, "T?"

Chapter Forty-Seven

*M**y 1969 Thoughts***

Dear Diary - the purpose of this journal is to sort through my thoughts, give a voice to my feelings and to vent. If your name is H or Little H, get out of my room and leave my personal items alone.

~Daisy

February 11, 1969
Dear Diary,

Father has been gone for ten days now. Mother hasn't stopped crying. She will hardly get out of bed. I wish I knew what to say to help her. I am helping by completing the household chores: laundry, cleaning, and cooking. Last night, after Little H and H were tucked into their beds, I went to her bedroom - not theirs anymore, weird to say that - and paused outside of her door when I heard her praying as she knelt beside her double bed.

"Dear Lord, tell me how to go on. Give me strength and the will to live. He has shamed me and our family one hundred percent. Dear Lord, give me courage to go on. Amen."

I have no idea what she was talking about. Who is he? And what did he do?

D

February 12, 1969
Dear Diary,
I asked Mother when she finally got out of bed who had shamed us. She turned towards me, extremely upset. She wanted to know who had told me. I told her I heard her while she was praying. She told me never to be so rude and listen to someone's private conversations with God. She slammed her bedroom door and didn't come out the rest of the evening.
I miss Father.

D

February 15, 1969
Dear Diary,
After school, I saw Mrs. Adams leaving her house with a large, brown travel case. She looked very distraught and sad. Tears were running down her face and blotching her makeup. She was a mess. She didn't pay me any regard before she ducked into a car that was waiting alongside the curb in front of her house. But Mr. Adams did see me. He gave me a strained smile before he shut the front door and returned inside.
This whole scene struck me as very strange, since we have lived next to Mr. and Mrs. Adams my whole life. They are like family to us. They are my parents' friends, and we all celebrated many holidays together. They didn't have any children of their own, so I think they enjoyed spoiling us as much as we appreciated the extra attention and gifts. Mrs. Adams loved to buy me jewelry and teach me how to apply makeup to accent my virtues.
"You won't need much makeup. You are going to be a knockout one day, Daisy. If I had a son, I am sure you would break his heart," she

always told me.

Mr. Adams enjoyed teaching me new things: how to play games - chess, bridge and Yahtzee - how to build campfires, and even how to square dance. He was a great teacher. He also had a lot of patience with the boys. We all looked forward to gathering with them on special occasions or a spontaneous backyard BBQ.

Therefore, no friendly acknowledgment from either of them seemed harsh considering Father had just died. And come to think of it, neither of them attended his funeral. In fact, I don't think I have talked or seen either of them in weeks. How incredibly strange…

I miss Father.

D

February 24, 1969
Dear Diary,
Over lunch the next day, I casually mentioned to Mother that I had witnessed Mrs. Adams with her travel case, and she seemed terribly upset. I wondered where she was going. Mother's response was completely out of her character; she actually said these words, but almost like she was talking to just herself:

"Hell's bell, the bitch is gone! Thank the Lord that one good thing is happening after this whole mess! One hundred percent good riddance! The devil is watching, you evil temptress."

I have no idea why she wants her friend to move out of her home next door. Seems bizarre to me. I miss Father.

D

April 2, 1969
Dear Diary,
Sorry, it has been a while, but Mother continues to be no help around the house. I have been busy with my schoolwork, taking care of Little H and H, and keeping up with the household chores. She consumed three gin and tonics even before we got

home from school today. I found the discarded limes in the kitchen sink.

To top it off, I got my first menstrual cycle tonight, and I have no one to talk to about it. Mother is too drunk and self-involved, and Mrs. Adams has not returned home. Thank goodness for Biology class. Some things make more sense now: my clothes have been fitting differently, my shirts stretch tightly across my bosom, and my pants creep up on my bottom. I needed a bra, so I went through Mother's drawer and found one in the back that fit.

I miss Father.

D

April 4, 1969
Dear Diary,

Since Mother is half in the bag most days by the time we arrive home from school, supper has become my responsibility. Some evenings, I make toast and oatmeal, and sometimes creativity strikes. Last night, we roasted hot dogs in the backyard over a pile of sticks we collected. Little H and H loved it! They pretended we were in a faraway land hiding from the enemy. It was refreshing to be acting like ourselves and laughing again.

From my lawn chair next to the little fire, I witnessed Mr. Adams watching us sadly out of his small kitchen window. I knocked on his back door to offer him one of our fire-roasted hot dogs. He answered the door right away. Told me I was sweet, thoughtful and responsible. He added he was so proud of the beautiful young lady I was "sprouting into" - at least someone noticed. His breath resmbled the same stale smell Mother's had after a good night of binge drinking.

My arms wrapped him in a big hug before I returned to our camp-fire. He held on a little tighter and longer after I let go, but it was okay - I knew he was lonely. But then the most unusual thing happened... He quickly kissed me...on the lips! When he finally removed his arms from around me, he acted like it wasn't a big deal, but it felt awfully strange to me.

'Lips are for lovers; cheeks are for friends.' That is what I was always told.

D

April 9, 1969
Dear Diary,
Since Daddy died, bedtime has also become my responsibility. H and Little H share a room across the hall from mine. After brushing their teeth, I tuck them into their twin beds in their shared bedroom. H really doesn't need it, but I can't help myself. Little H asked me to make up a fairytale like Daddy used to. Brought tears to my eyes. I had forgotten about that. What else am I gonna forget about Daddy? His smile? His hands? His voice? I sure hope not.

To keep his memory alive, I told Little H about a princess who lived in the sea. She was a mermaid with a long fish's tale. But she wanted legs so she could walk on the beach. I can't remember all the details that Daddy included, but Little H didn't know the difference and loved the story. I miss Father.

D

April 10, 1969
Dear Diary,
Gin and tonics are Mother's new best friend. She even taught Little H how to mix them for her. Tonight, she must have reached her limit because her mouth was rambling. Something about how Mrs. Adams deserved to be in Hell. I asked her if Mrs. Adams died. She replied, "I wish." I am not sure what her rants are all about. I steer clear of her when she is like this. When Father was alive, she limited herself to one glass of wine with dinner or one gin and tonic after dinner with Father on the front porch. I miss Father.

D

April 15, 1969

Dear Diary,

Today was an unusually warm spring day. I pulled out a pair of shorts that barely covered my bottom and a tank top that I was sure would fit Little H now. I didn't have much choice, and honestly, I didn't look bad. I kinda like the curves I'm getting. I look like those girls in the teen magazines.

Our lawn needed to be cut. While I was struggling to remove the mower from the garage, Mr. Adams appeared and offered to mow our lawn for us.

"Daisy, let me be so kind as to mow your family's lawn. It is the least I can do." He had circles under his blue eyes. He looked tired and a bit lonely.

I offered a barter for the chore.

"Mr. Adams, what if we trade chores? If you mowed our lawn, I could do something you needed done at your house."

He agreed. While he cut our lawn, I dusted and vacuumed his main floor. We were both pleased with the task exchange. After he put our mower away, he enveloped me in a huge bear hug. When we parted, his hand tenderly touched my cheek, and he smiled adoringly at me.

Mr. Adams has always been a stable man in my life. He was a good friend of my father's. I have known him since I was a toddler. It felt good to be hugged again. God knows Mother hasn't hugged us in weeks. I miss Father.

D

April 20, 1969

Dear Diary,

Mr. Adams was sipping an iced tea on his front porch when I came walking home from school today. He still looked tired but seemed a bit lighter. Maybe this chore exchange was distracting him from dealing with his loneliness. He said he wanted to cut our lawn again if I dusted and vacuumed the upper level of his house. I didn't think our lawn needed the trim again but was willing to clean for him if he needed me to. I told him I needed to get my brothers home and settled in first. After I made them an after-school snack and set out food for dinner, I headed over to Mr. Adams' house. Mother was 'napping.'

After I was done cleaning and he was finished with the mowing, he offered me a glass of iced tea. We sat on his front porch. It was screened in and had matching, wooden rocking chairs to sit on. Mr. Adams was very chatty and asked me lots of questions.

"How old are you now, Daisy?" I told him sixteen, seventeen in a month. He couldn't believe it. "You are really growing into an amazing and beautiful lady. I bet you have your pick of boyfriends."

His attention made me blush. It felt good to be having a grown-up conversation with another adult. When I stood up to excuse myself, Mr. Adams sweetly grabbed onto my hand and smiled at me. "Daisy, I hope we can do this again tomorrow."

D

May 5, 1969
Dear Diary,

It is my seventeen birthday. Mother was too drunk to remember. H and Little H are too young to care. But Mr. Adams remembered. When I joined him for our afternoon iced tea, he had a cupcake with a single candle waiting for me. He even gave me a bouquet of lilies. He said they were his favorite flower, besides a daisy, of course. He has really been paying attention during our afternoon conversations on his front porch. His thoughtfulness made my day.

D

May 7, 1969
Dear Diary,

I had my first open-mouthed kiss! It was everything I ever dreamed about.

D

May 12, 1969

Dear Diary,

It has been three months and eleven days since Father has been gone. I've done my very best at keeping our family happy, healthy and fed, but I lost my temper today. Mother knew that I had plans to see a picture show, and she still proceeded to get herself completely drunk. I couldn't leave H and Little H with her in this condition. T was understanding, even though I didn't tell him the real reason I needed to cancel.

I spent the evening feeding, bathing and tucking in my brothers while Mother was passed out on the couch. I let her sleep it off. I sat in Father's old recliner in the living room patiently waiting. At midnight, when she finally woke up and seemed mildly sober, I yelled and yelled and yelled. She deserved it! I had been taking care of everything since Father died, and I was done!

"He is dead, Mother! We are all upset about that. We loved him too. We miss him too, but you need to pull it together!"

But her rebuttal pierced my heart like a sword.

She told me Father was no saint. Her exact words are still ringing in my ears, "You are one hundred percent right. I am sorry, Daisy, that I have been a shit for a mother. I can't seem to grasp that when your father took his last breath, it was in another woman's bed. It is hard to mourn his death and our relationship at the same time."

"What are you talking about? I thought he was here with you when he had his heart attack? The ambulance was parked in front of our house?"

"Yes, I did that. When I called 911, I gave them our address. I didn't need the whole town talking." She got up and left the room while I remained too shocked to understand what she told me.

Was Father sleeping with another woman? Who? How did she get his body here for the ambulance to pick up? Or is Mother still so drunk that she has no idea what she is saying?

D

May 29, 1969
Dear Diary,

T felt my breasts today. In his defense, my bra doesn't fit right. They were trying to escape anyway. They looked like two, very full water grenades tied in a tiny hammock.

It felt good to take my mind off Mother and the drama at home.

D

June 5, 1969
Dear Diary,

Mother drinks until she vomits sometimes. I don't understand.

She was in no shape to talk, but I tried to question her about the woman that Father was sleeping with. Her words were just one big slur.

D

June 7, 1969
Dear Diary,

Things are moving fast with T. He makes me feel special and loved. We have so much in common. We have intelligent conversations about politics, the Korean War and religion. He listens to me and values my opinion. We discussed civil rights and shared the same beliefs about equal treatment of all people no matter their race. We enjoy each other's company.

I may be only seventeen years old, but I have never felt more alive than when I am with him. Unfortunately, our relationship is secret, and I sneak out of the house during the middle of the night to see him. Thank goodness it is summer, and I don't have school. I would never be able to stay awake in class.

I think I am in love.

D

June 10, 1969
Dear Diary,

Tonight, I became a woman. I am not a square. I am a woman and am in love. T told me that he loved me as well. I am on cloud nine. Exhausted from all our lovemaking but still on cloud nine.

D

June 11, 1969
Dear Diary,

Thank God for T! Without him, I would be lost and alone. He listens to me and wants to make my life better. I love how he makes me feel. He adores me and has touched every inch of my body. And every inch feels more alive when he is next to me. His arms are slender but strong. When he smiles, my heart flutters. His blue diamond eyes light up whenever I am with him. I never want to stop feeling like this.

At night, I sneak back into my bed and get a few hours of sleep before I get up and take care of my brothers.

D

June 13, 1969
Dear Diary,

I can't believe how much life has changed since Father died a few months ago. Mother is literally drunk every night. I am not sure if she is ever sober anymore. Little H has grown two inches according to the markings on the kitchen wall. H has matured and wants to help around the house. He is becoming a little man. I sure appreciate how good he is at fixing things. Yesterday, a leg fell off the kitchen table - fell is an understatement because actually Mother broke it off when she tripped over her own two feet and landed hard onto the table - and he fixed it good as new! He is very handy and will make his bride a happy woman someday.

D

June 22, 1969

Dear Diary,

I have asked T when we can be together in the light of day. I want us to be an official couple. No more sneaking around. He isn't ready yet. He is worried about what people will say. We are from two different worlds. I told him I don't care, but he tells me to be patient. Our time will come. So, I try to act normal. Even Mother noticed something was different about me, and she is drunk all the time.

"Daisy, stop smiling and humming. You are giving me a headache." I ignored her and went about cleaning the kitchen floor. I even hummed a little bit louder.

D

July 10, 1969

Dear Diary,

T was quiet last night, early this morning. I can't quite put my finger on it, but after I lured him into bed, he loosened up. Afterwards when we lay in each other's arms, he was out of breath and told me, "Daisy, what you do to me is unreal!"

I told him, "Of all the things you have taught me, this is my favorite. You are a great teacher!"

We sure giggled about that!

D

July 17, 1969

Dear Diary,

I couldn't sneak out to spend time with T because Mother fell face first down the stairs. She claimed she tripped over one of Little H's toys, but we couldn't find anything near the stairs for her to trip over. She refused to go to the hospital, so H and I took care of her. I think she didn't want to see a doctor because she had too much to drink.

By the time we tucked her into her bed, her nose was swollen, and both eyes had started to swell shut. A couple of her fingers were bent into a weird position. H snapped them back into place before she could stop him. It was probably better that she was extremely drunk, so she didn't feel the pain.

I slept on the floor next to her bed to make sure she was okay. During the night while she was sleeping, she screamed Father's name and sobbed.

Just another day in my wonderful life.

D

July 22, 1969
Dear Diary,

It has been a long week. I haven't gotten to spend much time with T. Mother is in lots of pain but won't see a doctor. She simply kills the pain with alcohol. H and I take turns being with her. We are trying to minimize her alcohol consumption, but she gets meaner the more sober she becomes. We eventually gave in.

D

August 10, 1969
Dear Diary,

I think T wants to break up with me. After we made love last night, he was talking about our differences - age, life experiences and families. Even though he loves me, he thinks we should stop seeing each other for a while. I screamed and cried. He held me in his arms until I eventually cried myself to sleep.

I didn't even wake up until the morning sun was coming up. When I snuck back into my house, no one noticed I was missing. But I was worried about the neighbors seeing me creep around outside in the wee hours of the morning. I was careful. I had wrapped myself in T's home-made green afghan. It smelled like him.

D

August 15, 1969
Dear Diary,

After our love-making last night, T told me it was the last night we would be together. Our relationship was too dangerous. He should never have pursued me. Even though he loved me, he said he needed to let me go. If we were meant to be together, we would find a way back to each other. I could tell he was serious, and I won't be able to change his mind. I knew he was right, but I was deeply in love with him and couldn't bear the thought of not being in his arms again.

Doing the right thing is so hard!

D

August 20, 1969
Dear Diary,

I haven't seen T in five days. I am sleeping - or trying to - in my own bed at night snuggling his afghan. I miss him! Today, I placed five lilies - his favorite flower - in a plastic cup on his front steps.

I am keeping myself busy by giving our house some overdue deep cleaning. H and Little H are helping. Little H likes to scrub floors and vacuum while H can mow and fix anything that we need fixing. He even repaired our mower today - something with the belt. I don't know the details, but he is good with his hands. Sometimes after Little H goes to bed and Mother is passed out, H and I sit up and play cards. He is a joy to have around! Can't believe I am saying that about my kid brother.

D

August 21, 1969
Dear Diary,

It has been six days, and I am still crying myself to sleep. I formed six stones into a heart on his sidewalk today and left it there for him to find. I miss T.

D

August 22, 1969
Dear Diary,
Seven days... one whole week... My heart aches for him. I pretend it doesn't, but it hurts. I love him! He was my first love and lover! I miss T. I left him seven Tootsie Rolls in a lunch sack on his front door. I decorated the paper sack with crayoned hearts. Tootsie Rolls are his favorite candy.

D

August 25, 1969
Dear Diary,
I miss T. I miss him holding me. I miss his touch. I miss him telling me everything would be alright. I see him every now and then. I try to act normal, but I am breaking inside. I know that he is probably right. Our time together will come. I need to finish school and take care of my family right now. I am trying to be patient. Hoping he will miss me so much that he'll contact me. I try to go about my daily life as if our short love affair never happened.

D

August 30, 1969
Dear Diary,
When I went out to retrieve the newspaper from the sidewalk, T was collecting his as well. I opened my mouth to talk to him, and he put his hand up to stop me from saying anything. He shook his head and walked away. How did it come to this? We can't even be friendly towards each other? I am devastated!

D

September 10, 1969

Dear Diary,

Pardon me, but this is going to be a long entry. I need to tell some-one, and you are the only one who knows!

It was an ordinary autumn day. A light breeze was blowing. Birds were chirping in the tree branches. Some of the leaves were beginning to change colors. Temperatures were tolerable again. Mother was on her fourth tall gin and tonic. Neighbors' dogs were barking. It was just an ordinary day until a small brown four-door car pulled up along the curb of our neighbor's house. Slowly, the passenger door opened. First appeared a lady's leg covered in panty hose. The shoes were white, sensible flats. I knew before I saw more - it was Mrs. Adams. She was back. She came home.

A pit formed in the bottom of my stomach. I didn't mean to, but I heard myself take a sharp breath. She was wearing a beautiful pink and white floral dress. Her fuzzy auburn hair was pulled tight into a bun at the back of her head. She wore her signature bright red lipstick. She looked refreshed and calm compared to the last time she ducked into that same car. If it was possible, she looked more beautiful and classier than I'd ever seen her. I hated her. I envied her. She was elegant and graceful while remaining modest and polite.

She didn't see me sitting on our front porch working on my science homework. She was staring at her house - his house. I followed her gaze to their front porch where the screen door was being held slightly ajar - by him. His eyes were locked on her as she exited the car. He was smiling.

When she reached the three steps that led her to the front of the house, she paused and stared into his face. He bent down and kissed her tenderly and pulled her into a tight embrace. I felt like an intruder witnessing their reconciliation. It felt wrong to be sitting there, but I couldn't take my eyes off them. Thank goodness they did not see me. My cheeks were flushed, and the knuckles of my hands were white from holding my textbook so tightly.

Out of nowhere, Little H came barreling down our shared double driveway on his bike. He yelled, "Howdy, Mr. Adams and Mrs. Adams," as he was pedaling towards the street. They were caught off guard as well and looked towards him. They both smiled and gave Little H a small wave.

Then they noticed me a few yards away. Mrs. Adams smiled at me and also gave me a small wave. However, his smile quickly disappeared. He looked ashamed, like he was caught doing something he shouldn't be. He quickly escorted Mrs. Adams into the house and helped her with her travel case. When their door slammed shut, so did a piece of my heart.

D

September 11, 1969
Dear Diary,

And if you thought I was disappointed that Mrs. Adams returned home, you should have heard the words Mother spewed. She saw Mrs. Adams through the kitchen window when she was taking out the trash. Every curse word known to man came flying out of Mother's mouth. And Mrs. Adams even heard her through the glass of the window because she looked directly at us. She lowered her auburn head and disappeared into their house.

It was dinnertime, so I tried to cover Little H's ears, but he caught at least one phrase - "devil's bitch" - and kept repeating it like a broken record. I bet Father was rolling over in his grave. Mother never cursed when he was alive. I didn't even know curse words were part of her vocabulary. I miss him.

D

October 6, 1969
Dear Diary,

I missed my period. At first, I didn't even realize it. T broke up with me, school started back up, Mrs. Adams moved back home, Mother has been wicked rude, and I was distracted. I read that stress can delay your flow so I am crossing my fingers that it will arrive any day. I will keep you posted.

D

October 20, 1969
Dear Diary,
Still no period. I am scared! What will I do? I can't be a mother to a newborn! I am already responsible for my own mother and brothers! This can't be happening to me! I am all alone! I am only 17! Where will I live? Or will I be admitted into one of those girl hospitals?

Last year, there was a rumor at school about a sophomore named Carrie who got pregnant when she was sixteen. Her parents sent her away. Told everyone she was living with an ailing aunt. Everyone knew the truth that she was pregnant with Daniel's baby. When Carrie came home, she was pale and withdrawn. She was a ghost of her former self. I don't want to be like Carrie.

I miss him.

D

October 25, 1969
Dear Diary,
Still no period. I am seriously concerned. I need to talk to T. I don't know what to do. I am sure I am pregnant. I throw up in the mornings, my breasts are tender, and I am exhausted. All the signs we learned about in Health class.

D

October 26, 1969
Dear Diary,
I tried to catch T as he was getting into his car that was parked in our adjoining driveways. He was alone, but he sped off as soon as he saw me. I saw his intense, scared blue eyes in his rearview mirror looking back at me.

I am so angry! Who is acting like a child?

I left him a letter in his mailbox. If he doesn't talk to me soon, he will leave me no choice!

D

October 27, 1969

Dear Diary,

Who knew that a few heartfelt words written with blue ink on a single piece of lined paper would cause such destruction and heartache?

Fury and anger filled his eyes when T confronted me in the driveway after I arrived home from school. The letter upset him. Good, that means he still cares about me. His hands firmly rested on his hips, and his cheeks were flushed.

"You left me no choice. I have tried to have a civil conversation with you, but you avoid me."

"What is so urgent, Daisy? I told you that we can't see each other anymore. It has been two months." His tone started off angry but then morphed into more of a desperate plea. "I am back together with Annabelle. You can't keep doing this. You need to let go."

He wanted to erase me from his life. He wanted to forget our love affair. To him, our affair was nothing more than a big mistake. He had already moved on. He was back with his wife, and I was a conquest that he marked on his bedpost. But he wasn't getting off that easy. No way! He admitted to me once that he, in fact, pursued me. He seduced me. My pride and ignorance would not allow him to simply walk away.

Before he could say another word, I blurted, "I'm pregnant!"

And then that stubborn man with gorgeous gray-blue eyes had the nerve to question and doubt me. He didn't believe me! He proclaimed that he knew how teenage girls worked. This was my ploy to win him back. He started to pace the driveway.

"It isn't going to work, Daisy. I know how you are - all dramatic and needy. I've known you for years. Your deceit isn't going to work on me. I don't love you. I love Annabelle. You need to move on. Find a young man your own age. This conversation is over." He stormed off,

328

leaving me alone, crying in the driveway and holding my textbooks from school. How dare he talk to me like that! Who does he think he is?

As I yearned to cover my head in shame, I turned on my heel and dashed into the back door of my house where Mother was standing with her mouth wide open. She had heard every bit of our conversation while she was mixing herself her third gin and tonic in the kitchen. If he hadn't yelled so loud at me, maybe she would not have been drawn to the kitchen window to see what the commotion was all about.

I couldn't move. I could tell by the look on her face that there was no denying it. My secret was out, but unlike T, she wanted to hear what I had to say.

"Daisy... Daisy... dear God, please tell me that I heard wrong. Please tell me that you are not pregnant."

As I continued to sob, I simply nodded. I hung my head in shame.

"Dear Lord... it can't be true. And Mr. Thomas Adams is the father of the baby?" She sounded appalled and disgusted, which made it even harder to nod my head again. I heard her gasp and then drop her fresh gin and tonic glass on the hard kitchen floor. Glass shattered everywhere. I screamed, which brought the boys running from the living room.

Immediately, Little H started to sweep up the glass on the floor. He was oblivious to the cause of the broken glass. He simply wanted it cleaned up. H stared at me with a concerned look on his face. He seemed hurt that he hadn't known about my secret. Then the loud, loud yelling and rambling started.

"How the hell? What the hell were you thinking? What is wrong with that couple? Thomas Adams? How the hell did that happen? Never mind, I don't wanna know! Knocked up, are you sure? Those two are the devils' pawns! How could I have ever thought they were friends? I wish your father was still alive! He would beat that man into a bloody pulp."

I was rooted to my spot inside the doorway of the kitchen, clenching my textbooks to my chest as if to shield my heart.

I didn't know what to do or what to think. My life had blown up in a matter of a few crucial minutes. Nothing would ever be the same. T rejected me once again, Mother was angrier than I had ever seen her, and announcing out loud, "I'm pregnant," made it more real and absolutely terrifying. I hoped once Mother calmed down, she would know what to do. She continued to yell. I figured she needed to get it off her chest.

While she was ranting and yelling foreign curse words, Mother had managed to mix herself a fresh drink. The glass emptied quite quickly. One more time, the question was asked, "Are you sure you are pregnant, Daisy?"

"Yes, Mother. I haven't menstruated since August. I have many of the classic symptoms that a pregnant woman has." My head dropped down, my eyes on the floor. I was too ashamed to look her in the eye and see her disappointment. Plus, it was super awkward to have this conversation in front of H.

"And you are one hundred percent sure Thomas Adams is the father?"

I couldn't believe she thought I would bed more than one man at a time. I know she was disappointed in me, but I was not easy.

"Yes, he is the only possibility. He is the only man I have ever made love with."

It was as if this was the first time hearing this news. She started throwing items that were resting on the kitchen counter. Bread, cereal boxes, bowls, silverware all flew and crashed into the opposite wall of the kitchen window. This time, Little H did not return to the kitchen. H and I watched our mother go mad.

"Calm down, Mother. We'll figure this out together." H mimicked his best imitation of Father's deep, calming voice to talk some sense into her.

"Calm down? It's a little late for that, isn't it? What a mess you have made for yourself, Daisy. And by Thomas' reaction, he wants nothing to do with you and the baby." She turned back to the counter. I thought she was looking for something more to throw. "Damn it! I am out of gin. Well, all for the best anyway."

My heart leaped in my chest. I imagined the words coming out of her mouth: "I might as well stop drinking." However, instead of those words, she grabbed her car keys and her purse.

"I need to go for a drive. I need to get out of this cursed house."

"Mother, you shouldn't be driving after you've had a drink." H tried to reason with her. He was being generous by saying she had only one drink when we knew that wasn't the case.

"Harry, don't concern yourself with me. You have much more to worry about now that your slutty older sister is pregnant. People will talk, and it won't be kind. There will be rumors all over school about how fast she is and who the father is. You are going to lose your friends. You need to concern yourself with protecting your own reputation because Daisy has ruined hers."

H grabbed her wrists, perhaps thinking physical touch would help her calm down and give her some perspective on the situation.

"Don't say things like that, Mother. We are a family, and we will get through this together."

"Family? You call this" - with her arms, she motioned to the three of us - "a family? We are hardly getting by, and now Daisy is adding another mouth for us to feed. Nope, this is our own living hell that your saintly father created."

She shook her wrists free from H's grasp and called for Little H. Summoned, he came running into the kitchen.

"Come on. You and I are going out." She circled her hand around his little neck and steered him towards the door. I stepped to the side to let them pass by. I didn't have the strength or willpower to stop them.

Unfortunately for Mrs. Adams, she had momentarily returned home from the grocery store when Mother stepped out of our house. A tumultuous storm raged in Mother's eyes as she noticed her fresh enemy standing only a few feet away. Mother spewed words at her that will be forever engraved in my brain.

"You and your husband are the spawns of the devil!"

Mrs. Adams was bent over retrieving grocery bags from her trunk when Mother came barreling towards her. Mrs. Adams jumped as Mother's loud words of hatred shattered and tainted the quiet neighborhood. She looked frightened and worried about what hurtful words

Mother was going to confront her with. H and I headed out of the door as well. We followed Mother outside in case we needed to pull Mother off Mrs. Adams and honestly, out of pure curiosity. We were like moths to a flame. Couldn't stop ourselves.

"For years, you teased and taunted my powerless, weak husband. Telling him what a great father he was, how awesome you thought his grilling abilities were and asking him advice on financial investments. Touching his forearm, batting your eyelashes at him. You enticed him with your affections. You charmed him with your sinful intent. Then you seduced him into your own marital bed. The devil will collect when it is your time, Annabelle. I am one hundred percent sure that you will rot in Hell."

The two women, who were obviously no longer friends, were within spitting distance of each other. "And now your precious husband, Thomas, does the exact same thing to my daughter, teases her with attention, tempts her with his vulnerability, and charms her with words any naive, budding young woman would want to hear. His constant lies and devoted attention drew her in. She pleasured your husband in the same bed that my husband took his final breath. How ironic is that?"

My heart skipped a beat. In a matter of minutes, our lives came crashing down. H and I looked at each other... Father was having sex with Mrs. Adams? Annabelle? Mrs. Adams was Father's mistress? How could that be? He had his fatal heart attack in her bed? Were they in love? Did T know about them? Is that why she moved out? My father and I had sex in the same bed with spouses of the same married couple? Gross!

My mind was reeling. This was too much to take in. It did make sense though - why neither Mrs. Adams or T attended Father's funeral, why Mother simply called the ambulance to our house since they lived next door, why Mrs. Adams, Annabelle, moved out, and why Mother was completely insane the last few months. Puzzle pieces fit together. It was a disgusting, sordid puzzle but a puzzle, nonetheless.

Mrs. Adams appeared as stunned as H and me. She couldn't form a sentence, "Iris? What are... when did she... how... what happened...?"

A wicked laugh escaped Mother's throat.

"You had no idea either? Well, hell's bells! What fun for me to be the one to break the news! About time something goes my way."

A smirk of pleasure erupted on Mother's face. She licked her lips and surveyed her audience. She was going to enjoy this. She pointed her finger straight at Mrs. Adams.

"You seduced and screwed my husband, and then your husband seduced and screwed my underage, virgin daughter. You killed my husband with your wicked ways and temptations, and then Thomas - your crazy, sick husband - raped and knocked up Daisy. I believe the Lord is talking to you, Annabelle."

Mother has always believed very powerfully in Heaven and Hell. Her belief was that your time on earth was a testament on where you would reside for eternity. I wondered if she believed Father was in Hell and that she would never see him again. Maybe she didn't even care.

It was then that I noticed Little H. He had witnessed this whole awful scene. His innocent, tender ears were burning with knowledge that his young brain could not process. H and I were teenagers, and this new knowledge was scarring us. But Little H was only eight years old. This was too much for his young brain to process. He stared straight ahead with Mother's hand still around his neck, steering him as she walked. He was like a crutch for her. He was unable to move on his own. He was her puppet. I tried to gently pull him away from her, but he wouldn't budge. He was in a state of shock, rubbing his lucky, two-headed coin.

Mrs. Adams looked like she wanted to throw up. She was holding tight to the trunk of her car. Resting her hip on the car to hold herself up. Tears were now flowing in a steady stream down her face.

"Iris, I am so sorry. I have…wanted…to tell you… I am -"

"I don't want to hear it! Don't unload your lies and false apologies on me. You aren't sorry. You are sorry that you got caught and that your lover died in your bed. I don't wanna hear how you have felt badly for months and how you can't even face the day. No! That is how I feel. I am ashamed of my family. I am ashamed of my own husband and his last minutes before he died. And now, as if that wasn't enough, I am ashamed of my teenage daughter who is pregnant with your

cheating husband's baby. You go about your daily life and aren't even concerned with the lives next door that you ruined. We were friends - I trusted you both! I trusted your friendship with my husband. I allowed your husband to be a second father to my children. By seducing my family, you have destroyed our lives. And what for? Sex!" Mother shook her head. "I pity you, Annabelle. You are damned to Hell. I am one hundred percent sure that the devil will be knocking on your door. He will come to collect you and your perverted husband."

Mother turned her back and started walking towards her car as T opened the back door of their house. She stopped walking and turned her rage on him. He must have had no idea what was happening just outside of his door. His eyes were wide open in fear as he realized what he had entered into.

"Great timing, Thomas! If I were you, I would turn right back around and return into your house made of sins and lies. If I ever see you standing in the driveway, I will run over your sick, perverted ass!"

T must have believed every word she said because he quickly retreated into his house, leaving his wife outside to withstand the verbal abuse from his neighbor all alone. It was at that very moment that I realized what a coward he was. He seduced a young teenage virgin - me! - and he did it knowing about my father and his wife's affair.

Did he do it to get revenge on my family? Did he use me to get back at my dead father? Did he fake the entire relationship? Did he care about me at all or was it all revenge? Not only did he abandon me when I needed him most, but now he abandoned his wife at the hands of a deranged woman. He was weak. Mother was right: he abused my trust and loyalty and then seduced me.

Suddenly, our family car roared to life as the three of us left in the driveway were brought sharply back to reality. Each of us knew she was capable of running us over by the intense fury we had witnessed, so we all backed up away from her path.

Mother took off like a bat out of hell down our driveway and into the street. The last thing I noticed before her taillights hit the street were Little H's eyes, sitting stiffly next to Mother in the front seat. His big brown eyes were wide with fear and sadness. I fought the urge to jump in front of her car and remove him from her grasp. I will regret not having acted on that urge for the rest of my life. Those beautiful, innocent eyes will forever haunt me.

Within seconds of her tires squealing down the street, we heard a violent crash of metal. It was one of those moments in life that seems to happen in slow motion. The brain slowly pauses to process the information that the ears heard.

H's brain materialized the facts first, and he sprinted down the street in the same direction that Mother had turned the car.

Mother and Little H? Crashing metal?

A silent prayer escaped my mouth. "Lord, please let us be wrong."

I ran after him but couldn't keep up. After about two blocks of running, the first thing I noticed was the smell of burning metal. The crisp autumn afternoon was poisoned by the strong smell of gas fumes. The remains of a four-door, brown Plymouth were wrapped around a tall oak tree. The car's engine hissed its protest. Mother and Little H's names were being shouted by H as he tried to free them from the wreckage.

My vision became cloudy. I thought it was the smoke from the car crash. I batted it away with my hands. Small freckles of light sparked in my vision, and my skin felt warm. I felt dizzy. I stopped running to catch my breath, and before I knew what happened, everything went black.

D

November 15, 1969

Dear Diary,

I haven't been able to write to you in a while. My heart is shattered. If I thought things looked awful during my last entry, I was mistaken. Little H and Mother are gone. I can only pray that they are in Heaven and had a wonderful, joyful reunion with Father.

At first, Mrs. Adams and Mr. Adams appeared to pity us, brought over meals and informed Social Services that they were our family.

However, as soon as SS told them that they needed to fill out some necessary paperwork to have us come live with them, the help and kindness came to an abrupt halt. They couldn't and wouldn't lie to the authorities no matter how badly they felt. H and I were on our own.

We closed all the curtains. We locked all the doors. We stopped answering the front door. We even stopped going to school. We feared for our freedom and what future we would have without each other. We were all we had, and we couldn't lose each other after all we have been through.

D

November 20, 1969
Dear Diary,
Sometimes my mind wanders and imagines that things are different.

What if Father hadn't died in the arms of another woman? What if he had his fatal heart attack at home in his recliner as he fell asleep to the evening news? What if Mom would have been tucking in one of us kids? Little H would have required one more kiss on the head before she joined Father in the living room to put closure on the day. Maybe she would have discovered him limp and lifeless. Then we would never have known about his affair with Mrs. Adams.

Things would have been so different. Mom wouldn't have become an alcoholic. Mrs. Adams would have remained her best friend. I wouldn't have falled in love with T. I would have never had to take over the maternal role in our house and never resented Mother.

D

December 1, 1969
Dear Diary,
Neither of us want to be in foster care. We most likely won't stay together. No one wants one teenager, let alone two. I only have a few months left before I'm eighteen. I can't do it.

We have no one. We only have each other. No one cares about us anymore.

D

December 30, 1969
Dear Diary,
We have run out of food in the house. Our last meal was a can of beans. We split it and dipped our last piece of bread in the gravy at the bottom of the can. I sucked my spoon to make sure I got every last drop. I need to come up with a plan.

D

December 31, 1969
Dear Diary,
H and I can't hide from Social Services anymore. We are running away. We don't know what else to do. But I have a plan. We will start over in a new town, a new state - we will have a new life. We will tell everyone that we are newlyweds who are expecting a baby. No one will question it. We'll say we were robbed or there was a house fire - that is why we don't have any identification. We'll figure that out later.

I have secretly packed a few things that I can't tell H about because we agreed to leave all family memorabilia behind. But someday he will want to remember Little H and our childhood. I found little H's stuffed, gray bunny whom he fondly named Cottontail.

I also collected a few family photos. One of little H and H after a family picnic. We had gotten all dressed up for Father's Day. I had chosen what the boys were wearing. I wanted them to look like mini versions of Father. They sure did. We packed a picnic filled with all of Father's favorite foods: bologna sandwiches with mayonnaise, apples and sliced cheese. It was a special occasion, so Mother had purchased everyone a bottle of Coke.

I also grabbed a picture of me with them both on the first day of school. We were so excited about going back to school and seeing our friends. Of course, I took a couple pictures of Mother and Father. I never wanted to forget them. Even though Father hurt our family with his lies and betrayal, he was still the man who taught me to ride a bike, showed me how to properly wash and wax a car, and always encouraged me to follow my dreams. I knew he loved us.

Mother may have been a drunk and neglectful in the end, but before Father's death she always made sure we felt loved, tucked us in each night, and made sure we were grateful for all the wonderful things in our life. I knew she loved us.

In the extra box that I secretly packed, I added this journal, T's old green afghan and a handwritten letter Father had written to me years ago. For H, I made sure to grab his favorite record, a first-place ribbon he had won for his homemade, one-of-a-kind science project, and his pocket watch that Father had given to him.

We had both packed clothes. Just plain, no personalization. We didn't want anything to tie us to home. We were planning on starting the new year of 1970 on our own.

I am seventeen years old with a baby growing inside of me.

Harry, who renamed himself as Ben, is almost fifteen and growing like a weed. He could pass for nineteen or twenty, and I am sure once I start showing, people won't doubt our story - we are a young, married couple with an infant. Our families forbid our love, so we ventured out on our own and have fallen on hard times.

1970 will be the year we find happiness. Who knows where this adventure will take us? I am optimistic that together we can do this!

Life can't get any worse, can it?

D

Epilogue

It was a boiling hot summer day in Why, Arizona - which simply meant a raw egg would boil on the sidewalk because it was so hot. So, when I opened the front door to my Mexican-style stucco house in the desert, the air-conditioned breeze was beyond welcomed. My evening plans consisted of laying on my couch and watching old movies.

Why was my current hometown, mainly for Daddy's - couldn't begin to think of him as anything but Daddy - admiration of strange town names. I know he would approve of how the town earned its name. As two state highways come together, the letter 'Y' was formed by the combining pavement. Eventually, Arizona law required towns to have at least three letters in their name, so 'Why' became the established name instead of just the letter.

I'd been working at the border control station for six months, just enough time to understand why natives don't cause much trouble in July and August - it is too damn hot!

I pushed the red beeping light on my answering machine to hear a familiar voice from my past. It was Flo. Her southern drawl tugged at my heart strings and made me miss her.

"Hey, Lily. Are you there? Pick up the phone. I got some spankin' good news! Molly's lawyer explained that the journals can be admissible in court as long as there is other physical evidence to indicate that what the writer described is true, not hearsay. And you ain't gonna believe this, Lily, but to lessen her own sentence, Lisa coughed up some pictures of that nasty room. And glory-be! It is just as Daisy detailed. Naked ladies dressed in only shoes and jewelry, all cozied up to smokin', boozin', sweatin' businessmen. It is truly pornographic, and I ain't even a fuddy-duddy. You better call me back, girl."

Five years ago, after I said my final farewell to Daisy and T - my biological father - at the nursing home, I relinquished the diaries to Flo. Neither of us had much hope that Pastor Tony would get what he deserved. But as the pressure mounted, his wife Lisa cracked. She admitted that she loved her husband but wouldn't take credit for his evil, sometimes involuntary sexual adventures. She made a deal with the lawyers. The photographs were a new discovery.

After I listened to Flo's answering machine message explaining that Daisy's diaries were going to be used in court the following week, I knew that I needed to be there to give *them* an extra punch. To prepare for my visit to Canby's courthouse, I packed a light suitcase and a newly purchased blonde hair coloring kit and asked for a week off work.

As my own mother quoted in her infamous diary, "It's gonna be a doozy."

SINCE IT WAS A CRIMINAL TRIAL, the defendant and the public had a right to an open court. Many people were drawn to see such a scandal. It was the talk of the entire tri-state area.

I arrived fashionably late at the Canby courthouse to make a dramatic entrance. I was right to believe by being late there would be standing room only. As the oversized wooden door creaked open, the last few rows of viewers turned to see the late arrival - a tall, attractive *blonde* dressed in a bright red tank top, white short shorts and a pair of black, ridiculously high heels. Not court-appropriate clothing, but I was dressed as *Daisy*, and that was the point.

My timing could not have been more perfect because there was a moment of silence in the court proceedings. Karma was working with me, unlike how she seemed to always be punishing Daisy. My heels clicked and clacked as I made my way down the aisle to get as close as I could to the front. I was drawing a lot of attention.

I selected the crowded row that I wanted to squeeze into. "Excuse me. Pardon me." Politely, I tried to force my way through the row of people, who were all taking notes - reporters. Walking in eight-inch heels was not something I did on a regular basis, so my clumsy fall onto one of the reporters' laps didn't need to be rehearsed. "Oh, dear! I'm so sorry."

When the young, eager reporter jumped to his feet to help me up from the floor, he dropped his pen, paper and briefcase onto the hard, unforgiving tile floor. The loud disruption echoed through the walls of the old courtroom. Everyone turned to see what had happened and who was going to receive the tongue lashing from the judge.

Just as the judge beat his gavel and demanded order in his courtroom, Pastor Tony caught my eye. He looked like he'd seen a ghost. His skin, which was already pale from time spent locked indoors, turned translucent. His eyes bulged out of his head. His jaw dropped open as he gaped at...my mother, Daisy.

Being true to her character, I gave him a small flirtatious wave and a wink. He looked like he was going to pass out. It was too loud in the old room to hear his question, but I read his lips, as did a few of the reporters.

"Daisy?"

I am sure the judge ruled the jury to strike my disruption from the record. Maybe even suggested removing it from their memory. Either way, the jurors were only human. They were subconsciously swayed. The ghost of the woman from the pornographic photos walked in, made a scene and was escorted out. That left an impression. My goal.

The trial concluded two weeks later, and after only twelve hours of deliberation, the jury came back with a guilty verdict. Pastor Tony was going to rot in prison, right where he deserved to be. Karma corrected this wrong.

To celebrate the court victory, Flo was hosting a big party at the Canby Diner. She invited everyone she knew. "You gotta come, Lily. You can finally meet my Molly. She wants to thank you for everythin'. But I gotta know, are you comin' as your mother or yourself? The press is gonna be here and what a hoot it would be to have a ghost show up. Did I tell you that the local paper titled their article, 'Pastor Anthony Shade haunted by ex-mistress'?"

Flo was disappointed when I told her that Lily was attending. She wanted a show.

"You were extremely convincin' as your mother. A bit scary though! You should've told me you were doin' that. You almost put old Flo in the graveyard."

The diner was packed with the locals and a few reporters from nearby towns. They were hanging around in case another surprise ghost appearance happened. The story of a popular, respected pastor with a secret sex room and illegitimate child was causing quite a bit of publicity for the little town, making all the local establishments quite busy. No one was complaining.

Meeting Molly and Lucy was the highlight of the evening. Molly's rounded cheeks perked up at the mention of my name. When I held out my hand after Flo's introduction, she grabbed it and pulled me into a big embrace.

Thankfully, Lucy appeared healthy and happy. Her hair - cut into a short, stylish bob - was a natural brown color, and her once very pale skin was now a healthy peach color. After our introduction, we acknowledged each other with a slight nod. No words needed to be spoken.

For Flo and Molly, this party marked the end of their worries about Pastor Tony influencing Lucy and her daughter. With Pastor Tony living behind bars and suffering a tarnished reputation, Lucy and Camille could heal, move on and lead normal lives.

However, for Lucy, the party was a bit more delicate. The town was celebrating the fact that the father of her baby was found guilty of many, many sexual offenses. He was the first man she had sex with.

She believed he loved her and wanted to take care of her. So, if her smile seemed forced, it was.

I understood how she felt: sometimes silently walking away from a toxic relationship was enough of a celebration. Balloons, a cake and party music were not necessary. Some celebrations were better alone and in private.

After a few hours of small talk and a tearful goodbye with Flo, I jumped in my trusty Subaru and headed south. Before I made my way back to Arizona, I was going to drive through Normal. The road trip was just what I needed to bring some peace and closure to my past. I popped in a cassette of my favorite band, Ace of Base, rolled down the windows, and sang along with the music.

Before I knew it, I rolled into sleepy Normal, Iowa. The streets were quiet. I turned off my radio and breathed in the crisp, cool summer air. It was the middle of the night, so I slowly idled down the street of my old neighborhood. My stomach tangled in a knot. It had been five years since I packed up and left. Never regretted my decision. I needed to make a new life for myself. I didn't want to be known as Daisy's daughter anymore.

A new family had moved into our house years ago and painted it pale yellow. There was a small purple bike with training wheels left on the front lawn. A new tree had been planted in the front yard. From outward appearances, it looked well-loved. But I knew from experience that looks could be deceiving.

A couple blocks south, I parked my car at the curb, got out of my car and shut the door. The evening moisture dampened my shoes, and the full moon lit my path. Usually, a cemetery visit at two in the morning included some giggly teenagers on a dare. However, on this night, it was only me. I wasn't giggling, and I wasn't crying...yet.

I found his tombstone under the big oak tree. Even though biology told me that he wasn't my actual father, my heart had a hard time accepting it. Therefore, his tombstone read 'Beloved Daddy.'

"Hi, Daddy. I know it has been a while, but I think about you all the time. I wanted to make sure you knew that I was fine and living my best life. I hope I'm making you proud."

Next to his tombstone was a newly marked, smaller one. I had not purchased it, so I assumed that Thomas Adams had.

I turned my head a bit but didn't get physically any closer. Unspoken words that had gathered like abandoned water in a well lapped at the edges of my mind. *I forgive you. I forgive you for not loving and respecting me enough to be truthful. I forgive you for hurting and punishing me for something that was not my fault. I am not like you. I am a better person. I will not make the same mistakes that you did.*

But instead of any of that, all I said was, "Hey, Daisy."

"Acceptance doesn't mean that life gets better:
it just means that my way of living life
on life's terms improves."
(Sharon E. Rainey)

Acknowledgments

First and foremost, I need to thank my man. Since the first day, you have believed, pushed - and shoved - me to pursue this dream. You are my cheerleader, my friend, my partner and my husband. Thank you for your unwavering support!

Kramer, PJ and Fitzy - you helped me so much with your insightful suggestions and untamed enthusiasm. Your donated time to my project and loyal friendship means a great deal to me. I could not have done it without you.

My author friends - Larry and Jen - thank you for your advice and guidance. As a virgin author, your helpful responses were the answer to my anxious prayers. And, Jen, I love the cover! Thank you for making my idea come to life.

Clara Abigail, my editor - you make me sparkle! You polished my dream and made it shine. Thank you for endless help and continued patience! Without you, my dream would still be a dull, jumbled pile of words.

My friends, my witches - there are so many of you to thank. You inspired many of these characters and for that I thank you for simply being you. Keep feeding me ideas! Without you, I wouldn't have these juicy stories to write.

Made in the USA
Coppell, TX
21 September 2021